INTRIGUE

Seek thrills. Solve crimes. Justice served.

Cold Case Protection
Nicole Helm

Wyoming Christmas Conspiracy
Juno Rushdan

MILLS & BOON

COLD CASE PROTECTION
© 2024 by Nicole Helm
Philippine Copyright 2024
Australian Copyright 2024
New Zealand Copyright 2024

First Published 2024
First Australian Paperback Edition 2024
ISBN 978 1 038 93898 5

WYOMING CHRISTMAS CONSPIRACY
© 2024 by Juno Rushdan
Philippine Copyright 2024
Australian Copyright 2024
New Zealand Copyright 2024

First Published 2024
First Australian Paperback Edition 2024
ISBN 978 1 038 93898 5

MIX
Paper | Supporting
responsible forestry
FSC® C001695
www.fsc.org

Published by
Harlequin Mills & Boon
An imprint of Harlequin Enterprises (Australia) Pty Limited (ABN 47 001 180 918), a subsidiary of HarperCollins Publishers Australia Pty Limited
(ABN 36 009 913 517)
Level 19, 201 Elizabeth Street
SYDNEY NSW 2000 AUSTRALIA

Cover art used by arrangement with Harlequin Books S.A.. All rights reserved.

Printed and bound in Australia by McPherson's Printing Group

Cold Case Protection
Nicole Helm

MILLS & BOON

Nicole Helm grew up with her nose in a book and the dream of one day becoming a writer. Luckily, after a few failed career choices, she gets to follow that dream—writing down-to-earth contemporary romance and romantic suspense. From farmers to cowboys, Midwest to *the* West, Nicole writes stories about people finding themselves and finding love in the process. She lives in Missouri with her husband and two sons, and dreams of someday owning a barn.

Books by Nicole Helm

Harlequin Intrigue

Hudson Sibling Solutions

Cold Case Kidnapping
Cold Case Identity
Cold Case Investigation
Cold Case Protection

Covert Cowboy Soldiers

The Lost Hart Triplet
Small Town Vanishing
One Night Standoff
Shot in the Dark
Casing the Copycat
Clandestine Baby

Visit the Author Profile page at millsandboon.com.au.

For the dogs we miss.

CAST OF CHARACTERS

Cash Hudson—The middle Hudson sibling. Keeps his distance from the Hudson Sibling Solutions work and focuses on training dogs.

Izzy Hudson—Cash's twelve-year-old daughter.

Carlyle Daniels—Works for Cash. Her brother married into the Hudson family, so she lives on Hudson Ranch.

Walker and Mary Daniels—Carlyle's brother and Cash's sister. They are married.

Anna and Hawk Steele—Cash's sister and her husband, who's an arson investigator.

Palmer Hudson and Louisa O'Brien, and Grant Hudson and Dahlia Easton—Hudson brothers and their girlfriends.

Jack Hudson—Oldest Hudson brother. Head of Hudson Sibling Solutions and also the sheriff of Sunrise, Wyoming.

Detective Laurel Delaney-Carson—Detective at Bent County investigating the kidnapping attempt and then murder.

Chessa Scott—Cash's ex-wife and Izzy's mother.

Chapter One

Carlyle Daniels had grown up in a tight-knit family. Dysfunctional, trauma-bonded—no doubt—but close. She supposed that's why she loved being absorbed into the Hudson clan. Their tight-knit was familiar, but bigger—because there were so many more of them.

So, yeah, a few more overprotective males in the mix, but she had *sisters* now—both honorary and in-law, because her oldest brother, Walker, had married Mary Hudson last fall.

Carlyle liked to talk a big game. She *really* liked to tease her oldest brother about how lame it was he'd gotten old and settled down, but deep down she could not have been happier for him. After spending most of his adult life trying to keep *her* safe while they tried to figure out who killed their mother, he now got to settle into just…normal. He worked as a cold case investigator for Hudson Sibling Solutions and helped out on the Hudson Ranch and was going to be a *dad* in a few months.

Her heart nearly burst from all the happy. Not that she admitted that to anyone.

She'd been working as Cash Hudson's assistant at his dog-training business on the ranch for almost a year now. She'd settled into life on the Hudson Ranch and in Sunrise, Wyoming. It was still weird to stay put, to not always have to look over her shoulder, to know she just got to…make a life, but she was handling it.

What she was not handling so well was a very inappropriate crush on her boss—who was also her sister-in-law's brother, which meant she probably *shouldn't* ever fantasize about kissing him.

But she did. Far too often. And normally she was an act-first-and-think-later type of woman, but there were two problems with that. First, she no longer got to bail if she didn't like her circumstances. She was building a life and all that, and bailing would bum Walker out which just felt mean and ungrateful.

Second, Cash had a daughter, who Carlyle adored. Izzy Hudson was twelve, smart as a whip, sweet and funny. She also had a little flash of something Carlyle recognized. Carlyle didn't know how to explain it, but she knew Cash didn't see it. She didn't think any of Izzy's family saw it, because the girl didn't *want* them to see it.

Carlyle saw through Izzy's masks all too well. She'd been the same all those years ago, keeping secrets so big and so well, her brothers hadn't found out until last year. So, she felt honor bound to keep an eye on the girl, because no doubt one of these days she was going to run headfirst into trouble.

Carlyle knew the lifelong bruises that could come from that, so she wanted to be…well, if not the thing that stopped the girl, the cushion to any catastrophic falls. She considered herself something of a been-there-done-that guardian angel.

Carlyle looked up from the obstacle course she'd been setting up for the level-one dogs and surveyed her work. She was satisfied and knew Cash would be too. He hadn't been super excited about hiring her. The fact he'd even done it had been because Mary had insisted or persuaded him to—but Carlyle knew that was more about him being a control freak than anything *against* her.

She liked to think she'd proved herself the past year—as a hard worker, as someone he could trust. She glanced over at the cabin that was Cash and Izzy's residence, while everyone else lived up in the main house. Palmer and Louisa were just a few weeks out from a wedding and finishing up their house on the other end of the property, but everyone else seemed content to stay in the main house. It was certainly big enough.

Carlyle sometimes felt like the odd man out. She wanted to be like Zeke, her other brother, and have her own place in town, but staying on the property made a lot more sense for what her work schedule was like.

And for keeping an eye on Izzy.

Who, speak of the devil, stepped out of the front door of her cabin, followed by her father and then Copper, one of the dogs retired from cold case and search and rescue work.

Carlyle sighed, in spite of herself. There was something *really* detrimental to a woman's sense when watching a man be good with animals and a really good dad whose top priority, always, was his daughter's safety.

Or maybe that was just her daddy issues. Considering her fathers—both the one she'd thought was hers, and the one who'd actually been hers—had tried to kill her. More than once.

But Don, the fake dad, was dead. Connor, the real dad, was in jail for the rest of his life. So, no dads. Just brothers who'd acted *like* fathers.

And now, for the first time in her life, safety. A place to stay. A place to put down roots. She had not just her brothers, but a whole network of people to belong to.

Copper pranced up to her and she crouched to pet his soft, silky face. "There's a boy," she murmured.

She glanced up as Cash and Izzy approached. Cash was a tall, dark mountain of a guy. All broad shoulders and cowboy swagger—down to the cowboy hat on his head and the boots on his feet. His dark eyes studied her in a way she had yet to figure out. Not assessing, exactly, but certainly not with the ease or warmth with which he looked at his family.

And still, it made silly little butterflies camp out in her stomach. She felt the heat of a blush warming her cheeks like she was some giggly, virginal teenager when she decidedly was *not*.

She was a hard-hearted, whirling dervish of a woman who'd grown up fast and hard and had somehow survived. Survival had led her here.

Things were good. She was happy. She wouldn't ruin that by throwing herself at Cash, and she wouldn't ruin it by failing at this job or messing up being part of this family network.

No, for the first time in her life, Carlyle was going to do things right.

CARLYLE DANIELS WAS a problem. Worse, Cash Hudson couldn't even admit that to *anyone* in his life. She was a good worker, Izzy *loved* her, the animals *loved* her and she was an even better assistant than he'd imagined she'd be.

But he found himself thinking about her way too much, long before he'd stepped out of the cabin this morning to see her across the yard getting work for the day set up.

He too often found himself trying to make her laugh, because she didn't do it often enough and the sound made him smile...which he also knew *he* didn't do enough. As his siblings and daughter routinely told him so.

But if anyone had *any* clue he smiled more around Carlyle than he did around anyone other than Izzy, he'd be flayed alive.

He was too old for her—in years and experience. He was a father, and he had one disastrous marriage under his belt. He could look back and give himself a break—he'd been sixteen, reckless enough to get his high school girlfriend pregnant, and foolish enough to think marriage would make everything okay.

Maybe he was older, wiser, more mature these days, but that didn't mean he could ever be *good* for anyone. Didn't mean he'd ever risk Izzy's feelings again when she already had oceans of hurt over the mother she hadn't gotten to choose.

He wasn't even interested in Carlyle. He just thought she was hot and all the settling down going on around the Hudson Ranch was getting to him. Grant and Mary were fine enough. They were calm, settle-down-type people. Mary might be younger than him, but he'd always figured her for the marriage-and-kids type—and even if he liked to play disapproving older brother, Walker Daniels was about as besotted with Mary as a brother could want for his sister.

Grant was older, far more serious, and he and Dahlia had taken what felt like forever to finally even get engaged, so that was all well and good. Cash could take all those little blows that reminded him time marched on.

But it was Palmer and Anna who *really* got to him. Younger than him. The reckless ones. The wild ones. He'd never have pinned Palmer for marriage, and he'd never thought anyone would want to put up with the tornado that was Anna.

But Palmer was getting married in a few weeks, and by all accounts Louisa was the answer to any wildness inside of him. Anna was a *mother* now, and a damn good one, and somehow she'd found a man who thought all her sharp edges were just the thing to shackle him down forever.

Someday, sooner than he'd ever want, Izzy would be an adult. Making her own choices like his siblings were doing. Izzy would go off into that dangerous world and *then what*?

Cash pushed out an irritated breath. Well, there was always Jack. Single forever, likely, being that he was the oldest and Cash couldn't remember the last time he'd been on a date, or even gone out for a night of fun.

They could be two old men bemoaning the future and the world together.

And no one would ever know he had an uncomfortable *thing* for Carlyle. He blew out a breath before they finally approached the obstacle course. "Morning," he offered gruffly.

"Good morning," she said brightly, grinning at Izzy as she stood up from petting Copper.

"I'm going to walk Izzy over to the main house, then we'll get started."

"Dad," Izzy groaned, making the simple word about ten syllables long. "I can walk to the house by myself. It's *right there*." She pointed at the house in question. Yes, within his sight, but...

Too much had happened. Too much *could* happen. As long as his ex-wife was out there, Izzy wouldn't leave his side, unless she was with one of his family members.

"I'll be right back," he said to Carlyle.

Izzy didn't groan or grumble any more. He supposed she was too used to it. Or knew he wasn't going to bend. He wished he could. He wished he could give her everything she wanted, but there'd been too many close calls.

They climbed up the porch to the main house in silence and he opened the back door that led into a mudroom.

"I'm not a baby," Izzy grumbled. Probably since she knew he would follow her right into the house until he found someone to keep an eye on her.

He didn't say what he wanted to. *You're* my *baby*. "I know, and I'm sorry." They walked into the dining room, and Mary was already situated at the table with her big agenda book and a couple different colored pens.

She looked up as they entered and smiled at Izzy.

Cash would never not feel guilty that Izzy ended up with such a terrible mom, but Mary as an aunt was the next best thing, he knew.

"I'm craving cookies. What do you think? Should we make chocolate chip or peanut butter?"

Izzy didn't smile at her aunt, she just gave Cash a kind of killing look and then sighed. "What do you think the baby wants?" She went over and took the seat next to Mary at the table.

Mary slung an arm around Izzy's shoulders, and Izzy leaned in, putting a hand over Mary's little bump.

Izzy didn't want to be treated like a baby, she didn't want him being so overprotective, but she also loved her family. She was excited about cousins after being the only kid on the ranch for so long, and she *liked* spending time with her aunts and uncles.

So this wasn't a punishment. He tried to remind himself of that as he retraced his steps back to where Carlyle was waiting. She'd brought out the level-one dogs, and they were lined up waiting for their orders.

Because they were level one, there was still some tail wagging, some whining, some irregular lining up, but they were good dogs getting close to moving to level two. They all kept their gazes trained on Carlyle, and she stood there looking like some kind of queen of dogs. Her long, dark ponytail dancing in the wind, chin slightly raised, gray-blue eyes surveying her kingdom of furry subjects.

He came to stand next to her and didn't say anything at first. Ignored the way his chest got a little tight when she glanced his way, like he was part of that array of subjects she ruled.

She could, he had no doubt. If he was someone else in a totally different situation, she no doubt would.

"She's tough," Carlyle said, not bothering to explain she was talking about Izzy.

As if he didn't know that about his daughter. As if he hadn't raised her to be tough. As if life hadn't forced her to be. "Yeah, and the world is mean."

"Take it from someone who's been there and done that, it doesn't matter how well-intentioned the protection is, at a certain point, it just chafes."

Cash knew she wasn't wrong, but it didn't matter. "I'd rather a little chafing than any of the other alternatives."

Carlyle sighed, but she didn't argue with him. She surveyed the lineup of dogs. "Well, you want to start or should I?"

Carlyle was good at this. A natural. "Take them through the whole thing."

She raised an eyebrow. He hadn't let her do that before all on her own, but...it was time. He couldn't give his daughter the space she needed to *breathe*, so he might as well unclench here where it didn't matter so much. "You can do it."

She grinned at him, eyes dancing with a mischief that was far too inviting, and completely not allowed in his life.

"I know," she said, then turned to the dogs and took them through the training course. Perfectly. A natural.

A *problem*.

Chapter Two

Carlyle had never been a good sleeper in the best of times. She wouldn't admit it to anybody, but she preferred to sleep with the lights on. The dark freaked her out when she was alone. Too many shadows. Too many unknowns.

But she'd learned that first night at the Hudson house that living with too many people meant they noticed. A light under the door at all hours, or when they woke up before her and walked by her window outside, off to do their chores. Then there were questions.

So, she dealt with the dark the best she could. She focused on how safe the Hudson ranch was. Due to the nature of solving cold cases, and the danger they'd seen over the past year, they had all kinds of security systems and surveillance.

Besides, the man who wanted her dead was safe behind maximum security prison-bars. But a lifetime's worth of running—because even before her mother had been murdered they'd been on the run—meant she had a hard time shaking fear loose.

Tonight was no different. Lately, she'd been sort of letting fantasies of Cash lull her off to sleep, but she was beginning to think that wasn't very healthy. She'd gone to the Lariat last night—the local bar—with Chloe Brink, one of

Jack's deputies at Sunrise Sheriff's Department, and three different men had hit on her.

She hadn't been the slightest bit interested. Worse than all that, Chloe had called her out on it.

Uh oh. You've got the look.

What's the look?

The look of a woman hung up on a Hudson who is perennially in the dark.

Carlyle wasn't sure she'd felt that embarrassed since Walker had tried to give her a sex talk when she'd been fourteen.

So, which one is it? Chloe had asked, like it was just a foregone conclusion she was hung up on a Hudson. *A single one, I hope.*

Oh my God, yes. Which was an admission, and she couldn't believe she'd been stupid enough to fall for such an easy ploy.

Chloe had grinned. *Doesn't leave too many of them these days. Cash is more age appropriate.*

Does that make Jack more age appropriate for you? Carlyle had retorted. Getting too bent out of shape about the truth, but not being able to stop herself.

Chloe had looked at her bottle with a hard kind of unreadable stare. *Jack is my boss.*

Cash is my *boss.*

Chloe had finished off her one and only beer, because she was driving. *Maybe we've both got issues.* Which had made Carlyle snort out a laugh.

Then Chloe had driven her back to the ranch and idled outside the big house, staring at it with an opaque expression. She'd sighed, a world's worth of knowing in her voice. *They'll mess you up, Car. If I were you, I'd steer clear.*

Carlyle hadn't known what to say to that. Chloe was the first friend she'd made outside of the Hudson ranch, and she didn't want to be a jerk. She liked the feeling of having someone to go to who didn't revolve around *family*. Like she was a normal, functioning adult who had not just a strong family life, but friends. Interests. Things outside this sprawling ranch.

Maybe a boyfriend who was *not* her boss.

She decided then and there she was not going to fantasize about Cash to fall asleep anymore. She would think about the dogs. About work. About Izzy.

But all those things just circled back to Cash.

Eventually, she got irritated enough with herself that she slid out of bed. She went over to the armchair next to the window. She sat down on it and rested her arms on the windowsill and looked out at the great, vast night around Hudson Ranch.

The stars sparkled above. This place was so beautiful. She'd grown up jumping from city to city, but she was certain— deep in her bones—she'd been made for *this*. Mountains and sky and fresh air.

She knew her brother Zeke didn't feel comfortable taking too much from the Hudsons, but Carlyle liked to think they'd earned it with the way they'd grown up. Why not enjoy the generosity of people who could spare it?

Not that the Hudsons had seen only sunshine and roses. Their parents had disappeared when they'd been kids, and only the determined, taciturn dedication of their oldest brother, Jack, had kept the family together.

But they'd had this ranch, they'd had money and the community of Sunrise. They'd even built their own cold case investigation company. All Carlyle had ever had since her mother had been murdered was Walker and Zeke.

She'd damn well enjoy a nice house and pretty surroundings now no matter how they came along.

Except just as she was thinking it, like some kind of grand cosmic joke, the security light kept on at all hours—since the trouble last year—went out. Just one moment it was on, the next it wasn't.

She frowned. It was supposed to stay on all night. Still, the landscape was well lit by the moon and stars and... Was that a shadow over by Cash's cabin?

"You're being ridiculous," she whispered to herself. "Paranoid." But she pressed closer to the window, squinting in the dark. It was probably a dog. Or a bear.

But it looked damn human. And the security light had gone off.

"Don't overreact," she whispered to herself again. She went back to her bed and reached for the lamp. She'd spend the next hour or so reading or something. She turned the switch.

Nothing happened.

She sucked in a shaky breath, let it out. *Coincidence.* The bulb had just burned out at an inopportune time. Something normal. Boring. If she went around waking everyone up and screaming, she would look panic-addled. They'd all start treating her with kid gloves, like she was some kind of victim.

When she was a *survivor.* She swallowed and moved over to the switch by the door. She flipped the switch.

Once again, nothing happened.

She flipped it again. Once, twice. Three times.

The lights wouldn't go on. Terror swept through her. Not an accident. Not a figment of her overactive imagination. But it could be a perfectly innocent loss of power, she tried to remind herself over the panic. Even though it wasn't storming. Even though this had never happened the whole time she'd been living here.

She rushed back over to the window, hoping she'd look out into the night and not see a thing.

But *something* was moving around Cash's cabin in the moonlight. No power shouldn't matter when it came to the security systems. They should have a backup, but...

Maybe it was nothing. Maybe the security system would catch it. So many maybes.

She couldn't just stay here and do nothing. She thought about texting Cash, but again... If it was nothing, she couldn't stand looking like she didn't have a handle on everything she'd been through.

She strode over to her closet and keyed in the code for the gun safe she kept on the top shelf. She pulled out her gun and then left her room. She considered knocking on Jack's bedroom door since it was the only other bedroom on the main floor, but no. It would be too embarrassing to be wrong with any of these people.

Besides, she had a gun. She knew how to use it. She knew how to handle danger. So, she'd handle this on her own because it was *nothing*, and no one would have to know she'd overreacted.

It was fine. She'd check it out, make *sure* it was fine, then wake someone up about the power outage. Once she was sure there was no other danger.

She unlocked the side door and slid out without making a sound. She looked up to where she knew a camera was situated. They were motion activated and should have moved with her. Even in the dark.

They didn't.

Power outage. Backup outage. It was...fine. It had to be.

She moved off the porch and toward Cash's cabin, led by moonlight and a spiraling fear that made it hard to breathe evenly. But the closer she got, the more she could see the outline of a shadow. At the side of the house. The side she knew Izzy's room was on. She wanted it to be a dog, but when no growls or barks broke out, she knew it couldn't be true.

Carlyle crept closer. Her heart was thundering in her chest, but she'd been in positions like this before. Once she was close enough, she cocked her gun.

"Freeze," she ordered sharply.

The shadow stopped. It turned toward her. He or she was standing right next to the window to Izzy's room. The window was open a crack, a little light shining on the other side of that curtain. Izzy's night-light no doubt.

Oh God. Carlyle should have called someone. Said something. She should have trusted her gut. When had she stopped doing that?

"If you don't tell me who you are in two seconds, I'm going to shoot," Carlyle said. Luckily, a life of danger meant that even though her insides shook and terror had taken hold, she sounded cool and in charge.

But the figure didn't speak. Carlyle heard the soft sound of a growl from inside. No doubt Copper. Hopefully alerting Cash or Izzy that there was trouble.

Still the figure didn't speak.

Carlyle raised her voice, held the gun steady. "Okay then. One—"

A high, piercing scream tore through the world around them. Then raucous barking followed.

Izzy. Copper. Cash.

But they were inside. Was someone in there with them? Was someone hurting Izzy in the cabin? What would have happened to Cash if that was the case?

So focused on thoughts of Izzy and Cash, Carlyle forgot about the present danger and turned toward the cabin.

The blow was so hard, it seemed to rattle her bones and

she lost her footing, her balance. She fell onto the hard, cold ground, the blow now burning. Like she'd been…stabbed in the process?

But the hard sound of footsteps retreating meant whoever had been there was running away. They'd never spoken.

But…the scream. Someone was inside with Izzy. Carlyle had to get… She tried to get up, but the pain about took her out. She rolled over onto her stomach, tried to get to her hands and knees. She managed, but only just barely. She had to grit her teeth against the pain, and the fuzzy light-headedness that wanted to take over.

She heard the slam of a door, footsteps. Copper ran up to her first and licked her face, whimpering. "Thanks, bud," she muttered. She looked beyond the dog to the other footsteps.

Cash. Barefoot, hair haphazard, gun in one hand and flashlight in the other. But he was standing and whole.

"Carlyle," he said, clearly with nothing but confusion.

"They got away." Had she lost consciousness? "Izzy?"

"I'm okay," came the girl's wavering voice. She was huddled behind Cash, holding on to him for dear life.

"Cops are on their way," Cash said as he approached. "What the hell happened?" He swept the flashlight over her head, then down her shoulders.

"I saw someone outside Izzy's window. I…"

"Daddy, she's bleeding."

Cash swore, immediately kneeling at Carlyle's side. "Come on." Then he lifted her up into his arms.

It was too dark to walk her across the yard to the main house safely. Someone had been out here and gotten away, so he couldn't risk Izzy out in the open.

"Hold the door open for me, Iz."

She scrambled to do just that as Cash carried Carlyle to the cabin porch. "You still with me?" he asked through gritted teeth as he maneuvered her into the dark entryway.

"I'm okay. Really. They just knocked into me. I think I hit my head."

That would explain the blood, hopefully. Head wounds usually bled more than was necessary. It needed to be… something like that. He needed to get a good look at her though, see for himself. He laid her down on the couch in the living room as Izzy flipped on the lights. He didn't need to tell Izzy to lock all the doors or stay close. She was too used to this.

He wanted to swear again, but he kept it inside his head. He studied Carlyle's face, saw no traces of blood. "Where'd you hit your head?"

"Uh…" She reached up, patted around. "I guess I didn't. I'm okay."

But there'd been blood. He frowned at her. What the hell was she… His thoughts trailed off as his gaze tracked down her shirt. There on her side, her shirt was all bloody…and the blood was soaking into his couch.

This time he did swear, and Izzy didn't even scold him. "Why didn't you tell me?" he demanded, reaching forward to lift her shirt.

Carlyle's eyes darted behind him as she grabbed his wrist to stop him from lifting up her shirt.

She was looking worriedly at Izzy. She was trying to protect Izzy. "It's okay. Really. Got any Band-Aids?" She tried to laugh, but it clearly hurt because she squeezed her eyes shut.

She was going to need *stitches*, not a Band-Aid, with that amount of blood. Cash didn't know how to sort through every terrible emotion battering him. She was injured, Izzy was terrified. Hell, *he* was terrified, but he wanted Izzy out of earshot before he asked Carlyle what happened.

A knock sounded at the door, and even though Cash knew bad guys didn't *knock*, he grabbed onto Izzy before she could rush to answer.

"Who is it?" he called out.

"Jack."

Since he recognized his brother's voice, he let Izzy go. "Go ahead."

Izzy scrambled for the front door and let Jack in. Jack locked the door behind him and then strode forward.

"Grant, Hawk and Palmer are checking the perimeter. Anna's trying to figure out what happened to the security system. Fill me in," he demanded, all sheriff even though he was in pajamas. He held his gun in one hand, cell in the other.

Cash looked at Carlyle. Her worried gaze was on Izzy. Something twisted in his gut, sharp and complicated, but he pushed it away. Had to focus on the task at hand.

"Iz?" he forced himself to say. "Can you go grab a wash-cloth and some bandages? Some of the antibiotic ointment. We'll get Carlyle all fixed up." Which was a lie, but it would get Izzy out of earshot for a minute or two.

She nodded and ran for the hallway.

Cash looked at Jack, kept his voice low. "Carlyle needs to go to the hospital."

"The 911 call should pull in an ambulance. If not, one of my deputies will run her there on code. Let's try to sort out what happened so she can go straight there."

"I couldn't sleep," Carlyle said. And she *sounded* alert and with it. Maybe the bleeding wasn't so bad.

"I was just sitting in my room, looking at the stars out the window, and the security light went off." She swallowed. "At first, I thought…it was just nothing. Then the lights didn't work. I thought I saw a shadow so I…came to check it out."

"Without telling anyone?"

"Yeah, without telling anyone," she replied, not bitterly exactly, but certainly with some acid in her tone. "That shadow could have been anything, including a figment of my imagination."

"But it wasn't," Cash said. Because Izzy had screamed. He'd rushed to her bedroom to find Copper growling at the window and Izzy cowering in the corner.

"I don't have any great details," Carlyle continued. "It was all shadows. There was someone by Izzy's window. I had my gun, so I told them to stop. Tell me who they were. But then Izzy screamed, and Copper went nuts inside and I… I got distracted. So the person rushed me." She looked down at the bloody shirt. "I guess stabbed me too."

Jack nodded, no doubt filing away all the information. And his brothers and brother-in-law checking the perimeter would look for prints. Any evidence of whoever had been here.

But someone had been right outside his daughter's window, and he hadn't even *known*. He'd come to rely on those security cameras and look where it had led him.

Izzy rushed back in with the first aid kit and a dripping washcloth. Cash took them from her and then maneuvered her so she was facing Jack, not Carlyle and her bloody shirt.

Jack knelt in front of Izzy, put his hand on her shoulder. "What made you scream?"

She swallowed and Cash was overwhelmed with the guilt of how little he'd been able to protect her from danger. She was only twelve and she'd already seen far too much for a grown woman, let alone a middle schooler. He'd tried to shelter her from so much and failed. Every single time.

Cash lifted up Carlyle's shirt. The bloody gash on her side, just above her hip—where an intricate and colorful tattoo wound around pale skin—would definitely need stitches, and that was probably his fault too. He pressed the washcloth to it, then put her shirt back down. He took her hand and pressed it on the shirt over the lump of wash-cloth. "Can you hold it?"

She nodded as Izzy began to answer Jack's question.

"Copper was growling," she said. "It woke me up. I was getting out of bed to get you, Dad. But then… I heard a weird noise. It took me a minute to figure out it was some-one opening my window. Then I heard voices and I just… screamed."

"What kind of voices, honey?" Jack asked, rubbing a hand up and down her arm.

"I heard someone say *stop*." She looked over her shoul-der at Carlyle. "You, right?"

Carlyle nodded.

"Then I heard this kind of…creepy breathing. Right by my window. Copper was really growling now and I… I didn't know what else to do."

"You did good," Carlyle said firmly.

Izzy's bottom lip wobbled before she steadied it. "You're hurt."

Carlyle shrugged. "I'm fine."

A pounding started at the door. Not police yet, from the sounds of it. Carlyle's expression went grim. "You better let him in before he tears the door down with his bare hands."

Jack sighed and got up, unlocked the door and opened it for one of Carlyle's brothers.

Walker was barefoot. Hair wild. Eyes hot and angry.

Yeah, Cash couldn't blame him. He'd be looking the same if situations were reversed.

"What the hell is going..." His gaze landed on Carlyle on the couch, and even though she was holding pressure on the wound, the blood was visible on her shirt and the couch. Walker started to swear as he crossed the room to her.

"Come on, Walker," she said firmly, even though she was too pale and this was taking too damn long. "Not in front of the kid."

Walker came up short as if finally realizing there were other people in the room, one of them a twelve-year-old girl. He blinked once at Izzy, then his expression went blank. "Someone explain to me what's happening."

"No big deal. Just got a little knocked around when I found someone outside Izzy's window. Cops are on the way."

"An ambulance too, I hope."

"It's okay. She's going to be okay. She said so," Izzy said, sounding very close to tears.

Cash pulled her into him, gave her a squeeze. "She's going to be just fine, but we'll have a doctor check her out just in case."

"Hopefully he'll be cute," Carlyle said, making Walker groan.

But it also did what it was supposed to do, Cash supposed. Izzy didn't look *quite* so distraught. Walker didn't look *quite* so murderous. She'd lightened the tone, made them think that because she could crack a joke all was well.

The door opened behind Walker, this time Hawk. "Didn't find anything," he said, his expression cool and blank. "Cops are coming up the drive. Why don't we move up to the main house for questioning. They're going to want to search around the cabin anyway."

"I'm going to take Carlyle to the damn hospital myself," Walker said.

"Barefoot?" Carlyle replied with a raised eyebrow. "Going to toss me in your truck too?"

Her brother scowled deeply, but by that time a police cruiser had parked outside the cabin. Then it became the usual. The far too usual. Cops and an EMT and moving to the main house while Carlyle and Walker went to the hospital.

There were questions, so many questions, and an exhausted Izzy curled up on his lap because she was afraid. Terrified. So terrified that he didn't even bother to bundle her up into one of the guest rooms upstairs. He just sat on the couch and let her sleep in his lap long after everyone had gone or retreated back to bed.

Like she was a baby again. He brushed a hand over her tangled hair. "I'm sorry I haven't done a better job, baby," he muttered. Like he had so many times over the years. No matter how hard he tried, he couldn't seem to give her the life she deserved.

The police had no answers, but Jack was down at the sheriff's department to find out what he could. They'd all work together to figure it out, to get answers, to protect Izzy. But Cash was so tired of this...constant battle. Every time he eased into some new season of his life, something like this happened.

Sometime before dawn, he heard light footsteps and looked up to see Anna enter the room, carrying a fussy Caroline. Anna sank into the rocking chair across from the couch where he sat, Izzy asleep across his lap.

Cash had a very vivid memory of being sick one winter not long after Anna had been born, sleeping on this couch, and waking up to his mother in the same position with baby Anna.

Now Anna was the mother, and he hadn't seen his own for half his life. Time just kept inching on.

"The obvious answer is Chessa," Anna whispered, her expression hot and mean even as she snuggled Caroline to her chest. Anna and Chessa hadn't gotten along even when Cash had still been married to Izzy's mother.

"Maybe," Cash said. He knew she was talking about who was outside Izzy's window overnight, but it didn't sit right. Chessa was tiny. Granted, when she was high she could inflict some damage, but it was hard to believe she could do the damage done to Carlyle.

An even bigger stretch was Chessa having the know-how to cut the electricity. She might know the ranch well enough, but she wouldn't know how to tamper with the generator and make sure all the security system batteries were dead *along* with cutting the electricity.

"Not on her own. No, but who else would be after Izzy?" Anna demanded.

"I don't know," Cash muttered, looking down at his sleeping daughter. But they needed an answer this time.

A final one.

Chapter Three

Carlyle was bitter about the stitches. She hated needles and hospitals and know-it-all doctors even when they *were* cute.

She was bitter about Walker hulking about like some kind of overprotective dad when she was *fine*. "Go home to your wife."

"I'm going to have the doctor check you for brain damage."

She rolled her eyes. This lousy hospital bed was uncomfortable, and the IV in her arm was making her want to crawl out of her skin. Made worse when Walker finally stopped *pacing* and sat down on the hospital bed next to her.

"What were you doing out there, Car?"

"Checking out a threat."

"Why didn't you come get me?"

"I'm not a kid. You gotta get that through your head. I wasn't going to wake you and your pregnant wife up when I wasn't even sure it *was* a threat."

"You should have. Or called Cash. Or grabbed Jack. Literally an entire ranch full of people who would have helped at your fingertips, and you walk out into the dark alone. Everything could have gone so much worse."

Carlyle looked hard out the window. Day had risen. Cars came and went from the parking lot. She had to blink back tears. It could have been so much worse, but this was bad enough because if she'd had backup, maybe whoever it was wouldn't have gotten away.

"I feel guilty enough, thanks."

He sighed and patted her IV-less arm. "I'm not trying to make you feel guilty."

"Doing a hell of a job anyway."

"Whether or not they track down who it was, you stopped something from happening to that little girl, Carlyle."

"The police don't have anything, do they?"

"Not yet. Mary's updating me as she hears, but we won't know what Jack's found until he's done."

"It just means she's going to keep being in danger."

"And she's got an army of people protecting her, Car. It's not the same. All you had was us."

She hated that he could see through her so easily, that he might be feeling his own guilt. "You two were pretty top notch."

"Not like the Hudsons."

No, they hadn't had a ranch or a community or much of anything the Hudsons offered Izzy. A sheriff as an uncle among them.

"We did the best with what we had. Not exactly your fault."

"Nah." He squeezed her hand. "But the things we blame ourselves for don't have to be our actual fault to feel like we should have made a different choice. But there's no different choice. There's only the one you make in the moment, and then how you learn from it. Don't go it alone, Car. Not anymore. None of us needs to."

"This feels like a pep talk for our brother."

"Yeah, but he's not chained to a hospital bed, so he just leaves when I try."

"I know it's not my fault," she said, both because it was

true and because he needed to hear her say it. "I know it worked out that I happened to look out there when someone was sneaking around." Or maybe if she didn't *know* it, she tried to convince herself of it. "It had to be her mom, right?"

"That's what most of them think."

"Most?"

"According to Mary, Cash isn't totally sold, at least on it just being her. Doesn't think the mom has it in her to orchestrate that kind of attack on her own."

Carlyle frowned at that. It *was* pretty orchestrated. It was a lot for one person to handle, because it wasn't just cutting the security light and the electricity, it was debilitating all the security backups and getting to Izzy all in a short period of time. But *why*?

"We'll get to the bottom of it," Walker said. "And more, we'll all protect Izzy. She's lucky she's got so many people who've got her back."

But it wasn't luck to be a little girl who felt like a target. Carlyle should know. Luckily, the doctor came in, because she didn't know how to convince Walker she was fine, or that she didn't feel guilt, or that she was going to magically not worry about Izzy no matter how many people were looking after her.

It took another couple hours, mostly of waiting until she wanted to scream, before they finally released her and Walker drove her back to Hudson Ranch. Walker walked her right to her room—no detours allowed. Mary was waiting there for her, and it was clear she'd tidied up Carlyle's room, changed the sheets, had a tray of snacks waiting.

"I don't want to be fussed over," Carlyle grumbled as she got into her bed, hating that it was a lie. She absolutely wanted pillows fluffed and snacks delivered and Mary's soft, easy presence. She was so perfect, and Carlyle might have hated her for it if Mary didn't love Walker so much, if she wasn't going to make the best mom to Carlyle's future niece or nephew.

"Oh, dear," Mary said, sounding truly perplexed. "You sure got messed up with the wrong family, then." She arranged the tray on the nightstand and shot Carlyle a grin.

Carlyle wanted to keep pouting, but it was too hard. Mary really did embody that old saying about glowing while pregnant. And Walker sliding his arm around her waist and looking down at her like she hung the moon only added to it.

It was everything she wanted for her brother, but if she thought too much about it, the lack of sleep and pain medicine would likely make her cry and she didn't want to indulge in that just yet.

"You know, a girl who's been stabbed deserves to know the gender of her first niece or nephew."

Mary looked up at Walker, who gave a nod. "It's a boy," Mary said, her smile soft and wide.

Carlyle hadn't expected Mary to actually answer. She really hadn't. It made her want to cry all over again.

Luckily, Izzy popped her head in the doorway. Mary moved out of the way to let Izzy in. "Can you keep an eye on her for me, Izzy? I've got some brownies in the oven I need to check on and Walker has some work to do."

Izzy nodded solemnly, and when they left the room Izzy produced a little clutch of wildflowers she'd clearly picked and tied together with a pretty little ribbon. She walked over to where Carlyle sat on the bed and held them out.

"Do you like them?"

"I *love* them." Carlyle took the outstretched flowers and a took a deep sniff of the blooms, then patted the space on the bed next to her. "Hop up. I'm not fragile."

Izzy was studying her with big, worried eyes, but eventually she crawled up onto the other side of the bed. Carlyle lifted her shirt high enough so Izzy could see the small bandage over her stitches.

"See? It's nothing."

Izzy reached out and touched the edge of the bandage, then Carlyle's tattoo, her mouth all pursed together in a frown. "My friend's aunt got shot in the leg. It was a long time ago, but it still hurts her sometimes."

"My God, what's in the water around here?"

That *almost* made Izzy smile. She cocked her head. "What's your tattoo of?"

Carlyle dropped her shirt. She didn't think Cash seemed like the type of person who'd be thrilled with his daughter getting a tour of Carlyle's tattoos. She had a few, all easily hidden by normal clothes.

Izzy sighed at Carlyle's lack of response, but she didn't push it. "I know this has something to do with my mother. I don't know why she... I don't know. But I'm sorry that—"

Carlyle pulled her as close as she could without causing too much physical pain under the weird numbness of pain meds. "Listen." *Life's a bitch and then you die* was on the tip of her tongue, but Cash probably wouldn't like that one piece of advice, even if it was borderline suitable for a twelve-year-old. "I don't do sorrys. Because I don't do anything I don't want. So no one's gotta be sorry when I wade in, because I did it because I wanted to."

"But—"

"No buts. Them's the breaks, kid. Now, I went through some scary stuff when I was your age too. And it's not that different. My mom was okay, and I had some pretty good older brothers, but my dad sucked. Hard. The kind that put us all in danger. So, I know how it feels. I do."

Izzy didn't say anything, just looked down at her hands

in her lap. But slowly, ever so slowly, she leaned her head on Carlyle's shoulder.

Carlyle might have lost it right there, but she knew she had to be strong for Izzy. "It makes you feel helpless, but... It's a good lesson. You can't control anyone but yourself. So you focus on being the best version of yourself you can be. And sometimes you go through hard stuff that makes you wonder *why*, but then...there's all this."

Carlyle pointed out the window. Izzy's eyebrows drew together as if she didn't understand what Carlyle meant.

"I've been holding my own for the past two years because I wanted some space from my brothers. I was alone, and I was lonely. And scared. It was hard to get through that, but now I get to be here. Horses. Dogs. I'm going to be an aunt. And you're going to be a cousin. That's pretty cool."

Izzy nodded after a while. "I like babies. Caroline cries a lot, but she's so cute."

"Yeah. I'm not saying you don't get to be scared or unhappy because you've got an awesome family and place to live, but what I want you to understand, accept, *know* is that everyone in this place will do whatever they can to keep you safe, and that's nothing to be sorry about. Even though sometimes it doesn't feel like it, that's a gift. We'll all keep you safe. That doesn't mean you're weak, or a burden. Because you've got some responsibility too. You were going to get your dad. You screamed. You did the right things."

"Maybe," Izzy said, but she was clearly not fully buying it. "Can I ask you a favor?"

"Anything."

She lifted her head, turned those big blue eyes on Carlyle. "I want to learn how to shoot a gun, Carlyle. And you're the only one who'll teach me."

Ahh... Hell.

LITERALLY LESS THAN forty-eight hours after she'd been *stabbed*, Carlyle was in the dog pens, being a pain in his ass.

"You aren't working," Cash said. Ordered. "Go back to the house."

"If I don't have something to do, I'm going to lose my mind."

"Take up knitting."

"I'd rather bleed out, thanks."

He laughed in spite of himself. Which was bad because she grinned at him and wouldn't take him seriously now.

"The doctor said no heavy lifting," she continued. "But the nurse said I should keep mobile. I don't want to get all stiff and weak over a few stitches. Besides, I needed to talk to you about something away from Izzy. Work seemed about the only option."

Cash frowned. He didn't like the sound of that. At all. Particularly when Carlyle looked…nervous.

"How do you feel about Izzy and… Look. She came and talked to me yesterday… The thing is…"

"Spit it out, Carlyle," he snapped, because he couldn't begin to fathom what this was that would have Carlyle, of all people, stumbling over her words. About *his* daughter.

"She wants me to teach her how to shoot a gun."

Cash barked out a laugh, and not a nice one. "She knows that's not happening. I've told her she has to wait until she's sixteen. And I don't appreciate her trying to talk you into going against that very clear rule. I'm going to go over there right now and—"

Carlyle grabbed him, held him in place. "You can't tell her I told you. She'll never tell me anything again."

"Good! She shouldn't be telling *you* anything anyway."

Her head drew back like he'd slapped her, and it took him a second, but he got it. Too late, but he got it.

"I didn't mean it like that."

She stepped away from him and crossed her arms over her chest, her expression cool and detached. Trying to hide the hurt. "Oh, yeah? How did you mean it?"

He blew out a long breath. *This* was why he'd kept their lives somewhat isolated. *This* was why he hadn't wanted an assistant. Why he and Izzy lived in their own space.

He was in charge of his daughter, and he didn't do well with anyone butting in telling him how to do that.

Now he had to somehow apologize to Carlyle for something he *hadn't* meant, while making it clear she could in no way get involved in this decision regarding his daughter.

"You don't understand." He shoved a hand through his hair, trying to find the words. "How hard this..." He blew out a breath. Maybe he didn't have the right words, but he had a very clear truth. "My daughter *loves* you, straight through."

Carlyle looked at him with that expression she very rarely showed. It was a little too vulnerable for her usual badass bravado. And it weakened his defenses against her, because he knew better than most that soft spots and hurts lived under a tough exterior.

"I love her too," Carlyle said, very quietly. Seriously.

"Yeah. I know. I do...know that. Hell, Car, you've got a stab wound to prove it. But she came to you on this because she knows I'll say no. She wants it to be a secret. I can't accept that. I won't, not with all this going on. Secrets between us aren't safe, and I know she hates it, but sometimes you hate the things people do to protect you."

Carlyle swallowed visibly. But she nodded. "I'm not going to do it against your wishes. If I was going to do that, I wouldn't have told you in the first place. Just let me... Let me try to make it her idea to tell you, okay? I'll try to convince her to tell you before we do anything, but you can't go storming in there yelling at her that she can't. She's *scared*, Cash. And she has every right to want to do something about it."

"Nothing is happening to her."

"No, nothing is. I know you're scared too. We *all* are. But she's a kid who feels like everything is happening *to* her. Why wait four years? What's that going to change? I know you have to be the worried, careful dad. I get that, I really do. But you don't get how it feels to be that kid. You're an adult who gets to feel like you have some kind of control."

"You think I feel like I have *any* kind of control?" he shot back. He hadn't felt in control of a damn thing since his parents disappeared when he was fourteen.

Carlyle crossed over to him, put her hand on his arm. "But when we're adults, we get to *do* stuff about that feeling. You can't expect her to just sit there and be protected. Trust me, Cash. I know your family has been through some bad stuff, and no doubt Jack did annoying things to try to protect you, but it's got nothing on being the youngest kid in a group full of people who think they know what's best."

He tried to take that on board because it was true. Carlyle had been more in Izzy's shoes than he ever had been. Maybe he'd felt like his entire adult life had been about rolling with a hundred different punches, but he supposed Carlyle was right. He could punch back whenever he wanted, and he was always telling Izzy to let him handle it.

"I don't like the idea of her dealing with guns. Not at this age. Maybe I'm wrong, but that was always the family rule. Unless you wanted to go hunting, no guns until sixteen."

"Can't you make a compromise for special life circumstances? Can't you at least teach her how to *shoot* one, even if you don't want her to have access to a firearm?"

"What'd be the point of that?"

"Knowledge, Cash. Knowing how to do stuff makes you feel like you can…handle things. I don't know how else to explain it. Knowledge is power."

Cash didn't know how to take that fully on board. It wasn't that he thought she was wrong. Worse, it felt like she was right. And all the ways he'd tried to protect Izzy from things—from her knowing bad things, understanding awful things—might have been the wrong choice.

"She's the most important person in the world to me. I just want to protect her."

"I know." Carlyle swallowed, like this was hard for *her*. "I think I know better than most. And while I can't know how you are feeling as a parent, I have been in her situation. I know what she needs, Cash. I know what it's like to know someone out there is after you, and it doesn't matter. I had the two best brothers in the world protecting me, but it didn't *matter*. I kept secrets I shouldn't have, secrets that got my brother shot, and put all of us, including you guys, in danger. I just… If I can help her and you not go through that, I will stick my nose where it doesn't belong. Sorry."

Her hand was still on his arm, and he understood that she was trying to *help*. He had so much help, so much support in his family, but Carlyle really was the only one who had a kind of insight into what it felt like to be in Izzy's position. Cash had never really thought of that before.

He patted her hand. "I appreciate it, even when I don't."

She laughed at that, her mouth curving and her blue-gray eyes taking on that little sparkle of mischief that was so much *her*. "I guess it helps I don't mind ticking people off."

"You?" he replied, with mock surprise, which made her laugh again.

There was something about the sound of it. Like a magnet. He always found himself moving closer. Getting a little lost in that dimple in her cheek.

Someone behind him cleared their throat and Carlyle jumped while Cash dropped his hand from over hers, like they'd been caught doing something other than *talking about his daughter*.

"Sorry to interrupt," Jack said as Cash turned to face him.

"Not interrupting," Cash muttered, shoving his hands into his pockets. He would have felt embarrassed, or worried what Jack thought, if he hadn't recognized that blank, cop look on his brother's face. Bad news. Cash moved forward. "What is it? Iz—"

"It isn't about Izzy," Jack said, quick and concise. "She's at the house and is fine."

"Then what is it?"

"Bent County found Chessa."

"Good." Cash knew it wouldn't be that simple, but it was a start. "Are you going to go question her or are they? I'd like you to be there. I'd…"

Jack let out a breath. Stepped forward. Bad news, all around, Cash could feel it. Like Mom and Dad all over again. Jack reached out, put a hand on his shoulder. "She's dead, Cash."

Cash had no idea how to absorb that. But that wasn't all.

"It's looking like murder."

Chapter Four

Carlyle knew she couldn't possibly feel as shocked as Cash, but it was close. Dead. Murder. A kidnapping attempt that now made even less sense.

And the two Hudson brothers, standing there *so* still. Jack's hand on Cash's shoulder and Cash barely even taking a breath.

"I don't understand," he finally said, his voice little more than a scrape. "She...she was murdered?"

"That's the premise they're operating under. I'm still working on getting more details out of Bent County. It's an ongoing investigation and they know I've got personal ties, so I'm getting shut out. I sent Chloe over to the coroner's office to see if she could get something for us to go on. But I have a bad feeling this will work its way through the town grapevine, so I wanted to tell you before you got exaggerated word of it from someone else."

Carlyle had an uncomfortable, vivid flashback of Walker telling her what had happened when she'd been at school that she...she had to look away, take a few steps back.

This wasn't about her. This wasn't...the past. Not her mother murdered all because Carlyle had been tired of moving around, had thrown a fit because she wanted to stay in one place.

It was just the horrible roll of the dice that scattered similar tragedies around the world. And how her mother had dealt with the man who'd wanted her dead was hardly Carlyle's fault, no matter how often she felt like it was.

"I have to tell Izzy," Cash said, his voice still that awful, pained gasp of a man drowning.

"You could wait," Jack said. "Give us some time to find more answers. She's not leaving the ranch, so it's not like she'll have contact with anyone running their mouth. Let's take some time to get all the information."

"She'll know." Carlyle knew she should have kept her mouth shut, this wasn't her family, her business. But she... Even more so now, she had been in Izzy's shoes. Her mother had been murdered when she'd been a kid. And Carlyle had *loved* her mother, depended on her for everything, blamed herself for her death, so it was different. It was so different.

But right now, it felt the same. It was too many commonalities, and too much understanding Izzy's position to keep her mouth shut. She retraced her steps to stand next to Cash again, to face off against Jack.

"She won't know if no one tells her," Jack said, a clear warning in his hard tone.

Carlyle should nod and agree because this wasn't her family or her business, and it'd be smart to heed Jack's warning. But... She turned to Cash. "It doesn't matter how careful you all are. If *you* know something *she* doesn't, that's this big and this important, she'll feel it. And she'll worry it's about what happened at the cabin. She'll make it into something else, she will feel...like an outsider. Trust me, when you feel like that, you make bad choices."

Cash turned to look at her, but every move seemed weighed down. Like he was swimming through molasses. In his head, it probably felt like it.

"What do you mean, Carlyle?" he asked, with the weight of the world on his shoulders.

She wished she could heft some of the load. "I just mean..." She looked from Cash to Jack then back again because Cash was clearly the only receptive audience. "My mother was murdered too, you know. When I was Izzy's age. Walker and Zeke... They tried to shelter me, keep the sordid details from me, but the thing was, I already was too deep in. I knew secrets, but they tried to keep me separate. I know it was to protect me. I know they were trying to do the right thing, the *good* thing, but it put us at cross purposes. We spent too many years..." She trailed off. She didn't need to go down the full tangent of her life. "I know this isn't the same situation. You aren't Walker and I'm not Izzy, but I just know what it's like to be in her position. You feel powerless, and you'll do some pretty reckless things to find some power. Especially if everyone you love is keeping something from you."

"*You* felt that way," Jack pointed out.

Carlyle tried not to scowl at him, but hiding her frustration with him was a hard-won thing. She managed not to scowl, but her tone was snappish when she spoke. "Yeah. You got a lot of experience being a twelve-year-old girl whose mother was murdered?"

Jack, predictably, said nothing in response. That was the problem with all this childhood trauma bred into the very fabric of this ranch. They thought because they'd had it rough, they understood all the layers of what was rough for anyone else.

But Carlyle could see, very clearly, there was something very different about losing your parents suddenly and without knowing what really happened, and knowing that someone had *killed* one of them, on purpose, for you to find.

The Hudsons looked at Izzy and saw their own problems, but even Carlyle couldn't begin to guess what the little girl felt about the terrible mother she'd barely known—by all accounts—being murdered.

What Carlyle *did* understand was being the little girl left out of the discussion, someone not *part* of what was going on.

"I know you guys had stuff too," Carlyle said, her focus on Cash because he's who she had to convince. He had the final say in his daughter's life. "I can't imagine what it's like to have your parents disappear into thin air, but it's not the same." Of course, Carlyle couldn't resist a *little* dig. "You were in charge, Jack. She's not. And she knows it."

Jack's scowl was epic. He crossed his impressive arms over his chest, all tall and glowering and intimidating.

Too bad Carlyle had grown up at the feet of intimidating. She didn't so much as *blink* at him.

"You know I'm right," she said to Cash. "I think you have to know I'm right."

Cash didn't look at her. He looked at some spot on the ground. Making Carlyle realize this wasn't *just* about Izzy. Maybe this Chessa was his *ex*-wife, maybe he didn't love her anymore, but he'd married her once. Had a kid.

He'd lost something too.

Sympathy swept through her, and she reached out to touch his arm or something, but he chose that moment to move forward. "I'm going to go tell her," Cash muttered, pushing past Jack.

Leaving Carlyle to face off against a clearly very disapproving Jack. Which she should have left alone, but disapproving authority had never sat well with her, no matter how well-meaning.

"You don't have to agree with him or me, Jack. She's not my kid and she's not your kid."

"They're all mine," he muttered, but he didn't argue anymore, just turned and strode away as Cash had.

Leaving Carlyle alone with the dogs. Her side throbbing, her heart aching and far too many memories making it all too easy to worry about what Izzy might do next.

But the one thing she was reminded of quite plainly by Jack's parting words hurt just as much.

None of them were *hers*.

CASH WENT FOR whiskey that night. He rarely drank anymore. At most, a beer here or there. Never hard liquor. Never with Izzy under the same roof. It tended to remind him a little too much of the hell he'd raised when he was far too young.

It was hard to remember that kid. He was nothing like the boy who'd lost his parents—angry and confused and scared, but too much of a fourteen-year-old to admit it. So he'd caused trouble, fought with Jack, drank, ran with the wrong crowd.

Everything had changed at seventeen when Izzy had been born. So tiny. So *his*. A responsibility he owed to everyone in his life to see through. To take more seriously than any other responsibility he'd ever been gifted. He'd given up everything wild in that moment.

Chessa had never felt that. At the core of all their marital issues, that was number one. Everything in Cash's life had changed when Izzy had taken her first breath, and Chessa had wanted nothing to change. Cash hadn't struggled to give up their wild, reckless ways. Chessa had always been desperate for one more hit.

Now Chessa was dead. He'd always known she was heading in that direction. Too much drinking. Drugs. Getting mixed up with dangerous people all for a hit. He'd felt at turns guilty about it, and at turns—which made the guilt nearly swamp him now—wished she'd just get it over with so he wouldn't have to worry about her hurting Izzy anymore.

She'd lost the ability to hurt him a long time ago, if she'd ever had it to begin with.

A sad state of affairs, through and through.

Now he'd had to tell his daughter her mother was dead. At someone else's hand. He'd planned on just telling her Chessa had died, leave the details out of it, but Carlyle's words had haunted him.

So he'd told Izzy the truth. A slightly sanitized version of what little he knew, but definitely the important parts.

Izzy hadn't cried. She'd been upset, he knew. She hadn't tried to hide the hurt. But it was more fear and confusion.

And definitely hiding something. He wouldn't have seen it if Carlyle hadn't brought up her own experiences, but she was right. Trying to protect Izzy had only led him to this place where his little girl didn't trust him with everything.

He let out a long breath. Why not get really drunk? There were a hundred people in this house to take care of things, and as long as no one fully knew what had happened with Chessa, and the kidnapping attempt, Izzy would be sleeping at the big house. More eyes, more bodies, more protection.

But not more answers.

The storm door squeaked open and Carlyle slid out into the dark, one of his dogs trailing after her. Copper would be up in Izzy's room, but Swiftie—who should be sleeping out at the dog barn—had clearly latched on to Carlyle.

Both woman and dog surveyed him, then Carlyle jutted her chin at the porch chair. "Mind if I join you?"

"Would it matter if I did mind?"

Her mouth curved at that, and she went over and settled herself next to him on the porch swing rather than the open chair. Swiftie settled under her feet.

He didn't scowl, but he wanted to.

"I don't want to butt in," she began.

He snorted. "Don't you?"

She sighed, then grabbed his drink—right out of his hand—and took a deep swig like it was a shot. *Hers* for the taking.

"Are you even old enough to drink?" Because he liked to remind himself—when he was feeling a little too bruised and bloody and tempted to lean on her—that she was over five years younger than him, and he had no business wanting her company.

She gave him a killing look. "It wouldn't matter to me if I was, but I'm not *that* young, Cash. In fact, I'll be twenty-four next month." She handed the glass back to him.

He grunted. "I had a seven-year-old by the time I was twenty-four."

"And I had put a famous and powerful senator in jail by the time I was twenty-three. Want to keep playing this game?"

She really was something else. Everything inside him felt too heavy to allow a laugh to escape, but she made him *almost* want to.

"I'm too tired, and not drunk enough, to play any games."

"Well, if I were you, I wouldn't go down the drunk route. I know how this goes. I can't tell if Jack knows and is sparing you, or if he's in denial because you're all upstanding Hudsons. They're going to look at you first."

"Who?"

She turned to him then, her gray-blue eyes as serious as her expression in the dim light of the repaired security pole. *Some security.*

"The cops. When someone is murdered, the significant other is the first person they start digging into."

"I haven't been Chessa's significant other for a decade. I haven't even had contact with her in close to five years. The few times she's come sniffing around, someone else dealt with her."

"Doesn't matter. The *ex* with custody of their kid? Especially a kid who's been a target? Primo suspect."

"No one who knows me is going to think I killed my own daughter's mother. No one with any sense is going to think I waited all these years to do it, either. Why now? I *do* have custody. I have everything. Chessa was the one with nothing." Because of her own choices, he had to remind himself.

"Jack isn't investigating. Bent County is. And even if he was, even if someone who 'knows you' was, they shouldn't."

"Why the hell not?"

"Because he's your *brother*. Because personal connection is a red flag, Cash. You want people thinking you did it? You want to be a true crime podcast in ten years so people can look at Izzy and wonder? You can list all the reasons people shouldn't suspect you, but all anyone is going to see is that you're the ex-husband."

If he sat with what she was saying, he understood. If he could detach himself from the situation, he'd probably agree with her.

But they were talking about *him*. And Izzy. And Chessa. And murder.

"I didn't kill anyone."

"Well, I know that. But do you have a good enough alibi? Was that weird kidnapping attempt some kind of...decoy?

You gotta start thinking with that investigator brain of yours, because the cops are slow and wrong half the time."

"I'm not an investigator anymore."

"You try to stay out of it for Izzy. I get that and I haven't been around that long. But I also see how much you *want* to be involved. You've got the skills. If not by use, by osmosis. And lucky for you, I've got the knowledge of how this goes down. You're on their list of suspects, and once they have a time of death, they're going to want to know where you were."

Sometimes, she made no sense and yet he felt like she saw right through him all at the same time.

"I happen to trust the cops, Carlyle."

"You shouldn't. They're not gods, Cash. Not saying they're bad or evil. They're just people. Human, capable of error and getting drowned in too much red tape. And if I'm trusting just people, it's going to be the people I know and love who don't have to worry about paperwork. We need to look into it ourselves, and *you* need an ironclad alibi."

He wanted to beat his head against a wall, but that wouldn't change anything. If there was one thing he understood in this life, it was that the blows never stopped coming, no matter how many you'd already had.

"Look, I appreciate the advice. Maybe you're not even wrong. I don't know. But I know I didn't do it. There can't be any proof I did, because I didn't. I'm just going to keep my head down and make sure Izzy's okay. No investigating around the cops, no worrying about alibis. Just her well-being."

Carlyle paused for a very long time, abnormally still and looking out at the twinkling night with a serious expression on her face when she was usually a whirl of excess energy and movement.

When she finally spoke, it was quietly and seriously. "She's never going to thank you for martyring yourself for her. She's going to wonder why her dad didn't have a life." She took another long sip of his drink. "And then probably blame herself for it."

She looked a little miserable, which was unfair since she was telling him *he* was about to be a prime suspect for murder. "Speaking from experience again?"

"Yeah. I had to kick Walker out of my life so he'd go live his." She turned, flashed that smile that always looked a little dangerous, but in this light he saw it for what it was. Deflection. "Look at him now. Married. About to be a dad. I did that, and has he thanked me?"

Cash could see the similarities between him and Walker whether he wanted to or not. Between Carlyle and Izzy. But... "I get it. You lived this weird version of what she's going through, but you're not the same." He took the glass from her, finished off the drink. Not enough to get drunk, but she was probably right about that being a bad idea.

"No. No two people are the same. Maybe it's different when it's your dad giving up everything he enjoys for you. But you've walked a little in our shoes too, Cash. Don't you ever worry about Jack and all he's given up to keep you guys going?"

He wanted to swear, because of course he worried about that. Because it was true. Jack had sacrificed a million times over, to keep them together, to keep the ranch going, to start Hudson Sibling Solutions. And on and on it went.

Cash looked at the empty glass in his hands. He knew he shouldn't say any more. Shouldn't prolong whatever this was. A pep talk or advice or whatever. But he felt like the words...had to be said. She was the only safe place to say them.

It was the strangest realization, in this already strange moment, that he didn't really *have* much of a safe place. Not when he was so busy trying to protect his daughter, his siblings, himself.

He didn't need to do that with Carlyle. "I used to wish she was dead. I just thought it'd be easier."

She was quiet, but only for a second or two. Then she put her hand on his shoulder, much like Jack had earlier today when he'd delivered the news.

But Carlyle's slim hand felt different than his brother's. Like comfort without the strings of who they were. Because she was right about too many things. And she understood these…strange, twisted, tenuous trauma-laden relationships.

"I don't blame you, Cash. I doubt you're the only person in your family to feel the same. Izzy included. But don't tell it to the cops. My bet? They'll be sniffing around first thing in the morning. Have an alibi. Even if you have to lie."

"Why would I lie?"

"Because if the murder happened some night you and Izzy were sleeping in the cabin out there, that's not enough of an alibi. They'll ask you to prove you didn't sneak out and do it and sneak back."

"With Izzy sleeping *alone*?"

Carlyle shrugged. "She's twelve, Cash. Not an infant. And *I* know you wouldn't leave her alone. Anyone here knows you wouldn't, but that doesn't mean much to cops looking for someone to lay the blame on. You have to be smart about this. Izzy needs you to be smart about this. Sometimes being smart means bending the truth a bit. You've got this big mess of a family behind you, and you're innocent, so that helps, but you can't let it make you complacent."

He studied her. So serious and earnest, which was not her usual MO. "Which one of them sent you out to pep talk me?"

She frowned quizzically, as if she didn't understand what he meant at first. Then she looked at the house, and something in her expression changed again. But he couldn't read it.

But he got the feeling it meant *no one* had sent her out. She had come out all on her own. Wanting to offer him advice to protect himself.

He didn't know what to do with that.

She got up off the swing. "I'm your guardian angel, obviously." She flashed that mischievous grin, but it didn't land. She was making a joke out of it because she was uncomfortable.

And since she was, he played a long. "Angel? Hardly."

"I am *reformed.*"

He snorted, but he got to his feet too. She moved for the door, but he reached out, got ahold of her hand to stop her. He gave it a squeeze.

"Thanks. I do appreciate the butting in, even when I don't like it. Because Izzy is the most important thing. I'll listen to anyone if I think it'll keep her safe. So butt in, be annoying. If it's for her benefit, I'll deal."

She looked down at their hands, but she didn't pull away or act like she was uncomfortable. He couldn't see her expression, but they just stood there on his family's porch holding hands.

Which suddenly made *him* feel uncomfortable, because it felt like all those intimate connections he'd spent years avoiding. Shrank his world down to not feel anything that didn't involve his family. Because shrinking down was *safe*, and he had to be safe. For Izzy. No matter what Carlyle said.

He dropped her hand, and she looked up. But she didn't quite meet his gaze.

"Any time," she said breezily, grabbing the storm door and opening it. Swiftie trailed behind her as she stepped inside and away from him.

He watched them disappear inside and wondered why it felt like a mistake.

Chapter Five

Carlyle shook out her hand as she walked back to her room. Not the time or place to get all...*whatever* over a little hand-holding. Over actually helping someone, instead of always being the one who had to be helped.

Cash thought she was young, and wrong.

But he'd listened to her. Thanked her. Squeezed her hand like what she had offered meant something. It did a hell of a number on that pointless soft heart of hers she was always trying to bury.

She opened her bedroom door. "You, Carlyle Daniels, are a grade A—" Before she could finish insulting herself, she stopped short. Froze.

Izzy was sitting in the middle of Carlyle's bed. Crying.

What Carlyle wanted to do was cross the room and gather Izzy up in her arms and tell the little girl she would literally fight every last demon to the death if she stopped crying.

But that was what no one—men in particular—ever understood. Sometimes, it wasn't about someone fighting the battles *for* you. Sometimes, it was about feeling you had the power to fight them yourself.

So Carlyle did her best to take her time, to tack on a smile. To give Izzy a little space at first.

"Hey. What are you doing in here? Pretty sure your dad

will have a meltdown if he goes to check in on you and you're not in bed." Carlyle moved to the bed and took a seat on the edge.

Izzy sniffled, wiping her nose with her sleeve of her pajamas. "I've got ten more minutes. He's like clockwork."

Oof. How well she knew these little games. The way some kids observed too much, filed far too much away. All to hopefully never be caught off guard again.

But the off guard always came.

Carlyle gently laid her hand on Izzy's shoulder. Much like she had with Cash outside. Two hurting people, so determined to hurt *away* from each other, rather than show each other their vulnerable underbellies.

Oof times a million.

"I know you're scared. You've got every right to be right now. And you're probably tired of hearing it, but it's true. No one's going to hurt you, Izzy. You are the most protected girl in Wyoming. I'm working on convincing your dad to let you learn how to shoot. Because you should feel like you can protect yourself too, but he's gotta be on board with it. You've both got to be honest with each other."

But Izzy was shaking her head before Carlyle even finished. "I'm not worried about protecting *me*," Izzy said, like Carlyle was crazy. "I don't want anyone to hurt my dad."

Carlyle felt a bit like she'd been stabbed all over again. But she tried not to let it show. "Why would anyone hurt your dad? Look, I realize I'm relatively new to the situation, but it sounds like Chessa was mixed up in some dangerous stuff. Stuff your dad wouldn't touch with a million-foot pole."

Izzy's expression was stubborn. Her eyes were shiny and puffy, but she'd stopped actively crying. "I don't think someone tries to get me one night, and Chessa shows up two days later dead, and it doesn't connect. It *has* to connect. I'm worried it connects to my dad, not me."

She sounded so adult. So like her father. But she brought up an interesting and terrifying point. With Chessa out of the way, what did anyone want with Izzy? What had Chessa even wanted with Izzy if, by all accounts, she hadn't wanted to be a mother?

Didn't that mean Cash might be the *actual* target? What better way to get to him than through the daughter he cherished and protected above all else?

Carlyle studied the girl, trying to find a good place for her whirling thoughts to land. There were still tears in Izzy's eyes, but underneath was a quick mind that caught on. That understood.

No matter how little her family wanted her to.

"The two things might not connect," Carlyle offered, even though she didn't know how that would possibly be true. "Maybe it's just bad timing Chessa was murdered."

"Maybe," Izzy agreed, still reminding Carlyle a bit too much of Cash right then. The careful, measured way she didn't *argue* with what Carlyle had said, but was clearly internally working through all the ways she didn't agree.

And she was going to keep those thoughts bottled up and to herself, because she didn't think the adults listened. Carlyle squeezed her shoulder. "So, how *could* it connect? What do you think?"

Izzy blinked. Once. Then looked down at her hands. "No one cares what I think," she muttered.

"First of all, I know that isn't true. You all care about each other more than just about anybody. But I think all that care, mixed up with danger, tends to a lot of...isolating yourselves and keeping secrets. You're here, in my room, crying, because you don't want your dad to see you're upset, right?"

"I know it hurts his feelings when I cry. I know... He's like the *best* dad. I do know that. I don't think he does."

Stab me in the heart, kid. "I mean, maybe you could tell him. Or not keep secrets from him."

She watched the mutinous expression begin to storm across Izzy's face and quickly changed tactics.

"Tell me how you think it connects, Izzy. Let's see what we can figure out."

The girl frowned. "Well, it's not the first time my mom tried to take me, right? If it *was* my mom who hurt you."

Carlyle hadn't heard the whole story of that, but there'd been rumblings from the Hudson contingent about an incident a while back.

"Last year," Izzy continued. "She helped that guy who tried to hurt Aunt Anna and shot Uncle Hawk? She told Uncle Hawk that she..." Izzy curled her hand into the bedspread. "She wanted to sell me or something. I don't really get that, but everyone was pretty upset about it."

Carlyle felt like she couldn't *breathe*. Sell... What an absolutely awful thing. Surely...

"No one told you about it?" Izzy asked, clearly reading Carlyle's shock.

Carlyle shook her head, unable to find her voice. Sell your own kid? Hell, her biological father had tried to have her killed, so she shouldn't be surprised at how terrible parents could be, but...

"They didn't tell me either, but I heard them talking. I always hear them talking, no matter how sneaky they think they're being." She picked at the bedspread. "But Aunt Anna and Uncle Hawk and Dad and everybody stopped that whole thing. They outsmarted the guy. Well, mostly. He shot Uncle Hawk."

Carlyle was struggling to come up with words. She'd always thought she had it pretty rough, but this girl had seen her damn share.

Izzy looked up at Carlyle earnestly. "That guy was mad because Hudson Sibling Solutions hadn't found his son alive. He wanted like revenge or something. So, what if all this is like…revenge? My mother didn't like Dad or our family. Maybe someone else didn't either. Maybe someone doesn't want to hurt *me*. They want to hurt my dad. Take me. Murder my mother. I don't know how *that* would hurt him, but maybe someone thought it would because she was my mother."

Carlyle could think of a reason someone would murder Chessa to hurt Cash. If they were going to have him take the fall.

But as much as she was all about the truth and not keeping secrets, Izzy didn't need to know that. Not yet.

"That's possible," she agreed, though it killed her to put that look of worry in the girl's eyes. "But right now, it's just as possible as anything else. Do you…know anyone who'd want to hurt your dad?"

"I know my mother hated him. Hated all of us. So maybe someone who knew her?"

"Not a bad thread to tug." But someone who had a relationship with Chessa probably hadn't killed her. Probably. But if the Hudsons had enemies… "I'll look into it."

"Really?"

"Really. And if you think of anyone, or anything that seems fishy—not just lately but even years ago—you tell me. We'll see if we can put it all together."

"We?" Izzy asked suspiciously.

"Look, I'm not going to go behind your dad's back. I'm

not going to lie to him. The way I see it, you all need to do better at working together. Not separately."

"He won't listen. He'll just keep hiding me away. Telling me to stay safe and stay out of it."

"Maybe," Carlyle agreed equitably. "But he'll be wrong to do it, and I'll tell him so. We're going to work together on this one. All of us. I'll see to it." Because Izzy's thought process was a good one, and maybe they didn't need to terrify her with all the possibilities, but she had to feel like she wasn't just someone to be hidden away.

Izzy studied her with big, serious blue eyes. Carlyle didn't know what to do with the intense gaze, so she just… took it.

"I don't want anything to happen to him, Carlyle," Izzy said, her voice little more than a whisper. "Even when I'm mad, I…"

"Listen…" She figured if it worked for the father, why not for the daughter? "You don't have to worry about your dad. I'm going to look after him. I'm going to be his guardian angel." Then she couldn't resist it anymore. She pulled Izzy into a tight hug. "I swear, Iz. I'll keep him safe." *Both of you.* "Whatever I have to do."

She'd keep that promise, no matter what it took.

CARLYLE HAD BEEN RIGHT. First thing in the morning, two Bent County detectives were waiting in the living room before Cash had even gotten his coffee. He sidestepped them and took the back way into the kitchen before they saw him.

He needed to prepare himself.

Mary was already looking fresh and neat per usual, had coffee mercifully brewing, and a whole breakfast spread on its way.

"Don't you ever have morning sickness?"

"Why do you think I'm up this early? Wakes me up before the sun, but then when the sun comes up, I'm *starving*." She nodded toward the front of the house. "They want to talk to all of us, but you first. I told them to wait," Mary said, frowning over the tray of breakfast foods she was putting together. "And suggested that the next time they wanted to do some questioning they should maybe call first. Or appear at a decent hour."

"Did they point out they're trying to solve a murder?"

Mary puffed out a breath. "Regardless. That's no excuse for bad manners."

"It probably is exactly the excuse for that."

Mary clearly did not agree, but she was not an arguer. "Take your time. Drink your coffee in here. I'll keep them busy until you're ready."

"I'll never be ready," Cash muttered. How did a person answer questions about their ex-wife's murder? His daughter's awful mother? He studied Mary, Carlyle's words from last night haunting him now that she'd been right about the cops' appearance.

"Carlyle's worried about my alibi."

Mary stopped what she was doing, looked at him, a slightly arrested expression on her face. "Walker said the same thing."

"Did you tell him the police know what they're doing, and I'm innocent so he's overreacting?"

Mary blinked. "Well. Yes."

"Yeah. I'm starting to wonder if we're *underreacting*."

"We have security footage," Mary said, her umbrage fully in place. "That will prove that you were here and—"

"Yeah, about that?" Palmer said, also coming into the kitchen through the back way. No doubt avoiding the cops too. "We don't have security footage."

"What?" Mary and Cash demanded in unison.

"I was up all night dealing with the security network. I figured the cops would want proof of where we all were, and that's easy enough, right?" Palmer poured himself a big mug of coffee. "It's all been wiped. Everything before the kidnapping attempt. It looks like some kind of...reset put in motion by the backup batteries failing, and maybe it is, but the timing is suspect."

Cash set his coffee down. This was...bad. Really, really bad.

"If Chessa was killed *after* the night Carlyle got stabbed, we've got all the footage we need. But..."

"It's going to be before," Cash finished for him.

"You don't know that," Mary insisted.

But he did. In his bones. Coincidences didn't just *happen*. Not like this.

"Just tell the truth," Mary said, even with worry etched into every inch of her expression. "You don't have anything to hide."

"Yeah," Cash agreed. He didn't have anything to hide, but he couldn't help but wonder if Carlyle would be right yet again. He took the mug of coffee. "Might as well get this over with," he grumbled, then he pushed off the counter and headed for the living room.

He knew the male detective. Thomas Hart was with Bent County and had worked on a few of their cases last year. He didn't know the blonde woman.

"Hart," he greeted. "Mary said you have some questions for me?"

They both stood up, and Thomas gestured toward the woman. "My partner, Detective Delaney-Carson."

"Ma'am."

She nodded and shook his hand, then they sat.

The woman took the lead. "A lot of this is just procedure. Outlining the players. Trying to get a sense of who might have seen Ms. Scott alive last."

Cash nodded. "I can guarantee you it wasn't me. I haven't actually seen her in years."

"There was a report from last year and the year before that she was on your property."

"The first time, she dealt with Anna and only Anna as far as I know. Second time, she was involved in the kidnapping and attempted murder, if I recall correctly, of Hawk Steele. All dealt with by other members of my family and the Sunrise Sheriff's Department."

"Where your brother is sheriff?" she asked lightly.

But it wasn't a question.

The detective made some notes on a pad of paper. Then continued to ask the usual inquiries. What was their relationship like? Non-existent. How did he feel about Chessa's lack of mothering? Ticked off but philosophical considering he didn't want Izzy around her when she was high. What did he know about Chessa's drug use and on and on.

But Cash *was* too much of an investigator at heart, even if he tried not to be. They were asking a lot of roundabout questions, but they were working up to something specific.

He waited them out, refusing to let his impatience show. They wouldn't hear anger or frustration when they listened to the interview tape back. They'd hear boredom and compliance.

"So, where were you the night of June first?"

And there it was. They had a time of death—some time the evening of June first. The day *before* the kidnap attempt. Now, they wanted his alibi. Cash blew out a breath. Trying to think of both the truth and how the hell he was going to get out of this. "Monday, right? Izzy's on summer break so our schedule is a little looser than normal, but I spend every night in the same place. In my cabin, on this property, with my daughter."

"Can you take us through that particular night?"

"I don't remember anything specific. But the usual pattern is eating dinner around six. Sometimes here at the main house, but if I remember correctly, we had spaghetti night at the cabin. Then we go play with the dogs until sunset. We go inside, Izzy takes a shower while I clean up the dinner mess. She goes to bed, then I watch TV, or do some reading, and then go to sleep."

"Alone, presumably?"

Cash wanted to scowl. Wanted to yell. Carlyle had been right. They didn't see it as enough of an alibi.

"It's okay. You can tell them."

Cash jerked at the new voice, looked over his shoulder at where Carlyle stood in the entrance to the room. She looked tired, but she was dressed for a morning of dog training. Swiftie sat at her feet, tail softly swishing back and forth.

"Tell them what?" he asked, wholly and utterly confused at what she thought she was doing.

"We've been keeping it on the down-low, but he wasn't alone. We were together."

What the hell was she doing? *Lying* to the cops? He stood and turned to face her, to try to get it through to her whatever she was doing was *not* the way to handle this, without giving anything away to the cops. "Carlyle."

But her gaze was steady on the detectives, her expression stubborn. "It's kind of a secret, but I'd rather tell the truth than have you guys looking in the wrong direction. I was with him. In his cabin. In his bedroom. For most of the night that night."

Chapter Six

"Can anyone corroborate that story?" the detective asked, keeping any thoughts she had on the subject closed behind an easygoing expression.

But Carlyle knew how to lie to cops. She knew how to make them believe it. She *knew*, and she'd made a promise to Izzy. "Like I said, it's a bit of a secret. We've been sneaking around. You know, family can be complicated, and we wanted to see where it went before Izzy got involved. Not to mention my brothers."

Carlyle watched as the two detectives exchanged a look. It wasn't disbelief exactly, but they certainly weren't falling for it hook, line and sinker. The woman wrote down a few lines in her notebook.

Carlyle moved farther into the room. She didn't dare look at Cash's expression. He was probably blowing the whole thing, so she had to focus on the cops. Focus on saving him from his noble self.

"I bet if you asked anyone around here, they'd say the same thing. Maybe they didn't *see* me at Cash's cabin, or know anything was going on, but they've wondered. Noticed little things. Maybe someone will remember something from that night, even."

"So, you're saying you were in Cash Hudson's cabin—"

"*Bedroom*," Carlyle corrected the male cop, hoping to

God her cheeks weren't turning red. She could not actually *think* about being in Cash's bedroom, even as she convinced these cops that was just the usual.

"I saw Carlyle sneak into the main house very early that morning. Coming from the direction of Cash's cabin."

Everyone turned to Mary, who was pushing a little cart with a tray of food on top. She stopped the cart in front of the detectives. "Please, help yourselves. But Carlyle is right. I did see something, and I didn't say anything to anyone about it."

"Why not?"

"My husband is her very protective older brother, and Cash is *my* brother. I thought I'd just keep it to myself until they were ready to be open about it. It wasn't really any of my business what my adult brother and adult sister-in-law were getting up to in the middle of the night."

Carlyle wanted to cheer. Mary was lying. *Mary.* Carlyle might have expected the quick thinking and subterfuge of Anna, but Mary was so proper, so upstanding. But she was also always surprising people.

"What time was this?" the female detective asked, pen poised on the pad of paper.

"I don't know exactly. I'm up and down with morning sickness all night half the time. After midnight, definitely. So morning, but very early. Before the sun was up."

She was so smooth, and not too specific. *Just* specific enough to corroborate Carlyle's story and give a large window of an alibi to Cash. It was a *revelation*.

Carlyle had to look back at the detectives to keep from grinning. She couldn't look at Cash. It would ruin her act, she knew.

"Thank you for your cooperation. We'd like to speak to Anna Hudson-Steele next. She had a run-in with Chessa Scott a while back?"

"She did," Mary said primly. "Help yourselves to food, detectives. My sister will be down once she's done *feeding* her baby." And with that, Mary sailed back into the kitchen.

"What about Hawk Steele? Can he be bothered this morning?" the man asked, with only a *hint* of sarcasm in his tone.

"Yeah, we'll go get him," Cash said. He took Carlyle by the elbow, and she realized she was the *we* in this situation. He pulled her out of the room, down the hallway, and didn't say a word.

When she finally worked up the nerve to look at his expression, it was a cold kind of fury she'd only ever seen on his face that night of the would-be kidnapping.

"If you're going to yell at me, you should probably wait until they're gone," Carlyle muttered under her breath. He didn't drop her arm even though they were out of earshot. He just dragged her along and up the stairs.

"I'm not going to yell at you," he muttered. He knocked softly on Anna and Hawk's door.

Hawk opened it, scowling already. But he was dressed, and Anna was rocking baby Caroline in the corner in her pajamas.

"I take it the cops want to talk to me."

"News travels fast. They asked for Anna first, though."

Hawk's scowl deepened. "I'll handle it."

"Oh, I don't mind talking to them once Caroline's done," Anna said. "Considering how often I have to feed this ravenous barnacle, it's going to be very hard to pin this one on me. They ask you for an alibi?" Anna asked Cash.

"Yeah," Cash said. He kept his expression carefully neutral. "For the night of June first. Carlyle supplied one."

"How did Carlyle supply an alibi for the whole night..."

Anna trailed off. "Oh." Her gaze was sharp—from Cash to Carlyle then back again. "Well."

Carlyle had to fight off another wave of embarrassment as Cash didn't explain it away. He let Hawk and Anna just... believe it was true. And she'd never been one for embarrassment, but this was just...weird.

"I'll go talk to them until you're ready," Hawk said darkly. He bent over and brushed a kiss across Anna's cheek, then Caroline's. "And when you come down, do not be yourself."

Anna grinned up at him. "I could not possibly fathom what you mean, darling."

He grunted, but turned and left the room. He closed the door behind him so Cash, Hawk and Carlyle all stood in the hall.

Hawk paused. "If they get too hung up looking at any of us, whoever actually did it is going to disappear."

Cash nodded grimly, but Carlyle didn't need to nod because hadn't that been her whole point with the fake alibi? This needed to be a concerted effort to not just rely on the cops who had to follow procedures and every viable option.

Hawk strode down the hallway toward the stairs. Carlyle moved to follow, but Cash took her by the arm again and pulled her down the hallway to a room at the end of it. She assumed it was the room he slept in when he stayed at the main house.

He closed the door behind them, and Carlyle tried not to feel nervous. She didn't do nervous. She'd done what was right, what would help. He could be mad at her all he wanted, but she was *right*.

And still, her stomach jittered with worry.

"You were right." He blew out a long breath. "They'll look into Anna because she had a fight with Chessa a long time ago. They'll look into Hawk because Chessa was involved in hurting him, but mostly they think I'm the prime suspect."

"So are you going to thank me for my quick thinking?" she asked, trying for her usual flippant tone.

He glared at her. "I don't like this. Lies come back to bite. Why do you think I let Anna think..." He shook his head. "It's best that only you, me and Mary know the alibi is a lie. I need you to agree to that."

"What about Walker? I don't mind lying to him, but you're going to have to make sure Mary is okay with it."

"Hell, I don't know. I guess that's up to Mary."

"What about Izzy? They're going to want to question her."

"They can go to hell."

"Cash—"

"Don't. Don't start on the she needs to have some choice or power or whatever."

He sounded so...at the end of his rope. Just barely hanging on by a thread. She wanted to soothe him somehow. But now wasn't the time. They had to act. He had to get over this hang-up. "Okay. I won't start on that, but... Izzy has some theories."

"Theories?"

"About how the events might connect. About who the actual target might be. She's smart. She's—"

"Twelve."

"Yeah, Cash. *Twelve*. Not two. She's looking for patterns, links, and she's worried about you. Scared to death *you'll* get hurt in all this. We have to work together. All of us. Maybe the cops will beat us to answers, but maybe they won't. So, let's *all* work together. On the same page. *With* Izzy. If you let her in on this, at least a little, she's not going to be crying in my room worrying that you're going to end up like Chessa."

She hadn't *meant* to let the crying part spill, but she didn't know how to get through his thick skull.

He closed his eyes, clearly in pain—emotional pain. And she couldn't stop herself anymore. She crossed the room to him, put her hand over his heart.

"You're both trying so hard to protect each other that you are shutting each other out, and I don't think that's what either of you want, Cash."

He opened his eyes and looked down at her. A million things swam in the dark depths, mostly bad things. Hurt and worry and she just wanted to *fix* it for him. Her free hand came up and touched his cheek.

"I promise, letting her in isn't going to ruin her life. Giving her some agency isn't going to fling her into danger. She's already *in* danger. Let's give her the tools to find some power. And protect the hell out of her while we do. All of us. Your siblings. Mine. And your amazing daughter. I have faith in the Hudson-Daniels machine, Cash. Do you?"

He inhaled slowly and she knew she should take her hand off his face. She knew she should step away.

But she didn't. As the moment stretched out, she just stood there, while he slowly let out his breath and didn't move away.

But when he inhaled again, he patted her hand, as if she was a child, and then stepped back. "Thanks, Carlyle," he said, though his voice was rough. "You're right. Let's get everyone together and go from there."

Then he left her in that room, heart feeling bruised and wrung out, tears she didn't understand in her eyes. But she'd gotten her point across.

Everyone together.

She had to believe that would matter.

CASH TENDED TO avoid big family meetings. He didn't like Izzy getting too involved in whatever was going on, particularly ever since Izzy had witnessed a gun to Anna's head last year. But Carlyle had been insistent and… He wanted her to be wrong about it, but no matter how he looked at it, he couldn't convince himself she was.

She understood Izzy's position too well. And she was right, the Hudson-Daniels machine was better than any police department in the world.

She just kept being right. He rubbed at his chest, where she'd put her hand. Like she could impress upon him all these truths he'd been avoiding for years. Like she could just crumble all those walls he'd built to keep his daughter safe.

And failed, time and time again.

He could admit failure. You couldn't be a parent for twelve years, particularly under the circumstances in which he'd been a parent, and think you couldn't fail, but gathering up all his siblings to discuss that failure felt a bit *much*.

But they all gathered, in the big living room with his siblings where they'd once crushed together on the couch to watch movies. Their parents would always make a huge batch of popcorn and then curl up on the love seat that he now had at his cabin.

He'd always thought those first few years without them would be the hardest. Being a teenager, not knowing what happened to them. But it was now. With Izzy nearing the age he'd been when he lost them. With his memories of them getting fuzzier and fuzzier.

When he was so tired, so exhausted and wrung out he wanted to lay the weight of all this awfulness on someone else's lap. Just for a minute or two.

He supposed, if he let himself get over the whole *failure* part, this was as close to that as he was going to get. Anna in Hawk's lap on the armchair, Caroline's baby monitor on the little table next to them. Palmer and Louisa and Grant and Dahlia shoved together on the couch, in the almost exact same position—his brother's arm around his fiancée. Walker and Mary on the window seat. Zeke, Walker and Carlyle's brother who lived in Sunrise and kept somewhat more separate from everyone else, stood next to them, arms crossed over his chest.

He almost perfectly mirrored Jack, who stood on the other side of the room, looking grim, while Izzy and Carlyle lay on the floor with the dogs.

Cash never ran these meetings. He'd been as separate as he could be. Now, this was his problem and he had to take charge.

"So, we all know what happened. Chessa was murdered on June first. Sometime at night. The police have now questioned me, Hawk, Anna and Jack. What's next?" Cash looked at Jack. Since he was the sheriff, had even worked for Bent County for the first few years of his police career, he'd have an idea of their investigative tactics.

"Now that they have a time of death, likely, they'll start looking into her movements that night. If they can narrow down the location of the last place she was seen alive, they'll try to find people who saw her, get their impressions."

"Any idea where she was found?"

"They're being really careful because they don't want me to know too much and pass it on to you. But Chloe talked to the coroner. Didn't get much, but she thinks she was found *in* Bent."

"My money is on Rightful Claim. The saloon there? If Chessa was in Bent, she didn't pass up going to a bar." Anna turned to her husband. "We could go have a night on the town. Ask some questions."

Hawk shook his head. "The guy who owns that saloon is married to Detective Delaney-Carson," Hawk said, referring to the female detective. "I don't think going there and questioning anyone is a good idea if it might get back to the detective. We need Bent County to think we're just waiting for them to solve it."

"I could do it," Zeke said. "I know how to be stealthy, and I don't have as known of a connection to you guys. At least in Bent." He turned his gaze from Anna and Hawk to Cash.

Because, apparently, this was somehow *his* deal, when he'd avoided making these kinds of decisions for twelve years.

Cash gave him a nod. "That'll work. Palmer, any fixes for the missing security footage?"

Palmer shook his head. "It's been wiped, that's for sure. I've got a friend over in Wilde seeing if he can't do better than me, but it's not looking good. But to that point, Chessa wasn't acting alone. Clearly. She didn't have that kind of skill or background. By my way of thinking, whoever killed her worked with her on that kidnapping attempt."

"It wasn't Chessa at my window the other night," Izzy said. She'd moved so she was pressed against Carlyle, like she was looking for some comfort. Cash waited to feel some kind of…discomfort or jealousy, but he could only feel gratitude that Izzy had different people to lean on, gain confidence from.

God knew Carlyle had more than her share.

"How do you know that?" Jack asked gently.

"I don't know. It just…wasn't. She…she's like…" Izzy threw her hands in the air, clearly struggling to find the words she wanted to. "She's just not careful. She would have just…like bashed in the window or something. Aunt

Anna, when she came here that one Christmas, you said she was a bull in a china shop. Always had been."

Anna nodded. "Yeah, *careful* isn't Chessa's usual style, but... She knew how much trouble she could get into. Maybe she figured out how to be stealthy."

Izzy shook her head and so did Carlyle.

"Whoever ran into me was pretty...solid," Carlyle said. "From everything you guys have told me, Chessa was shorter, less substantial. Whoever knocked me to the ground was taller than me. Wider. If Chessa was involved, it wasn't her at the window, and it wasn't her doing the security stuff. Maybe we need to consider the fact she wasn't involved at all?"

Cash looked at her. *Knocked me to the ground* when she'd been stabbed. Because there was the whole truth and then there was being careful about not overwhelming Izzy with it. He had to appreciate the fact Carlyle saw some nuance and balance to the situation.

Carlyle dipped her head, whispered something into Izzy's ear. Izzy frowned, but then she nodded. "I don't think the kidnapping thing was about me. Or Chessa, really. I know she told Uncle Hawk she wanted to sell me or whatever, but that was just about getting money."

Cash felt like he'd been stabbed. She'd *heard* that? When he'd worked so hard to keep her in the dark about the worst things Chessa could be.

"Go on. Say the rest," Carlyle encouraged, while Cash reeled. But Izzy wasn't done dropping bombs.

Izzy took a deep breath. "I think someone wants to hurt *you*, Dad. Or maybe the whole family. But mostly you."

And Cash was left utterly speechless.

Chapter Seven

Carlyle watched as the color simply leached out of Cash's face. It made Carlyle feel awful for him, but at the same time, she thought that reaction was good. He wasn't denying it out of hand.

He knew it wasn't just possible, it was a *reasonable* theory. Which meant they could act on it, instead of wasting time trying to convince him it was possible.

It had taken Izzy a lot of courage to say it to a room full of adults, and no one was arguing with her or discounting her. It warmed Carlyle's heart, because her brothers had *always* meant well, but they'd been young men saddled with the responsibility of a little sister. They'd discounted her, scoffed at her, and often made her feel foolish without *meaning* to.

But the Hudsons knew better. They were mature, and had the experiences and enough of a framework to all instinctively give Izzy the feeling she'd helped.

"If someone was targeting Cash, Chessa would be at the top of the list," Jack said, not as a counterpoint, but more thoughtfully. Like thinking Izzy's point through. "Izzy is on to something, but I don't think we can fully discount Chessa's involvement."

"Absolutely. Chessa could very well be involved," Carlyle offered. "But she's not the *point*. She's…"

"A pawn," Anna finished for Carlyle. "She was a pawn last year. Darrin Monroe used her because she hated us. But his goal wasn't her goal. She wasn't...with it enough to have a clear goal. It was about feeding the addiction. Not about like...actual plots and plans."

"She could have gotten mixed up with someone who had the plots and plans, and she was the one who chose the target," Cash said grimly, and with a careful look at his daughter.

Because even though by all accounts Chessa was a bit of a monster, wanting to sell her own child, Cash cared about how that affected his daughter.

"I think we should go back and look through what happened with the guy who wanted revenge on you guys. Who was involved, beyond him and Chessa. Let me look at the file or report or whatever. Yours or Sunrise's. Maybe I'll see something you guys didn't since you know all the players." Carlyle looked around the room. She couldn't make out what everyone's expressions meant, but there was really only one person who mattered.

She glanced at Cash.

But it was Jack who spoke. "He just had a personal vendetta against us. Darrin is in a high-security psychiatric hospital, so I just don't see how it could connect."

"I don't either. Not yet. And maybe it doesn't. But isn't that what we do?" Mary asked. "Pull threads until something unravels. This is another thread to pull, and it's less likely to draw the attention of Bent County. Zeke sees if he can gather anything in Bent. Carlyle goes over that case. Chloe keeps trying to see what other information she can get out of Bent County to pass along to Jack."

The conversation from then on was more logistics than anything else, and Izzy practically climbed into Carlyle's lap. Carlyle held the girl close, hoping Cash didn't see this as a failure. That just because Izzy was upset didn't mean she shouldn't be here. Upset was just part of the deal when your mother was murdered, whether you loved her or not.

When they finally started to scatter, Cash reached down and helped Izzy to her feet. "Come on. Time for bed." Copper got up too, so Carlyle got to her feet. Before Cash led Izzy away, Izzy turned and threw her arms around Carlyle.

She hugged the girl back, reluctant to let go. There was no way to convince Izzy she was safe. Carlyle knew that better than anyone, but she was understanding more and more the lengths her brothers had gone to try. The lengths Cash and his family went to try.

When Izzy finally released her from the hug, she grabbed her hand. "Come with," she said.

Carlyle didn't know where she was coming with to, but she wasn't about to argue with the girl. She let Izzy lead her, side by side with Cash, deeper into the house and up the stairs, Copper and Swiftie following along.

They stopped at a door and Izzy turned to Carlyle and wrapped her arms around her one more time. "Thank you," she whispered, and squeezed tight.

Carlyle hugged her back, running a hand over her braid. "No thanks necessary, Iz. Friends help each other out."

Izzy's mouth curved, the first smile Carlyle had seen on her face all day. Cash opened the door and silently led Izzy inside with Copper. She was sharing Caroline's nursery, because it was in the center of the house, and because there was a video baby monitor in there.

Caroline was already asleep in her crib, so Izzy had to sneak in quietly. Cash moved behind her, tucked her in. They whispered something to each other, and Carlyle knew she shouldn't stand there and *watch*, but she couldn't help herself.

He loved his daughter *so* much. There was no doubt he'd do anything and everything to keep her safe, and the fact he wasn't perfect at it only made the whole thing...that much more poignant. That you could love someone so hard, and fail again and again, and just keep trying.

It put a weird lump in her throat, and a longing in her heart she didn't understand.

When Cash exited the room, pulling the door carefully closed behind him, he gestured for her to follow him. She didn't know what else to do. All worked up internally, she really wanted to go hide in her room and work on some kind of...protection against all this *feeling*.

Instead, she followed him into the bedroom from yesterday.

The bedroom he was staying in.

He closed the door behind them, leaving the dog on the other side.

It was nothing, Carlyle *knew* it was nothing and yet she could also feel the heat climbing into her cheeks. Her stomach fluttered at the mere...thought.

Get it together.

"That was productive," she offered, trying to sound her usual irreverent self...and fearing it came out more like the squeaky words of a coward. "The Hudson-Daniels show is on a roll."

"Between Zeke going to Bent and you going over an old case, it's sounding more like the Daniels show."

"Does it matter who's doing it if it gets done?" she countered, feeling defensive and sympathetic all at the same time.

"No, it doesn't," he said, with a kind of firmness that brooked no argument. Or the kind of firmness someone used when they were trying to convince themselves of something.

He said nothing else, made no effort to break the silence or explain to her why she was here.

"So…" She had no idea why he'd brought her in here, and the longer they stood, in his room, alone, on opposite sides of a messily made *bed*, the more she wanted to jump out of her own skin.

"Look, there needs to be some effort to…" He trailed off, never finishing his sentence.

"To what?" she asked, since she sincerely had no idea what he was talking about.

He opened his mouth, closed it, then a knock interrupted whatever he was going to come up with. He sighed heavily, then gave her a sharp look.

"Look rumpled."

"What?"

"You came up with this alibi. Now you gotta play along with it." Then he stalked over to the door, clearly unhappy with the whole situation. Cash opened the door, and her brother stood at the threshold.

When Walker saw *her*, looking rumpled as ordered, sitting on the edge of the bed, his eyes hardened.

So, she grinned at him. "Heya, Walk."

CASH WISHED IT WAS…literally anyone else. Except maybe Zeke. He did not want to deal with either of Carlyle's brothers over something that wasn't even true.

No matter how she'd blushed when he'd closed the door behind them. Which was not something he could think about. Certainly not his body's response to it. Not now. Not ever.

He wasn't thrilled about this turn of events, but he had

to see it through. And if Walker was standing there look-ing like he might actually take a piece out of him, it meant Mary hadn't spilled the beans about this all being fake.

Which was something. Not that Cash particularly wanted to play along with this fiction, but he felt like he didn't have a choice. They'd used it with the cops, now it just had to be...

"What the hell are you two doing?" Walker demanded.

Carlyle's eyes got real wide, comically wide. Clearly, she was needling her brother. "Talking, Walker. Whatever else could we be up to?" She walked over and stood next to Cash. Too close, judging by the way Walker's gaze got even harder. Cash wouldn't know because he was keeping his gaze resolutely anywhere but on her.

"Laying it on a little thick, Car," Cash muttered, torn between a dark kind of amusement, because it *was* funny, and just...wishing he was not in the middle of any part of this situation.

Carlyle moved to face him, so he *had* to look at her, and she trailed her finger down his chest—*Jesus*—and smirked. "That's what I do, babe."

Then she flounced out of the room, over Walker's sput-tering. Swiftie got up and followed her down the hallway.

Cash regretted every decision that had led him here.

Particularly when Walker's rather large hands clenched into fists. "I want to know what's going on between you and Carlyle. What you think you're doing with my baby sister, who's a good seven years younger than you."

Cash might have felt some sympathy for Walker, what with having two younger sisters of his own. He understood the need to be protective, to maybe warn a guy off. But one of those sisters was Walker's wife, so... "What's the age difference between you and Mary again?"

"Less than seven," Walker said darkly.

"Yeah, by like a *month*," Cash replied with as much sarcasm as he could muster. "You don't have much of a leg to stand on, you know. My sister got kidnapped because of you. I don't recall getting involved." Because he never did, did he? And it hadn't helped him at all. "So far, I've given your sister a job and—"

"Yeah, *and*. The *and* is what I'm ticked about."

Cash scrubbed his hands over his face. "Isn't my current circumstance enough of a disaster without whatever this is?"

"Yeah, and you've got my sister involved in it."

"She got herself involved. I tried to stop her. A million, trillion people could try to stop her. She doesn't *stop*. Don't pretend you don't know that."

"She's got a bad habit of wanting to help a lost cause."

Cash laughed, a little bitterly, because boy was he a damn lost cause. "What do you want me to say, Walker? To do? Because unless it involves mind control, we both know *she* is going to do whatever the hell she wants."

"You just steer clear. She doesn't need to get messed up in this. She shouldn't be at those meetings, or in your room, or getting *stabbed*, Cash." Then he turned around, like he'd given a directive he expected to be followed wholesale, no argument.

Which was right. Cash shouldn't be able to argue with it, because it was all things he'd said about his daughter, and if he didn't have a daughter, things he'd likely be saying about his sisters.

But…maybe Carlyle had gotten to him because he could see this too easily from *her* point of view. Not Walker's or his.

"Maybe you don't give her enough credit, Walker."

Walker stopped at the doorway. Turned, slowly. Cash

was sure it was meant to be intimidating, but he was too tired and Walker wasn't any older or stronger or different than him.

If anything, they were too damn much alike.

"Excuse me?" he asked, very slowly.

"So far, your sister has proven my instincts wrong at just about every turn. You think I was going to let my daughter sit in the middle of that meeting, talking about her mother's murder? Hell no. That was all Carlyle. Because as she likes to keep telling me, she's been in Izzy's shoes."

There was a flicker of something in Walker's expression that Cash recognized all too well. Guilt. Because boy had they walked damn similar paths.

"I get it. Better than anyone, probably. The way you feel. The things you do to protect someone you love who you see as more vulnerable. But Carlyle's not. No more vulnerable than you. Than me. She's smart and she's strong. Not invincible, though she might think it, but the thing she seems most adamant about is that she doesn't need someone to swoop in and save her or hide her away from the bad things. And I realize I'm not a great catch, but I'm hardly a bad thing you need to save her from."

"Maybe. I know she can't see it that way, but for *me*, I have been Carlyle's dad from the time she was Izzy's age, whether any of us liked it or not. So it doesn't matter how old, how not-vulnerable, how whatever she gets, I'm always going to do what I can to protect her. It's what fathers do, and I know you know that."

"Yeah, I do know that. Understand it. But recall, we've got our own orphan situation over here. There's a reason no one bashed your face in when you started up with Mary. Because we could all see you were so head over heels in love with her, you'd destroy yourself before you hurt her on purpose. It isn't always about…protecting them from every difficulty."

"You saying you're in love with my sister?" Walker asked, a little *too* casually.

Damn. "I'm saying, do you really think I'm going to do anything to mess her up? Do you, knowing my family, knowing me, really think she needs you to butt in? Bud, she'll kick my ass from here to Kentucky if she sees fit. And I can't go anywhere, so I'll just have to suck it up and have my ass kicked."

"Maybe if you didn't have the kid, but she's got a soft spot for Izzy. She won't hurt you if it'd hurt your daughter."

Cash wondered if the blows would ever just stop, give him a chance to breathe, adjust, move on and heal one bruise before another came. "Fine, I give you permission to kick my ass if it comes to it. Happy?"

Walker studied him. "I'll send Zeke to do it. He's meaner." But he grinned, a bit too much like Carlyle for comfort. Then he sobered up. "I know you're a good guy, Cash. That's not the issue. The issue is you got a kid to put first, and at some point… Carlyle deserves a life where she gets to come in first."

"I'm sure she does," Cash agreed, surprised to find that it…hurt more than it should that he agreed with Walker. Because this was all pretend. Not real. So it didn't matter what he couldn't give her.

And never would.

Chapter Eight

With extra people in the main house, Carlyle felt even less like she could sleep with the lights on. Which meant sleeping was a bit of a bust, and now that she'd been traumatized and stabbed from something as simple as looking out the window on a starry night, that was hardly the relaxing pastime it had once been.

Maybe she just needed a snack. Something heavy and fatty that would make her nice and sleepy. She left her room, ready to sneak over to the kitchen, but something...creaked above.

Someone was moving around upstairs. And considering there were what felt like a hundred people in this house, it could be anyone. Hell, it could be the house settling.

But her gut had been right last time. Someone bad *had* been outside. Maybe it was unlikely anyone *bad* had gotten upstairs, but it wasn't *impossible*.

She looked at Swiftie. The dog would make too much noise if she followed. Carlyle crouched, looked the dog in the eye. "Stay," she whispered firmly.

Heart pounding, nerves humming, she snuck her way up the stairs, being careful to try and avoid the ones that squeaked. She'd learned long ago to make sure she knew how to move around anywhere she was living without making a noise.

But when she carefully crested the stairs, the hallway was illuminated by a night-light plugged into the wall. There was no lurking shadow or stranger.

Just Cash.

Not walking up and down the hallway, not going from one room to another. Just sitting on the hallway floor, his back to the wall right next to Izzy's door. Carlyle figured she should probably turn around, sneak back downstairs and…leave it. Leave this.

But he looked so *alone*, and she just couldn't stand it. She purposefully made some noise before stepping into his line of vision.

His head snapped up, but once he recognized her, some of the tenseness in his shoulders released. "What are you doing up?" he asked in a whisper when she got close enough.

"Can't sleep." She didn't need to ask him what he was doing. It was pretty obvious. She went ahead and moved into a sitting position on the floor next to him. "Going to sit out here all night?"

"No." He had his legs out in front of him, his head resting back against the wall. Kind of the picture of defeat, but she knew he wasn't defeated. Because he'd never give up while his daughter might be in danger. That was just the kind of guy he was. Why else would she be halfway to messed up over him?

"I know she's okay," he said, like Carlyle had demanded an explanation when she hadn't. "But sometimes…"

"I think you've got all the fairest reasons to be a little paranoid. But you know what I do when I can't sleep?"

He looked over at her, one eyebrow raised. "Roam the house? Sneak around in the dark getting stabbed?"

She kept her laugh quiet. "Yeah, that. And find something

productive to do. Let's go unearth that case file you guys were talking about tonight. We can go over it together until we're too sleepy to fight it."

"I wasn't involved in that case. I don't get involved in cases." He said it so firmly.

She understood this wasn't stubbornness for the sake of being stubborn, but something he needed to believe. That by keeping his nose out of things, he wasn't just protecting Izzy *now*, but always had been. That the choice, the sacrifice had been the *right* one.

But Carlyle knew all too well sometimes there was no *right* choice, there was only what you did to survive. Physically. Emotionally.

Sometimes it felt like she understood him better than she understood herself. Because she understood what he felt, but not why she was being all soft and gooey over this mess of a man in the privacy of her own head.

But here she was. "Involved or not, you were there. And so was Izzy." *And so was Chessa,* but she didn't say that out loud because she didn't think it needed to be said. She got back to her feet, held out a hand. "Come on. Better than sitting here like a sad weirdo."

He snorted, and it took him a second or two, but he finally took her offered hand and let her help him up. She wanted to keep holding onto his hand, but she dropped it. She might be gooey, but she was no fool.

"She wouldn't be happy to find you out here," Carlyle said. Not an admonition, just a reminder.

He shook his head. "I know."

Carlyle nodded, then turned away from him and the urge to put her arms around him and *comfort* him. She headed back downstairs, where they'd be able to talk at a more reasonable level and Carlyle knew there was a room full of files.

And they could focus on *that*, not this feeling inside of her.

Swiftie was waiting at the bottom of the stairs, then followed as they made their way to the office.

"Wait here, I'll get the keys," Cash said.

So she waited by the door to the office. She reminded herself she was just…helping him out. Giving him something to do. Giving herself something to do. It was better than going stir-crazy in that little bedroom, desperately trying *not* to think about him.

And his bed.

She nearly jumped a foot high when he returned, because she'd been too busy trying to push that thought away that she hadn't even been listening. He unlocked the door and pushed it open, moving inside first. He went right for a file cabinet, shuffled through some folders, then pulled one out.

He turned to face her, but the room was so crowded with stuff—filing cabinets and security equipment and an array of computers and printers—there wasn't much space at all.

Just them facing each other in a small, dim room. Even the dog had stayed outside the doorway.

It was too small. They were too close. It was too…

"Let's go out into the living room," he suggested.

Carlyle nodded and followed him out to the spacious living room. She sat down on the couch, but then he sat right next to her.

So much for distance.

He opened the file and spread out the contents on the coffee table as Swiftie settled herself under the table. "Jack double-checked earlier. Darrin is still in the state hospital under maximum guard. Jack should have a list of anyone who's visited him by tomorrow, the next day at the latest. So, we'll look into it, but it just feels like a dead end."

Carlyle picked up a few pieces of paper stapled together. It outlined everything that had happened. "Who wrote this account?"

"Everyone. Anna started it with everything she knew, then we each went over it and added things."

Carlyle read the entire document, then went through it line by line to try to work out any players the Hudsons might have overlooked. Chessa had been arrested before Darrin had made an appearance. She'd worked with him to take Hawk against his will, but Chessa was the one who got caught and arrested.

But then she'd been let go. Her bail posted by one of the Hudson ranch hands. A traitor, basically.

"What about this cop who let Chessa go?" she asked, pointing at the name *Bryan Ferguson*.

"What about him? He just followed procedure. Tripp Anthony, on the order of Darrin Monroe, is the one who paid her bail and got her out because Darrin was paying him too. There was nothing out of the ordinary on the cop's side. Just a mistake."

"But wouldn't he know that Chessa wasn't your average jailbird? Wouldn't he know Jack was involved and give him some warning? It seems like an epic screwup to let her go and two hours pass before Jack finds out."

"Jack chewed him a new one, I'm pretty sure. It was all on the up and up, procedure wise. I don't know that it's some great conspiracy when it had been an honest mistake. Jack trusts his team."

She was about to argue with that, but he held up a hand. "*But* we can see what Jack has to say in the morning. Mary's right, it's all just pulling at threads. We pull at them all, no matter how seemingly pointless or wrong, until we have answers."

Carlyle nodded. But she looked at the name. Honest mistakes happened all the time, but a cop should know better.

Cash yawned. "And I think I've hit the wall of exhaustion that *might* let me get a few hours before chores. We should try to get some sleep."

Carlyle nodded and knew she should just…agree. Not chase the desperate desire to keep him right here. "You know, I could hang out in your room. Emerge in the morning. Really let everyone talk. I could sleep in a chair or on the floor or something. Not suggesting we share a bed or anything."

He paused—midstretch—like she'd done something really shocking. But then he dropped his arms, and expressly did *not* look her in the eye.

"Not a terrible idea, but Izzy might see, and I wouldn't want Izzy to get the wrong idea. I'm not sure how she'd feel. I know she loves you, but she's never seen me with anyone before."

Carlyle knew Cash leaned toward *monk*, but she thought it was more a recent phenomenon. He'd been like seventeen when Izzy was born, probably not even twenty when he'd gotten divorced. Surely in his younger years he'd… "Never?"

Cash shrugged. "Weirdly, the disastrous end of my marriage made me a little leery of trying to start something up with someone and a toddler at home makes it a little hard to take a night off and…have fun."

"I call baloney. You've always had like five built-in babysitters."

"Not *always*. Between Jack's work schedule, and Grant being deployed for a while, Anna and Palmer doing the rodeo, Mary going to college. It's not like now. Everyone scattered."

Except him. He'd always been right here. Because of Izzy. "So you just…" She shook her head. She just couldn't believe it. She'd found time to have a little *fun* when she'd been the target of a murderer, so… She narrowed her eyes at him. "You just didn't want anyone to *know* you were off to get laid."

He made a choking noise, which of course was why she'd put it like that.

"Regardless of *why*, I wasn't. I…" He shook his head. "Why are we having this discussion?"

"You're not saying… Like, *all* this what? Decade? Since you've been divorced you haven't once—"

"Please don't say *get laid* again. Carlyle, this is not…" But he clearly couldn't find the words. She didn't know if it was embarrassment or what. She did know she should let it go.

But she couldn't.

"That's a long, long time not to…have *fun*."

"Good night, Carlyle," he said firmly, and stalked off. She heard the stairs squeak under his weight, could track his progress to his room down the hallway.

She sighed. *Ten years.* All because he had a kid at home? No, it had to be more complicated than that. It had to be something about his marriage, about Chessa.

Who was dead. Murdered. And the real thing she needed to focus on. She stayed in the living room, forced herself to go over the report, and not consider any *fun* she could have with Cash Hudson.

CASH WOKE UP in a foul mood. He could blame it on murder and being a suspect and not being able to sleep in his own damn house, but mostly it was the fact that Carlyle asking him about *fun* had really messed with his mind.

Because it was far too easy to imagine having fun with *her*, and considering his ex-wife was dead and he was suspect number one, that was really not the place his mind should be drifting.

Ever. But especially now.

He had long ago convinced himself that sex was unnecessary. That the enjoyment of it—just like booze and carelessness—was for the young and unencumbered. While Palmer had been sleeping his way through half of Sunrise, Cash had considered himself *better*. Or tried to.

Now...

He threw the covers off, trying not to groan out loud. It was early yet, but an early breakfast, a gallon of coffee and some work with the dogs could maybe take his mind off all the annoying caveats it seemed bound and determined to wander down.

Once downstairs, the smell of breakfast filled the air like it usually did. Mary had already been up and about, whipping up her normal spread. They'd really be in for it once she had the baby and had to take some time off from being the organizer and cook and keeping them all in line.

Mary wasn't in the kitchen, but he helped himself to the food out on warmers. When Cash got to the dining room, there was no one to be found except Jack. He was dressed in his sheriff uniform—khaki pants and a perfectly pressed Sunrise polo. He had his phone in one hand and a fork in the other.

"Morning," Cash offered.

"Morning," Jack replied, setting down his phone. "Sleep okay?"

Cash chuckled, only a little bitterly. "Sure. Nothing like a little possible murder charge to really help a guy sleep."

Jack's return smile was wry.

"Carlyle and I went over the file last night. Couldn't sleep. She wants us to look deeper into Deputy Ferguson."

Jack's expression darkened. "I haven't let him forget what a colossal mistake that was. But the kid is ineffectual at best. Not a cold-blooded killer."

"I know. But what have we got to lose to let her poke into him? Maybe it unties some other knot."

Jack nodded. Not because he thought he was wrong about Ferguson, but because this was how you investigated. And maybe their expertise was cold cases, but it was the same. The way he saw it, they were trying to avoid a cold case.

Just as much as they were trying to avoid him going to jail.

And as much as he should focus on Ferguson, avoiding jail, etcetera, all he could think about was Carlyle. What she'd said last night, and why she'd made him question if he'd been doing the right thing all these years by avoid-ing *fun.*

In front of him sat his role model, so to speak. "You've been single forever."

Jack paused with the fork full of egg halfway up to his mouth, then set it down on the plate. "I'm sorry. What?"

"If you have a night out on the town, you certainly keep it on the down-low. I've never once met a woman you were dating. At least, not since *you* were in high school, which I'll be kind and point out was a very long time ago."

Jack blinked. Once. His face had gotten very carefully blank. "I'll repeat myself. *What?*"

"I'm just trying to work out why you've kept yourself

living like a monk all these years. I know why *I* do. It made sense for a while, but it doesn't anymore."

Jack's voice took on that holier-than-thou, I'm-in-charge iciness. "I don't see what business it is of yours, Cash. I don't see why we're having this conversation."

"I spent ten years quite convinced I was making the best, most right choice for Izzy by staying away from even a hint of...fun. I assumed you were making the same choice for us. But here we are, all adults. Most of your little chicks married. Why still live like a monk?"

"If this is because you decided to hook up with Carlyle and think I need some kind of...encouragement to go have *fun*, I feel like I should remind you of something far more important. You are the main suspect in the murder investigation of your ex-wife and your daughter's mother. Don't concern yourself with my personal life."

"Or lack thereof?"

"Sure. Right. Just... Can we focus on Ferguson?"

Cash had the totally foundation-crumbling realization that his brother was lying. He *did* have a personal life, or thought he did. Hidden somewhere.

But now was not the time to dig into it.

Probably.

He heard someone in the kitchen, and since Swiftie pranced in and took a seat under the table, Cash figured it was Carlyle.

Then Carlyle appeared, plate piled high. "Morning, boys," she said, sliding into the seat next to Cash. She gave the first bite of food to Swiftie, which Cash should scold her for.

But he didn't.

"Sounded a bit tense. Are we bickering in here?" She made a little tsk-tsking sound.

And Cash had the fully out-of-body, out-of-character impulse to follow Carlyle's example. Irreverent. Never afraid to say the wrong thing, the shocking thing.

"I was just talking to Jack about relationships."

"Juicy."

"I'm beginning to think he has a secret one."

Carlyle's eyes widened. Jack's glare was *glacial*. Cash couldn't help but grin.

"You've really rubbed off on him, Carlyle," Jack said, standing. "Enjoy each other's company while it lasts, I suppose. Because if we don't figure out the *true* concerns of the day, Cash might be spending his mornings talking with the other inmates in Bent County Jail."

And with that, he left.

Carlyle let out a low whistle. "I've never seen him react that way, even to Anna. Why are you picking on your poor brother?"

"Misery loves company?"

She laughed. "What did he say about Bryan Ferguson?"

"He stuck with his initial assessment but gave you free rein to poke into him as you see fit. If you find a lead, he'll follow it." She shoveled some eggs into her mouth and nodded along.

"Excellent," she said.

And he found he couldn't quite stop looking at her. She wasn't fear*less*, but she did a hell of a job acting it. She wasn't reckless with things that were important, but she clearly only counted *people* as important, and his daughter was one of those people. She had a whole different outlook on the world, but at its core the things she valued were the same as the things he valued.

A strange, twisting and oddly weight-lifting realization to have.

She must have noticed his staring. She turned to him,

those expressive blue-gray eyes confused as she wiped at her face. "What? Egg on my face?"

"No. Nothing," he replied, because he didn't have the words for *what*, but he was starting to think he needed to figure them out.

Chapter Nine

Carlyle used her beat-up old laptop to do a rudimentary search on Bryan Ferguson. While she was at it, she started looking into the ranch hand who'd facilitated the payment of the bail. He'd died, but that didn't mean there weren't connections somewhere.

Her entire life had been about following the strange, twisting turns of connection. And then avoiding them when she could.

When she thought her eyes would cross, she went outside and over to the dog barn. It was technically her day off, but she would needle Cash into giving her some work to do. She had to work out her body so her mind—which was going in circles—didn't drive her over the edge.

She'd have liked to have been the one teaching Izzy how to shoot, but in the end that job had gone to Grant, who had the most patience out of anyone. Besides, with the stitches, no one wanted her repeatedly shooting a weapon, no matter how well she could handle it.

So, she went to the dog barn instead. Cash had all kinds of dogs. So there was always all kinds of work to do. She tended to avoid the paperwork if she could. She much preferred the training and being outside.

Swiftie followed her over to where Cash had three of

his younger dogs. He had Izzy up on a horse, and Carlyle quickly realized this was less about training the dogs themselves, and more about giving Izzy the opportunity to train.

He stood, elbows resting on the top of the fence while Izzy took the horse through a walk then a gallop, and shouted different commands to the dogs. Carlyle came to stand beside Cash.

"It's your day off," he said by way of greeting.

"I knew you were going to throw that in my face. I needed a break from my computer. Consider today volunteer work."

He rolled his eyes, but they both stood and watched as Izzy expertly put the dogs and horse through their paces. Carlyle grinned. "Damn, she's a natural, isn't she?"

"It comes with growing up on a ranch surrounded by animals, but she's got a special touch with them, that's for sure." All proud dad. She wanted to lean her head against his shoulder and just enjoy the moment.

If she said that to anyone, they'd think it out of character. She was loud. She was wild. Not traditional, not *soft*.

But sometimes, that armor she'd spent so long building started to feel heavy, like it needed to be taken off.

She sighed and watched Izzy maneuver the horse and command the dogs, all the while keeping a respectable space between her and Cash. Little glimpses of the woman Izzy would grow up to be someday flashed through her mind.

Carlyle watched, but no matter how much she wanted a distraction, her mind kept going back to the problem at hand. Izzy as a kid. Izzy as a woman. It got her thinking. Did she need to look back *further* into the cop's and the former ranch hand's lives? Not just rap sheets—Tripp a small, petty one up to his involvement last year, Ferguson nothing—but maybe earlier in their lives to try and find a connection to each other.

Izzy gave a sharp command to the dogs, and two of the three immediately obeyed. Carlyle tapped her fingers on the fence, watching, thinking.

Cash put his hand over her tapping fingers, stilling them. "Worrying?"

"Thinking," she replied.

He did *not* withdraw his hand, and she held herself very still, trying not to react. Trying not to think anything of it. Friendly gesture. Simple gesture. Clearly just annoyed with her tapping.

"I feel like that should be concerning to me."

She grinned at him. "Me thinking *is* very concerning. This Ferguson guy. What are the chances I can sweet-talk him into saying something he shouldn't?"

Cash's expression was very...odd. She kind of expected him to laugh or lecture her about not getting too involved. But this was neither of those things, and she didn't know what to do with it.

"Probably not the right tactic. Ferguson says to anyone you were...whatever, that's going to poke a hole in that alibi you just had to give me. *We're* supposed to be secretly engaging in sleepovers, remember?"

She glanced over at him, meeting that dark gaze. And there *was* something different in it. Or her brain was a little fuzzy because his very *large*, calloused hand was still resting over hers. "Yeah, I remember," she said.

Breathlessly. Like some kind of *fool*.

"If you've got some questions for Ferguson, let's bring them to Jack. See if he can ask them."

"Is Jack talking to you right now?"

Cash laughed, the corners of his eyes crinkling. He adjusted his cowboy hat, finally took his hand back. "Ah, he's just a bit prickly in the mornings."

"And every other time I've interacted with him. Well, unless Izzy is around. He does have a soft spot for her." Carlyle kept her gaze on the little girl, the whole thing... overwhelming for reasons she couldn't quite articulate.

She just knew that she'd been hard on Cash when it came to how he treated Izzy. She'd been telling him what he'd done wrong. So maybe he deserved to know what he'd done right too. "For anything you think you didn't give her, family matters. My brothers were everything, even when I was trying to get them to give me some space. They were my foundation. She doesn't just have you, she has all of them, and all of this."

"Kinda luck of the draw."

"Maybe. But you could have moved somewhere else. Gotten farther away from cold cases and danger. They don't need you to run the ranch and you don't need them to run your dog business. You stayed for yourself, but you stayed for her too."

"And how are you so sure about that?"

When she looked over at him, her heart hammered against her chest. His expression was...different. Not that *woe is me* or determined, protective dad mode. Something more open. Something more...

She didn't know. So she put her armor back in place, flashed that grin. "I am a keen observer of human nature." But she couldn't keep up the act. "You're not so hard to figure out."

"You are," he replied, so seriously.

She scoffed, or tried to, but her throat was a little tight. "I don't see how."

"You're an excellent mask wearer. I should know. But, per usual, Izzy gets under it. No one can resist Izzy."

"She's the best."

"Yeah. And there's a softy under all the *Carlyle* of it all."

Carlyle gave a fake injured sniff. "I do not know what you're referring to."

He laughed. *Again.* He was smiling. *At her.* And there was something warm and wonderful and *awful* blooming in her chest. She should look away, walk away, lock herself up with the computer and find him some answers.

But her phone rang, and she jumped at the loud, surprising jangle. Less than steady, she pulled her phone out of her pocket. She had to clear her throat to talk.

"It's Zeke. I'll, uh, be right back." She swiped her finger across the screen, turned her back on Cash and took a few steps away. "What?" she demanded.

"Hi to you too."

"I'm working."

"Today's your day off."

"Yeah, but I'm working on case stuff."

"Yeah, me too. I was just calling to see if you'd come up with anything I should be on the lookout for tonight in Bent. Any people I should ask around about being seen with Chessa, that kind of thing."

Not a bad idea. "Bryan Ferguson and Tripp Anthony. Don't necessarily bring up Chessa connecting to them. Just see if you get any kind of reaction from it, some idea of if anyone knew them or what they think about them."

"And if I do get some information?"

"Just file it away. Come out to the ranch for breakfast tomorrow and we'll go over what you find."

"You getting too deep in this, Car?"

"Probably. Why?"

Zeke sighed. "You should be out having some fun or

something. Not getting dragged into more investigations and danger and running. Haven't you had enough of that?"

"Maybe I *like* danger. I'd think *you'd* understand that, mister spy operative."

"Former. I'm enjoying the quiet life."

"My butt," she muttered, turning to look back at Cash and Izzy. Izzy had gotten off the horse and she and Cash were standing next to it, watching the dogs run and tumble over each other.

In the middle of all this, they were laughing.

Carlyle didn't care what kind of fool it made her, she wanted to be part of it.

CASH KNEW SHE'D walked away to talk to her brother in private because they were discussing the murder case and what *they* were doing about it. Which made him uneasy, because he didn't like the idea of them planning something on their own.

And it had nothing to do with her suggesting sweet-talking anybody. Or mostly not about that.

Izzy was chattering on about music and concerts and her usual twelve-year-old stuff and it made him want to believe everything was going to be okay. If she could be worried about cute drummers and the importance of musical *eras*, then maybe he could...do that too.

Maybe not worry about cute drummers but allow himself the bandwidth to focus on more than danger and protection. He wasn't sure he knew how to do that anymore. It had become such a habit, such a comfort zone. Shrank his world down until it was just him, Izzy and dogs.

But it hadn't saved her from trauma, from danger. Maybe he needed to...open up again. Maybe the real lesson in all of this was that he couldn't control the world or the people around him, but he could control the hours and minutes here, and how he thought about them.

He went through the rest of the day making a conscious effort to do just that. To engage in frivolous conversations with Izzy, even when he was walking her to and from the stables to the house in a nod toward keeping her safe. To take a fussy Caroline from a very frustrated and frazzled Anna.

"She's a demon bent on world destruction," Anna said darkly, collapsing onto the couch.

"Like mother, like daughter," Cash replied, making Anna laugh. He walked Caroline in the same relentless circle he used to walk Izzy in when it was the only thing that would put her to sleep. Once Caroline was asleep, and so was Anna, Cash put Caroline in her crib in her room, put the baby monitor speaker next to a sleeping Anna, then checked in on Mary and Izzy. They had their heads together, cooking up something for dinner. He did his routine chores, and he didn't let the darkness of Chessa's murder invalidate all the light in his life.

Carlyle had been right. He could have left. He could have secreted Izzy away any of the times danger came knocking at their door. And he had, in a way, by keeping her cooped up in that cabin. But he'd never been able to dream of raising her without his family, without the legacy of this ranch. Even when trauma and tragedy followed, this was home.

So when the house was dark and quiet, and Izzy was tucked safely into bed, he went down to Carlyle's room.

Because she was a different kind of light he'd *never* allowed himself to have, and maybe it was time to change that.

When she opened her door, she didn't *startle* exactly, but she definitely hadn't been expecting him. Maybe she hadn't really been expecting anyone.

"Hey. What's up?" Swiftie's tail thumped over in the corner. Cash gave her a little hand signal that had the dog trotting out of the room.

"Nothing in particular. Just thought I'd see if you'd found anything new about Ferguson or Tripp." Starting with murder cases. Lame, even for someone as rusty as him.

She was frowning at Swiftie's retreating tail, but then shook her head and turned and walked toward her bed, where a laptop and a notebook and papers were strewn about. She gestured toward them with some frustration. "Not really. There has to be a connection between these two. Why these two guys, you know? How did that Darrin guy get them to help him? But I'm coming up damn empty and it's irritating the hell out of me."

He should use that as a segue to discuss other things, but he couldn't seem to make himself. "Ferguson wasn't a target. He just happened to be the one handling bonds that night."

Carlyle shook her head. "I don't buy that. If it had been Jack or Chloe, would Darrin have sent Tripp to pay her bail? Hell no. It was more careful, more targeted. Too many people would have had to know Tripp was a ranch hand here."

"So they waited till the least likely person was handling it."

"Maybe." Probably, in fact. He didn't want to tell her that if there was a connection, surely someone would have found it by now, when it seemed so important to her to find one. So, he changed the subject.

"Any word from Zeke?"

"No. I told him to come over in the morning and give us an account of what he found, if anything. He'll probably hang out at the bar until at least around it closes. I don't think a lot of baddies are out at—" she glanced over at the clock on her nightstand "—ten fifteen."

"You never know."

She shrugged, and a silence stretched out. This wasn't that unusual. They worked together. Sometimes they dealt in silences. But this one wasn't easy, companionable, or all that comfortable.

So stop beating around the bush, dumbass. "Remember when we were talking about me not...having any fun?"

"Uh, yeah. Sure." She seemed...really uncertain with his change of topic, and maybe that shouldn't amuse him, but managing to set Carlyle a little off-balance—when that was usually her expertise—was kind of nice. "Gonna start hitting the bar scene?"

An attempt to put him off-balance, but not a good one. He only smiled. "No. I don't think so."

"Ah, so..." She cleared her throat, looked at the computer, then at him. No, not at him. Some spot on the wall behind him. "What about it?"

"I thought about it. All day. How I'd pretty much put *fun* out of my head the past twelve years, best I could. But then I got to thinking... In six years, Izzy is going to want to go off to college, I have no doubt, and I'll have to let her. I'll have to let her just...walk away." Which he just...couldn't think about right now. He still had six years. No use mourning something that wasn't here *yet*, even if he had to accept it would be here *someday*.

"Right. So, what, you're going to wait six more years to...have fun?"

He shook his head. "No, you were right. She's not going to thank me for making my entire life her protection. She's going to sit at this dinner table someday, like I did this morning with Jack, and wonder what the hell he's been doing with his life."

"You know, I do have a theory about what Jack's been doing. Or who."

Cash closed his eyes, shook his head. "I don't want to talk about Jack and theories."

"I'm just saying, I went to…"

She trailed off as he stepped closer. Close enough to see the way her dark hair had little glints of red. The way her eyes were too gray to be blue and too blue to be gray. The way her breath kind of caught and then she let it slowly out, watching him not warily, exactly.

Because she was fierce and strong and confident, but she wasn't made of impenetrable armor. He affected her in *some* way, and that was enough to reach out, touch her cheek.

"I like you, Carlyle. You've untied something inside of me that was tied so tight I didn't even know it was there. It was just a weight, holding me down. And you lifted it."

She made an odd kind of sound he didn't know how to characterize, except maybe as a little surprised. Her eyes went bright, and she cleared her throat.

"Just to be clear," she said, and he saw the effort it took her to sound a little cavalier. To not outwardly react to his hand on her cheek. "I had plenty of…*fun* before coming here."

"Hell, Carlyle." She really did have a way. He didn't know why it amused the hell out of him when it really shouldn't have.

"But it wasn't the kind that ever meant anything. Not serious. Not thinking I'd ever be in one place, put down roots, stick. So, I don't exactly know how to do that part."

"Yeah, I've kind of avoided it like the plague after one disastrous marriage."

"Well, look at us, two dysfunctional peas in a pod."

He put his other hand on her other cheek, cupping her face gently, drawing her just a hair closer. It had been so long since he'd felt this—allowed himself to feel it. The heavy thud of his heart, the warmth in his blood. A want he'd closed off a long time ago.

"You know, maybe we should give ourselves a break. Is it dysfunction if we've built fairly good, functioning lives with jobs and family relationships and a lack of jail time?"

Carlyle shrugged, but her mouth curved. "Define *jail time.*"

He shook his head, because it didn't matter *why* the things she said amused him, it only mattered that they did. That she lifted those weights away. That something here, between them, worked—no matter how little that made sense.

He lowered his mouth to hers. He paused, just a whisper from contact. Waited until her eyes lifted from his mouth to his gaze. Maybe that's what had first snuck under all his very impenetrable defenses. The unique color, the way—if he looked hard enough—that was the one place he could see that hint of vulnerability.

Then he kissed her, watching the way her eyes fluttered closed, feeling the way she softened into him like melted wax. Like she fit right here, in his arms.

That weight he'd been carrying so long lifted just enough to see the possibility of lifting more. Surviving the weights he couldn't lift. Expanding beyond the tight, hammered-down knot he'd pulled himself into for some bid at control and protection.

But life was in the opening up, not the closing down. So he opened up.

And Carlyle did too.

Chapter Ten

Carlyle woke up to the very odd sensation of her bed moving without *her* moving. And the realization she was very much *not* dressed.

But the *man* getting out of *her* bed was...or in the process of anyway. He reached for a sweatshirt, and she watched the play of muscles across his back. She couldn't imagine when he had time to work out, but as she'd had her hands all *over* those muscles last night, she knew they weren't just for show.

She allowed herself a little dreamy smile because he *was* dreamy. And last night had been...special. Which made a little wriggle of anxiety move through her. Since when did she get special?

He pulled on the sweatshirt and got up. When he looked over his shoulder and met her gaze, he smiled. He bent over the bed.

"You've got time to sleep yet. I've got chores." He brushed a kiss across her forehead, like that was the most natural thing in the world. Like he hadn't been dad-celibate for something like *twelve* years and knew what to do with...this.

She definitely did not know. Because he'd said all that about liking her and thinking she'd lifted some weight and what the hell was a woman supposed to do with *that*?

Particularly if he just…left. Like that was that. Off to do chores.

Was that that? Was this just some kind of…*fun*? Then what was she supposed to do with the whole *I like you* thing, and his daughter, and him? And her whole rooted life that had clearly been a really bad decision?

She could not stand the thought of going through the day not knowing what kind of punch this was so she could roll with it. "This is like…a thing, right?" she asked, before he opened the door to leave. "Not like a…random fun night to blow off a little steam? Because I can do either, but—"

He turned, then cocked his head and studied her from where he stood by the door. When he spoke, it was like he was choosing his words very carefully and she tried to brace herself for the disappointment.

"I don't have a life that allows for blowing off steam, Car."

"You could," she managed to say, though not quite as flippantly and *I-don't-care-what-you-do* as she might have liked. "If you needed to."

He didn't even hesitate. "I don't."

"Okay."

"Do *you* need to?"

She blinked. When she'd said all that stuff about roots? When he kissed her like the entire world had stopped existing? "No, I don't need to."

He smiled. "Good. I'll see you at breakfast."

She couldn't quite manage a smile back, even as he left. She felt a little too…raw and…and…*uncomfortable.*

She sat up in bed, ran her fingers through her tousled hair. *Sex*-tousled hair. Because she had had *sex* with Cash last night.

Multiple times.

Not just blowing off steam. Not *fun*. A physical reaction to the past year. Being friends and attracted to each other was probably always going to lead here. She'd have preferred less *murder* involved, but her life pretty much had always revolved around murder. Why should this be different?

And she was okay with that. She wouldn't be here if she wasn't, but there was something about going from what happened in *just* this room, and *just* between them, to out into the larger Hudson world.

Part of her wanted to crawl under the covers and just hide, and she didn't know why. Because she had never been afraid of anything—or at least hadn't *let* herself dwell in fear. She *acted*.

But this was… It wasn't about danger or fear or any of those things you could *fight*, it was just…her heart. It was easy, in a way, to brazen her way through life when it was all danger and protection and *threats*. Quite the opposite to Cash, she hadn't gone internal, shrunk her world with all the danger. She'd expanded it. Her whole life. It was the only way to survive in her circumstances, to fight out, to ignore fear, to be loud and present and *demanding*.

But both were extremes, and now it seemed they both had to find some middle ground. Maybe that made them good for each other. Maybe that made this all…positive.

But she still didn't know how to deal with his siblings, or hers, or—dear God—Izzy, knowing Cash Hudson had been *inside* her.

She allowed herself a groan then flung herself out of bed. Some old habits still helped a woman get through the day. Flinging her way into the thick of it was the only way she knew how to do this.

She got dressed, brushed out her *very* tousled hair. "You're not a coward. You've never been a coward," she lectured herself. Out loud. Then she opened the door, shook her hair back, squared her shoulders, ready to face whoever and—

Nearly jumped a foot.

Izzy was standing there. Swiftie and Copper on either side of her, like two little dog sentries.

"Jeez." Carlyle slammed a hand to her heart.

Izzy blinked. "I was just coming to get you for breakfast."

"Oh. Yeah, I'm coming." Carlyle tried to smile as she stepped out into the hallway, but she knew it stretched all wrong across her face. She was…uncomfortable. Because at the end of the day, everything that happened with Cash—and all his talk about living for himself—didn't matter if Izzy didn't like the idea.

Izzy came first, and she should. She'd spent her entire life with her dad apparently never even looking twice at a woman, and then Carlyle had come along and…

This was why people avoided roots. *This* was why Zeke had said no way to getting even deeper in the Hudson machine. It wasn't the kind of complicated someone could just shoot their way out of. She had to deal with untying all these awful, heavy knots weighted in her stomach.

"Is something wrong?" Izzy asked as they walked toward the dining room.

"No, of course not," Carlyle replied.

But Izzy stopped, blocking Carlyle's forward movement out of the hallway.

"You'd tell me, right?" she asked, eyebrows furrowed together as she frowned. A little suspiciously.

Which made Carlyle feel terrible. She bent over a little so she was eye level with Izzy, put her hand on the girl's shoulder.

"I promise. Nothing is *wrong*. I'm having a weird personal mental argument with myself about weird personal things. I promise."

Izzy smiled a little, but she studied Carlyle's face. "Is it because you like my dad?"

Carlyle had been calm in the face of so many crises, but none of that had prepared her for *this*. Her eyes widened, her mouth dropped open, and no slick words to talk herself out of this came out.

"So, that's a yes," Izzy said, a bit like... Carlyle was dim.

Carlyle found herself completely speechless.

"He doesn't really do that," Izzy said gently, patting Carlyle's shoulder. "But don't worry. You can be *my* friend. You don't need to be his."

"Uh..." This was...so much worse than she'd imagined. Because Carlyle had the distinct feeling she was...being warned off. When it was a bit too late for that.

"Come on. I'm starving." Then Izzy took her hand and practically dragged her into the dining room.

A lot of the Hudsons were already there. And Zeke was clearly just arriving. Carlyle tried to feel normal instead of like some kind of robot who had to learn to act like humans. Izzy was talking about how she'd helped make the muffins that were on the buffet laid out with food as they went down the line with their plates. Carlyle tried to engage, but she just kept looking at every new person who entered, both hoping it would be and hoping it wouldn't be Cash.

She was going to have to tell him about Izzy's reaction. She was going to have to...do something. But when he entered the room and smiled at her, she knew she shouldn't smile back. She should be...something. Aloof or...cool. But she smiled back because he was just so damn handsome and amazing and...

Really, what did she think she was doing?

He came right over, grabbed a plate, then greeted Izzy before putting some food on his plate. When they moved to sit down, she was standing right next to him, feeling like her heart was going to burst out of her chest. Because Izzy was *right there*, but so were very *visual* memories of last night, and the sweet thing he'd said about her lifting weights and...

Cash ran his hand down her spine before they sat. Casual, but not *friendly*. That was an intimacy, a little bit *more*. Carlyle didn't want to look at anyone, see if they caught that, but she couldn't quite stop herself from glancing at Izzy. Who was frowning at her.

Well, damn.

But she had to focus on Zeke. On the task at hand. Murder and framing and connections.

Not a little girl warning her off her dad.

"The bar was pretty busy. I made the rounds, dropped some crumbs. Lots of people remembered Chessa, but nothing specific about the night she was murdered. At Car's request, I mentioned the cop and the ranch hand. Nothing too obvious," Zeke said once everyone was settled at the table. "No one came out and said anything too direct, but I got the distinct impression that Bryan Ferguson and Tripp Anthony had, on occasion, before last year, not just been seen at Rightful Claim, but had been seen *together* there. And routinely."

"I knew there had to be a connection," Carlyle said, pointing her fork at Cash. Then, because she couldn't help herself even when she was a tangle of Izzy-nerves, at Jack.

"I'm not sure that proves anything," Jack said, but his expression was dark. Angry, clearly. "But we'll look deeper into it. It's a thread to pull." He was clearly mad that he hadn't been right about his employee. But then again, the whole family had been wrong about Tripp, so why should this be different?

Before anyone could say anything else, the doorbell echoed through the house. Everyone paused, but it was Mary as usual who got up to get it.

"Sit," Walker grumbled, standing up himself.

Mary raised an eyebrow at him. "Pardon me?"

He scowled. "With what's going on, you're not answering the door."

Mary's expression didn't change, but she remained very still. "I see."

"You're a brave man, Walker," Hawk muttered from his end of the table, where he held Caroline in one arm and ate with the other hand.

"With danger all around, I don't think it's wise for the—"

"Bud, you better watch every next word," Carlyle said under her breath. Honestly, the fact her brother could still be such a caveman sometimes was ridiculous.

But Mary didn't get all mad or bent out of shape. She didn't glare daggers at her husband—like Anna was currently doing.

The doorbell rang again.

"Go right ahead, Walker. Be a big strong man and answer the door." Mary settled her hands over her bump and gave her husband a bland smile.

Walker swore, clearly realizing he'd dug himself a hole he was going to have to grovel out of later. But whoever was at the door wouldn't wait, so he stalked out of the room.

"I would have punched him," Anna said.

"Some methods are more effective than punching," Mary replied, all pleasant and cool. She was going to rip him a new one.

Carlyle couldn't ignore the fact she wouldn't mind seeing it. She loved the way Mary handled Walker—and most people. Carlyle wished she could emulate it, but she was too much of a Daniels. Bull in a china shop.

Mary would know what to say to Izzy. Mary would know how to handle Cash. Carlyle had a bad feeling she was going to break a hell of a lot of china on this new road she found herself on.

Walker returned, leading the female detective from Bent County into the dining room. Whatever amusement there'd been was sucked out of the room. Everyone went immediately silent and wary. This just…couldn't be good.

The detective's smile was pleasant, but her eyes were sharp. "Good morning," she offered cheerfully. "Sorry to interrupt your meal, but this was a first-thing-in-the-morning kind of deal. And I didn't catch you at your place soon enough." She looked at Zeke. "So, let's talk about what you were doing in Bent last night." Then she helped herself to a seat.

CASH CONSIDERED MAKING an excuse to take Izzy out of the room. He was already on edge about having her listen to what Zeke had found out, but add the detective and it was too much. What twelve-year-old girl would be or should be involved in discussions about her mother's murder? No matter how not part of her life that mother had been.

Cash looked down at her, sitting next to him. She didn't look upset. She didn't seem overwrought. If anything, her expression reminded him a bit of Mary. Cool. Completely collected. Maybe even a little curious. He opened his mouth to say something, to tell her to leave, but hesitated before he could find some gentle way of doing it.

But she turned then looked up at him, all cool and *adult*, and shook her head. As if she knew what he was going to say. She was smart and had been his kid for all these twelve years, so she probably did know.

She didn't want to leave. She wanted to see this through. He didn't like it, but maybe he didn't have to. Maybe sometimes parents had to let their kids see something through, even if it hurt.

"Can I offer you something to eat?" Mary asked the detective.

The detective waved Mary's polite—if a little chilly—offer away. "No, thank you. And I don't want to interrupt your breakfast. I only want some answers as to why you were snooping around Rightful Claim last night, Mr. Daniels. And since you weren't at your apartment this morning, I had the sneaking suspicion you might be here."

"My family is here," Zeke replied.

The detective's smile didn't slip in the slightest. "But they weren't in Bent last night. You were."

"I was just enjoying a drink. I didn't realize your husband was on the Bent County PD payroll." Zeke's return smile was *not* polite. It was sharp and it was mean. Cash didn't know that it was the right tact to take, but God knew he wasn't in charge of Zeke.

The detective remained wholly unfazed by Zeke's demeanor. She'd likely dealt with worse. "My husband tends to notice when people are running a line of questioning in his bar. He *is* married to a detective. He also notices when someone goes poking around in the alley behind the bar. Particularly when it's been the site of a recent investigation."

Zeke had not shared that information with the class. Cash frowned at him.

But Zeke shrugged. "Detective, I talked to some people. I don't know what more you want to hear."

Her eyes flicked briefly to Izzy. Then to Cash. She smiled,

and it seemed genuinely kind. "Maybe we should discuss this more privately," she said to Zeke, but it was easy to see that *private* just meant away from Izzy.

"You don't have to," Izzy said firmly, sounding like an adult. But she took Cash's hand under the table, held on hard. "I know my mother was murdered, and I know you're trying to figure out who did it. I want to be here."

Detective Delaney-Carson studied Izzy's face, then smiled. "Okay. You're free to go whenever you need to though. You get to decide."

Cash wanted to hang on to his frustration and distrust of the woman who clearly had him on her list of suspects, but it was hard to do when she was thinking about Izzy at all, let alone giving her an out.

"Listen," she said, clearly to all of them. "I understand that you all have an investigative business. That you—" she pointed to Anna "—even have an independent private investigator license. I understand and, in fact, am not even opposed to the group of you investigating in whatever ways you can. Legally, and in a way that can actually be used in a court of law, and in a way that does *not* end in some sort of misguided attempt at vigilante justice. But you have to work *with* us."

"Are you going to work with *us*?" Cash demanded.

The detective sighed. "Look, my hands are tied to a certain extent. I have a police department to answer to and laws to follow. A code of conduct, standard operating procedure. I'm sure you're aware," she added, looking at Jack.

Who nodded. Icily.

"I want to hear what you all think Bryan Ferguson and the late Tripp Anthony have to do with Chessa Scott's murder. And next time you think to ask around about anyone, I don't want to hear it from my husband. I want you to come to me or Hart. It is not our goal to arrest the wrong man," she said, looking at Cash pointedly.

Zeke didn't say anything, but he looked over at Cash. Almost like he was asking permission. Which was...a nice thing to do, actually. Cash gave him a nod.

"Carlyle pointed out that it was strange, or at least something worth looking into, that Ferguson was the one who handled Chessa Scott bonding out with Tripp Anthony last year. She's been trying to find a connection between them. And I did last night. Not much to go on, but enough to know they were friendly. Seen together at Rightful Claim more than once."

The detective nodded thoughtfully. "When was the last time they were seen together?"

"It was unclear. Definitely last year before Tripp died, but I couldn't get a time frame."

"Did you make a list of who you spoke to?"

Zeke crossed his arms over his chest. "I didn't ask names."

She waved that away, clearly seeing through Zeke. "I'll want names. Trust me, my husband can give me a list of everyone you spoke with, but it'd be easier if you narrowed it down to the ones who'd seen the two men together. You can email them to me."

Zeke scowled, but the detective didn't seem to notice. "We've looked some into Bryan Ferguson. Just another reason it'd be better if you all came to us. Since Anthony is dead, he wasn't on our list, but he'd been dating Ms. Scott, yes?"

"That was what Chessa said when he bailed her out, according to Ferguson," Jack replied.

The detective nodded. "Does Ferguson know your family has been looking into him?"

Jack shook his head. "I certainly haven't told him or anyone at the department."

"I'm assuming the exception there is…" She trailed off, looked through her notebook. "Deputy Chloe Brink? The one who was questioning the coroner?"

Jack's expression got very hard. "She's looked into some things regarding the murder, but no. She doesn't know we've been looking into Ferguson."

"All right." The detective stood. "I'll have more questions likely, but I'm just going to reiterate that all of this goes a lot smoother if you trust me with what you find. We want the truth as much as you do." She turned her gaze to Cash. "Can you walk me out, Mr. Hudson?"

Cash didn't like that, but he didn't see what choice he had. He squeezed Izzy's hand then released it and stood to follow the detective out.

She didn't say anything until they got to the front door. "You've worked with Bent County before. You and your search dogs?"

Cash nodded, not sure where this was going. "A few years back when there was a missing boy over in the state park."

She nodded. "I read the report. Your dogs found him."

"In the nick of time."

"You've also helped Quinn Peterson at Fool's Gold Investigation."

Cash wasn't sure exactly what the detective knew about that case, what he should be straight about. It felt dangerous to let someone in, someone who thought he was capable of murder.

But she'd given Izzy some consideration and he couldn't ignore that went a long way in his book.

"She was looking for some specific evidence on a case.

Had a scent and an area she thought it might be in, so the dogs searched and found it."

"Yeah. I'd like to do that, Mr. Hudson. But it would be a conflict of interest to tell you why."

"Can't really have my dogs help out if I don't know for what."

"I know, but maybe you have an employee, someone you're not related to, a colleague somewhere else? Who your dogs would listen to?"

"Me."

They both turned to where Carlyle was. Not *hiding* per se, but she had definitely been stealthily following them and listening to that conversation.

The detective sighed. "You have a personal connection to—"

"To who? Your prime suspect?" Carlyle demanded, crossing her arms over her chest, just as Zeke had back there.

"Car."

She turned her slightly belligerent look on him. "Anyone who your dogs will follow, or is qualified to lead your dogs, is going to have a personal connection to you." She turned her attention back to the detective. "I don't think you're bad at your job, Detective, so I think you knew you wouldn't find some random person unconnected to all of this to help you out. And you don't have access to other search dogs, or you wouldn't be asking. So let's not waste time."

"Ms. Daniels—"

"I know how these things go. I can facilitate a search that doesn't discredit your investigation. You wouldn't be here, asking him about his dogs, if you didn't think it could be done."

"You said yourself you're involved with Mr. Hudson.

You're, in fact, his alibi. If you know how this goes, Ms. Daniels, then surely you understand how it looks."

"So, find a way to make it look good," Cash said. Because Carlyle was right. The detective wouldn't be wasting her time with this if she didn't think it could be done. "Carlyle is perfectly capable of handling the search dogs. If I stay out of it, and if you're with her the whole time, and it gets you what you're looking for...isn't it worth the risk that this one little thing doesn't hold up in court?"

She was quiet for a long-drawn-out moment. "Fine. When can you do it?"

"How about now?" Cash and Carlyle asked in unison.

Chapter Eleven

They immediately took the detective down to the dog barn. Carlyle tried not to feel nervous. She'd never taken the dogs off property on her own. She'd never led a full-on, nontraining search on her own.

But they were very carefully not giving away how unqualified Carlyle was to do this while the detective was in earshot.

"So, Carlyle and I will get the dogs loaded up in our Hudson Dog Services truck. We can drive out to the site—"

"You're going to have to stay here, Mr. Hudson."

"I'll stay in the truck and—"

The detective was already shaking her head. "This is already a stretch as is. I can't have you anywhere near the search area. You're going to have to stay here, Mr. Hudson. It's the only way."

Cash didn't look at her, but his expression was clear. He didn't like it.

"Ms. Daniels, I'm going to drive out to the site. I'm going to get everything ready on my end. When you've got the dogs loaded up, text me. I'll text you an address. I'm going to ask you not share that address with anyone. Is this the truck you'll be driving?"

"Yeah."

She noted down the make, model and license plate. "You'll

be cleared to drive up to the site. I'll see you soon." Then she turned and walked back toward the front of the main house where her police cruiser was parked.

Carlyle watched her go with mixed emotions. Then she looked at Cash with even *more* mixed emotions.

His expression was...concerned, she supposed. But not frustrated or angry like she'd expected.

"I can do this," she said, not because she was confident, but because she wanted to assure him. There was just...so much at stake that was *outside* her control. Usually she was only ever risking herself when she was storming through a bad decision.

"I know you can," Cash said, but he was looking at her, still with that concern, like he could *see* the anxiety on her even as she tried to hide it. "The dogs know what they're doing. All you have to do is facilitate. Just like anything else you've done with them. They're the pros. You've been doing this for a year. You know the ropes."

Carlyle nodded, and she knew she was doing a terrible job of keeping the worry off her face because Cash took her by the shoulders, gave them a squeeze. "You can do this. I know you can."

"I know I can." But he saw through her, so why not be honest? Maybe he could temper his expectations if she was. "It's just...a lot of pressure. I don't want to mess it up."

"You can't. All you're doing is taking them out there. Giving them some direction. They're the ones doing the job. If they mess up, Hick just won't get a special treat tonight."

He was trying to make a joke—she knew him well enough he wouldn't deny a dog a treat. But she couldn't force herself to smile or laugh.

"Even if this is a dead end, I'll tell you guys where we

do the search. I don't care what she said. We'll investigate it ourselves later if we have to and—"

Cash shook his head. "It won't be the place. She's testing you. She'll meet you there then take you to a second location."

She hadn't thought of that, but he was right. Of course he was right. The detective wasn't about to make this *easy*.

"Just let the dogs do the work, okay?" Cash said, squeezing her shoulders again. "They'll find what's there, *if* it's there."

Carlyle wasn't so sure about that. If she didn't lead the dogs the right way, she could mess everything up. But this was what had to be done, and she was a *doer*. "I better get going," she said. Because she wanted to keep that worry to herself, not end up blurting it out to him so *he* worried more.

"Be careful. And don't go pissing off the detective just because she's pissing you off."

Carlyle pouted, if only to add some levity to this whole awful situation. "But that's my favorite pastime."

"Try to play this one by the book, Daniels." Then he leaned down and kissed her. And lingered there, his mouth on hers. Unfurling all that warmth and yearning inside of her. Not just a physical yearning, but an ache for something she hadn't let herself want before.

Something she was still too afraid to name, even in the privacy of her own mind. Especially when she was reminded of her run-in with Izzy earlier. She had to warn him lest he walk into that minefield without any preparation.

But part of her was worried he'd drop her like a hot poker. And she wouldn't even be able to blame him. His daughter came first. Should come first.

So, because she was her, she ripped off the bandage. She pulled her mouth away, cleared her throat and tried her best to appear unaffected. "Just FYI, I don't think Izzy is too keen on this whole thing."

"What whole thing?"

"The...us thing. Not like she thinks something's going on. Just that I think she picked up on my feelings for you, and she made it clear I should steer myself elsewhere."

His eyebrows furrowed. "She loves you."

"Yeah, but... She loves you more. The best and most. Sharing you is a pretty new concept. She's not a fan."

"I'll talk to her."

Carlyle immediately shook her head. "Look, this isn't my business, I know that, but you can't go *talk* to her after she warns me off. Then she thinks I'm some whiny tattletale. And that doesn't help anyone." Least of all Carlyle herself. It would just kill her if Izzy suddenly stopped trusting her.

"I'm going to have to talk to her anyway, Car. I'm not sneaking around pretending this isn't happening."

Oh, how her traitorous, silly little heart fluttered at that. "Okay, fine, but don't mention me. Don't mention not liking it. And when she tells you she doesn't, you listen. You can kick me to the curb over it." She was talking too fast, saying too much, but she couldn't quite stop herself. "No hard feelings. Just be straight with me, okay? No...beating around the bush or trying to make it nice. Just straight out."

He looked so...concerned. She didn't know what to do with that reaction. She wanted to run in the opposite direction. She didn't want...concern. She was tough. She was brave. She was...

He reached out and cupped her face in his hands. She was *toast*.

"My daughter dictates a lot of parts of my life, and rightfully so, but not everything," he said, so very seriously. "I still have to...be able... She can't dictate everything without any discussion. Without getting to the heart of it. That isn't fair to me and it's not raising my daughter the right way to let her just...always gets what she wants."

"You're going to keep...whatever we're doing...even if she hates it? Hates me because of it? Hates you because of it?" Carlyle didn't want that. As much as she wanted *him*, she didn't want that.

"I'm going to talk to her, Carlyle. Because there's no reason for her to not like me having a relationship with you—which is what we're doing. It might be uncomfortable for her at first, for all of us. It's new, and I don't expect it to be easy. But she doesn't get to decide wholesale. It has to be a discussion."

"And if after you've discussed it, she's still against it?"

"Let's take it one step at a time, Car. Like, step one. Go find this evidence the detective wants."

Carlyle wrinkled her nose. "What if it hurts your case?"

Cash sighed, dropped his hands. He looked out at where the detective had gone. "Did you see her when she looked at Izzy?"

"Yeah, she wanted her gone, but then when Izzy spoke up for herself, she gave her an out. Treated her like...a whole person, not just a kid to be shunted off. It was good."

"I wanted to take against her for having me on her list, but she's doing her due diligence. She also didn't stop Zeke last night, when it's clear her husband gave her the opportunity to. She's not telling us to butt out. She's bringing us even more in. Maybe it'll bite me in the ass, but I think I trust her."

Carlyle blew out a breath. "Yeah, I do too. But I don't trust this *whole thing*. Something's off and I don't like it."

"Agreed. All we can do is take it one step at a time." He tucked a strand of hair behind her ear, waited until she met his gaze. "Be careful, Car," he said seriously.

She'd never spent much time being careful, but she figured now was a good time to start. So, she smiled. "I will be."

CASH HAD BEEN forced to have a lot of tough conversations with his daughter over the years. Between everything with Chessa, to the danger the Hudsons routinely dealt in, to Anna getting pregnant *before* she was married to Hawk and where *did* babies come from then, to—quite frankly, the worst—puberty.

He hadn't done a good job every time, but he'd tried. If there was anything he'd had to accept in being a parent, it was that the best you could do was *try*, and if your trying sucked, you just had to get better. Lean on his family a little bit.

So, as Cash—plagued by uncertainty—walked toward the dog barn with his daughter, knowing he had to have this potentially difficult conversation, he realized it was not anything new.

But it *was* a new subject. Him being involved with someone. Finding the right balance between including Izzy and not letting her think she got to make his decisions *for* him. They were a family, but some things were private. Someday, she'd want to date, and he doubted very much he'd have a say.

He wanted to go jump off the nearest mountain at the thought.

"Can we work with the horses again today?" Izzy asked, swinging her arms in the pretty morning like she didn't have a care in the world. He wished she could always feel that way, particularly after this morning's breakfast.

"Well, technically it's Crew Three's turn, and Carlyle had to take them with her to work with the detective this morning." They should take Crew Two out on the trail, but

Cash wanted this whole murder thing solved before they went too far from home base. "What if we take the puppies through the obstacle course instead?"

"Pita too?"

"I'll text Hawk." He pulled out his phone and texted Hawk to send his dog out. None of them were puppies anymore, but until they had a new batch, they'd be known as the puppies.

"Before you get the rest of them out, I want to talk to you about something."

All the ease and happiness leaked out of her quickly. Her arms slumped and she shaded her eyes to look up at him.

"Nothing bad happened. This is a good thing I want to talk to you about, I like to think." He crouched to make himself eye level, though it wasn't much of a crouch anymore. She was going to be a tall one, and that ache of too much joy and wistfulness wrapped around his heart like it always did.

But that frown did not leave Izzy's face. She watched him with deep, deep suspicion as he tried to come up with the words.

He knew he should start out quickly, so she didn't invent terrible scenarios in her head, but he was struggling to find the words to start. "Iz… You… You like Carlyle."

Her frown deepened. Which wasn't exactly expected, but maybe it should have been with what Carlyle had told him.

"So?" she said, a little belligerently.

"So. I…like her too."

"She works for you."

"Yes, and she's a…friend."

"Cool," Izzy said, trying to turn away from him, but he reached out for her arm, kept her in place. Because her *cool* sounded anything but.

"I like her a lot, actually," he said firmly. Because he could interrogate Izzy's feelings on the matter instead of be clear about his own, but that felt like a bit of a cop-out. He'd already initiated this relationship with Carlyle. He wasn't going back on it. No matter how she'd assured him he *could*.

She had heartbreak in her eyes like no one had ever chosen her over anything. And maybe they hadn't, and he couldn't *choose* her over Izzy, but this wasn't...so cut-and-dried. Life never was. It wasn't about *choosing* over anyone else.

It was just life.

"As more than a friend," he continued, while Izzy scowled at him. "I wanted to let you know that."

"What? That she's suddenly your girlfriend?" Izzy said, with the snotty kind of look that usually irritated him.

He was not an old man, but man, the word *girlfriend* made him feel old and out of place. Still, it was a word that made sense to Izzy. No matter how snottily she'd said it.

"Yeah. You seem to have a problem with that. Which I have to say, I don't understand because I know you love her."

"Yeah, I do." She jerked her arm away from him. "Because she's *my* friend," Izzy said, exploding. "She's on *my* side. Finally, there's someone who doesn't listen to *you*. She listened to *me*. She cared about *me*." Izzy spun around and pointed at him. "Now...she's yours. And she'll listen to *you*."

There was a well of anger there that he hadn't anticipated. That he didn't know what to do with. But beyond just not understanding, her words hit at just about every little insecurity he had. "Izzy... Do you really think I don't listen? I don't care?"

Her face got all crumpled looking, like right before she cried. But before he could reach out for her, she stomped away from him. Not far. Just to the entrance of the barn.

"I just…"

Cash didn't know if she didn't have the words, or just couldn't squeeze them out. So he found some of his own to give her.

"You are the most important thing in my world. You always will be. I know I'm not perfect, but I know if I've made anything clear to you, it's that. That doesn't mean I don't have other important things. I always have. We are very lucky to have a big family, getting bigger every year, who we love and loves us back. They're all important."

Izzy turned very slowly. If she'd let any tears fall, she'd wiped them away first. "You love her?" she asked, her voice wavery and those tears still visible in her eyes, even if they didn't fall.

What was with everyone asking him that question? "I don't…know."

"Shouldn't you?"

"It's just complicated. Adult relationships aren't so cut-and-dried. And there are…extenuating circumstances." And now he just wished he could reverse time and *not* do this here. Or anywhere. Ever.

Izzy swallowed. "Everything keeps changing."

And how. "I know, baby. I can't promise you that'll stop. Life is change. You're going to grow up on me. And you're going to make your own decisions, and I don't have to like them. Though I hope I will. But I can promise… Nothing comes in front of you for me, Iz. And if we talk about it, we can work through whatever comes."

She looked down at the ground, and he knew she was trying so hard not to cry. "I just… Aunt Mary is going to have a baby, and she won't have time for me like she used to. You'll spend time with Carlyle, just like all the aunts and uncles… Except Jack." She looked up at him, all those tears making her blue eyes bluer. "Where do I fit if you all get married and have babies?"

He pulled her into his chest, and she didn't push him away. "You fit right here, baby. Because you are my baby. You're our first baby here on this ranch. Nothing changes that. Not more kids, not more people. You'll *always* be ours. Long before everyone else."

She leaned her head on his shoulder, and he felt the tell-tale tears seeping through his shirt. He rubbed her back, tried to find the words to ease this change in the midst of all this danger.

"You'll help with Mary's baby. Just like you're doing with Caroline. And…just think. You're going to middle school in the fall. There will be sports and clubs and all sorts of things." Things he'd always been leery about letting her join, but he clearly needed to…let go. Find a way to give her a bigger life, not a smaller one.

"I know it's hard to feel like everything is changing around you, but it's just…life moving along. You add people, you lose people." He pulled her back, so she had to look at him. "But nothing ever changes that you're part of this." He pointed out at the ranch, at the main house— where Pita was racing across the yard toward them. "Love just expands, baby. It's not something that can get used up."

She took a deep, shaky breath. "Chessa… She stopped loving me. She used it all up and then there was nothing left."

Cash wished there was some way to heal that wound, but he'd had to accept that he couldn't. Only time and growing up and being there for her could. Or maybe he just hoped it could.

"Your mom never loved much beyond herself. There are probably some reasons why that was, but I could never get to the heart of them. I tried, but... Nothing that Chessa ever felt or didn't, did or didn't, is about you. Nothing. And I know it might be hard to believe that, and maybe you can't just yet. But I want you to look at *all* the people who are here and think about them and their place in your life. Not the one person who isn't."

Izzy swallowed. "I just...don't want things to change. I want Carlyle to be my friend and..."

"She will be. Whatever is going on between Carlyle and me at any time isn't ever going to be about how you guys feel about each other. And I think you know Carlyle well enough to know she's not afraid of making me mad. She loves you, independently of me. She sticks up for you when she thinks it's right, because she's been in very similar shoes. That doesn't change just because we...date," he finished lamely. "I promise."

She let out a long breath, then nodded. "Okay. I guess... I guess it's okay then."

Cash didn't point out he hadn't been asking for permission, because it was nice to have. Because having her blessing meant something. "I love you, Iz. Nothing ever in a million years changes that. Nothing."

She curled into him, holding on tight. "I love you too, Dad."

Pita arrived with delighted yips and barks, jumping in between them with enthusiasm. Izzy laughed and released Cash to throw her arms around Pita and wrestle with him a bit. And for a moment, Cash let himself forget about murder, and Carlyle out on a search job, and the hole Chessa had left in his daughter's heart.

And just enjoyed the moment.

Chapter Twelve

Carlyle pulled up to the address the detective had texted her. Like Cash had said, it clearly wasn't the end location. The detective was alone, standing next to her police cruiser, in a kind of abandoned parking lot outside of Bent.

The detective held up her hand in a wave. Her other hand held a cell phone to her ear. Carlyle went ahead and parked and got out of the van, then took a surreptitious look around.

This location wasn't in the boundaries of the town of Bent, but it was close. The saloon Zeke had cased the other night couldn't be more than a mile or two away from this spot.

"Did you look under the potty stool?" the detective was saying into her phone.

Carlyle raised an eyebrow. What the hell was a *potty stool*?

"That's where I found it last time. I have to go. Yeah. Love you too, bye." She hit a button on her phone and pocketed it, smiling at Carlyle. "Sorry. Family emergency."

"A lot of potty stool-related emergencies?"

The detective laughed. "I have three kids under the age of six. So, yes."

Carlyle blinked. It was hard to imagine this very professional and with-it detective with *three* little kids. Not to mention, Carlyle had been to Rightful Claim, the bar the detective's husband owned. She knew what he looked like. "You're really married to that hot, tattooed saloon guy?"

"Yep."

"That's really hard to believe." She remembered Cash's words to not irritate the detective a little too late.

But the detective didn't get offended. She didn't even frown. She grinned. "Oh, Ms. Daniels, you have *no* idea." Then she pointed to Carlyle's truck. "Am I okay to ride with you in the truck to the search site?"

"Allergic to dogs?"

"No."

"Then you're good to go." Carlyle thought about bringing up the fact this wasn't how the detective said it would go, but then she decided to just roll with it. Let the detective dictate how this would go and just observe.

A woman could glean a lot just from observing. If she could keep her big mouth shut. Well, she'd *try*.

"Once we're inside the truck, I'm going to turn my body cam on. That way, we've got everything documented should we need it for a trial. Once we get to the site, Hart and two other Bent County deputies will be there. We've got the search area blocked off."

"And something for the dogs to use to search off of, I assume?"

"When we get there. Everything is going to go on camera. The more transparent we can be, the better off we'll be come trial."

"You keep talking about a trial, but we don't even have a suspect yet." The detective said *nothing*. "I thought we were working together."

"We are, Ms. Daniels. Believe it or not, I don't want to arrest Mr. Hudson. Off the record? I don't think he did it, and it's a waste of time trying to pin it on him."

"On the record?" Carlyle asked, because she wasn't dumb enough to be swayed by a little good cop, even without the presence of a bad cop.

"We're exploring every possible and reasonable avenue," she said, sounding very formal and official.

Carlyle really didn't want to like her, but she was making it hard. "Well, let's go find something for the record then."

The detective nodded. "Just remember. We're recording *everything.*" She patted the little attachment to her police vest.

Carlyle nodded, appreciating the clarity. No attempt to get her to say something dumb and incriminating on camera. They got in the truck, and the dogs whined a little bit at the newcomer, but they were well trained enough to stay put.

The detective gave directions as Carlyle drove. They passed Rightful Claim, rounded the corner and entered the back alley.

Where Zeke had been *poking around*, as the detective had called it this morning. Carlyle didn't say anything about it. With the camera running, she figured it best she said as little as possible.

The detective got out, so Carlyle did too. Detective Hart and two uniformed deputies were waiting, and there was an area of the alley and the building behind the saloon sectioned off with crime-scene tape.

"The area taped off is what we're searching," Detective Delaney-Carson explained as they walked over to the other officers.

"What do you have for the dogs to get a scent?"

Hart produced a plastic bag. Inside was a torn scrap of fabric. Carlyle figured the streak of brown on the gray-and-pink fabric was blood. Chessa's blood.

She set that thought away as best she could.

"We can go in this building through that open door, but only the ground floor. They can also search around out here within the tape, but not beyond."

"I'll have to be the one who gives the scent to them," Carlyle said, which wasn't *exactly* true, but true enough. "They won't understand what they're supposed to do if it's any of you. You'll also want to stand out of the way and remain mostly still so they're not distracted by you. I've got six dogs. They'll take turns in teams of two. When they're out in the field, you want to just stay out of their way."

"What if they want to go beyond the borders of the search?" one of the officers asked.

"I'll stop them." Carlyle looked around the blocked off area. It seemed such an odd location to be cordoned off. Had Chessa been found here? She glanced around, looking for security cameras, but didn't see any. "What if they hit on something beyond the borders? Can't I just let them go for it?"

"We don't have a search warrant for any area beyond," Detective Delaney-Carson said. "The street is fine, but inside or around certain buildings is private property. But if they're pointing to that area, we can work on expanding our search warrant with that due cause. So, you'll just let us know and we'll go from there."

Carlyle didn't know what to think of that, but she supposed it was just something to file away. Maybe Jack would have an idea what it meant and why.

She moved to the truck and unleashed the first two dogs. She prepped them for the search, then took the bag of evidence from Hart and opened it. Then she let the dogs do their thing. She followed them, and Detective Delaney-Carson followed her. The other three stayed where they were in different corners, patrolling the area so no one happened upon them, Carlyle guessed.

Both dogs immediately went for the building. Carlyle shared a look with Detective Delaney-Carson then followed the dogs. The detective kept right by Carlyle's side, then stopped her before she entered the building.

"We already gave it a sweep, but we can't go upstairs, so let me go first."

Carlyle nodded and the woman drew her gun and went in first. Carlyle followed her in. The dogs sniffed around the empty room. More like a warehouse than anything. All concrete and grimy windows, which let in a little light but not much visibility. The detective kept her weapon drawn, but she motioned Carlyle forward.

There was definitely something going on here that Carlyle hadn't been let in on, and she didn't know what to make of that. She figured it wasn't malicious, but that didn't mean it didn't make her nervous.

Carlyle watched as the dogs headed for the stairs.

"You can't let them go up there," the detective said.

Carlyle gave the order to stop, and both dogs sat obediently. Right there at the bottom of the stairs.

"You sure they can't go upstairs?"

"You have reason to believe they scent something upstairs?"

Carlyle pointed to both of them, sitting at attention, waiting for the okay signal. "Clearly."

The detective nodded. She pulled her radio to her mouth. "Hart. The dogs want upstairs. Call it in. See if someone can expand that search warrant for us."

The return came back staticky but affirmative. The detective still held her gun, her eyes focused on the stairs. She had a frown on her face.

She wanted up there. She *suspected* something up there.

Carlyle wondered if she could just…go. She wasn't a cop. Search warrants didn't matter to her. But then one of the dogs let out two low *woofs*. Carlyle frowned. It wasn't one of the normal search responses, but she thought Cash had told her something about that indication one time. A long time ago. When he'd first been introducing her to all the dogs.

She looked at the dog who'd made the noise. Colby. Colby hadn't always been search and rescue. Or she had, but it had been for something else… What was it?

When Carlyle remembered, her body went a little cold. "Detective, I think we better get out of here."

"Why?"

"These dogs are trained for search and rescue, but this one in particular also has some training with finding drugs, weapons and explosives." Carlyle didn't know the exact signs for all of those, but she knew the dog's reaction just… wasn't good.

"All right."

Carlyle signaled the dogs out of the building, she and the detective following. But just as they reached the doorway something…exploded. Loud and bright, and then the ceiling rained down on them.

Hot. Bright. *Hell.* Something—or *somethings*—crashed on top of her. Painful, but nothing heavy or sharp enough to do real damage. She hoped.

The dogs were out, and Carlyle was about to jump forward to follow them, but she heard swearing and looked behind her. The detective was on the ground, conscious, but when she tried to get up, she swore even harder and didn't manage. That's when Carlyle noticed she had something stuck in her leg.

But worse, all around them were flames. The entire upstairs had exploded and collapsed, and none of the sounds the fire and building were making could be good. The roof was crumbling. Carlyle had to get them out of here. She grabbed the detective's arm. "This might hurt, but it's better than staying put." Then she dragged her out through the doorway.

They'd likely sustained some burns, and if the blood dripping on the ground was anything to go by, she had a bit of a head wound. And *maybe* dragging the detective was hell on her stitches from the other day. But she was on her own two feet and of sound mind.

She managed to drag the detective away from the flames. She thought—hoped—she heard sirens in the distance but mostly it was just the crackle and creak of a building going up in flames.

Carlyle kept dragging Laurel, but she was running out of steam. She managed to make it around the corner before she stumbled a little bit and fell on her butt. She scooted her back against the brick building and the detective did the same.

"Well, thanks. Probably saved my life, Ms. Daniels."

"Any time."

"Your head's bleeding."

"Yeah, so's your leg. Don't look at it," Carlyle immediately told her, because the giant piece of debris sticking out of the woman's leg was about to cause Carlyle to lose her lunch, and she'd seen worse, she liked to think.

But yikes.

"Don't worry. Been hurt once or twice. Know the drill." But the detective closed her eyes, leaned her head against the wall. Then she swore. Loudly. "This better not put me off the damn case."

Hart came running up to them, crouched in front of the detective, worry all over him. "You okay?"

"Yeah, thanks to her."

"Paramedics are on their way with fire, plus another unit." Hart looked at the detective's leg, blanched, swallowed, but didn't shake or faint. He looked over at Carlyle. "Anything beside that gash on your head?"

The old stab wound throbbed, but she didn't think that was relevant. Besides, her heart was beating too hard, and her limbs were too shaky to really take stock. "No. Where are my dogs?"

"They ran straight for the truck, so we leashed them up with the others. That okay?"

Carlyle nodded. She didn't want to have to tell Cash what happened. "Yeah, listen. I better get them back to the ranch." Of course she felt about as sturdy as a dead tree branch, but no one needed to know that.

"No. You'll get checked out. Sit tight. I've got some phone calls to make. Do you want to call someone from the ranch to come pick up the dogs?"

Carlyle nodded. "I left my phone in the truck though."

"Use mine," Detective Delaney-Carson said, holding out her cell phone, but before Carlyle could make the call, the detective grabbed Hart by the pants' leg.

"Hart," the detective said, sounding like she was trying to be more firm than she actually *sounded* firm. "Don't you dare call my husband."

"Grady'll kill me if I don't."

"Yeah, well. The price you pay for being my partner, I guess. He'll find out soon enough, hopefully once I'm all bandaged up. You tell him now? *I* kill you."

But there wasn't any more to say because an ambulance pulled up. One EMT went straight for the detective and one for Carlyle. They poked and prodded at her head, asked her too many questions to count. And fully ignored her when she said she was fine.

"We'll transport you both to the hospital in the same ambulance. Easier that way. You need a stretcher, Detective. Ms. Daniels, you can walk on your own accord if you feel up to it."

Carlyle nodded, then steeled herself to look at the detective. But they'd removed the debris and there was bloody gauze over her thigh.

She was conscious though. Talking to the EMT with the stretcher, every bit the in-charge detective even after what had happened.

What *had* happened?

Carlyle got one last glimpse of the building. Something had exploded on that top floor they weren't allowed in. And that was fishy. But the detective had been acting weird. Like she knew something she wasn't letting on.

Once they were all loaded up in the ambulance, Carlyle didn't make her phone call. She looked at the detective. "That thing off?" she said, pointing to the body cam.

The woman reached up, switched something on it. "Now it is."

"Detective, you know what happened in there, don't you?"

"I think you earned the right to call me Laurel. And maybe be the namesake of our next kid."

"Jeez. Isn't three enough?"

"We make cute babies."

It *almost* made Carlyle laugh. "I bet."

The detective—*Laurel*—sighed. "We have some theories. I'll tell you about it. Make your phone call first."

WHEN CASH'S PHONE RANG, he didn't recognize the number, but with Carlyle off searching for things with his dogs, he couldn't just ignore it. So he answered, with a pit of dread in his stomach. "Hello?"

"Hey."

"This isn't your number."

"No, it's the detective's. I'm helping her out with something, but we've got to leave the dogs behind. Can you come pick them up? Detective Hart will have the truck and the dogs at the Sheriff's Office."

"What are you working on?" Cash asked.

"I can't explain just yet. I will tonight though, promise."

"Carl—"

"Really, Cash. It's fine. I promise. We just need the dogs picked up. I'll be home tonight, and I'll be able to explain everything. Just too many…people around right now. Okay?"

He didn't like this at all, but he understood why she might not be able to talk. But then why not text? "You sure you're okay?"

She laughed, and *that* sounded more like her. "Yeah, I'm sure. If I was in some kind of trouble, I'd be too busy fighting my way out of it to call you."

Fair enough, even though the idea made him frown. "Okay, I'll come pick up the truck. Zeke's still out here, he can drop me off. He was talking about doing some more poking around Bent anyway."

"Oh, he doesn't need to do that."

"Why not?"

"Listen, I've got lots of stuff to tell you guys, but can you just stay away from Bent for now? It's not dangerous, I promise. I just want to make sure we aren't messing with this case. That detective was right. We need to make sure she can build a case."

Now he was *really* worried. "Carlyle, I have never once heard you admit someone else was right."

"I didn't say the *male* detective was right. Then you'd really have to worry."

Which was fair enough, and almost made him want to laugh if he could around the little weight of worry in his stomach. But she was a grown woman, and everything she said made *sense*, even if it didn't land right.

"Just get the dogs back to the ranch," she said. "I'll call you when I need a ride if I can't hitch one home with one of the cops."

"Car..." He couldn't get over the feeling she was holding out on him. That something was *wrong*. But she'd called the ranch...home, and that felt...important. "All right. Just promise you'll call. And come home soon."

"I promise. By dinner. Get the dogs. We'll talk soon. Bye."

"Bye." He pulled the phone away from his ear, trying to tell himself everything was fine. If there was a problem, she would have at least hinted at one. She'd only hide something to protect him, and he couldn't think of what she'd be protecting him from.

But he was damn well taking Zeke with him. First, he hunted down Mary to make sure she'd keep Izzy within someone's eyesight at all times. Then he found Zeke and explained the phone call.

"Since when is she about listening to detectives' orders?"

"I don't know," Cash said. "I don't like it."

"Yeah, me neither," Zeke said. "All right. Ready?"

Cash nodded, but before they could make way for the door, Hawk entered the room with a phone to his ear. He made a stopping motion to them, and though Cash felt impatience snapping, he waited. And so did Zeke.

When Hawk finally pulled the phone away from his ear, his expression was blank. Cop blank. "I just got called into a fire. There was an explosion. One Bent County detective and one civilian were hurt and taken to the hospital."

Cash was already moving—and so was Zeke, swearing a blue streak.

"You can't just go tearing off—" Hawk called after them, but they were outside and in Zeke's truck before he finished.

"Hold on," Zeke muttered, and then he drove like a bat out of hell for the hospital.

Cash only wished he'd go faster.

Chapter Thirteen

Carlyle managed to downplay her injuries to the nurse. There was enough confusion that she didn't even have to take her shirt off. They just cleaned up her head—no stitches this time—and let her go with a little printout about painkillers and what to look for.

Carlyle knew she should head out. Call Cash to pick her up. Or maybe call Chloe so she didn't have to tell Cash about this at all. Maybe if she took off the bandage before she got back to the ranch, he wouldn't even know.

But she hadn't gotten much out of Laurel about what the detective knew in the short ambulance ride, and Carlyle was determined to return to the ranch with more information than when she'd left.

So, she poked around the hospital until she figured out where Laurel had gone—she'd had to be admitted due to the severity of her injury. Carlyle waited until the hallway was empty and no one appeared to be in her room, then slipped in.

Laurel looked up from where she'd been messing with the IV in her arm and frowned a little at Carlyle. "Are you supposed to be in here?"

"Are you supposed to be trying to take that IV out?"

"That is *not* what I was doing."

"Uh-huh."

"You get the green light or are you sneaking off?"

"Green light. Just a little scrape on my head," she said, pointing to her bandage and ignoring the throbbing pain in her side. "You need surgery?"

"Still some discussion on that. I'll riot," she muttered irritably. And since Carlyle understood the feeling so well, she smiled.

"No one out there?" Laurel asked, jerking her chin toward the door.

Carlyle shook her head. "Pretty empty."

"Okay, come here so I can talk softly. I don't think anyone would be listening, but we're not going to be too careful with small towns where everyone knows everyone. Pull up that chair."

Carlyle did as she was told and was grateful when Laurel didn't beat around the bush.

"I'm going to tell you a few things. I shouldn't name names, but I'm going to because your people probably need to be on the lookout, and because I don't know how long I'll be stuck here. Hart will keep working on your case, and he's as good as me. I should leave it at that, but I figure you and yours will poke around anyway, so why not poke in the right direction?"

"That sounds very un-cop of you."

Laurel smiled. "I would have been highly insulted by that when I first started out, but these days, I'll take it as a compliment. I feel like we're on the cusp of something. It's complicated, and I haven't been able to untie all the little knots yet. But there's a correlation between Bryan Ferguson, Tripp Anthony and Butch Scott."

Carlyle hadn't heard of Butch before, but Scott was Chessa's last name.

"Chessa's brother," Laurel confirmed. "Half-brother,

anyway, according to his birth certificate. And Butch's stepmother owned that building across from Rightful Claim. Where we found Chessa's body. Butch and Bryan were stepsiblings once upon a time, and Butch, Bryan and Tripp all graduated high school together. Not uncommon out here, and I haven't gotten far enough to know if they were ever friends, kept being friends, but the ownership of that building was suspect."

"Even more so now."

"Yeah."

"Look, Hart will keep tugging on the line. I might need a day or two to talk my way around doctors and my husband to get back on the case, but we're not going anywhere. We're going to solve this."

The door flew open. "Speak of the devil," Laurel muttered. "Run. Hide. Save yourself."

The man did look a bit like a devil. He was *very* large, one arm nearly covered in tattoos. He had a beard, and his hair was a little wild. He looked like he would tear down the foundations of the earth, and Carlyle had enough experience with men—particularly the protective sort—to see it was about the fact his wife had been hurt, and there was nothing he could do about it. So he was just going to be… loudly and impotently angry about it.

"What are you doing here?" the detective—*Laurel*—demanded of the man who was her husband. "You are supposed to be on kid duty."

"And now your sister is. What the hell, princess?"

Princess? People really did have secret lives you couldn't guess at.

"Grady, this is Carlyle. Carlyle, my husband."

"Don't pull that polite BS with me," the man grumbled

as he strode to the other side of Laurel's hospital bed, but he looked over at Carlyle and gave her a nod. "Hi."

"Hey."

"I assume the two guys yelling in the waiting room who I used as a diversion belong to you."

Carlyle blinked. *Two* men. Her brothers? Well, no reason to feel bummed about that. She *had* lied to Cash about where she was. Well. Only sorta. She was fine. Cleared and on her way out.

But apparently, first she had to deal with her brothers and how they'd gotten wind of her situation. "I guess I should go...put a stop to that."

But the man's attention was already back on his wife, and Carlyle could still see all that anger, but she could also see the gentle way he took Laurel's hand, and that anger was just love and worry all tangled up in something that might feel useful.

She supposed that's what married people with three kids who wanted another one did. Carlyle didn't know what to do with the weird feeling in her gut, so she went to find her brothers.

But it wasn't them out at the nurse's station yelling. Well, one of the angry men in the waiting room was. The other one was Cash.

It was an odd realization, to see some of that violent anger in his eyes that had been in the detective's husband's. Like she might matter to him *that* much.

And something inside of her—something she'd shored up so many times in her life, plugged all the cracks and holes, fought tooth and nail to keep it intact—came crumbling down.

The tears spilled over, and she walked over to Cash. Her breathing hitched, and she didn't want to sob, but she was a little afraid that noise that came out of her was exactly that. As he turned, he frowned, but pulled her into his arms.

She supposed it was all of it. Explosions and tangled webs of people they hadn't figured out. Cash in her bed and Izzy's not-so-subtle disapproval. That look in his eyes. The detective and potty chairs and tattooed husbands and debris sticking out of her leg, all because she wanted to find the truth.

God, Carlyle was so tired of people getting hurt to find the truth. Her whole life. The *whole* of it.

"Hey." She heard the surprise in Cash's voice, but he held her there, tight and close, rubbing a comforting hand up and down her back. "It's okay. You're okay," he murmured.

And the silly thing was, she knew that, but it made everything better when he said it.

IN A TURN of events Cash didn't quite know what to do with, Zeke handed him the keys to his truck. "You take her home. I'll get the dogs."

Cash had figured he'd have to fight him on it. Zeke was the more formidable brother, mostly because Mary had Walker wrapped around her little finger. Walker had been threaded into the Hudson family and ranch life. Zeke kept himself apart.

But this was an acknowledgement of…something. So, Cash handed the keys to the dog truck over to Zeke. He had a million admonitions to offer about how to drive with the dogs, how to leash them properly, how to make everything okay.

But in the end, he offered none. Zeke would figure it out. The important thing was getting Carlyle back to the ranch where she could rest. The woman was *crying*, despite the fact she was on her own two feet and seemed to be okay.

Carlyle sniffled into his shoulder, then gradually pulled herself back. Zeke put his hand on her shoulder, and she looked over at him.

"You really okay, kid?" he asked, with a gentleness Cash had never heard out of him.

She nodded. Didn't give her brother a hard time for calling her *kid*. Cash and Zeke exchanged a worried look over her head, but what was there to do?

Zeke left and Cash led Carlyle back out to the parking lot. He'd never seen her cry like that, never expected to. She brazened through everything, and he knew there were deeper feelings under all that bravado, but he hadn't expected a...breakdown, he supposed.

They climbed into Zeke's truck without saying a word. She'd stopped crying, but the evidence of it was all over her face. He'd *planned* on chewing her out for not telling them what was going on, but now he didn't have the heart to. So he just...drove.

She laid her head on his shoulder the whole way back. She didn't say anything, and while he occasionally opened his mouth to say something, in the end, he just kept it shut. Sometimes, comfortable silence was the best medicine.

When he pulled up to a stop in front of the ranch, he made a move to get out, but Carlyle didn't. She just sat there staring at the house.

"Everything okay?"

She didn't look at him, but she answered his question. "You haven't even been mad about me not telling you the truth."

"You seem upset enough without me adding to it."

"That's nice."

"Is it?"

She finally looked over. "Yeah. Because I probably would have been a jerk about it if the situation was reversed."

"I'm beginning to think you're a big old softy, Carlyle. And not a jerk at all."

She let out a little huff of a sound, *almost* a laugh. "That's nice that you think that."

"That's me. Mr. Nice."

"But you're hot too, if it makes you feel better."

It was his turn to laugh. She was sounding more and more like herself, even if he didn't know what to do with that. "You need some rest. I assume they gave you instructions for dealing with that?" he said, finally addressing the bandage on her head.

"Yeah, in my pocket."

"So, we'll go take care of it."

"I need to tell everyone some stuff Laurel, the detective, told me. About the case, about the connections."

"Come on, Car. You're beat."

"Yeah, but the detective who was on your side is in the hospital, and I have information that we should be looking at." She leaned toward him, across the center console. So serious, so...*worried*. "Being beat can take a back seat." She pushed herself out of the truck, hopped down before he could rush around to stop her.

He frowned. "You have to take care of yourself."

"If there's anything I've learned, it's sometimes the only way to take care of yourself is to see the damn thing through so it can stop hanging over your head. This is too big to tiptoe around. We've got to dive in, no matter how we feel."

If nothing else, she was back to her normal go-getting self, but... That was not him. Not anymore. He'd left all that *dive in* thinking behind when Izzy came along. But that was the extreme again.

Maybe what the two of them needed most from each other was the balancing act. The compromise. "All right. We'll compromise. I'll get Jack and whoever else is within reach right now. Get this over with. Anyone who doesn't make it, Jack will spread the info. You've got fifteen minutes, then you're in bed. And you're going to hand over those instructions."

She frowned, but she eventually slid the paper out of her pocket as they entered the house.

"Sit," he said, pointing to the couch. "I'll be right back."

He went through the house, found Jack, Anna with Caroline on her hip, and Walker standing in the kitchen over a pan of brownies.

"She's in the living room," Cash told Walker before he could make the angry demand that was clearly on the tip of his tongue.

Walker left quickly.

"Where's Iz?"

"She and Mary are up in Mary's room going over nursery colors," Anna said. "It's keeping her occupied. What's going on? Zeke already called and said Carlyle's okay."

"Come on out to the living room. Carlyle will explain. Anyone else around?"

Jack shook his head. "Palmer and Louisa are up at their house site. Grant and Dahlia are still out visiting her sister. Hawk's dealing with the fire."

"We'll do this just us then. Fill in everyone else after the fact."

"Hawk should be home soon," Anna said. "We can needle him for more information on the fire."

Cash nodded as they walked out to the living room. Walker sat next to Carlyle, who was rolling her eyes. A good sign, Cash thought.

Once everyone got situated, Carlyle jumped right into it. "Did any of you know Chessa's brother?"

"Chessa only has sisters," Cash replied.

"Laurel said—"

"You're on a first-name basis with the detective now?" Walker interrupted suspiciously.

"Yeah, saved her life and all."

"Jesus," Cash and Walker said in unison.

But Cash couldn't think about lives in danger. He had to focus on the problem at hand. "Chessa doesn't have a brother." *Didn't* have a brother, he reminded himself internally. Because she was gone this time. Really gone. Such a strange ribbon of grief and relief every day over that, and he wasn't sure he'd ever fully come to terms with it. Which made him think of Izzy upstairs with Mary, worried about how things would change, how she would fit. Knowing the answer had never been Chessa, and now never could be.

"Laurel said it was a half-brother. And this half-brother's stepmother owned the building that exploded."

As if on cue with the word *exploded*, Hawk came in.

"What can you tell us?" Anna demanded.

"Not much, yet. Sent some things away to be tested." He took Caroline from Anna, kissed the baby's head. "What I can say is, the explosion set at the building Carlyle and the detective were searching was deliberate."

"Obviously," Carlyle muttered.

"And we...found some human remains in the debris."

An echo of shock went through the room, and Cash was glad Izzy wasn't here to hear that. Maybe she'd have to know eventually, but for right now they could stick to one murder.

"We'll do some tests there too. Determine if the fire was the cause of death or something before."

"I don't think it was the fire," Carlyle said. "The detective and I were in the building. I think the police were in and out of the building before I got there. They only had a search warrant for the downstairs, but... We would have heard someone upstairs. The dogs would have sensed someone upstairs, right?"

She looked at Cash, so he nodded. "They might not have reacted to it though, if they were searching for the scent."

Hawk nodded. "It's all good information to have. The police are tracking down the property owner. Luckily, they already had contact with her regarding the search warrant so it's just a matter of finding her. I've done what I can do today in terms of the fire. Now, it's a bit of a waiting game until tests come back and more questioning is done."

"There's more though. This half brother you guys apparently didn't know about, Butch Scott—"

"Butch Scott. Wait. We know Butch Scott. I thought they were...cousins or something?" Anna said, looking at Cash.

"That's what she always told us."

"Maybe he was," Carlyle said, as if this strange mistake didn't mean anything. "More important, Butch Scott and Bryan Ferguson were stepbrothers at one point."

All eyes turned to Jack. His expression was not as cop-cool as Cash had expected it to be.

"I had some news of my own I wanted to share once we got everyone together. Bryan didn't show up for work tonight. No one knows where he went." He looked up at Hawk. "Do you have any more information on that corpse in your building?"

Hawk took a breath. "The initial consensus is adult male, but most identifying characteristics had been burned away. Until the tests are run. One happenstance missing person doesn't mean it'll be Bryan."

"But it could be," Jack said firmly.

Hawk nodded. "Yeah, it could be."

"Laurel said she and Hart would keep trying to untangle the connections, but she also sort of gave me the go-ahead to try our hand at it. She wants to figure out who did this almost as much as we do."

"So, that's what we'll do," Jack said.

Chapter Fourteen

"So, let's get started," Carlyle said. Even though her head and side throbbed. Even though her eyes felt weirdly prickly. Even though she kind of wanted to crawl into her bed and cry for a hundred years.

But that was a feeling to be avoided, so why not go whole-hog on this? Familiar territory, all in all. Push down the emotional garbage and focus on the danger, on solving the mystery. What else could matter?

"No, you're going to bed, Car."

She was about to argue with Cash—no one got to tell her what to do and so on and so forth, but Walker gave her the subtlest shake of the head. And she had no idea *why* that made her feel something close to ashamed. Like maybe he understood what it felt like...to deal with the garbage rather than the danger. Like, maybe just maybe, that's why he had a wife and a kid on the way.

Because he'd let the garbage go.

She didn't know why everything suddenly felt *different*. Like that unbelievable explosion—ranking pretty damn low on the list of traumatic events on her life—felt like it had detonated something inside of her.

Or maybe it was watching that detective—so sure of her-self, so professional, so kick-butt—be worried about potty stools and be happily married to a husband who looked like he'd move heaven and earth to reverse time and not have her hurt, even though she was in this dangerous job.

Cash helped Carlyle to her feet, and she didn't fight him. She felt like spun glass, and the wrong move would shatter her—like she had in the hospital. If she cried in front of him twice in one day, she was quite certain she would literally die of embarrassment.

So she just let herself be led away, and tried to turn off all the vulnerable parts of her brain. Disassociate. Find some detached place to be.

But she just kept seeing Laurel's husband storming into her hospital room. Walker shaking his head at her. Cash angrily standing in that waiting room demanding to see her.

"I keep thinking you're feeling more yourself, then you get real, real quiet. I know they checked you out, but are you sure you don't have a concussion?"

"Not a concussion." *Just a mental crisis.*

He pulled the instructions he'd taken from her out of his pocket. "It says you can take a shower. Let's do that."

"Together?"

He laughed. "As enticing an offer as that is, *you* are resting tonight. Shower. Are you hungry? I can go hunt you down a snack. Then, *sleep.* Lots of sleep. No staying up late. No getting up early."

"Sure, Dad."

He winced, which *almost* brought her some joy. Not *everything* inside of her had been rearranged today if she could enjoy making him uncomfortable, and that was a relief.

"Go on," he said, not rising to the bait. "Can you handle the shower on your own?" He looked over the paper once more. "Don't wash your hair," he instructed.

She plucked the paper from his hands. "I'll handle it."

He opened his mouth, then shut it. "Okay, you can handle it."

She thought that was going to be that. He'd turn and leave, and she could take her shower in peace and figure out how to shore up all these cracks in her armor. Put all these rearranged pieces of herself back in the right order so that she didn't want to cry. So she didn't want to ask him ridiculous things like *where is this going? Will you ever love me like that detective's husband loves her? Like Walker loves Mary?*

But Cash didn't walk away. He kept *talking.* "But sometimes, you let other people handle it. Because I can't take that scrape on your head away. Or the fact you got *stabbed* to save my daughter. So you could just let me do this. You take a shower, I'll get you some food, and you'll give me a bit of room to fuss over you before you go to sleep."

Fuss. She hated to be fussed over. Wasn't that why she was always saying the shocking thing? When her brothers had gotten all soft over her, it had made her miss her mother so much she thought she wouldn't survive the *weight* of it. "I really don't want to cry in front of you again," she said, because if *anything* made her brothers run, it was that.

Cash, on the other hand, shrugged. Unbothered. "I have a kid. I can handle tears. It's one of my few talents."

It was true. At the hospital he'd just held her. Let her not talk. He'd just...acted like it was a perfectly fine and normal thing to do to cry. He was just doing all this *taking care*, and what had she done for him? What *could* she do?

She sucked at taking care. The only thing she was good at was diving into things headfirst—like this afternoon with the detective, which hadn't gone well at all.

And she'd had to watch the detective's real life. That

man's expression when he looked at his wife. Love and worry and just this perfect picture of *life*.

Like what Mary and Walker were building. Like so many of the people here, and she'd sworn to herself she never wanted all that, but now she was *surrounded* and…and…

God, she had to make this stop. And she knew how. Face it head-on. Freak him out so he bailed. "We need to have the talk."

Cash's eyebrows drew together. "What talk?"

"The talk. The you-and-me talk. The…what-the-hell-are-we-doing talk. Because there's just…all these threads, and we can't keep knotting them."

He studied her like he was afraid she'd suffered the concussion he was so worried about, when she knew her head was just fine. Even if her words weren't. Even if *she* wasn't, at the heart of things.

"I know I'm doing this wrong. Hell, that's how I do things, so why not? You just dive right in."

"Get in the shower. I'll get you something to eat. You'll rest and—"

"I don't want that! I don't want *this*!" She pointed a little erratically at herself because she had no words for what she felt. Only this anxiety-fueled gesture. Only this need to put a stop to all this before…before…before…

She didn't know before *what*. Just *before*.

"Car, I'd love to follow, but I just plain don't."

"I know that. You think I don't know that?" She was off the rails, and she didn't know how to get back on them except to explode everything. "I don't need you to tell me you're in love with me. I just need to know that you could be, eventually. That…eventually… That… It's just… You've been married. Had a kid. I haven't. And I never thought I'd want something so…boring. But I guess, I think, maybe I do. Not like, *today*. Just…someday. So, we should be on the same page about that, because there's too much tangled and rooted here to just…bump up against that someday in the future and need to walk away."

For a moment, he stood there like a statue. An awful statue. Because she couldn't read what he thought of any of that, and so she had the space to think of all the worst-case scenarios she'd just introduced.

Because that's what you do, Carlyle Daniels. Create worst-case scenarios.

But when he spoke, his voice was strangely…raspy. Like each word held such great weight it scraped against his throat.

"Hawk came in and said a civilian had been hurt, and we knew it had to be you. I just…went dark. Hollowed out. I know fear. I've lived with that bastard most of my life, and this was that. The kind you just… It takes over. You are reminded you have *no* control."

She'd been there—more times than she could count. So many times she'd given up on the idea of control a long time ago.

"Your brother asks me about love," he said disgustedly. "Fair enough, I guess, but then my *daughter* asks me. Now you…and I don't know." He raked his fingers through his hair, leaving it unruly. "My track record sucks. My…radar sucks."

She didn't understand where he was going with this, and she wanted to poke and prod more about her brother and Izzy asking him about *love*, but something about his panic eased her own. "*You* don't suck."

He sighed and met her gaze. Not quite so panicked, but she didn't know what had taken over. Something…resigned. "I'm glad you think so. But… You have to understand. A while back, I figured that was it. I made my mistake, was going to pay for it forever, so that was *it*."

Ouch. Well, she hadn't expected it to be that quite cut-and-dried, but now she had to get rid of him so she could cry in peace. "That's all you had to say. We don't have to drag it out." She moved for the bathroom door—because like hell she'd cry again. "We don't have to—"

But he stepped into the bathroom doorway so she couldn't answer, his expression stormy. "Would you shut up and let me finish? You think *you're* panicking? I know how wrong this can go, and I've got a daughter to think about. My panic wins."

"I actually prefer to win," she grumbled, crossing her arms over her chest.

He made a huffing sound, almost like a laugh. But then he got all serious again. "Carlyle, I don't know how to answer all your questions. I'm still…sorting everything out. But let's start with that I am not sitting here thinking… *I could never marry or have kids with this woman.* It's certainly not some…off-the-table thing."

That was not romantic. It really shouldn't be romantic. Was her bar so low? Or was it she just understood how much that must…mess with him. How much *she* must mess with a man who cut off everything he could for so long.

So she nodded. "Well, I guess that's all I was asking."

"Maybe you should ask for a hell of a lot more," he said, looking downright *sad*.

They really were just two messed up, messy people. But she didn't mind that, didn't think it was too terrible. Not when they really wanted to…be good people, help people. Maybe they had a lot of stuff to work through, but they weren't *bad*.

So maybe all this *more* everyone kept talking about

wasn't *more* at all. It was just having the kind of self-aware-ness to know what she really wanted—outside of what any-one else thought.

"You know, I don't have a kid. I think that makes fear different. It must. But I've also been pretty well acquainted with fear most my life. I know far too intimately how tenu-ous it all is. How little control *anyone* has. So no, I don't need to ask for *more*, Cash." She moved forward and wrapped her arms around him and squeezed tight—even though it sent a bolt of pain through her side. "Not from you. I think you're physically and psychologically incapa-ble of giving less than you've got."

He ran a hand down her back. "I hope that's true."

But she didn't hope. She knew.

Just like she knew she couldn't rest. They couldn't rest until they found something. Because they were all in dan-ger until this mystery got solved.

But for a little while, she'd give him what he asked for. The space to fuss. And she'd try really hard not to hate it.

CASH FINALLY CONVINCED Carlyle to get into the shower, then he went to the kitchen and put together some food on a tray like Mary usually did. It wasn't as nice as when Mary did it, but it would get the job done.

Fuel. Carlyle needed rest and fuel. And once he made sure she got those things, he could go figure out this whole Butch Scott thing. And once he did *that*, maybe they could figure out the personal stuff.

He had to breathe through the tightness in his chest. A panic born of...well, failure. Everything with Chessa had been such a spectacular failure. Here he was twelve years later, still dealing with it. Even though she was dead. It wasn't that he thought Carlyle was like that. It was more...

Well, he supposed he couldn't help but blame himself for not finding a way to make things work with Chessa, for not finding a way to get through to her.

Intellectually, he knew better. Love didn't solve addiction. It couldn't erase the marks of an unsteady and abusive childhood. Even if he'd been able to find it within himself to love her, he couldn't change her.

But the guilt stayed. Because he'd wanted a better outcome for Izzy, and for her mother.

So, for the time being, he'd turn his attention to trying to figure out who killed Chessa. Maybe that could ease some of his guilt, and then...then he could really think about what a future with Carlyle looked like.

The future and thinking about it scared the living daylights out of him ever since he'd first dropped Izzy off at kindergarten.

He shook it all away. Focused on the task at hand. That's what had gotten him through for the past few years. One step before the other.

So he took the tray of food to Carlyle's room. She was sitting at the window, looking out at the night sky. That must have been what she'd been doing the night someone had been at Izzy's window. Had that wistful, sad look been on her face then too?

He wanted to find some way to take that wistfulness, that sadness away. She deserved so much more than *this*. But didn't they all? Maybe *deserved* just flat-out didn't matter. Maybe there was only making the best out of what you had.

And the fact she was here. Carlyle being whole and wholly her was a best. A bright spot. "All right. You should eat."

She turned to look at him, then her eyes dropped to the tray. She swallowed, hard. "I thought you'd have Mary put something together."

"She and Izzy had their heads together ordering stuff for the baby. Didn't want to interrupt. Sorry if it's not up to par." He set it on the table within reach of where she was sitting.

She shook her head, her eyes bright. "It's great. I'm... I'm pretty used to doing everything on my own. I guess it's been easy to let Mary swoop in because she's just...her."

"It's what she does."

"Yeah, and it's what you do too, I'm starting to realize." She reached forward, picked up a piece of cheese. "But I also know that means you'll try to tell me to eat, to sleep, and it's not going to happen. You're not doing the work without me. Either we both sleep or we both work. The end. But I think we need to work. I think we need to figure out who this half-brother you didn't know about is."

"I knew about him. Chessa just claimed...less of a familial connection. Which makes sense. Chessa's parents were a bit of a mess. She used to say her father had impregnated half the county. He was an addict himself. Abusive."

"I'm not going to feel sorry for her. Even if she's dead. Anyone who'd sell their daughter doesn't get my sympathy. I don't care if it's the addiction talking."

Cash knew he would always have a complicated relationship with feeling sympathy and grief toward Chessa. But he'd always found some comfort in that his family got to just wholesale hate her, blame her. It was simple for them, and even though he couldn't partake, it felt good it could be simple for someone.

And this felt good in a different way. Because no matter what Izzy thought or worried about, Carlyle was so wholly on her side. Always.

"I'm not asking you to feel sorry for her. I'm just trying to make it clear. She could have half siblings everywhere.

It doesn't necessarily mean Chessa had a relationship with Butch, or knew they were siblings. Even with the same last name."

"But they were. So maybe *he* did, even if she didn't?"

"Maybe. I don't remember meeting him. He was more Anna's age. I think that's why she remembered the name. I'm sure he was trouble like the rest of the Scotts. Nobody really had a chance, growing up like that."

"I imagine Jack is already looking into what kind of trouble he's been in," she said, continuing to eat.

"Yes. Palmer will be doing his own searches too. So there's no reason for you to—"

"From here on out, we're in this together, bud. No more independent work. So, unless you're planning on taking a break, I'm not either."

He sighed. She was pale, and her hair was in a messy knot on her head as she'd followed the instructions and had not washed it. She looked in desperate need of that break. "*I* haven't been stabbed and nearly exploded, Carlyle."

She shook her head, unmoved. "Lucky you. Doesn't change anything."

He sighed. There would be no getting through to her, so he supposed he had to just give in. But not without conditions. "You finish your food. Drink some water. Take something for that headache I know you're pretending you don't have. Once you do all that, we'll join Jack and Palmer downstairs. But not before you take a little care of yourself."

"I always take care of myself," she replied, that typical flash of defiance in her eyes.

He crouched next to her seat so they were eye to eye. "It's not *yourself* anymore, Car. Got it?"

She held his gaze for a very long time. Then she nodded.

And leaned forward and pressed her mouth to his, gently. Cash let the kiss linger, until she pulled away.

"That goes both ways, Cash. You got that?"

"Yeah, I think we both got it."

Chapter Fifteen

When they went down to the living room, there was what Carlyle could only describe as a war room set up. They were treating it like one of their cold cases.

Palmer had joined the fray, sitting in a chair with a laptop in his lap. Zeke was back from picking up the dogs and was conferring with Grant over a bulletin board on wheels they must have rolled out once she'd gone upstairs. Anna rocked Caroline in the corner chair, while telling Grant to add things or take things off the bulletin board. Hawk stood closer to the entryway, speaking into his phone in low tones.

When Zeke spotted Carlyle enter the room, he scowled. "You should rest."

"There's no point. I'm not going to sleep knowing you all are down here working this out." She walked over to the bulletin board, ignoring the way Zeke's glare was now aimed at Cash.

Honestly. *Men.*

"What have you all come up with in the past hour?"

Jack was the one who took the reins first. "It's looking more and more like Ferguson was the body in the building. We'll need dental records to confirm, but no one's seen him, and everything Bent County would release to Brink leans toward Ferguson."

"No whereabouts on Chessa's half-brother?" Carlyle asked.

Jack shook his head. "They're looking, thanks to Detective Delaney-Carson. But he likely knows he's being looked for, so that'll make it more difficult."

Carlyle stared at all the seemingly disparate events on the bulletin board. "What's the endgame here? We have a failed kidnapping, a murder—probably two—and an explosion. What is the goal?"

"Maybe there isn't one," Anna replied, considering. "Just destruction? Pain? They wanted to frame Cash, like Izzy said. So maybe that's it?"

But they were doing a really bad job of framing Cash, Carlyle thought to herself, frowning at the bulletin board as she tried to find a thread that made any sense. Maybe they couldn't have predicted her as an alibi for Chessa's murder, but they had to know he'd have one for the explosion. Unless there was something about that which would point to Cash?

"Some guy messes with *my* sister, I'm going to mess him up." Zeke looked over at Cash pointedly.

"I hardly *messed* with Chessa," Cash said darkly. "Quite the opposite."

"It wouldn't have to be true. Could have just been how Chessa framed things to her brother."

Carlyle rolled her eyes. "But Cash didn't think she had much of a relationship with this Butch. Chessa claimed him as a cousin when they were together. It's possible they didn't even know or care they were related. Just because they had the same father named on their birth certificate doesn't mean much—as you and I both know." After all, the name of the father on her birth certificate had not been accurate.

"Maybe something changed in the past few years," Grant

suggested. "Maybe they didn't know about each other a decade ago or didn't care. But something brought them together more recently and they figured the connection out?" Grant pointed at a paper tacked to the bulletin board. "Butch Scott has had trouble with the law since he was a minor. As an adult, a lot of the charges deal with drugs. Could be they started to run in the same circles."

"Then how does Bryan Ferguson get messed up in this?" Jack said. He'd apparently at least accepted his employee was part of it, but Carlyle got the feeling Jack didn't believe in Ferguson having full-on involvement. Maybe because he'd likely ended up dead.

Maybe Jack was right, to an extent. He knew Ferguson. Had worked with him. Been his boss. Jack was hardly the type to believe in someone who didn't prove they were trustworthy. Carlyle wasn't even sure he trusted *her*.

"Whether intentionally or not, we know Ferguson helped Tripp get Chessa out of jail on bond that night last year. Or at least kept it from Jack for as long as possible," Cash said. "Whether it was true or not, Chessa said Tripp was her boyfriend at the time. Chessa escapes, Tripp dies. But Chessa doesn't just escape, she disappears. She lies very low for a *year*."

"And that was abnormal?" Carlyle asked Cash, but it was Anna who answered.

"She never went more than a few months without demanding money from somebody around here."

"Did you all pay her off?"

"At first," Cash said, clearly unhappy that he had. "But once the drug addiction became evident, we cut it off. She never stopped asking though. Until this all happened. I figured she was just…finally aware enough that she'd crossed that final line. She'd engaged in actively harming one of us, talked too freely of getting her hands on Izzy. I thought maybe she'd figured out nothing good was going to come from messing with us."

Carlyle shook her head. She was no addict expert, but she understood patterns. "If she stayed away that long, she had access to money to buy drugs, or just access to the drugs themselves. That pattern doesn't stop because someone finally becomes self-aware. Especially someone who paints themselves a victim. She didn't realize anything. She found a steady mark."

"Butch Scott?" Anna suggested.

"Maybe."

"Well, we can't do anything with that information until the cops find him. And you're not going off in the middle of the night to search, so I guess it's bedtime."

Carlyle didn't even bother to acknowledge Zeke had spoken. She was studying Butch's rap sheet. She tapped the end of it. "He's also kept his nose clean for the past year almost. After *years* of not going more than four months without getting some kind of arrest." She looked at Jack. "We want to find out where he is, sure. But we also want to know where they *were*. Them both going quiet makes me think they were together."

"Together not getting into trouble?" Grant asked dubiously.

Carlyle shook her head and looked at Zeke. Because she knew he had to be thinking the same thing she was. "Sure, you can stay out of trouble by not finding any, but that's not their MO. So the other option is they found someone to *hide* their trouble. Someone—or *someones*—who could hide it *for* them."

"You're suggesting Ferguson kept them from getting

in trouble," Jack said, and though his voice was detached, even Carlyle could tell this was eating at him.

As much as Carlyle wanted to go easy on him, because she was that softy Cash had accused her of being and didn't want to hurt Jack worse than he was hurting himself, they had to follow the truth to find the truth. "He knew the ins and outs of Sunrise Sheriff's Department, didn't he? And likely Bent County too."

Jack didn't reply, but that was reply enough.

"You guys searched his apartment when you looked for him?"

"Bent County did," Jack said. "They're making sure Sunrise is staying as far away from this as possible."

Carlyle nodded, thinking. "What about other property he owned? Or Tripp Anthony? Just because he's dead doesn't mean he doesn't connect to the big picture here."

"Tripp lived on our property, in the cabin Walker stayed at when he first came here. Before that, he lived at home with his parents in Hardy," Anna said. "They would have been the ones in charge of everything when he died. And he's been dead this whole time."

"Still, it wouldn't hurt to look into what he had. Into *his* known associates, as well as Bryan's. Find those little connections that might lead to bigger ones. The cops are going to do what they can, and I know Laurel wants to get to the truth of this, but she's been hurt."

"So, we pick up the slack," Zeke said.

Carlyle nodded, turning her attention to Jack. "You know how they'll go about it. How they'll approach these connections. We need to do it differently. So we're not just treading the same water. Where are they going to look first?"

Jack was quiet for a moment, but eventually seemed to relent. "They'll focus on Butch. How he relates to the case, to Chessa—only to Ferguson if and when he's identified as the dead man. But right now? They're going to focus on finding Butch and getting info about him."

Carlyle nodded, because she'd figured as much. "Okay, so let's focus on Ferguson. And Tripp, to an extent. Let them focus on the Butch angle, we'll focus on this one."

"I'll text Brink to look into any property Ferguson *and* Tripp might have had access to," Jack said. "Maybe it leads us to something before this started, but it won't stop anything. Ferguson being dead means whoever killed him will know we'll look into him. They won't be anywhere that ties them to him."

"If they're smart," Carlyle agreed. She studied the bulletin board, because so many things didn't add up. It was possible everyone was just so clever that even the Bent County detectives and this group of trained investigators couldn't see their pattern, but Carlyle was beginning to wonder if it didn't make any sense because it was scattershot. Because there was no *solid* goal.

She glanced at Cash.

Except maybe...revenge.

CASH BOWED OUT of the discussions a little early to go put Izzy to bed. He wasn't surprised exactly that Carlyle had decided to come with him. He'd thought the case and wanting to crack it would come first, but she walked away without a backward glance.

For her, Izzy was a priority too. And that mattered a great deal.

"She's going to ask about the bandage," he said to Carlyle. It was his first instinct to hide it, or lie to Izzy about it, but as much as Izzy was *his* daughter to care for and protect, it was Carlyle's injury, because she'd gotten messed up in his life. Maybe it was her call on this one.

"She didn't know I was at the hospital?"

"I doubt Mary told her or she would have insisted on seeing you a lot earlier. They've been so happily busy with baby stuff, I didn't want to interrupt."

Cash didn't know why that made Carlyle frown, but he didn't have a chance to ask because they'd reached Mary's open door.

Not only were Mary and Izzy sitting next to each other, heads practically touching as they looked at something on Mary's laptop, but Walker was sitting in the armchair in the corner flipping through a pregnancy book. Copper was curled in the corner, but he lifted his head when Cash and Carlyle stepped in the room. Walker eyed Carlyle though didn't say anything.

"Time for bed, Iz," Cash said.

Izzy rolled her eyes, but she got up at the same time. "It's summer. Why can't I stay up late?"

"It's late enough. And you've got chores in the morning, just like the rest of us."

She groaned, but before she left the room, she turned back to Mary. "*I* like the name Levi."

"We are not naming our kid after some boy band singer," Walker said from his spot in the corner. Clearly this little argument had been going on for a while now.

"He plays the *drums*, Uncle Walker," Izzy said with the kind of contempt only a twelve-year-old girl can muster. Walker hid a smile.

"Oh, Levi Jones?" Carlyle said, perking up. "He's *hot*."

Izzy nodded emphatically and Cash couldn't stop himself from pulling a face, but Carlyle grinned at him, and it was nice to see these parts of her back. The clearheaded investigator she'd been downstairs. The mischievous woman who liked to tease.

He liked the softer sides of her too, hoped she'd get more used to those coming out, but he knew she was *feeling* her best when she could cause a little discomfort. He had no idea why he found that so damn attractive.

They got Izzy through her bedtime routine, and Cash tucked her in while Carlyle waited outside the door.

"How come she has a bandage on her head?" Izzy asked, surprising Cash that she'd noticed and hadn't said anything to Carlyle. He'd been ready to let Carlyle take the lead on this, but Izzy was asking out of earshot.

"She just had a little accident when she went to help the detective." Which was mostly true. "She's good. I promise." And that was the important part. She was good.

Izzy nodded, but she was chewing on her lip. Clearly still worried. Cash brushed some hair off her forehead. He couldn't promise everything would be fine like he wanted to. "We're getting to the bottom of everything. One step at a time. We'll get there." He kissed her forehead, then moved to leave the room, Copper settled into his dog bed under the window.

But Izzy spoke before he'd made it to the door.

"You know, if you and Carlyle got married and had a baby, that'd be okay."

He froze. Inside and out. What the hell was he supposed to say to *that*? Except maybe no more days with Mary baby planning.

Cash had to clear his throat to speak as he turned to look at her, but he couldn't see her expression in the dark. "Ah, well, it's a bit...soon for all that, Iz."

"That's okay. But I like babies, so..."

"I... Okay," he agreed, because he didn't know what else

to do. Because that was *quite* the one-eighty from earlier. Because this whole Carlyle thing wasn't even a *week* old, and everyone was already throwing all this at him. "Night, Izzy. I love you."

This was why people didn't live with their families into adulthood.

He stepped into the hallway, closing the door behind him.

Carlyle studied him. "Looking a little pale," she said, as if concerned, but he saw the amusement in her eyes.

"You heard her, didn't you?"

She laughed, hooked her arm with his and leaned into him as they walked down the hallway to his room. "Yeah. Don't worry, I'm sure I went a little pale too. I do not know that *I* like babies. Particularly coming out of me."

Cash only grunted. They walked into his bedroom, still arm in arm, but once inside his room, he pulled his arm away from her. He pointed at her.

"Now, no funny business."

She grinned, sliding her arms around his waist. "Aw, come on. Just a little." That grin stayed in place, and he saw a kind of relaxed happy that hadn't been in her eyes all day. Understandably. But there were shadows under her eyes and that bandage on her head.

"You need your rest." But he dropped his mouth to hers, because good in the midst of bad was starting to become… not the distraction he always feared, but a foundation to get through the bad.

Still, he bundled her into his bed, and it didn't take much for her to fall asleep. She was exhausted and injured. He was a little exhausted himself apparently, because the next thing he knew he woke with a start, not quite sure what it was that had woken him up. Carlyle was curled up next to him and as he lay there and listened to the sounds of the house in the dark, he didn't hear a thing. He glanced at the clock. Four in the morning.

Early yet, even before Mary's usual ungodly wake-up call, but Cash knew he had lots to do today, and there was no point trying to get another hour's sleep when he'd likely lay there and make too many mental to-do lists to count. Might as well get up and start the *do* portion of his day.

Palmer and Zeke had handled the dogs last night, but the truck would need cleaning out. There was paperwork to do from yesterday's events with the dogs—he'd have to have Carlyle write up a report for what had happened. Much as he didn't want her to have to relive the explosion part, it was important to keep records of everything the dogs did outside the ranch.

He slid out of bed, being careful not to wake Carlyle. She stirred a little, but rolled over and was quickly breathing evenly again. Swiftie stayed put on her side of the bed. He grabbed his clothes, his phone, then carefully eased out of the room.

Clearly, everyone in the house was still asleep, which was good. Often, in the middle of danger or investigations there was always someone up and about, putting too much time and worry into it. But everyone upstairs was paired off now, and there were kids and kids-to-be in the house besides Izzy. Life—real life—was starting to take over all the ways they'd isolated themselves since their parents had died.

Except for maybe Jack, who very well could be awake in his room working on something, but Cash hoped he was asleep.

It was dark and still as he walked downstairs. Not even the telltale sound of a baby crying or a rocking chair creaking. He decided to forgo coffee. He didn't want to chance waking anyone up, particularly when a lot of them had likely been up too late looking into Bryan Ferguson.

Cash disengaged the security system so he could step outside into the cool, dark morning. On a normal morning, he would have left it off, knowing people would be coming and going for the rest of the day, but it was early and dark enough he thought it best to reengage the system once he was out. The cameras always ran no matter what, but the alarms were usually only in place overnight.

Once that was taken care of, he turned and looked out into the dark night around the ranch. He lifted his face to the sky. The moon was a tiny sliver above his cabin in the distance, clear and bright despite its diminished size. The sky sparkled and pulsed. And for a moment, Cash just stood there and absorbed this odd time of night, this quiet.

Home. This had always been his home. Through good times and very bad times, Hudson Ranch had been the roots that had kept him tethered. Izzy had come along and only sunk those roots deeper—but he'd only been able to do that for her because of his family and this place.

He didn't let himself wallow in self-pity as a rule. It always felt too close to going down Chessa's line of thinking about the world, but Cash realized he'd gotten very bad about counting his blessings. He had shrunk his world down to Izzy and just Izzy. He *knew* he'd been lucky in the face of tragedy, but he hadn't *felt* it in a long time.

Even with the danger going on around them, he felt that gratitude in this moment. He'd had this place, this foundation to keep Izzy safe all these years. And he could manage all the years to come.

A streak of a shooting star flashed across the sky. Like a good omen.

He was ready for a few good omens. He'd been white-knuckling it for so long, and there was a part of his brain telling him to keep at it. There were murders and explosions. Now was not the time to *relax and enjoy.*

But for all the *wrong,* there was good. His daughter. His family. His dogs and business. And the surprising detour that was Carlyle Daniels. A good reminder of what he'd realized himself last night. No matter the bad, the foundation of good was how you muddled through.

Between Bent County, the Sunrise Sheriff's Department, his family and the Daniels siblings, they would get to the bottom of this. He'd long ago stopped depending on answers for a great many things—when your parents disappeared into thin air never to be heard from again, that was the life lesson.

But today, he was going to believe they'd find this problem's answers. He'd give Izzy the answers about her mother's death that he'd never been able to find about his own. No matter what it took.

He set out across the yard, heading for the dog barns. He'd get his chores done early, then move into investigation mode. They could afford a full break from training for a day or two, as long as the dogs got exercise.

So focused on this plan of action, he almost didn't stop his forward progress even as his gaze went over the dark shadow of his cabin. But a few steps beyond the cabin, the image of it, the wrongness of *something,* caught up with him.

He paused, frowned, then turned back toward it. He'd seen…something. Probably just the reflection of the moon. But could they be too careful right now?

He retraced his steps silently. He studied the shadowy cabin. Everything was barely visible in the dim light of the moon and stars. It was all dark now. No light. No flash of anything. Definitely just a random reflection, he told himself. Mentally urging himself to move on.

But his body didn't listen. It was rooted to the spot as he squinted through the dark at the cabin. He didn't see anything this time, but...he *heard* something. A rustle, an exhale. *Something.*

He should go back to the house and get a gun. He should text one of his brothers. There were a lot of things he should do, but the closer he got to the cabin, the more he could discern that the noise was a voice. Someone was inside the cabin. *Talking.* He couldn't make out words, but a window or door must have been open because he could hear the tone and tenor of the voice.

Normally, that would have sent him back to the house immediately. Normally, he would have made all the right choices in this moment.

But the voice clearly said, "You have to." In a voice he *recognized.*

It wasn't possible. It couldn't be possible.

But he *knew* that voice.

So he moved toward the cabin, rather than away like he should.

Chapter Sixteen

Once Cash reached the porch, he could tell the front door was cracked open. It was too dark to determine if it had been forced or not, but it didn't matter when he knew that voice. It was clearly coming from inside, and they were either talking to themselves or their audience was completely silent.

Cash crept up the stairs, listening to every word that was spoken. It couldn't be possible, but...

"I told you it was a bad idea." There was a beat, the speaker clearly listening.

Then it dawned on him. She was on the phone. Had the flash of light he'd seen been a phone screen?

"You're the one who had to do the explosion," she said, her voice getting louder in frustration. A frustration he was so well acquainted with.

Was this some dream? A break with reality? Everyone had said she was dead. *Dead.* People he trusted. People he loved. Everyone certain she was murdered. There were cops who thought *he* was a suspect.

But that was Chessa's voice. He knew Chessa's voice. Maybe they hadn't spent much time together in the past few years, but her voice had haunted him for years. He had listened and watched for her vigilantly for so long now, it was hard to believe he'd be wrong. He couldn't imagine anyone sounding this much like her and not *being* her. Or talking about explosions—the one that was clearly connected to his current predicament.

Cash crept closer to the door. Maybe if he could get some glimpse at the person talking, he could convince himself there was no possible way—

But the door swung open, and he had to jump back to avoid being smacked in the face by it.

The woman who stepped out into the night was… It was Chessa. Maybe it was dark, but the moon and stars offered *some* light. Maybe someone out there looked *a lot* like her in the shadows. But he knew this woman, and even in the dark he just knew it was…her. Short and slightly built. That I'll-mess-anyone-up posture he'd once found attractive, when he'd wanted to see *everyone* messed up.

Chessa wasn't dead. No matter what anyone had said. She was *here*.

"We've got company," she said into the phone at her ear. She didn't seem surprised to see him. Just sort of grim about it. She shoved the phone in her pocket. "Where's your posse?" she asked dismissively, the shadow of her chin jerking toward the house.

Just like always. Such a *Chessa* movement and statement. It was *her*.

Cash couldn't get over the pure shock of it all. Even now. Standing here, staring at her. It was real and he didn't know how to process it.

He didn't think she was high. He'd spent that first year of Izzy's life learning the signs in Chessa. There was a *movement* to her when she was high. Tonight she seemed still, controlled and stone-cold sober. That was honestly more of a concern than her being alive. High Chessa was volatile and dangerous, but Sober Chessa used all that rage and trauma to cause true, focused damage.

"You're alive," he managed to say, no matter how pointless that sounded in the quiet night around them. "How the hell did you convince people you were dead?"

She made a noise, not quite a laugh, but sort of amused. "I can't believe that worked. Pays to have friends on the inside."

"Ferguson?"

She didn't act surprised he knew. "Poor guy. All *riddled* with guilt with pulling one over on his little cop buddies. He was going to break. Had to take care of it." She sighed like she was upset over a broken nail. "Oh well. He did what we needed."

"Who's *we*?"

"Wouldn't you like to know?" She shook her head. "You really thought you'd ever be rid of me, baby?"

Sometimes, it made his skin crawl that she was Izzy's mother, but this was beyond all of those old guilts and frustrations. She had somehow convinced an entire law enforcement agency she was dead. But she wasn't, and she was *here*, sneaking around the ranch.

"What are you doing here, Chessa?" he asked, doing his best to sound bored instead of enraged.

"What do you think? I'm going to get my hands on her. I'll never stop trying. *Never.*" She moved forward, but Cash didn't see any kind of weapon on her. She just poked her finger into his chest.

He would never understand. She hadn't wanted to be a mother, hadn't wanted to stick around. She'd *left*, and he hadn't made that hard on her so he couldn't ever understand this need to keep popping back up. To keep trying to *hurt* the daughter she didn't want.

Because she was a damn wound every day of his life. And Izzy's.

But her poke turned into a shove, almost like she couldn't quite stop herself, and he was still reeling from her being *alive* that it landed hard enough that he stumbled back.

"I'm going to take her," Chessa said, giving him another push, though he was ready for it this time. He held his ground.

"Why do you think it's going to go differently this time?" And it made him uneasy, because she might not be the most rational person on the planet—high or sober—but Izzy was just as protected as she always was, and Chessa had never once succeeded at getting her hands on their daughter.

Chessa didn't respond to his question. Instead, she lunged at him. A terrible attempt at a tackle, but then she kicked his shin, and he went down just enough that she jumped on top of him.

It was all so…surreally ridiculous. Cash wasn't quite sure how to proceed, except to protect himself from her weak attempts at punching and kicking. She was short and never'd had much meat on her bones, but she seemed nothing but skin and bones now.

He had the height and the weight to easily stop her blows. He couldn't fathom why she was trying to fight him when he had the physical upper hand. He rolled over on top of her, pinning her hands above her head. She stopped moving, but he could see the way she grinned up at him in the breaking light of dawn.

"You won't hit me, Cash. All that noble Hudson blood. You won't do anything except sit there and take it." She lifted her leg, clearly trying to land a knee, and failing as she tried to free her arms from his grasp. "I'm your daughter's mother. You wouldn't do *anything* to hurt me."

"That's where you're wrong, Chessa. Because I'd do anything and hurt any damn person to protect my daughter."

"I'm counting on it," Chessa said, then she smiled up at him and it was clue enough for what was coming. But he wasn't quite fast enough. The blow hit him from behind, from someone much bigger than him. It didn't knock him out, though it hurt like the devil, but it did knock him off Chessa.

And before he could get to his feet, she rolled over and jabbed something sharp and painful into his thigh.

And then everything went black.

CARLYLE COULDN'T BELIEVE how long she'd slept, or that she'd slept through Cash leaving the room. She was usually a light sleeper, but she supposed the past few days had really taken it out of her.

She sat up in Cash's bed, then yawned and stretched as she blinked at the bright sun streaming through the windows. Her body hurt. All over. She lifted her shirt to peek at her stitches.

She frowned a little. They'd bled through the bandage she'd slapped on last night after she'd showered. Maybe she should have mentioned something at the hospital the other day, but she had just wanted to get out of there.

And she definitely didn't want to go *back*. So, she'd just slap another bandage on and hope the problem went away. Because there was too much to do today. Way too much.

And Cash had let her sleep the entire morning away. She was going to have to have a talking to with that man. She didn't mind being taken care of *a little*, but not when so many important things were going on. Hopefully, there'd been some kind of break in the case.

If there wasn't, well, she was damn well going to find one.

She slid out of bed with a wince. Her head wasn't too bad, but man, her side was really killing her. She'd need to take something for the pain when she changed the bandage. All of her supplies were down in her room, so that'd be the first stop.

She let Swiftie out. "Have you been up here the whole time?" she asked, giving the dog a pat on the head as she walked out into the hallway.

But she stopped abruptly. Izzy was coming out of her own room down the hallway. She came to the same abrupt halt.

A deep, awkward silence ensued as Izzy studied Carlyle, then the door behind her. Swiftie trotted past Izzy to head downstairs, likely to be let out.

Carlyle didn't know how to sit in an awkward silence, so she cleared her throat. "Uh, you sleep in too?"

"No. I was just up here to get Caroline her doggy," Izzy said, holding up the stuffed animal.

"Your dad isn't…in there," Carlyle said. God knew why. She might love this little girl, but she hardly owed her an *explanation*. She definitely wasn't going to tell a twelve-year-old everything had been perfectly hands-off. Last night at least.

Izzy frowned. "He isn't? I haven't seen him all morning."

"I'm sure he's just…out doing chores." It was the only explanation, but it was strange Izzy hadn't seen him at *all*. He usually made a point of eating breakfast with her. "Did you text him?"

Izzy shook her head. "We all thought he was sleeping in, so we were leaving him to it."

Because they'd likely known *she* was in the room, allegedly with him. The whole family, no doubt. *We all*. Oh, Carlyle wasn't ready to think about *we all*. She knew they all *thought* things, and that was easy to brazen through when it wasn't *true*. But it was true now and...

She blew out a breath. Well, she was going to have to deal with it, wasn't she? *She'd* been the one to bring up all that future junk. She could hardly get a little gun-shy now that they had an audience.

Carlyle pulled her phone out of her pocket. She sent Cash a quick *where are you* text, then forced herself to smile reassuringly at Izzy. "I bet he's out with the dogs. I just have to grab a few things then I'll go look for him if he doesn't answer."

Izzy chewed on her bottom lip, but she nodded. They headed downstairs and Izzy trailed after her to her bedroom. Carlyle didn't want Izzy to worry, so she decided to forgo the bandage and the painkillers and just grab her work boots and a hat to hide the bump and bandage on her head.

"Have you eaten break—" But before she could shoo Izzy out of the bedroom and to the kitchen, Izzy practically leapt forward.

"Carlyle! You've got blood on your shirt."

Carlyle looked down at her side. Damn stitches. "Oh, that's nothing."

"That's where you had your stitches," Izzy said, frowning so deeply a line formed on her forehead. "Carlyle, you need to go to the doctor!"

Carlyle shook her head. "Nah. I'm good. I just need to change the bandage. No worries. I'll just..."

Izzy took her hand and pulled her into the little half bathroom attached to her room. She grabbed a washcloth and ran the hot water. "It could be infected," she said, sounding very adult. Her expression was very stern. Carlyle could certainly physically move past the girl, but she found herself standing in the bathroom, feeling like a child herself.

"It's fine."

Izzy sighed very heavily. "Lift your shirt," she instructed.

Carlyle wasn't much for taking orders, but coming from a *child* she really didn't know how to be a jerk in response, so she did as she was told.

Izzy tutted over the bloody bandage, carefully removed it and threw it in the trash. She gently washed away the blood, sighed over the broken stitches, then applied a new bandage over the gash with adept hands. She had Mary's cool, collected nature about her, and the calm, authoritarian voice Cash used with the dogs.

"You really should go to the doctor if that's not better by tomorrow." She looked up at Carlyle very sternly.

Carlyle could only smile and brush a hand over Izzy's flyaway hair. No wonder she was crazy about her. "You're something, kid."

Izzy's mouth curved a little. "I could be an EMT when I grow up. Help people in emergencies. Sometimes I help the vet when he comes out, but that just makes me sad. The animals don't know what you're saying to them, but people know you're trying to help them. So, I think I'll do that. I'd be good at it."

"Bet your ass you would." Carlyle had no problem seeing her do just that.

This caused Izzy to give her a full-blown smile. But it died quickly. "What if my dad is having an emergency? What if—"

"He has his phone. His dogs. And his brain. I can't promise you he's not... Let's just focus on finding him, and we'll go from there. But no matter what, he's going to be okay." Which she also couldn't promise, but she needed it to be true for herself just as much for Izzy. He had to be fine. He *would* be fine. He was Cash.

Izzy nodded and they walked toward the kitchen. Carlyle slid her arm around Izzy's shoulders, gave them a reassuring squeeze. Again, the move was as much for the girl as it was for herself.

Mary was sitting at the kitchen table with Walker. They both looked up at their entrance, but then Mary frowned. "Where's Cash?"

"He was up early. Really early. I haven't seen him since. Are we sure no one's seen him out and about this morning?"

Mary blinked once, then smiled over at Izzy. "Caroline probably wants that, honey," she said, pointing to the stuffed animal still in Izzy's hand.

"I'll get it to her in a second. So *no one* knows where Dad is?" she demanded, looking at Carlyle, then back at Mary and Walker.

"I'm sure he's out doing chores," Carlyle managed to say, but he hadn't texted her back. So she was getting less and less sure. Still, where would he have gone? People didn't just…disappear.

She thought of the Hudson parents and had to swallow the lump of fear that lodged in her throat.

"He didn't get coffee this morning," Mary said quietly, pointing to the carafe. "His mugs—kitchen and travel—are still right there." She looked over to Walker, who nodded.

"I'll grab Palmer to look at the security footage. Grant and I will go find him," Walker said, making it sound easy. Light and casual as he got to his feet. "Probably hip-deep in dogs somewhere," he said, and flashed Izzy a grin. He gave his wife a quick squeeze on the way out.

Mary nodded. Her expression was calm, but she wrung her hands together in a sign of nerves as Walker strode out of the kitchen.

"The uncles will take care of it," Izzy said, sounding

so calm and collected just like her aunt, but Carlyle saw the terror in her eyes, so she didn't argue. She took Izzy's hand in hers.

"Yeah, besides, if he's with the dogs, we all know he's fine. Those dogs are fierce."

Izzy swallowed and nodded, but her gaze was worried and she stared at the back door. If he'd left, it would be on the security footage. If he was out there on the ranch, Walker and Grant would find him.

If he was in trouble… Well, the Hudsons and the Daniels would come together to get him out of it.

No matter what.

Chapter Seventeen

Cash came to in the dark. His head pounded. His stomach threatened to heave out its contents. He felt fuzzy headed and a little drunk. But he hadn't been drinking. He'd been...

He tried to cast back and remember. Tried to lift a hand, but he couldn't move at all.

He was tied up. To a chair. He looked around, even as his vision seemed to swim. Inside his cabin. That was good, even if nothing else was. Like the roiling nausea in his gut, the complete immobility. None of that was *good*, but he was in his own kitchen, which meant help was not that far away.

He took a breath, trying to steady himself. Bad but not terrible. He could work with this. He would have to.

"This might just be the *best* day," Chessa said.

He turned his head toward her voice. She was smiling at him. Her eyes were bright now, her movements jerky. How he'd gotten in this predicament was a little fuzzy, but he remembered her. Alive. She'd been sober before, but now it was clear she'd taken a hit of something.

Behind her, rifling through his kitchen pantry was a big man.

"Butch, right?" Cash managed. His mouth was dry and trying to speak caused a coughing fit he immediately regretted.

The man didn't respond. Not to him. Not to Chessa. He just opened a jar of peanut butter and gave it a little sniff. As if satisfied by the smell, her re-capped the jar and tossed it into a bag on the ground. While Chessa moved around the kitchen, not doing anything. Just moving.

"I'm getting tired of waiting for him," she said, clearly aiming those words at Butch. That guy had to be Butch. Even though Cash had known of him, maybe seen him a few times, he had no clear recollection of what her cousin or half brother or whatever he was looked like, but they had to be in this together.

"You're always tired of waiting," Butch grumbled. "And it never got you anywhere, so why don't you shut up and let me handle it?"

She scowled at the man's back. Cash watched as her eyes darted toward the knife block on the counter, then back at the man. But she didn't make a move to grab the knives. She just turned to face Cash once more.

She sauntered over to him, got her face real close to his. "Maybe you'd like another hit?" she said, smirking. "A little lighter this time, so you don't pass full out. You never were one for the hard stuff, were you?"

He remembered now. The pain in his leg. She'd shot him up with something. "You were bad choice enough," he managed to say.

She reared back and slapped him across the face. It stung, and made the other side of his head throb, but the blow was hardly terrible and did little. He raised a condescending eyebrow at her.

"Feel big and important?" he asked her, working to keep his voice calm in the face of her increasing agitation so he didn't start coughing again.

She was clearly going to hit him again, but Butch grabbed her arm before she could swing. "Knock it off."

Chessa tried to wrestle her arm away from Butch, but he held firm. "I warned you." His voice was stone-cold. "You start acting this way, you won't get another hit. You'll end up as dead as everyone thinks you are."

Cash was very familiar with the look of seething hate on Chessa's face, but she stopped struggling. "How much longer?" she demanded of Butch through clenched teeth.

"Long as it takes. That's how we stay out of jail, re-member?"

She groaned and jerked her arm out of Butch's grasp, but she didn't say anything more, or do anything. Just stood in the corner of the kitchen, and when she couldn't stand that, simply began to pace. She complained, but quietly and under her breath.

Cash kept his gaze on her as he surreptitiously pulled at the cord that tied his arms and legs to the chair. Tied tight with almost no wiggle room. Likely Butch's doing. He was definitely the one in charge and worked with a clearer head and less explosive anger than Chessa.

Which might keep Cash alive longer, but it definitely meant he had less of a chance of escaping. He knew what buttons to push when it came to Chessa. Less so of Butch.

"So, who are we waiting on? You've killed Bryan Fer-guson, and I'm sure you're aware the police figured out that you all connect."

Butch didn't react, but Chessa kind of jerked at that, then whirled around so her back was to Cash. Butch went back to his pantry perusal and didn't say anything.

"They also know this is bigger than Bryan. It connects back to Tripp."

This time Butch paused what he was doing and looked

over his shoulder at Cash. "Please, keep talking." He smirked. "The more information, the better."

Cash didn't scowl, though he wanted to. "It's just not going to be rocket science to figure out the connection. Especially once they get ahold of your stepmother."

"Good luck there," Chessa said with a snort, earning her a glare from Butch.

Cash filed that away. Whatever Butch didn't want Chessa going on about was important. Information that could help. Once he got out of here.

Because he *would* get out of here. This was his house, his land and everyone who loved him was within arm's reach.

"This can't end well for you guys," Cash said.

"Don't worry about our plans, honey. We're going to be just fine. You, on the other hand? We're going to—"

"Shut up, Chessa. I'm warning you," Butch said, tossing a box of crackers into his pack. "Not another word."

"You think she's going to be quiet?" Cash said, forcing himself to laugh. If there was one thing he had on his side, it was the certainty that Chessa had a short fuse. "She can't control herself when it comes to anything."

Butch made a little noise, kind of like a laugh himself. "Women," he muttered.

"You've spent twelve years trying to beat me, Chess. You've never won."

"I've won. I'll *win*! Once I make this trade—"

"Hey!" Butch yelled, the volume of it hopefully traveling outside. *Please someone be outside.* "I told you to shut the hell up."

But Chessa was on a roll. Because high or not, controlling her anger had never been in her skill set. She moved toward him, hands in fists.

"You paint yourselves the heroes, but people hate you.

They're going to be so happy to think you're a bad guy. Just look at your parents. Someone hated them so much, they got rid of them without a trace."

"I said that's enough," Butch said angrily. He walked right over to Chessa. Cash braced himself for the blow he thought was coming to her, but it was worse. Butch put his hands around her throat. "You can't shut up. I'll make sure you never talk again." Then he clearly squeezed because Chessa started clawing at his arms and struggling. Her face started to turn purple as Butch choked her.

Cash couldn't just…watch her be killed. No matter what she'd done, who she'd been, this wasn't right. He tried to jerk his body enough to move the chair, to do anything. "Hey! Knock it off!"

Butch didn't pay him any mind. Cash looked around the kitchen, desperately hoping for some inspiration in how to get out of this, how to stop Butch, how to…

Then he saw the phone on the counter kind of shake. He couldn't hear it vibrating over Chessa's gurgles, but any sort of distraction would help.

"Hey! Isn't that your phone ringing?"

Butch looked over at the counter and sighed. He let go of Chessa and she dropped to the ground, gasping for air and pawing at her neck. Alive. Somehow, still alive.

Cash didn't feel relief, exactly. But he pushed all feeling away. He had to focus. Butch had answered the phone, but he didn't say anything besides *yes* or *no*.

Cash pulled at the bonds again. Tight. Too tight. He couldn't really move the chair. The only way he was going to get out of this was to wait it out. To somehow survive until…

Hell, he didn't know. But he wasn't about to give up.

"It's time," Butch said to Chessa. "But if you don't watch

your step, we're leaving the girl behind and maybe your corpse. No trade."

Chessa sneered at Butch, but she got to her feet on shaky legs. "Whatever," she muttered, her voice raspy.

The girl. Why did it always come back to Izzy? "How the hell do you think you're going to get your hands on Izzy? I'm *missing.* You think my family is just going to… what? Leave her home alone? Leave her unprotected? She's got an *army* keeping her safe. You'll never get your hands on her." He said it because it was true, and because it was a reminder to himself. No one was going to let Izzy get hurt.

"We have our ways." Then Chessa pulled out her phone and held it up, like she was taking a picture of him. "Smile, honey. We're about to send your family on a very wild goose chase."

WALKER AND GRANT walked into the kitchen a little while later, and they didn't need to speak for Carlyle to know they hadn't found Cash. Palmer was still looking through security footage, she assumed.

And Cash hadn't texted her back.

But she'd sat at the table and forced herself to eat, if only to keep Izzy company. Anna and Caroline had joined them in the kitchen, pretending not to be worried, but Anna's gaze kept tracking out the window.

Grant's gaze skirted over Izzy, but Walker dove right in. "There's no evidence he ever let the dogs out this morning."

"But he had to. He always does," Izzy said, grabbing onto Carlyle's arm.

"I'm going to go get Palmer," Anna muttered. She passed off Caroline to Mary and left the kitchen.

Izzy leaned into Carlyle and Carlyle held her tight, trying not to let her mind zoom ahead. One step at a time. If he hadn't let the dogs out, something had stopped him. It would be on the security footage. Palmer would have found something, and they'd know how to proceed.

But before Palmer came in or Anna returned, Jack strode in through the back door in his Sunrise SD polo. "Anything?" he demanded.

Mary shook her head. "No."

Jack didn't say anything to that, and Carlyle couldn't read his expression. She supposed Jack, more than any of them, had the most practice keeping a blank expression in the face of potential trauma.

There had to be something to *do*. Something that wasn't just sitting around *waiting*. Carlyle was about to insist upon it when Anna returned, Palmer at her heels.

"He left the house just after four," Palmer said grimly. "Turned off the alarm, then reset it. The footage loses him between the house and the dog barns. There's no sign of him on the barn cameras."

"What about the cabin?"

"The cameras at the cabin are wired. The wires were cut sometime yesterday. But there's no evidence of anyone getting on the property from any of the entrance points."

There was a little chorus of swearing.

"The ranch is just too big to ever be fully secure," Palmer said. "But the fact we've had this kind of trouble multiple times suggests someone knew enough about the setup to circumnavigate it."

"Chessa," Izzy said, her voice wavering.

"But Chessa is dead," Anna pointed out.

"Yes, but she knew the place," Palmer said. Like the rest of them, he glanced at Izzy as if not quite sure how much to say. "She was also allegedly friends with Tripp before he died. He was our ranch hand. He knew the place *and* the security quite well. They might both be dead, but they might have passed along some information to someone who's not."

"We'll start a search party," Jack said. "We know he left on foot. If he got waylaid by someone, the chances are they were on foot as well unless we find tracks. So, we'll split up. In threes. Izzy will stay here with Mary, Dahlia, the baby, some dogs and..." He looked over everyone. "Carlyle."

"Uh-uh. No way."

"You're injured, and we need someone here who's good with a gun."

He was full of it, but as much as she wanted to go look for Cash, Izzy was gripping her hand with such force it almost hurt. The little girl needed her, and Mary might be good at comforting, but Jack was right. Carlyle knew her way around a firearm, and how to protect.

This would be the best thing she could do for Cash, so she nodded.

Jack started deciding groups, but his phone trilled, and he pulled it out of his pocket with a frown. Then swore. Viciously.

But then he looked from Izzy to Mary. "Mary, why don't you take—"

"No," Izzy shouted, jumping to her feet. "What happened? You know something. Don't take me away." She looked up at Carlyle, tears in her eyes but a stubborn set to her mouth. Carlyle wrapped her arm around her shoulders.

"Tell us, Jack."

Jack's mouth hardened, but he nodded. "Someone just texted me a picture of Cash. They're asking for a ransom. So he's fine. He's alive." Carlyle knew Jack said that just for Izzy. "They just want us to pay money to get him back."

"Money, but why?"

Jack didn't answer her. "I'm going to forward Hart the

text. And Brink and have her bring some Sunrise officers out here so we can decide how to proceed."

Carlyle and everyone—but Mary—pushed in close to Jack to see the picture on his screen. How to proceed? Someone had Cash and...

In the picture he was tied up. He had a big bruise on his head and for a moment, a fleeting, terrible moment, she thought he must be dead. But he was scowling. Scowling at the picture-taker.

"They said they're in a hotel in Hardy. They've given me a money drop off point."

"They're not going to give him up," Grant said in a low voice, meant just for the adults.

Carlyle agreed with him, but she wasn't sure what else could be done. They wouldn't just give an address that could be surrounded. "He won't be at the place they're saying. They know you'll go to the cops."

Jack nodded. "No doubt, but we'll have to at least begin to play it their way."

"I want to see," Izzy said, trying to reach up and take the phone from Jack.

"There's nothing to see, sweetie. It's just a picture to show us he's alive and well. They can't get a ransom if he's not. The police will take it from here. It'll be okay."

But Izzy didn't drop her hand. "Let. Me. See."

Carlyle looked from the girl to the picture. It wasn't that bad, and it was clear he was alive. She wasn't sure Izzy needed this stuck in her head, but sometimes knowing was better than the unknown.

"Let her. It'll be better. She won't wonder. She'll know." And they'd find a way to get Cash back here, so this terrible picture wouldn't have to be anyone's last memory. Carlyle swallowed the heavy lump in her throat.

Jack sighed deeply, but then lowered himself into a chair. He motioned Izzy over, then put his arm around her reassuringly as he tipped the phone screen toward her. "He's going to be okay, Izzy. We're going to make sure of it."

Her chin wobbled, and her eyes filled with tears, but then her eyebrows drew together. "That's not a hotel. That's not Hardy."

"What?" Carlyle demanded…along with everyone else.

"Look." Izzy pointed at the bottom edge of the screen, and everyone leaned closer. "That's our kitchen. In the cabin."

Carlyle couldn't figure out what Izzy was pointing at. The picture was mostly just Cash's face, with very little hints at the room around him. She did see a little pink dot behind his ear. Carlyle looked around at the other adults at the table. They were all frowning too.

Izzy pushed Jack's hand out of the way and used her fingers to zoom in on the picture. "There," she said, pointing to the tiny pink dot nearly completely hidden behind Cash's ear. "That's my fairy stained glass thing that hangs in the kitchen window. I *know* it is."

Carlyle let out a breath. It was a stretch, a real reach. She looked behind her, out the kitchen window. The cabin was right there across the yard. She moved over to the window along with everyone else.

"You think they could be in there *now*?" Carlyle asked. She wanted to run across the yard right now and find out, but they all clearly knew on the off chance Cash *was* in there, they had to be very, very careful.

"Why though?" Jack asked. "Why hold him here so close to all of us?"

"Because they told you to go to Hardy," Carlyle said. She didn't want to say the rest in front of Izzy, but maybe it was best if the girl knew. "This isn't about Cash, or not only about him. What has Chessa said she wanted every single time?"

Anna swept a hand over Izzy's hair. "Chessa's dead," she said, once again.

"Sure, but that doesn't mean what she was after just stops. Especially if she was working with people. Butch. Bryan. Whoever. What purpose does it serve to send you off property when we know he's not? To put fewer people on Izzy. Because what were you going to do before the picture, Jack? Have two people and some dogs stay here with Izzy while the rest of you scattered."

Jack said nothing, but she could see a flash of irritation in his eyes. Not because she *was* right, but because he hadn't seen it himself.

"All right. We wait for the police to get here. We surround the cabin. We—"

"That'll take too long and put Cash too much at risk. We have to be sneaky," Carlyle insisted. "We can't go about it the way you normally would. This is about Cash and Izzy, but it's also kind of about you guys as a whole, right? Cash was the one to kick Chessa out, to refuse to pay her, but you all played a role in that. And if Chessa knew you, and passed that along to whoever is part of that, then she knows what you'd do."

"Chessa would have to think about someone besides herself for more than five seconds to know what we'd do," Anna said darkly.

But Jack's gaze never left Carlyle. "What do you suggest then?"

"I think we should give them what they want."

Chapter Eighteen

The response to Carlyle's suggestion was loud. Carlyle let out a sharp whistle to stop it. "Let me finish! Calm down. You guys. Seriously? I am not suggesting we put Izzy in danger. I'm suggesting we lay a trap. Let them think you've gone to Hardy, that we've scattered. Let them think you've handled this in the typical Sheriff Jack Hudson fashion, and then pull the rug out from under them."

"We need to make sure they're still in the cabin first," Grant said. "There's no point to this if they've moved location."

"My phone," Izzy said. "We can track Dad's phone with my phone. But I don't know where Dad puts it at night."

"I do," Mary said, and she hurried out of the kitchen.

Carlyle gave Izzy a squeeze. "Good thinking, kid."

Izzy nodded. She was clutching Carlyle's arm for dear life, but she was holding up. And that was what was holding them all up, Carlyle thought. They couldn't fall apart when they had to come together. They couldn't dissolve when Cash needed them to be strong.

Carlyle looked out the window. She could see just the edge of the cabin. What she really wanted to do was run across the yard, beat down the door and deal with whatever.

But it just didn't make sense. Whoever had Cash had a

plan. Whether they had him in that cabin, in the hotel in Hardy or somewhere completely else, they wanted something. And this would never end until they got to the bottom of what.

And who.

If Chessa was still alive, Carlyle could believe this was all about Izzy. But with her dead, that made less and less sense.

"Did they ever find the stepmother who owned the building?" she asked Jack.

He shook his head. "She's been reported missing by a friend."

"Missing? Not like she took off?"

"It's unclear, but there's some speculation something happened to her, rather than that she's avoiding questions about the explosion."

Carlyle sucked in a breath. Another murder? What could possibly be worth all of this? It didn't add up or make any sense.

Jack's phone rang, making everyone jump. "It's Hart," he muttered, then put the phone to his ear and walked out of the kitchen. Likely so he could speak freely without worrying about Izzy's reaction.

Mary reentered with Izzy's phone. "Here." Mary handed the phone to Izzy. Izzy immediately began to poke away at the screen. She held out the little map that popped up. "He's somewhere close on the property. That means he's in the cabin!"

"He could have left it behind," Anna said gently. Phrasing it in such a way it sounded like that would have been Cash's choice, not his kidnapper's.

"He could have, but I think we know he didn't," Carlyle said, working to keep her words calm. "If Izzy's phone tracks it on the property, and Izzy recognizes the background of that picture, chances are high he is in the cabin. Right *now*. We need to move forward with that plan."

Jack returned. "Hart is on his way. He's going to have a few men on standby at the entrances and exits of the ranch. He didn't think it sounded like a good idea to run code onto the ranch."

"You need to make it look like you're sending out your search teams," Carlyle said. "Mary and I will invite Hart inside when he gets here."

"We're not going anywhere," Jack said resolutely. "If Cash is in the cabin—"

"You don't have to *go*. You just have to make it look like you did. Make it look like Izzy is a sitting duck. But she won't be. Look, we could barge in there and get him out—God knows I'd like to—but we don't know what or who we're dealing with. We have to be more careful. Why not draw them out?"

"Because that takes time, Carlyle." She knew Jack wanted to say more—that it might be time Cash didn't have, but Carlyle refused to believe that. If they were holding him, demanding ransom, they'd keep him alive.

"Cash can handle time," Carlyle insisted. Because he had to. "We have the upper hand if we draw them out. We go in there guns blazing, they do. So we need to do something with the dogs too."

Jack didn't have a response to that. He was scowling, so clearly he didn't agree with her, but maybe he realized they really had no other options.

"Three of you go out together, armed and watchful, and saddle the horses like you're going on a search," Carlyle instructed. "The most likely thing is they're in that cabin, watching. Waiting for us to scatter. We have to act quickly."

There was a pause. Just about everyone in the kitchen—except her brother—looked to Jack. Carlyle wanted to be frustrated, but she understood the family's habitual looking to him to be the leader, to have the final say.

"Walker, Palmer and Grant. Go saddle up four horses. Walk them across the yard to the back of the house. Out of sight of the cabin. We'll tie them up there. Then we'll fan out and form an inner perimeter, out of sight. Any dogs not in a kennel or in the barn, get them there. Carlyle's right. We can't risk them posing a problem."

"Everyone should be armed," Carlyle said. "Every single person." She gave a meaningful jerk of her chin toward Izzy.

This earned Carlyle another glare from Jack. But then he sighed. His telltale sign of giving in. "All right. Palmer?"

"Got it." Palmer disappeared, likely to go gather the firearms in the house from their locked safe.

"I think it should look like as few people are with Izzy as possible, and that Izzy is within as close as reach to the cabin as possible. When Hart gets here, the two of us open the door. Together. And let him in."

"Don't you think we should hide somewhere?" Mary said, worry in every inch of her expression. "We have a great offense—all these people. There's nothing wrong with a little defense."

"We want to draw them out," Carlyle told her, with a gentleness she probably wouldn't have used with anyone else. "They need to get a glimpse of Izzy. They need to think they have this in the bag. The more they think they can easily take her, the better chance we have of doing this cleanly."

Mary didn't say anything to that, but Carlyle watched her reach out for Walker's hand as she placed her other over the slight bump of her stomach.

"You all need to go pretend to search, however Jack

wants that to look. Mary and Dahlia can watch the cabin from upstairs with Caroline. Any kind of binoculars you've got—see if you can get any glimpse inside. Izzy and I stay down here and wait for Hart."

There was another pause. Then Palmer returned with the guns. It was the strangest tableau, everyone standing in the Hudson kitchen, watching as guns were distributed to different people. Palmer hesitated at Izzy, but he handed her the one she'd been practicing with all the same.

"I know you know how to use it, Iz, and we trust you to. But remember, there are a lot of adults around here who can and will handle things. This is just a last resort."

Izzy took the gun and nodded. "I know."

Palmer let out a breath then turned to the remainder of the people in the kitchen. "We should move. The sooner we draw them out, the sooner Cash is safe."

Jack nodded and then everyone began to disperse. Most everyone left out the back door, leaving Carlyle, Izzy, Mary and Dahlia in the kitchen.

Carlyle pulled her phone out of her pocket. "I'm going to start a group call. That way we can all listen and communicate."

"Good idea."

Carlyle started the call on her phone, then shoved it into her pocket on speaker. They all separated, each going to their designated spots. Carlyle took Izzy into the living room, but the girl kept looking over her shoulder.

"Aunt Mary usually isn't scared," Izzy murmured, watching the staircase even though Mary had long disappeared.

Carlyle crouched to be eye level with Izzy and waited for the girl's gaze to meet hers. "There isn't anything wrong with being scared. This is scary. But we're going to fight, even if it's scary."

"I just want my dad to be okay."

"I know. We all do. So, he's going to be. Come on. Let's watch for Hart." She held Izzy's free hand and pulled her over to the big front window. They watched the lane that led up to the house without saying anything.

"I don't want to just sit around waiting, Carlyle," Izzy said, a frustrated and determined look on her face that concerned Carlyle almost as much as Cash being held so close without anyone understanding the situation.

In any other time in her life, Carlyle would have jumped in headfirst, but she was responsible for Izzy. Cash would never forgive her if she messed that up, and Carlyle would never forgive herself. So, for the first time in her life she had to go against her instincts and just stay put.

"I don't either, but sometimes… Man, I learned this one the hard way, but sometimes you've got to let other people help you out. You try to do everything on your own, everyone gets hurt."

Izzy didn't say anything to that, but a little cloud of dust started at the ridge. Then the police car appeared. Carlyle squeezed Izzy's hand. "We've got so much help."

The cruiser pulled to a stop at the front porch and Hart got out. He had a hand on his gun, and it was clear even though he was in detective plain clothes, he was wearing Kevlar underneath.

Carlyle pulled Izzy toward the door. She opened it, and fully stepped out herself. She then pulled Izzy behind her, so hopefully if someone in the cabin was watching they'd catch a glimpse of the little girl and know she was at Carlyle's side.

"Come on in, Hart."

"Where's Jack?" he asked as he followed Carlyle inside.

Carlyle explained her theory on what these people wanted.

She described the Hudson plan of keeping out of sight but close enough to know what was going on. She even explained where everyone in the house was and why she had Izzy with her.

Maybe she hadn't always trusted these cops, but now she had no choice.

"You're going to leave," she told him. "Drive all the way out. Then walk back in. Form an outer perimeter with your guys, and Zeke because he'll be here soon enough. We've got the inner. You start making a tighter and tighter circle, but the main directive is to stay out of sight from the cabin. They'll come out. Likely just one at first, but they'll come out. It's got to be more than one, so you don't want to intercede until we're sure there's no danger to Cash."

"This *is* my investigation."

"And this is my home. And the people I love," Carlyle replied. "My plan's good. The best you're going to get."

Hart glanced down at Izzy, who—to Carlyle's pride—had a lifted-chin, stubbornly defiant expression on her face. She shouldn't be holding a gun, worried about her father's life, but here she was, holding up. Holding true.

"All right. Here." He unhooked a radio from his vest. "You'll be able to hear us communicating with each other. Anything bad goes down inside, you radio out. Just press this button and talk."

Carlyle nodded. It was a good addition to her plan. Not that she was going to admit that to him.

"Anything strikes you as off, you're going to radio us, okay?"

She nodded. "I've got everyone else on a group call in my pocket. We'll do our best to communicate everything to everyone."

"Okay. I'm going to run code off the property, make it look like I'm off to Hardy and the address. Sound good?"

Better than good, but she only nodded. "You trust your guys on the perimeter?"

"With my life," Hart replied.

She hoped to God it wouldn't come to that. She opened the front door once more, letting Hart out then closing the door and locking it.

"Now what?" Izzie asked.

"Now, we have to wait."

Izzie nodded, but she was chewing on her bottom lip. A telltale sign something was bothering her.

Well, why wouldn't she be bothered? Her father was being held against his will in their home.

"It's going to be okay," Carlyle said. She would move hell and earth to make it okay.

Izzy nodded, but when she looked up at Carlyle, the expression in her eyes had Carlyle's stomach sinking.

"Carlyle, I think there's something I need to tell you."

CASH WAS FEELING worse and worse, the headache so bad he wished he could scoop his own brain out to stop the throbbing. Whatever Chessa had shot him up with was a hell of a drug.

Butch had finished with the pantry and was now stationed at the kitchen window. He hid behind the curtain but was watching through a gap. Cash couldn't quite turn his head enough to see out the gap himself, but he kept trying.

Chessa moved around. When it was clear Butch was getting agitated with her, she'd disappear into the living room for a bit, but she always came back. Edgy and pacing.

Cash could see the oven clock and knew it was creeping closer to ten in the morning. He'd been gone too long now. His family would be looking for him. It made no sense why they were keeping him this close to the people who could easily overtake *two* people. Even if they were armed.

"Finally," Butch muttered as the sounds of sirens filled the air.

Cash tried to turn in his seat again, but the bonds were too tight, cutting into his skin. Sirens, yes. But he frowned as the sound went from loud to soft—like the emergency vehicles were leaving the ranch, not coming toward it.

"Go on then," Butch said, jerking his chin at Chessa.

Chessa flashed Cash a self-satisfied grin then slipped out the back door. Cash tried to angle his head so he could see out of the kitchen window, but he couldn't manage it. Where did Chessa think she was going? What had those sirens been? He wanted to demand answers, but even if Butch gave them, Cash could hardly trust them to be true.

"You really think you can trust her to do anything?" he said instead to Butch, because it was a valid enough question. "Particularly when she's on something?"

"Not my rodeo, buddy," Butch muttered.

Cash frowned. Why would Butch pretend like he wasn't involved when it was clear he was? "This is a lot of work and effort if this isn't your rodeo."

"You have no idea the reward," Butch said with a harsh laugh. "Don't worry though. You won't be alive long enough to find out."

But he *was* still alive. For hours on end. Which meant they needed him alive for *something*. "I'm still alive, so…" Cash attempted a shrug despite his bonds. "I guess I'm not too worried about this alleged demise that's coming."

Butch spared him a glance. "For as long as we need you, you'll live. But that isn't much longer."

Chapter Nineteen

Carlyle slowly crouched down and put her hands on Izzy's shoulders. "What do you need to tell me?"

"I... I didn't think it mattered. It was...my little secret. And I would have told everybody, but I didn't think it would—"

"Iz, slow down. Take a breath. Just tell me. Tell me what you've been keeping a secret."

"There's a tunnel."

"A *what*?"

"A tunnel," she repeated, and her eyes were full of tears, her shoulders shaking underneath Carlyle's hands. "Between the cabin and the house. You just have to go into the cellar at the cabin, which is kind of creepy. Then there's this...tunnel. It comes here, through the basement. I don't go there much, but sometimes I just wanted to see... I just wanted to... I don't know. But if Dad is in the cabin, maybe we can get to him through the tunnel. The cellar opens right by the back door."

"Why didn't you tell anyone else?"

For a moment, Izzy didn't say anything. She looked at Carlyle's pocket, where the phone on speaker was, and chewed her bottom lip.

"It was somewhere I could go that nobody knew about. It

was just mine. Just for me and I got to make all the choices there and…"

Carlyle could hear Jack saying something over the speakerphone, but she couldn't focus enough for the words to make sense. She could only try to work through what Izzy was telling her.

A tunnel. To the cabin. To *Cash*.

"Show me," she said to Izzy. Because if she could get to that cabin undetected… They could stop this. "Just show me where the tunnel starts in the basement and—"

"That won't be necessary."

Carlyle jerked Izzy behind her and faced down a woman with a gun. The lady was short, wiry and looked really… rough. The look in her eye was maniacal enough it made Carlyle's whole body run ice-cold. But she held Izzy behind her. No matter what, she'd keep Izzy safe.

"Carlyle," Izzy said in a small voice. "Why did everyone say she was dead?"

Carlyle stared at the woman and realized those blue eyes were familiar because they were the same shade and shape as Izzy's.

Chessa. Not dead, like everyone had said, but here. Alive and with a gun.

"Because Hudsons *lie*, Izabelle," Chessa said, pointing the gun at Carlyle's chest.

"No we don't!" Izzy shouted, trying to come out from behind Carlyle, but Carlyle held her firm. Maybe she didn't know why, but she knew Chessa wanted Izzy, and that sure as hell wasn't going to happen.

"I don't know what you think you're doing, Chessa, but it isn't going to work," Carlyle said, very calmly as she tried to think of what she could do to get Izzy out of here.

Up the stairs. To Mary or Dahlia. She couldn't start shooting until Izzy was safe.

Then Carlyle could do what needed doing. But the staircase was on the other side of Chessa.

Whose finger was curled around the trigger of the gun.

"I don't need you," she said to Carlyle. "I thought Butch should have killed you when he had the chance." So Butch had been the attempted kidnapper. "He's so finicky and weird about things. So mad when I killed that two-bit cop. But he got to off his stepmother, didn't he?" She closed one eye, the gun clearly pointed at Carlyle. She was going to shoot, and Carlyle's only chance at survival was really that she was a bad shot.

Or help.

Because when the gunshot went off, it wasn't Chessa's gun. Or Izzy's or even Carlyle's. Chessa jerked and stumbled face-first onto the ground. Carlyle kept a hard grip on Izzy, keeping her behind her, but moving quickly forward to rip the gun out of Chessa's hand.

She made a low moaning sound as she writhed on the floor, but she didn't get up. Carlyle went ahead and lifted Izzy straight up off the ground and hurried her to the stairs where Dahlia sat on a stair, shaking.

"God, I hate guns," she muttered as Carlyle shoved Izzy at her. Dahlia wrapped her arms around Izzy, even though her arms shook.

"It's okay," Carlyle said. She gave Dahlia's arm a squeeze and looked her straight in the eye. "Hey, you saved the day. Take Izzy upstairs. Be with Mary this time. Lock the door."

"Carlyle—"

But Carlyle wasn't listening. There was a tunnel in the basement. And Cash on the other end.

She looked at Izzy. "Stay safe." Then she ran.

CASH HEARD THE *pop* of what could have only been a gun-shot. Somewhere far off, but distinctive enough to know it was a gun. A gun.

Cash looked at Butch, who gave nothing away. He just kept looking out the gap in the curtains.

The minutes that passed were interminable, but as Cash watched Butch, the man's expression began to change. From neutral to more and more irritated. He looked at the clock on the wall more than once.

"Chessa late?" Cash asked.

"Shut up," Butch replied, standing. He walked over to Cash.

Cash didn't know why he didn't stay quiet, didn't know why he was dead set on pissing off the big guy when he was tied to a chair. Maybe Carlyle had gotten to him after all. "Big surprise that Chessa messed everything up."

Butch leaned in and Cash used it as his chance. Maybe he couldn't escape his bonds, but if he could knock Butch out or incapacitate him in some way, then at least there was no threat he'd die.

He used his head to land the hardest blow to Butch's nose that he possibly could. Pain radiated through his own skull on contact, but Butch outright *howled*, and blood spurted from his nose. Butch swore a blue streak as he stumbled back and landed on his butt.

Fury blazed in his expression, and he scrambled over to what Cash had assumed was just a bag of food pilfered from his pantry. But Butch pulled out a gun.

Well, that wasn't good. But he couldn't work up much fear over the radiating pain in his head, the blurred vision. Maybe he'd given himself a concussion? But he was about to get a gunshot wound for the trouble.

"I wouldn't," a female voice said from the kitchen entryway.

Cash could only stare as Carlyle appeared. Butch whirled, but Carlyle was faster. She shot and Butch stumbled back, crashing into the kitchen counter. Carlyle moved over to him while Butch made terrible, pained moans.

She grabbed a knife from the block on the counter and began to saw at the ties around Cash's wrists behind the chair.

"Izzy?" he asked.

"Mary and Dahlia have her."

"They're working for someone. There could be more people out there."

"Cops and your entire family have the whole ranch surrounded." The bonds on his arms fell away and he nearly gasped in relief. "The ransom attempt wasn't the smartest move. No one fell for it. We're safe. She's safe."

She cut the ties at his feet then helped him up. She studied his face. "That's a hell of a knock," she said. He didn't know if she was seeing the mark from hitting Butch, or from earlier, but it didn't matter.

Somehow she was here, and Izzy was safe, and Butch...

Cash wasn't steady on his feet, but he used the counter and the wall to balance as he walked over to where Butch sat.

Butch had pushed himself against the wall. His complexion was gray. Blood poured out of his nose and the bullet wound in his stomach. His eyes were glassy, but they looked from Cash to Carlyle with a kind of resigned hate.

"Who sent you?" Cash demanded. "What do you want with my daughter?"

Butch looked at him, then Carlyle, then at the gun she

held pointed at him. Cash didn't expect an answer. But Butch surprised him.

"Rob Scott."

Cash frowned. "I never had anything to do with Chessa's father. Neither did she."

"Yeah, and that was fine and dandy when she didn't have anything to offer him, but then he got into selling and Chessa helped him out. Got him customers. Worked in a little prostitution ring. She kept talking up how much money she could get for Izzy, how much you'd wronged her. Eventually, he decided to fund her delusion, but she's a loose cannon. I tried to tell him that, but he didn't care if it came with a payday."

"That's a nice story that leaves you completely out of it," Carlyle said while Cash reeled over all of that...truly awful information.

"I don't see anything wrong with wanting to make a profit. I'm not fool enough to use the product like her." He jerked his chin like he was aiming it at Chessa even though she wasn't there. "I'm just muscle. I do what I'm told. And I didn't kill anyone, so what? I'll do a few years' jail time. I ain't worried about it. Probably cut me a deal if I tell them everything. That's the only reason I'm bothering to tell you anything. I don't have any loyalty to Scott."

"Then why work for him?"

"Why not? The money's good, the women are better." He shrugged, even as rivulets of blood flowed out of his nose and stomach. Even as he sat there knowing that even if he survived, he was going to jail. "Better than busting my ass at some minimum-wage job."

Cash didn't see how, but he didn't have to. The sirens were getting closer. "Go open the front door, Car."

Carlyle opened a drawer, pulled out some dish towels. "Push that in there. If he doesn't die, he can testify."

Cash supposed she was right, so he did as he was told. Butch just stared at him. Not with hate, not with interest. Cash stared right back.

"She isn't right, you know," Butch said, then he grunted in pain as Cash pushed harder to stop the bleeding. "You crossed her. She'll never let it go. And now that you got in Rob's way? That's two lunatics with you on their hit list."

Cash supposed, deep down, he'd known that even if he couldn't understand it. In Chessa's mind, he was the villain, and Izzy was hers for the taking. "That a warning, Butch?"

"Nah. Just the truth. I hope it hangs over your head for the rest of your life."

Before Cash could say anything to that, two EMTs rushed in with a stretcher. They pushed Cash out of the way and went to work on Butch, but Carlyle was dragging in another one. "He needs one too," she said, pointing at him.

The EMT walked over to him, took one look at his head and nodded. "Yeah, you've earned yourself a hospital trip."

"Is he good enough to go with me?"

Cash looked behind the EMT to see Detective Hart, but the EMT took him by the chin, moved his head this way and that. Asked him to follow her finger with his eyes. "Yes. But straight to the hospital."

Hart nodded and the EMT released him and strode over to where they were working on Butch. Carlyle led him outside and to the Bent County police cruiser Hart must have been driving.

"I'll go with and—"

Cash cut her off. "Stay here. With Izzy. Please?"

She took a breath, studied him, then nodded. She leaned in, pressed her mouth to his. "Like glue, Cash."

"Thanks."

She helped him into the back of Hart's cruiser, gave his hand one last squeeze, and then didn't just walk off to the cabin, but jogged. He knew she'd keep her promise.

"You up to telling me what happened?" Hart asked as he started the engine.

"Yeah, let's get this over with."

Chapter Twenty

Carlyle woke up feeling fuzzy headed. She was too warm, and under a blanket that smelled like strawberries.

When she blinked her eyes open, she realized she'd fallen asleep with Izzy in Izzy's bed in the kids' room. Izzy was curled up next to her, her fingers wrapped around Carlyle's wrist. For a moment, Carlyle could only watch the girl sleep.

Her heart ached in a million ways, for a hundred reasons. She nearly cried, then and there, but she'd hate to have Izzy wake up to tears.

Because the bad stuff was over now. She didn't know the prognosis on Chessa, or Butch for that matter, but she knew that Izzy was safe. Butch had been happy to rat out who was behind it, and there was no way any of them would be let out of jail for a very long time.

Carlyle would do everything in her power to make certain.

Izzy stirred next to her, yawning as she blinked her eyes open. She met Carlyle's gaze then sat straight up. "Do you think Dad's home?"

Carlyle sat up too and swung her legs over the side. "If he's not, you and I are going to the hospital and demanding to see him."

"Demanding?"

"Oh yeah. Or sneaking into his room. We'll work it out."

Izzy *almost* smiled at that, and they both got up off the bed and walked out into the hallway, the two dogs trailing behind them. Carlyle had no sense of what time it was, or even what day at this point. When they walked down the stairs, Izzy gripped her hand.

They both looked at where Chessa had been, and Carlyle figured she was holding onto Izzy as much as Izzy was holding onto her at this point. They were about to head for the kitchen, but a noise in the living room had them changing course, and as they walked through the hallway, they caught sight of Cash walking in the front door, flanked by Jack and Grant.

"Daddy!" Izzy tried to run over to him, but Carlyle held her firm for a minute.

But Cash nodded, so Carlyle let her go. The little girl raced over to Cash, who knelt to catch her. It was Grant standing behind Cash that clearly kept him from being knocked over by Izzy.

Carlyle stayed where she was, the lump in her throat making it impossible to speak anyway.

"Let's get Cash sitting down," Grant said, helping Cash back up to his feet while Izzy clung to him.

"I'll fill everyone in on the case once we get situated," Jack offered.

There was a bit of a commotion then, people talking at once as the big group of them settled into the living room. Carlyle figured she'd go stand next to Walker, but as she passed the couch where Cash and Izzy were situated, Izzy reached out and gave her arm a tug, so Carlyle had to take a seat right next to her.

With her arms wrapped tight around Cash's arm, she

laid her head on Carlyle's shoulder. Like they were a little unit. Or could be.

"We're questioning Chessa's father," Jack said. "Zeke talked to some of his contacts at a federal agency. It looks like they can build a particularly big case against him—beyond just this. Especially if Butch makes it and testifies, which is looking possible."

"How did Chessa make everyone think she'd been murdered?" Cash asked. His voice was a little raspy, and it looked like he hadn't slept, but he looked…relaxed. Because his daughter was right here.

He moved his arm over Izzy's shoulders, resting his hand on Carlyle's. Carlyle had to blink back the tears stinging her eyes.

Because it was over. Really over. Sure, there were legal steps left. If Chessa survived the gunshot wound, she could still be a threat if she didn't get much jail time. It wasn't some perfect happy ending.

But with so much of the danger neutralized, a happy ending felt like so much possibility Carlyle just wanted to weep.

Jack's expression was grim. "We're still working on identifying the body that was originally ID'd as Chessa's. It looks like they fake-identified the body as Chessa with the help of Ferguson and Rob Scott. Hart's theory is the body is one of her fellow—" Jack's gaze landed on Izzy "—coworkers," he finally said.

So, another prostitute. Carlyle supposed it made sense that Chessa and her father could manipulate things with a woman who worked for them, who they probably knew enough about to hide her identity.

"Butch and Chessa will be under guard at the hospital until they make a full recovery—if they do. Then they'll be transported to jail. Chessa's awake and eager to turn

on everyone. The information Butch gave you corrobo-
rates much of what Chessa said, and Chessa claims Butch
killed his stepmother. Police are looking into that too, but
even without full cooperation, they'll all be on the hook for
first-degree murder. They'll be locked up for a long while."

"What about this tunnel?" Cash asked.

"As far as we can tell, they were old cellars that were
connected," Jack said. "Old enough I'm not even sure our
parents knew about them. They were sealed off, kind of,
it looks like, until…"

"I found the one in the cabin when I was mad one day,"
Izzy said, looking at her lap. "Messing around in the cellar because Dad told me not to. Then I found the tunnel
entrance and it was like a book, and I was mad, so I kept
it a secret. Then it just became this…thing I did whenever
I was mad. Whenever everyone was talking about stuff or
doing stuff they were hiding from me. I didn't unseal the
other side though. I tried, but I couldn't do it." She looked
up at Jack, like she was desperate for him to believe her.

"No, that definitely looked more recent. I think the kidnapping attempt might have been a distraction in more ways
than one. It's possible Chessa and Butch have been hiding
out in the cabin since after that night."

Carlyle absorbed that like a blow. Painful, but what could
you do? It was over, and they'd survived.

"I'm sorry," Izzy said, her voice so small it was a wonder anyone but Carlyle and Cash heard her. "I didn't tell
anyone because… I just wanted to feel like… I just wanted
to have something nobody knew about. That no one could
protect me from. I'm sorry…"

"I'm sorry too, Iz," Cash said, pulling her close. "Sorry
you felt like you needed that."

Izzy nodded and snuggled into him. He glanced at Carlyle over Izzy's head and smiled. "We'll all get a little better at...talking to each other instead of trying to save each other, all on our own. Day by day."

Carlyle managed to smile back, even though she was overwhelmed with too many emotions to wade through. "Yeah." Because that was life. Day by day. Doing their best to do a little better. And she'd finally found a really good place to make her home, and good people to expand her family.

Danger or no, she was exactly where she wanted to be with the people she wanted to be with—all who'd worked together to keep each other safe and sound, no matter what threats were hurled at them.

What more could anyone ask for?

AFTER A FEW DAYS, Cash couldn't say he felt back to one hundred percent, but he felt more in control of his body. Felt like he'd dealt with what had happened, mostly.

Carlyle had handled working with the dogs for the past few days, with only moderate supervision from him as everyone was always fussing at him to rest. Then they ate their family dinner, put Izzy to bed together and came out onto the porch to watch the sunset, with Swiftie never leaving Carlyle's side for long.

It was a nice little routine. Rocking on the porch swing, her head in his lap as night slowly crept over the world.

Tonight, he was staring at his cabin. The place he'd raised his daughter, and then been held against his will.

"I don't think I can ever live there again." He twisted a lock of Carlyle's hair around his finger.

"So why not bulldoze it and start over?"

"Seems like a waste of a house."

"Sounds therapeutic to me. We can take a sledgehammer to it together. Have a destruction party."

Cash laughed, even though it hurt his head a little. "I'll keep that in mind."

And it was amazing, really. How she made everything feel infinitely possible. All those doors he'd closed and locked on himself, she'd busted open just by being her.

So, he figured tonight was as good a night as any. "You know I'm in love with you, right?"

She didn't say anything at first, but she did smile up at him. That brash, cocky smile that had first made her seem like some foreign beacon of light he couldn't resist.

"Yeah, I figured as much."

"You going to admit you're in love with me yet?"

She made a considering noise. "What's in it for me if I do?"

"Good question."

"I guess a hot guy in my bed," she said thoughtfully, as though she were ticking off points on a list.

He gave her a disapproving look. "Or my bed."

"And you're pretty decent when it comes to housework. That's a plus." She sat up and squinted out at the sunset as if considering.

He shook his head. "If you say so."

"And I like a man who can be a good dad to his daughter. If you couldn't, no amount of hotness could make up for it."

"You've got quite the criteria there."

"And the dogs. They can sense evil, so since they love you, you must not be evil."

"I'm glad the dogs are what convinced you of that."

She laughed then looked at him, her blue-gray eyes twinkling with mischief. "You're a pretty good package, Cash."

"Great," he muttered, because he knew she was messing with him, and he knew she got a kick out of it when he acted messed with.

She leaned her head on his shoulder and sighed. "I love you, Cash."

They watched the sun slip behind the horizon, not thinking about how everything would be happy and easy from here on out, but that no matter what was thrown at them, they'd always have that love.

* * * * *

Don't miss the stories in this mini series!

HUDSON SIBLING SOLUTIONS

Cold Case Protection
NICOLE HELM
December 2024

Cold Case Discovery
NICOLE HELM
January 2025

Cold Case Murder Mystery
NICOLE HELM
February 2025

MILLS & BOON

Wyoming Christmas Conspiracy

Juno Rushdan

MILLS & BOON

Juno Rushdan is a veteran US Air Force intelligence officer and award-winning author. Her books are action-packed and fast-paced. Critics from *Kirkus Reviews* and *Library Journal* have called her work "heart-pounding James Bond-ian adventure" that "will captivate lovers of romantic thrillers." For a free book, visit her website: www.junorushdan.com.

Books by Juno Rushdan

Harlequin Intrigue

Cowboy State Lawmen: Duty and Honor

Wyoming Mountain Investigation
Wyoming Ranch Justice
Wyoming Christmas Conspiracy

Cowboy State Lawmen

Wyoming Winter Rescue
Wyoming Christmas Stalker
Wyoming Mountain Hostage
Wyoming Mountain Murder
Wyoming Cowboy Undercover
Wyoming Mountain Cold Case

Fugitive Heroes: Topaz Unit

Rogue Christmas Operation
Alaskan Christmas Escape
Disavowed in Wyoming
An Operative's Last Stand

Visit the Author Profile page at millsandboon.com.au.

For Amber M., a caring, dedicated educator. While you were the principal at my children's elementary school, you became one of my personal heroes. Thank you for your service.

CAST OF CHARACTERS

Monty Powell—This part-time rancher and full-time state trooper refuses to let anyone else decide his destiny. Accused of murder, he must rely on help from his family and someone he least expected—the woman he let walk away years ago.

Amber Reyes—After Monty broke her heart, she left home and became a teacher. When her father's funeral brings her back, she is determined to prove the innocence of the only man she's ever loved.

Chance Reyes—Amber's brother and Monty's close childhood friend. He's also a lawyer with a secret that will change many lives.

Hannah Delaney—A strong-willed detective who must find balance between doing her job and maintaining her loyalty to her fiancé's family, the Powells.

Erica Egan—This journalist will cross any line for a scoop and to see her name in the byline.

Waylon White—Not thrilled to partner with Hannah Delaney, this detective won't do any favors for the Powell clan.

Holly Powell—Monty's mother and mayor of the town.

Chapter One

Friday, December 6
7:35 a.m.

Amber Reyes sped down the snow-covered road, clenching the steering wheel so tight her fingers grew numb. Even though it was freezing outside—30 degrees, which wasn't too bad for December in Wyoming—she was hot under the collar and not from the heat blasting out of the vent in her 4x4. She was headed to her half sister's place.

A half sister whose existence she hadn't been aware of until August, at the reading of her father's will when the details of a legal trust he'd established had been explained. Amber, along with everyone else in the small town, knew of Pandora Frye—the beautiful, eccentric, arrogant, wild child.

But she'd been shocked to discover Pandora was also the beautiful, eccentric, arrogant, illegitimate child of Carlos Reyes, the product of an extramarital affair twenty-two years ago.

Amber believed her mother had never known that her father had cheated. They'd always had a loving, picture-perfect marriage until her mother died ten years ago of cancer. Then everything had changed. At nineteen, Amber had learned the people closest to her couldn't be trusted.

Primarily her father. So she'd run from home to make her

own way in the world. And that was before she found out about her half sibling.

A decade later, she hadn't thought her father could top his previous conniving efforts to manipulate her into an arranged marriage—much less from the grave.

How wrong I was.

Though her father had bequeathed Amber most of the land, including the valuable river that ran through it, and the cattle, he had also stipulated ironclad conditions for her to receive it. The betrayal, his indomitable will to have things his way continued after his death.

But then came the real shocker. Her father had not only named Pandora in his living trust, claiming her as his daughter, but he had also given her the Reyes family home and one acre of land surrounding it, which she'd take ownership of at the beginning of the new year following his death. Giving Amber and her brother, Chance, one final holiday season in their home.

Thinking about it made Amber's blood boil. The house her parents had been married in. The house she and her brother had been born in. Land they had been raised on. The house that had been in the family for generations would soon belong to a virtual stranger.

Not if I have anything to say about it.

A wave of nausea swept over her. Slowing down and keeping her eyes on the road, she kept driving as she unzipped her purse in the passenger seat of her Jeep Wrangler. Inside the handbag, her fingers skimmed over the unopened letter from her father, but she didn't find what she was looking for. The saltine crackers were probably still sitting on the kitchen counter. She'd been in such a rush to speak with her sister—*half sister*—that she'd forgotten them.

Maybe she should've listened to her brother and stayed home.

But that was the problem. If she didn't convince Pandora

to sell them the house and the acre of land around it, she and Chance wouldn't have a family home for much longer.

Her cell phone rang. The caller ID showed up on the Bluetooth screen on the dash. Sometimes she thought she had a psychic link with her big brother.

She hit the Accept button, putting the call on speaker in the rugged SUV. "What is it? I'm almost there."

"You forgot your crackers."

Despite her anger, she smiled. "I just realized. I'm pretty nauseous."

"Pregnancy will do that to you," Chance said.

She put a hand to her belly. Only four months along, but if not for the baggy sweaters she'd started wearing, the rounded bump that had emerged one morning like magic would be visible to everyone. One careless, reckless night, swamped by grief, she'd given in to a moment of weakness and slept with Montgomery Powell. "We agreed not to use the P-word."

"Which one, Pandora, pregnancy or Powell? I can't keep track."

"Don't use any of them," she demanded, putting both hands back on the wheel. Best for things to be simple.

"You're going to have to tell Monty sooner or later. I think you should've done it by now."

"Thankfully it's not up to you and I choose later." *Much, much later.* "This is my body, my timeline. I won't be harassed or bullied by Monty or his family or you."

"Okay." Chance's snippy tone signaled he thought she was making a mistake.

Her death grip on the steering wheel made her forearms cramp. "I'd like to put out one dumpster fire before dealing with the next."

She switched on the wipers to prevent the falling snowflakes from sticking to the windshield. This time of year, it was typical to get several inches. She'd been gone so long, she'd forgotten how early the winter storms started here in Wyoming, in the valley where the small towns of Laramie and Bison Ridge were nestled.

"You're wasting your time," Chance said.

"I am not. She agreed to hear my proposal." Pandora, the leech, just as vicious as her mother, Fiona, had texted last night, telling Amber to come by for coffee at ten this morning. With flagrant disregard to the fact that Amber was filling in as a substitute teacher at the local elementary school and class started at nine. She had been up since five and decided to throw the young woman off-balance by showing up early. Inappropriately early. Outright rude, truth be told, but Amber didn't care.

"Only to see your face when she rejects it. The girl was over the moon at the reading of the will and so was her mother. The house isn't worth much, but she was ecstatic to get her grubby hands on it because it's ours. Or was. At least Dad left you everything of value with the land and cattle."

Everything but only one way to keep it, or lose all that, too, to Pandora.

"With that unconscionable proviso," she said through gritted teeth. "Why aren't you fuming? He left you nothing."

"Dad set me up for success. He paid for my bachelor's and law degrees, and I didn't have to work through school. I was able to focus on being the top of my class and got hired by a powerhouse company."

In a way, Chance was right. The day he started practicing, he did so debt-free. Not many of his colleagues had the privilege to say the same. Now he worked for Ironside Protection Services, earning a high six-figure salary, which was substantial compared to what she made as a schoolteacher.

A profession she'd chosen out of desperation after she fled the ranch, but surprisingly a rewarding one. "Still, he shouldn't have left you nothing."

"The simple watch he wore every day and his old rodeo buckles aren't nothing. They meant a great deal to him. Besides, I read the letter he wrote for me. I'm at peace with his decision. You should read yours. It might change how you feel."

Glancing at her purse, she seethed. "I have half a mind to burn mine."

"You'd regret it. Just like you're about to regret seeing Pandora."

She sighed, hoping he was wrong. For once. Though Chance seldom was. A fact that grated on her like sandpaper scraping her skin. "I'm almost at the harpy's abode. I'll call you afterward to tell you how it went." A long breath eased from her tight throat as she let up a bit on the accelerator.

"Don't bother calling me back. But would you mind grabbing us breakfast from Divine Treats? I'll take a bear claw. Also, one of those savory croissants. Ham and cheese."

Amber pulled up to the block of a recently constructed town house complex, consisting of ten units, in the center of downtown Laramie. Why their father had felt the need to buy Pandora one of these sleek, newly built places as well as give her the family home, too, was beyond Amber. She'd been here once after the funeral, in a failed attempt to get to know the young woman better. The finishes were top-notch, with custom cabinets and furnished with whimsical luxury. Stunning eye candy filled the interior. Their father had spared no expense.

"Don't you want the details on the meeting?" she asked.

"You can wait until you get home to fill me in," Chance said. "That way I can say *I told you so* to your face."

Shaking her head with irritation, she drove around the back to the parking lot. "You're unbelievable. Instead of being the annoying, know-it-all big brother, why can't you—" She lost the power of speech for a moment as her gut clenched.

"Amber? Are you all right? What's wrong?"

She slammed on the brakes, fixing her attention on the vehicle parked beside Pandora's sporty car behind her unit.

"Monty's truck is here." The words left a foul taste in her mouth.

For him to be here at seven forty-five in the morning could only mean one thing. He'd spent the night.

"Are you sure?" Chance sounded skeptical. "At least half the guys in town probably drive a Ford F-150."

She stared past the swirls of white flakes in disbelief at the truck. "How many drive one that's antimatter blue and has the vanity plate PWEL3?"

Buck Powell had a similar plate with the number one. Holly, domestic goddess extraordinaire and now mayor, had the designation number two. Their eldest son had the plate Amber was staring at right now.

Chance swore.

"That calculating, spiteful..." Amber swallowed the ugly words dancing on her tongue. "Is this the reason she agreed to meet me? Only to rub my face in the fact that she's bedding Monty."

"You're so early. Maybe it's coincidence." Her brother's words were comforting, but his tone full of doubt.

Unexpected tears filled her eyes. She didn't know what hurt more, her heart or her pride. "How could he?" she asked, her voice cracking.

"Not to sound like a callous guy on this one, but you two hadn't seen each other for almost ten years. You came home for the funeral, still angry over how things imploded between you two, and had a one-time slipup with him. Four months ago, might I add? You've avoided him ever since then, right?"

"Yeah, I guess so." Even though Monty had called, asking to see her, she'd rebuffed his attempts at contact because she didn't trust his motives and she didn't trust herself around him. With the unalterable stipulation in her father's living trust—Amber had to marry Monty within five months of her dad's death and stay hitched for two years, or everything, the entire property, the cattle, the money, went to Pandora—how could she believe anything he said? Especially if it was all the things her heart longed to hear.

"Plus," Chance added, "Pandora is easy on the eyes and comes across as, quite frankly, a floozy. It's probably nothing more than a one-night stand."

"But he didn't simply have sex and leave." Which would have been bad enough. "He spent the night." *With Pandora!*

Amber had only had the pleasure of a few nights with Monty herself. Even a lifetime ago, before she learned the horrible truth about why he'd taken a sudden interest in her, he had never stayed and cuddled until the sun came up with her.

She squeezed her eyes closed and saw Montgomery Beaumont Powell, six feet three inches of pure sex appeal. Tawny hair, the same as his father's. Intense brown eyes. A strong jaw with the perfect amount of stubble all the time, like he didn't even have to try. And a sweeping landscape of muscle. His sculpted physique was created by hard work on his family's ranch that was adjacent to hers, in addition to the extra effort he put into staying fit for his full-time job with the state police as a trooper. With his swagger and confidence, the man could've been a Hollywood heartthrob. Women swooned after him from Laramie to Jackson Hole. Not only for his heartbreaker looks, but also his status as heir apparent to the Powell fortune.

And Pandora Frye had sunk her claws into him.

The woman was taking everything that didn't belong to her.

Amber opened her eyes. She stared at the antimatter blue truck parked beside the cherry red Alfa Romeo Stelvio and slapped the steering wheel, letting a small scream slip.

"Get a grip," her brother muttered. "It's only sex. Even if he spent the night."

"He can sleep with whomever he likes. Except for her!" She whisked the tears from her eyes. *I will not cry.* Stupid hormones. "This may be a small town, but I'm sure there are tons of women willing to crawl into bed with him." Monty had never had a problem in that department. "He didn't have to sleep with *her.*" The living embodiment of her father's broken marital vow. The woman who would move into her family's house. "Yes, she's classically beautiful and nubile—" in fact, they were exact opposites: Pandora was slender, sophisticated, with creamy skin and red hair, whereas Amber was curvy and simple, and a brunette with brown skin "—but he knows something like this would bother me."

More like wound her to the marrow.

"Getting upset won't solve anything. You need to calm down, Tinker."

Tinker Bell. How she despised the nickname. It stopped being cute once she'd turned thirteen. At twenty-nine, it made her sound as ridiculous as she felt being back home. Still pining for Monty Powell, the veritable Peter Pan, who was only interested in using her for her pixie dust.

Straightening, she threw the truck in Park, blocking Monty's and Pandora's vehicles. No quick, clean exits for either party. "You're right. It doesn't matter what they do."

"It really doesn't so long as you marry Monty in twenty-nine days."

The five-month deadline was creeping up on her. One dumpster fire at a time, starting with this. "I'll show Pandora and him that I don't give two figs they're sleeping together. I just need her to agree to sell us back the house," she said in a voice so strained she almost didn't sound like herself.

"You're not still going in there, are you?"

Amber grabbed her purse, slinging it over her shoulder. "I most certainly am. I'm done running from things. This time I'm going to confront it head-on."

"Says the woman running from telling the father of her child that she's four months pregnant and wearing baggy clothes to conceal her burgeoning bump."

"Instead of lecturing me—"

"Reasoning with you."

She huffed. "You should be supporting me."

"You mean enabling you to make poor choices you'll regret."

Why was it so hard for him to be in her corner for once? "Before you can try to talk me out of it, I'm hanging up." She jabbed the red icon, ending the call.

Killing the engine, she pressed her door open against the frigid thrust of the wind. Another thing she'd forgotten about home: it was the second windiest state in the country. The town was in the perfect, or worst, spot depending on perspective. Rather than the mountains surrounding the valley blocking the wind, they made the jet stream faster. Add in high pressure from the Great Basin and low pressure from the plains and the town got squeezed, making the winters harsh.

Cold slapped her face as she climbed out. Icy flakes stung her cheeks. Crisp, clean air moved in the blustery wind, smelling of winter and snow and pine. Zipping up the oversize coat she'd recently purchased to hide that she was expecting, she marched up to the back door. Beside it a sign on the window read Pandora's Box Photography.

Her half sister was a glamour and boudoir photographer. The profession seemed better suited for a big city, but when one's father paid for their lifestyle in hush money, Amber supposed it didn't matter whether their career was profitable.

Bitterness welled inside her. She struggled to tamp it down. Since the day she left home, she hadn't taken one cent from her father or even spoken to him. Everything she had she'd earned and paid for herself, on a meager teacher's salary.

The name, *Pandora's Box*, was apropos, considering the

seven deadly sins seemed tied to the woman. She was the product of lust, had seduced Monty—unless there was some other explanation for him being here—was envious of their status as legitimate Reyes offspring and had, driven by greed, held on to their family home. The Reyes home.

What great evil was next?

Amber raised her fist, wanting to bang out her frustration rather than ring the bell, and knocked—only once because the door swung open on contact.

It must've been slightly ajar. She hadn't noticed. A gust of wind sprayed snow inside the entrance.

"Pandora!" she called out, crossing the threshold. She closed the door, keeping more cold air and snow from seeping in.

Music came from the first-floor bonus room Pandora used as her photography studio. A sultry Kacey Musgraves song just ended and a soulful one by Shawn Mendes started as Amber stood there.

A hopeful thought sprang to mind. Maybe Monty was here for some other reason. To get a portrait taken.

But at seven something in the morning with soft pop music playing?

Hope quickly withered. In its place, anxiety swelled, twisting through her.

Amber had no claim on Monty and no longer wanted any. Not after he'd deceived her right along with her father.

Only the house matters right now.

The door to the studio was cracked open. "Pandora!"

Still no answer. Hesitating at the entrance, Amber braced to encounter some tawdry scene inside, the two of them asleep or, worse, intimate. She set her mind to show no reaction.

Steeling her spine, she pushed on the door and strode inside.

She faltered to a stop and gasped. The blood in her veins froze, her stomach giving an acid twinge. A familiar copper scent wafted in the air.

Monty lay, utterly still, on his stomach on a curved, emerald colored velvet sofa, wearing nothing but black boxer briefs. His eyes were closed, his face slack. One long, muscular arm hung off the side, his knuckles on the floor.

A knife. An open butterfly knife was beside his hand. Covered in blood.

Her breath hitched in her lungs, but she forced herself to breathe as she shifted toward her half sister.

Pandora was sprawled on the floor in the center of the room, eyes frozen open and vacant, expression locked in an unnatural contortion, bruises on her pale face, her throat slit.

Squeezing her eyes shut, Amber turned away. Her mind spun. Steadying herself, she looked over the room.

Clothes were scattered about as though they had undressed in a hurry.

A bottle of whiskey was open on a side table next to the sofa along with a tumbler half-full of liquor. Another was broken on the floor. Lines of white powder were on a small mirror on top of a speaker from which music poured into the room.

Alcohol. Drugs.

Murder.

Sickening dread pooled in her chest.

This couldn't be happening, but it was. Blackness edged her vision and she swayed. For a second, she stood there, hyperventilating. Shaking. Trying to make sense of the sordid, horrible scene.

Grim urgency punched through the paralyzing fear. "Monty?" Why wasn't he moving? Was he dead, too?

Please be alive.

Snapping into action, she rushed to him. Red-lipstick kiss marks were on his cheek and neck. Along with some kind of rash. Hands trembling, she tugged off one of her leather gloves and pressed two fingers to the side of his throat.

He had a pulse. Thready and slow. But he was alive.

There was a strange sound. Was it coming from him?

She tipped her ear closer to his mouth. A wheeze came from him on every exhale.

Amber had never seen him like this, blacked out, wheezing, with a rash. What was wrong with him? And what had happened here?

Her gaze dropped to the bloody knife near his hand and then she looked back at Pandora.

Nausea churned her stomach. Amber had wanted this young woman out of her life from the second she became aware they were related, but not like this. Not murdered, dead, at twenty-two.

This was awful. She needed to call the police. Report it, and say what?

Monty was many things—a liar, a manipulative womanizer— but every cell in her body, every instinct in her gut, told her that he was not a killer.

She'd known him her entire life, once adored him, had kissed him, made love to him, created a baby together and still cared for him far more than she wanted to admit.

In spite of how this looked, and it did look as though he had killed Pandora, Amber knew he wasn't capable of such a thing.

She crouched beside the curved sofa and cupped his face, gripping his chin. "Monty." When he gave no response, she shook his shoulder. "Wake up."

Moaning, he stirred slightly.

"Monty!" She gave him a harder shake, rolling him onto his side. The wheeze became more pronounced and the rash covered his torso. "Please, wake up," she said, sick with worry.

His eyelids fluttered as if they might open but didn't.

Her mind spun like a carousel.

Think, Amber. Think.

All of Monty's brothers, even his cousin who also lived on the Powell ranch, were law enforcement. Any one of them would know exactly what to do and would protect Monty with his life. She took her phone from her purse, but she only had one of their cell phone numbers.

She dialed Logan, thankful he'd given her his number at her father's funeral. He was with the Wyoming State Attorney General's Office, Division of Criminal Investigation. She only prayed she'd catch him before he left Laramie to get on the road to Cheyenne, where he worked.

The line rang four times before he answered. "Powell."

"This is Amber." Her voice broke as she stared at Pandora's lifeless body again. "Where are you?"

Never in a million years had she thought she'd ever call him—the one Powell who had always been in love with her and would've married her in a heartbeat, happily, proudly, if she had felt the same.

"Leaving Divine Treats." Keys jangled over the line. "I had to satisfy my sweet tooth. I'm happy to hear from you. Finally."

The Divine Treats bakery was within easy walking distance, three blocks away. "I need you."

"What is it?" His voice tightened. "What's wrong?"

"It's Monty. You have to come, quickly."

"Did something happen to him? Where are you?"

"At Pandora Frye's." She rattled off the address. "Monty is out. I can't get him to wake up." Her voice was shaky, and she took a steadying breath to control it. "But Pandora…" Hot bile rose in her throat. "There's blood and a knife."

"Is she alive?"

Amber shook her head and then realized she had to use her voice. "No. She's dead."

"Are you sure?"

"Yes." Her gaze trained on the lifeless body, and she had to fight the urge to cover the poor woman. "I'm positive. You have to hurry."

"I'm climbing in my truck now. I'll be there in less than two minutes." A beat of silence. "Did you call 911?"

"No." She wasn't sure what to do. The right thing and the best thing might be different in this situation. Not once had she ever broken the law and she wasn't considering doing so now, but when it came to Monty, she never could think straight. One thing was certain. He needed someone on his side out in front of this. "Not yet."

"Okay. We have to hang up," he said, the sound of a car starting in the background. "Then you need to call 911."

But he didn't fully understand what he was about to walk into. What he was about to see. The bloody knife. The alcohol. The drugs. Pandora—naked, slain.

Oh, God. "Logan, the way this looks—"

"Whatever you're staring at will appear far worse if they pull our phone records and piece together the delay in calling 911." Another pause. "We've been on the line for too long already. I'll be there shortly."

Logan disconnected.

Had she made a mistake in phoning his brother first? She hadn't thought about the police looking at phone records. Would her actions make Monty look more guilty?

She only wanted to help, not hurt him.

A rush of mixed emotions battered Amber. She glanced back at Monty and desperately tried to rouse him. Heart pounding in her chest, she flicked another shocked look at Pandora.

No way Monty would've hurt her, much less kill her.

But someone had. Would anyone besides his family, her and Chance believe in his innocence? Half the town loved the Powells. The other half longed for their ruin.

Amber shook off the thought. The who and why behind this didn't matter at the moment. How many would stand beside Monty or stand against him didn't either. The only thing that did matter was proving his innocence and making sure Monty didn't go down for this murder.

She dialed 911.

Chapter Two

Friday, December 6
8:07 a.m.

Monty opened his eyes to glaring light and closed them again. His head was thick and throbbing, his throat dry as cotton. A bad taste was in his mouth.

"Mr. Powell! Can you open your eyes?" a strange male voice asked.

Pain thundered through his skull. Something was wrong. If only he could think.

Where was he? Why was someone shaking him? And shouting his name?

At least he was sitting up. Groaning, he forced his eyes open.

The room spun. Music played in the background. His breathing was strained to the point of wheezing. His fuzzy gaze veered past the stranger in front of him and locked onto Amber. She was blurry and then the sight of her cleared up. "What's going on?" he said, his voice low, his throat raw and scratchy.

Was she real? Was he dreaming?

"It's going to be okay, Monty." A warm, gentle palm pressed to his cheek. "You didn't do it. You couldn't have killed her."

Someone was dead.

None of the words coming from her made a lick of sense. "Killed...w-who?"

He was exhausted, like his brain and body were wading through sludge.

"Ma'am, we've already told you to step away from the suspect and to go back into the hall," a stern voice said.

Suspect. He refocused on the man in front of him. A police officer. Laramie PD.

"W-what's happening?" Monty asked, trying to piece things together. But his memories were jumbled.

"Get your hands off me!" Logan's voice was sharp, but his brother was out of sight. "Can't you see he needs help? At least let the EMT check him out."

"Sir, can you look at me?" a woman asked.

He was so thirsty. "Water."

"They need to take him to the hospital," Logan demanded.

The woman knelt in front of him. An EMT. She shone a penlight in his eyes, making him squint.

It felt like a jackhammer chiseled away in his head. "I need water."

"In a minute, sir." She lifted a gloved hand in front of his face, raising her index finger. "Please follow my finger." She moved it to the right and he dropped his head. "Do you know what day it is?"

He struggled to keep his eyes open, to come up with an answer. "S-Saturday? No. Friday. I think."

"What's the month?"

"December."

The EMT pressed something to his mouth. "I need you to blow, sir," she said, and Monty did his best until a strong wheeze forced him to stop. She slipped something on his arm that tightened. A blood pressure cuff. Once she finished, the EMT stepped aside. "He's not drunk. Blood alcohol level is zero. But his blood pressure is quite low and he appears to be having an allergic reaction to whatever drugs he took."

"No drugs," Monty said with a harsh wheeze. He'd never done drugs once in his life.

"He's not in anaphylactic shock and could be hauled in, but we'd advise against it. We should take him to the hospital to be examined," the EMT said.

"If he passes out in a holding cell or worse," Logan said, "it'll be on you. Do you want to risk suspension? Or losing your badge?"

"I'll take the chance to make sure a *Powell* doesn't wiggle out of this one," a cop said. "He's practically been caught red-handed, but your family has a lot of influence."

"He didn't do this." Amber's voice carried from the hall.

The other officer grabbed Monty by the arm and tugged him up, but he wasn't sure he could stand.

Monty swayed on his feet. His arms were wrenched at his lower back and cold cuffs were slapped on his wrists, the sound of metal ratcheting in his ears.

His blurry gaze drifted, landing on a pale body lying on the floor. A nude woman. Pandora Frye.

Dead.

Disbelief and confusion twisted together, spiraling and spreading in his brain.

"It's freezing outside." Amber rushed back into the room. "He needs shoes and a jacket."

One of the officers raised a palm, stopping her. "His clothes are evidence."

"Give him a minute," Logan said from the hall. "He can wear my boots. I can help him put them on."

The officer holding his arm in a vise grip yanked him forward. Monty took two steps. Swirling lights danced in front of his eyes. Then his legs gave out as everything faded to black.

10:35 a.m.

VOICES MURMURED NEARBY.

Amber?

Confusion fogged Monty's brain. Was he dreaming?

His throat ached as his eyelids slowly lifted. The fluorescent light overhead was painfully bright, blinding him for a moment. His thoughts scrambled like eggs in a sizzling hot pan.

The room came into focus. He was wearing a medical gown, lying in a hospital bed with several instruments attached to him, including an IV. A machine beeped nearby.

Amber hovered close to his bedside.

"You're real," Monty rasped. Jerking fully awake, he tried to sit up but winced when pain cut into his wrists and metal clanged.

"Take it easy." She put a palm on his chest.

His head pounded so hard he thought he might throw up. Closing his eyes and swallowing, he concentrated on breathing to help the dizziness pass.

"Do you want some water?" a familiar voice asked.

He turned his head to see Logan on the other side of the bed. His brother had been in his dream, too. With Amber. No, not a dream. A nightmare. "Yeah."

Logan grabbed a cup from a table and put the straw to his lips. "You're looking much better."

Better than what?

Monty drank, taking long, hard gulps, draining the cup of water.

"You're not wheezing anymore either," Amber said.

His gaze dropped to the metal bracelet on his wrist. "Why am I handcuffed? What am I doing in the hospital?" Taking another steady breath, he tried to calm his raging heart. He stared into Amber's hazel eyes and then at Logan's worried face. "What happened to me?"

The room door creaked opened. Both Amber and Logan shifted focus away from him in unison and moved closer to the bed, bodyguards shielding him from whatever was coming.

Hannah Delaney walked in. She was the fiancée of his cousin, Matt Granger.

Logan visibly relaxed. "They put you on the case?"

"What case?" Monty asked. "Would someone please tell me what's going on?"

Furtive glances were exchanged.

"Monty." Hannah stepped closer. She was petite, blonde and deceptively pretty, like a Disney princess but also tough as nails and capable of taking down a guy twice her size. Only a fool would underestimate her. "You should know I'm here in an official capacity."

Official. She was a detective. Worked mostly homicides.

"I'm assigned to the case for now," Hannah continued. "I could be pulled due to conflict of interest, but if I'm not, I won't be working this alone. Waylon Wright was put on it, too. He *asked* me to leave the scene and to come here." Her tone was sharp, and Monty gathered that she'd been kicked out. "He'll be here shortly."

Monty groaned. There was no love lost between him and the egotistical, caustic detective. They'd had an altercation as teens. Over the years, the animosity had only festered.

Hannah folded her arms. "Anything you say, I'll have to report."

"Then he has nothing to say until his lawyer gets here," Amber said.

Monty shook his head, trying to clear out the fog. "But I don't have a lawyer."

Amber took his hand. Her fingers wrapped tight around his. "Chance is on the way."

"But he's not a criminal lawyer," Logan whispered.

Amber pressed her lips into a tight line. "Chance will do until we can get the best attorney for this kind of thing."

"Explain what's happening." Monty squeezed Amber's hand.

"I found you at Pandora's place." Amber hesitated, swallowed hard. "She's dead. You were unconscious at first. Had difficulty breathing and a rash. They brought you here."

The words awakened a memory. Pandora on the floor. Pale. Still. Blood.

Not a dream or a nightmare.

A shudder ran through him.

"Turns out you were drugged," Logan said. "They're not sure with what yet. They're running tests, but whatever it was you had a bad allergic reaction. The doctor says you got lucky you didn't go into anaphylactic shock. They've had you on an IV drip of meds to counteract it. Your breathing is better. The rash is gone."

"I was at Pandora's," Monty said in a low voice, a statement, not a question, but everything was still cloudy. "But how? Why? What happened?"

Hannah eased closer to the foot of the bed. "You really can't remember?"

He shook his head, ready to expound.

Amber slid her hand over his lips. "That's enough. We need to wait for Chance to get here."

"You should be careful what you say." Hannah's face was neutral, her voice grim. "You're as good as family to me, but I will do my job." She looked over at Amber. "What were you doing at Pandora's this morning?"

Amber opened her mouth as if to answer but then pursed her lips tight.

"I can't help if I don't know." Hannah slid her gaze to Logan. "What were either of you doing there? Do you have any idea how this will look to Waylon?"

"Yes, I do." Logan sighed. "Are you here to help or to do your job?"

"Hopefully, both," Hannah said. "If you believe Monty is innocent and neither of you did anything wrong while at Pandora's, then you've got to talk to me."

Why had they been there?

An ugly thought crossed his mind. What if they had done something wrong, tampered with the crime scene, to help him?

But he shook off the idea. Logan was a sworn officer. His brother would never compromise his integrity. Not even for him.

At least Monty didn't think he would.

A woman wearing scrubs strode into the room. "You're awake. That's good." She checked his IV bag. "I'm Nurse Shelby. How are you feeling, Mr. Powell?"

"Like I've run a marathon, slept for days and still need more rest. And my head is pounding like it's going to split in two. Everything is foggy. I'm having trouble remembering."

"The doctor thinks you were dosed with a date rape drug and a boatload of it, too. We'll know for sure as soon as your blood work comes back." Nurse Shelby took his vitals. "But the mixture of the antihistamines and cortisone with whatever else is in your system is probably amplifying the drowsiness. Don't worry, it'll pass."

"How long until he can remember?" Hannah asked.

"Things will come back to him in a few hours, but he'll never recall what happened while he was blacked out if it was one of the drugs that we suspect."

Logan turned to the nurse. "Does the doctor think it was GHB?"

The nurse shrugged. "Could be. It's one of the most common date rape drugs right along with Rohypnol and ketamine."

But who had drugged him? And why?

"Monty, will you consent to have your medical record released to us?" Hannah asked.

Amber stiffened, tightening her grip on his hand. "Chance can advise us on what to do. If I had thought to call him sooner, he'd already be here. It's still hard to believe that you even need a lawyer."

"I only ask because based on what I've heard I think it will help," Hannah said. "Not hurt you."

Logan nodded. "I agree. I think it'll be the fastest way to get you out of these cuffs." His brother glanced down at the restraints on his wrists.

"Actually, I can take care of that now." Hannah took a handcuff key from her pocket and unshackled him.

"We told the officer who accompanied him here that he shouldn't be restrained in his condition," the nurse said.

"O'Brien." Logan huffed. "The man wouldn't listen to reason because he wants Monty to be guilty. End of story. Forget about due process."

"I'm sorry you went through that." Hannah frowned. "But there are quite a few on the force who'll feel that way simply because you're a Powell."

Monty rubbed his wrists. "Waylon will be one of them."

"No red flags in his record that I'm aware of," Hannah said. "He usually acts first and asks questions later, but a salt-of-the-earth straight shooter. I've known him to be a fair guy."

Logan swore. "Not when it comes to my brother."

Hannah's brow furrowed. "If they keep me on this, I'll make sure everything is handled aboveboard. The medical release?" she asked again.

"Okay." Monty rested back in bed. "If you think it'll help."

"I can see to it for you." Nurse Shelby headed for the door.

"Have it sent directly to the chief of police, Wilhelmina Nelson, as soon as possible," Hannah said.

"Sure. I'll do it right now." The nurse left the room.

Monty looked at his soon-to-be cousin-in-law. "Hey, Hannah. I want you to know, as family and as a detective, that I don't know what happened to Pandora, but I'm sure I didn't kill her."

"Not another word to the police," Amber whispered fiercely and then eyed Hannah with caution.

Everything he'd been told sounded bad. His hazy recollection of Pandora's studio, her dead on the floor, him incoherent, looked even worse. He simply needed Hannah to know that he wasn't guilty of something so heinous. Amber didn't understand how close he was to Hannah. His cousin Matt had been raised alongside him, like a brother, and Amber was aware he considered him as such. But that also meant Hannah was practically the sister he'd never had.

"You should listen to her." Hannah studied his face, her expression one of genuine concern. "If Matt were in your position, I'd advise the same."

He looked up at Amber—his pretty, sweet, fiery Tinker—grateful she was here with him. He'd spent thousands of sleepless nights aching to apologize for the way he'd treated her all those years back. Beg her forgiveness. The worst part, what he regretted most, was making love to her without telling her the truth first—that he'd intended for it to be a marriage of convenience for the land.

During their time together as a couple, everything had changed for him. He'd fallen for her so deeply, so unimaginably hard, he'd wanted forever with her. But when she found out his initial reasons for going after her, it had broken her heart and she'd run from him, from her family, from Wyoming. And it had crushed him.

At her father's funeral, he'd tried to voice the emotions slamming through him. For a moment, they'd gotten close, the clumsy words on the tip of his tongue, but her anger had turned into a different kind of heat, and he'd messed it all up by falling into bed with her instead. Seeing her, touching her, tasting her again was a gut-wrenching reminder of the grave error he'd made. Then she refused to see him anymore and stopped taking his calls.

He would've given anything for a chance to explain. Even though there wasn't any good justification for his actions. But he'd grown up since then. Not a day went by that he didn't hate himself for hurting her. Watching his younger brothers Holden Sawyer and Matt fall in love, with two of them now married and starting families—while he lived alone in the house he was supposed to share with Amber—had forced him to reassess his own empty life, opened his eyes to the fact that the only way to fill the gaping void plaguing him was to win Amber back.

But he'd never imagined that under such dire circumstances, where he might appear guilty of murder, she would support him rather than spit nails at him. A true testament to her character.

The nurse returned, coming into the room carrying a tablet. "I sent what we have so far over to the chief and made a note to have the results forwarded as soon as they're in." She handed Monty the electronic device. "Just need you to sign two forms. Also, there's someone at the nurses' station looking for you. Tall, commanding voice, ruggedly handsome and a rather abrasive man with a badge."

"That'd be Waylon." Monty finished signing the forms and returned the tablet.

"I think I'll leave before he gets in here." Nurse Shelby hurried out of the room.

"What's the deal between you two?" Hannah asked. "And how far back does it go?"

Monty glanced up at the ceiling. "Started in high school and never ended." It was too complicated to say more than that in the time they had.

The door swung open.

Waylon Wright strode in with all the swagger of a man on a mission, sucking the oxygen from the room.

Chapter Three

Friday, December 6
11:50 a.m.

Waylon shoved into the hospital room and clenched his jaw at the sight of Monty Powell, propped up in a hospital bed, playing the part of the victim when first glance of the damning crime scene made him look guilty as sin.

He tipped his Cutter-style hat to Amber Reyes, glossed over Logan Powell and briefly shifted his gaze to Detective Delaney. If common sense prevailed, she would be removed from the case post haste. But he wasn't going to hold his breath waiting for that to happen. In all likelihood, favoritism would continue to be showered on the powerful, wealthy Powells.

"I believe introductions are unnecessary," Waylon said, "so, let's cut to the chase, Monty. Yeah, you're a Powell and you also happen to be law enforcement." The latter Waylon respected, provided the cop was clean, but the influence and presence of the Powells was ubiquitous. They had enough money to buy senators and governors. Their spawn had infiltrated every corner of law enforcement. Monty was a state trooper. Logan was with the Wyoming Division of Criminal Investigation. Holden was the chief deputy of the sheriff's department. Sawyer was a fire marshal. Matt Granger—their cousin who they treated more like a brother—was the chief of the campus police at SWU, Southeastern Wyoming University. And the youngest, Jackson, was a US marshal in another state. Always craving more power, their mother, Holly, had been recently elected mayor. It was enough to make Waylon raise an eyebrow and wonder at their motives, if it wasn't the desire for control. Unfortunately for them, Waylon wasn't the kind of man who could be bought or easily swayed. "But I have no intention of doing you any favors in this investigation."

"Wouldn't expect you to," Monty said.

Waylon glanced down at his unrestrained wrists. Apparently, the favors had already started. He came to stand at the foot of the bed and eyed Delaney. "Why isn't he handcuffed?"

"The medical staff advised Officer O'Brien when he was brought in that he shouldn't be restrained in his current condition."

"Which at the moment is conscious," Waylon pointed out, "able to speak and quite possibly capable of running."

Delaney scoffed. "Give me a break. He's not going anywhere, and I was present the entire time they were off."

Waylon nudged the brim of his hat up with a knuckle and put a hand on his hip. "Is he a murder suspect?"

"I thought you were going to cut to it," Delaney said flatly, her face deadpan.

"Treat him as such. If you weren't sleeping with his cousin, he'd be in cuffs." When she narrowed her eyes and opened her mouth to respond, he raised a palm stopping her. "A woman is dead, throat slit practically from ear to ear. That man," he said, pointing at Monty while staying laser-focused on Delaney, "was at the scene of the crime, is our only suspect in the homicide, and his prints are on the murder weapon."

Amber Reyes gasped. Concern flooded Logan's face.

But there was only confusion in Monty's expression as he shook his head. "That can't be—"

"Say nothing," Amber said in a harsh whisper, cutting him off.

"I didn't know the prints came back already." Delaney lowered her gaze. "Listen, the cuffs were hurting him and like I said, I was here, watching him the entire time."

"I need everyone to leave the room." Waylon pivoted on his bootheel and glanced between Logan and Amber, but he also meant for Delaney to step outside, too. "I have some questions for the *suspect*."

Amber put a protective hand on Monty's shoulder. "Not without his lawyer present," she said, her voice tart, her cheeks reddening.

"Am I under arrest?" Monty asked, quietly.

"No," Waylon said, wishing that wasn't the case. "Not yet." As much as he'd love to see Monty behind bars, paying the price for any of his wrongdoings, his main concern was getting justice for the victim. Unfortunately, more than a few troubling elements to the case made him question whether Monty had actually committed this crime. It was by no means open-and-shut. He needed all his ducks in a nice, neat row before arresting a member of the Powell family. Especially the heir apparent. "But it doesn't look good for you."

"Looks can be deceiving," Chance Reyes said, sweeping into the room, wearing a crisp power suit and confidence like armor. "I'm Monty's attorney and this conversation is finished." He set down winter clothes and a pair of boots he'd been carrying, presumably for Monty.

"I'm only getting started." Waylon crossed his arms over his chest, irked that they were already preparing to get him out of the hospital. "I have questions for your client that need answering."

Chance plastered on a smug smile. "According to his doctor, it'll be hours before the effects of whatever he was drugged with will wear off completely and his memory will be restored.

She suspects some kind of date rape drug. The results should be in this afternoon."

If that were true, it would take quite a lot to knock out a guy Monty's size. But what reason would Pandora Frye have for drugging him?

"There are still a few questions that he's capable of answering right now," Waylon said. "Such as his whereabouts last night before he went to Ms. Frye's residence."

Chance stood beside his sister. "Is my client under arrest?"

Waylon shook his head. "No."

"Is he being taken into custody?" Chance asked.

They could only hold him for seventy-two hours. Then they'd have to charge and arraign him or release him. Based on everything they had so far, the district attorney would only insist on cutting him loose.

"Not at the moment," Waylon said, but he was a patient guy.

"Then this conversation is done because I'm advising Mr. Powell not to answer any questions and to exercise his right to remain silent."

"Let's make it official." Waylon redirected his gaze to Monty. "Are you willing to answer any of my questions at this time?"

Monty shook his head. "I invoke my right to remain silent."

"Satisfied?" Chance asked. "As soon as he is medically able to be released, he'll be at home."

"Don't try to leave town." Waylon turned for the door. "You'll be under surveillance."

"The heads-up is appreciated," Monty said. "Unexpectedly gracious of you."

"Grace has got nothing to do with it." Waylon flicked a glance at the other detective. "You'd know anyhow." And there was more than one way to get off a ranch that was thousands of acres without being seen by one cop parked at the front gate.

In all honesty, the measure was simply procedural. "Delaney, a word in the hall."

Waylon stepped out of the room and waited for her. He had questions for Amber Reyes and Logan, too. An officer at the scene of the crime had stated that both parties had been present when the authorities arrived and made things difficult.

With Chance present, Amber already acting cagey, Logan being tightlipped and not knowing if Delaney had already helped them get their stories straight, he figured it best to catch them off guard separately without a lawyer around. Sooner rather than later he'd find out exactly why they had been at Pandora Frye's home and no attorney was going to shut down the conversation.

Delaney joined him in the hall and looked him in the eye, shoulders squared and hands clenched at her sides like she was ready for a fist fight. "Do you have more griping to do over the removal of the handcuffs?"

"No. I want you off this case."

Delaney reeled back. "Why?"

"It's obvious, isn't it. You can't be impartial."

"The same could be said of you. I heard about the bad blood between you and the suspect."

He shrugged. "Grievances of teenagers. Nothing more to it than that," he said lightly, trying to dismiss it.

"Felt like a lot more in there to me. You were practically radiating rancor."

"Then you got your wires crossed. Sure, I don't like him, but I don't have to. What happened is ancient history unlike your current romantic relationship with a relative of the suspect. In fact, don't you live on the Shooting Star Ranch, making you a tenant of his parents?"

Her chin rose at that. "The house I live in with Matt and the land it's on belongs to him. I'm not the tenant of any Powell."

"Did he buy it from his aunt and uncle or was it given to him?"

"That's irrelevant and has no bearing on whether or not I should be working this case," she said, not answering the question, which told him everything he needed to know.

"Then you're not only lying to me, but also to yourself."

"Matt's property is legally separate and considered the Little Shooting Star. Some of the income from his ranch goes to the family. But it's his choice. He's under no financial obligation to do so."

"Still sounds like a relevant conflict of interest."

"The decision isn't your call to make. It's up to the chief."

His cell phone rang. He took it from his pocket and glanced at the caller ID. "Speak of the devil."

"Mind if I'm a part of the call?" Delaney asked.

Waylon didn't care. Whatever he had to say to the chief he could say in front of her. He answered, "Wright. I'm with Delaney. Putting you on speaker, Chief."

"Good to catch you both together."

"Speaking of together," Waylon said. "I believe it's best if I work this case alone or with another detective for reasons that you're already aware of, but I'm happy to list them in writing if necessary."

Delaney appeared unfazed.

"That won't be necessary," Chief Nelson said. "This case is rightfully hers. She was the first detective able to respond. I also assigned you to alleviate any possible concerns regarding impartiality. As for a conflict of interest, I believe she's far enough removed from the suspect to do her job and see justice served."

Waylon let a bitter chuckle slip out. "I'm not surprised you think that, Chief."

"What is that supposed to mean?" Nelson snapped.

His laughter curdled in his throat as he realized, though

his comment was rooted in fact, he had overstepped with a superior officer.

The truth was the chief had almost as much reason to give the Powells preferential treatment as Delaney. Chief Nelson was married to the sheriff. The sheriff's sister was Holden Powell's wife. To muddy the waters further, Logan had assisted Wilhelmina Nelson with cleaning up the LPD, cracking a huge case wide open and cementing her as the police chief. Forget about six degrees of separation. In this small town, when it came to the Powell clan, it was more like two.

"One might say you have a possible conflict of interest as well, ma'am," Waylon admitted.

"One might, but are you saying it?"

Waylon met Delaney's prying gaze "I am. Not only are you family for all intents and purposes, but your boss, the mayor, is also the suspect's mother."

Chief Nelson cleared her throat. "I notified Mayor Powell of the situation and informed her that I'll report directly to the governor regarding this case. She emphatically agreed and then assured me that she would in no way meddle in how this was investigated. In fact, she stated that she wouldn't even go to the hospital to check in on her son because she didn't want her presence to be a distraction. I handpicked you to be the lead detective on this homicide because your reputation is above reproach and your character is unimpeachable. So I'm going to let your comment slide. Just this once. Do we understand one another?"

He clenched his jaw at the hint of a grin on Delaney's face. "We do."

"Now that all that's settled, I'm aware the suspect's fingerprints are on the knife found at the scene of the crime. But the medical examiner gave us an estimated time of death between four and seven in the morning. According to Monty's medical record, it doesn't seem that he would have been in any condition to commit the murder. He couldn't even stand up when the EMTs evaluated him."

"Another theory is he was faking it," Waylon said. "Or perhaps he killed the victim first and then took whatever drug he was strung out on."

Delaney raised an eyebrow. "Well, he didn't fake a full-blown allergic reaction."

"This is such a high-profile case I ran it by Assistant District Attorney Merritt," Chief Nelson said. "She believes the DA won't touch this case with a ten-foot pole based on what we have so far. Once his blood work comes in and we know more, we'll reevaluate."

"Speaking of which, how do you have his medical file so fast?" Waylon asked. "The warrant hasn't even been signed yet."

"I asked the suspect to release them to us," Delaney said.

Only because she thought it would help him look less guilty. And so far, it had.

"The warrant just came through," the chief said. "I called the judge and asked him to expedite it."

Now, that was surprising, and also reassuring to see the chief doing everything possible to handle this properly. With the one exception of keeping Delaney assigned.

"I noticed a security camera mounted outside above the door of the victim's residence," Delaney said. "But I wasn't given a chance to see if there was any footage."

She referred to him booting her from the crime scene.

He'd made the right choice and would make it again given the chance. "We'll have to crack her password to access her main hub, but the camera had a micro SD card. Forensics happened to have a card reader. Everything had been deleted except for footage of the night prior showing Montgomery Powell parking beside her and entering the residence along with Pandora Frye at ten thirty. Then nothing else until Amber

Reyes arrived the next morning at seven forty-eight. Followed by Logan Powell at seven fifty-two. Then the ambulance and squad car shortly thereafter."

"Odd that everything else was deleted," Delaney said.

His thoughts exactly. "I figure the victim might've had it set to automatically back up to cloud storage. If so, we'll have access to the entire history in a day or two."

"On the footage, what was the dynamic between Pandora and Monty?" Delaney asked.

"She was smiling, excited, chatted almost nonstop while she unlocked the door. Monty on the other hand didn't look too pleased to be there, but he followed her inside. The camera on the front door was missing a micro SD card."

"Get access to the cloud storage as quickly as possible," the chief said. "And, Waylon, if you have any future concerns of corruption, malfeasance or whatever doesn't smell right to you, feel free to file a report with Internal Affairs in Cheyenne. Otherwise, no more crying about who your partner is. Get the job done and keep me updated. Are we clear?"

"Crystal."

The chief hung up.

He slipped his phone back in his pocket. "We may be partners on this, but I outrank you."

"That you do, Detective *Lieutenant*. Planning to pull rank?"

A detective lieutenant wasn't typical in a large city, but with smaller departments such as theirs, not only was he senior in the investigations division, but he also needed to remain hands-on. He found it easier and simpler to be referred to as a detective while working cases and dealing with others in the division unless circumstances required him to throw his weight around.

"Not at all." Delaney was an excellent cop but had a reputation for not working well with others and a habit of going rogue. It was the only reason she hadn't been promoted a long time ago. "I only bring it up because I don't want you to give me a reason to feel like I have to. That means no coloring outside the lines. You do this by the book, work it with me, every step of the way. If Monty or anyone in that family says a single word to incriminate him or another Powell, you've got to keep me in the loop."

She hesitated for a moment.

A moment too long for his liking. "Don't forget the oath you swore. Your loyalty has to be to the badge." Waylon blew out a heavy breath. "Or you should get out of my way, do the right thing by passing on this one."

"I'm clear on my loyalties."

No doubt she was, but since she neglected to clarify, he still wasn't clear on whether her loyalty was to the Laramie Police Department or to the Powells.

"The last thing I need is an IA investigation into my conduct," she added. "They'll go through my entire history with the department and I don't need that kind of headache."

True. IA would love nothing more than to dig into her file. They'd have a field day.

Delaney straightened her shoulders. "I'll do it by the book. If I learn anything incriminating, you'll know."

He wanted to believe her. Only time would tell.

Waylon nodded and started down the hall. "Pandora Frye's parents need to be notified. Let's find out who they are and see what they have to say."

"In the spirit of an honest partnership, I need to tell you something about her parents and some land she recently inherited. This is much bigger and complicated than you realize because it gives Monty a motive. Not just him, but most of the Powells."

"Sharing is caring." Waylon couldn't wait to hear this. Maybe Delaney would prove to be more a help than a hindrance. "I'm all ears."

Chapter Four

The cell phone on her desk rang. Valentina's heart leaped with expectation at seeing the name of her enforcer whom she'd made a lieutenant on the caller ID. "Please tell me it's done, and that SOB is in jail."

"There's been a problem," Roman said. "He's in the hospital."

"I don't understand." Valentina glanced at her Rolex. "The ketamine would have worn off by the time he was arrested. He should've appeared hungover but alert."

"I had to call the police sooner than intended. I watched them carry him out, handcuffed to a stretcher, and load him into an ambulance shortly after eight."

Eight! Her chest constricted. "That was way ahead of schedule. Why would you do that? What happened?"

"Not what. Who. Amber Reyes happened. She messed up everything."

Valentina sucked in a calming breath. "Explain."

"The Reyes woman showed up more than two hours early, throwing off the timing of things," Roman said. "I had gotten out of there just before she arrived. It's a good thing I spotted her before I left. At least I called 911 right after she went inside. I'm fairly certain I made the call before she did, *if she did*, but I'm not sure if the plan will still work."

Valentina restrained impulsive words of aggravation. "You assured me you had things under control."

"And I did. Until Reyes decided to ignore the time set in the text message that I had Pandora send to her. She also must have called one of the brothers because Logan Powell showed up there, too."

So many brothers and a cousin to boot. "Remind me, which one is Logan? Is he the fire marshal?" She knew that Holden was the sheriff's deputy but couldn't keep track of the rest.

"No, that's Sawyer. Logan is with DCI."

Valentina rolled her eyes. How was it possible for them to all be in law enforcement? "Did you take pictures of everything? Time stamps on their arrival?"

"Of course. Never know if we could use something later."

She shoved back from behind her desk and paced in the office that was once her beloved father's. "This could work to our advantage. Maybe Amber Reyes and Logan Powell might have done something stupid in an effort to help Montgomery." If anyone knew how to tamper with a crime scene, it was a cop. If so, then things would work out even better than she had originally hoped. She would not only take him down, but his law enforcement brother and former fiancée, too.

"If they tried, they wouldn't have had long," Roman said. "The police were on the scene only moments after Logan stepped foot inside. Not enough time to dispose of evidence that would point to Monty. Only enough rope to hang themselves."

"Their presence will be incriminating once the detective on the case finds out they were there before the authorities, especially if you were the only one to call 911. It'll beg the question of whether they corrupted the crime scene. Do you know who's assigned to the case?"

"I do. You won't like it."

She was never one to be coddled, not even as a child. Always ready to have the Band-Aid ripped off no matter how much it would hurt. "Tell me."

"Hannah Delaney was first on the scene and they're leaving her on the case."

Valentina had never heard of the detective. "What am I missing?"

"Delaney recently started a relationship with the cousin. Matt Granger. It's serious. They're engaged. Live together on the family ranch."

Letting out a growl of frustration, she picked up her coffee cup and threw it against the wall, smashing the mug to pieces. For a reckless second, she considered ordering Roman to shoot Montgomery Powell in the head. But then she remembered the promise she'd made to her father—his dying wish for Montgomery to suffer the way her brother had—and stopped herself.

"There is good news," Roman said. "Waylon Wright was made the lead detective. From what I've heard, he hates the Powells. Any shred of evidence that points to Montgomery being guilty, he'll chase it. The man is a bloodhound. Nothing and no one will get in his way."

One small consolation in the face of this unmitigated disaster. "Why did that wretched woman have to show up so early and ruin months of meticulous planning?" Amber Reyes would have to pay.

"It was way too soon for the authorities to find Montgomery. We needed at least another ninety minutes. Possibly two hours. I gave him a precise dose for his body weight. He would've been awake on his own by then. The authorities only would've run a general tox screen to check his blood alcohol content and to see if he did any of the cocaine that I left in the studio, but now they'll order a full panel. They'll find the ketamine in his system."

I should've taken care of it myself.

She dropped down in her chair. Tapping her long finger-nails—painted the color of blackened berries—on her desk, she considered the situation. Forced herself to focus on the things going in their favor. "This is simply a hiccup." Concentrating on the positives and how to maximize them was the only way forward. She never wallowed.

"No. This is worse than that. There's more. It's my under-standing that he had a reaction to ketamine. I couldn't have known he'd be allergic, but it's still my fault. *Perdóname.*"

Roman—once her father's right-hand man and now hers—made it difficult to remain angry with him. He was fiercely loyal. Took responsibility for his mistakes, which were rare. When they did occur, he always asked for forgiveness.

He was also quite attractive. Slick bald head and a touch of stubble, giving him that rough appeal she found alluring. An excellent lover, too. She'd sampled his goods herself. If only she didn't need him for the dirty work, like seducing Pandora Frye and killing her, she might've given him a place at her side. As her partner. Not as equals, of course. She would remain in charge of her father's empire, as queen, while he could've been her prince consort.

It was lonely at the top. The seat of power was never meant to fall to her. Santiago was supposed to take over the cartel, but with her brother's brutal death, she was the only one left to reign.

Her heart ached. She could use her father's wise counsel now. He would know precisely what to do to avenge Santiago.

All she could do was trust in the plan. And in Roman. The one person she could count on.

"You're taking great risks for me," she said. *For her father. For Santiago.* Far beyond the scope of anyone else in her or-ganization. "Thank you. Now we have to do damage control."

"I don't know how it'll play out," Roman said, "but I don't think they're going to arrest him just yet."

Focus on the endgame. "Whether or not he ends up in jail today matters little." Ultimately, his final destination would be a cell behind bars, where he would watch, helpless to do anything, while she tore apart his family. Only then would he die. While incarcerated. Painfully. Slowly. The way her brother had. "The first seed of doubt has been planted. His character and motives will be questioned. Opportunity, means and motive are clearly there. He won't be allowed to return to his position with the state police unless this is resolved in his favor. This will give us the chance we need for the next step."

"I won't be able to be your eyes and ears at the hospital. I'm not sure when he'll be discharged."

Roman was working on something else equally important for her.

"Never mind that. I'll send Leo to get an update. It'll be easier for him to contact me." Her driver was a capable man, interested in taking on a larger role in the organization.

"I'm sorry. If this murder doesn't stick to him—"

"We can't wait to find out. We need to expedite the rest of the plan. Starting today."

"Move up the timeline on everything?"

"Yes."

"Are you sure that's wise? It could raise unwanted suspicion."

"We have no choice now. Do your part. On my end, I'll get Leo to help me. It'll be the perfect test for him," Valentina said. There was more than one way to make a person suffer. "I've got to go. I need to reach out to our contact inside the highway patrol."

The day after Montgomery hit her family's radar, she'd begun her search for the perfect person to infiltrate the state troopers. One thing her father taught her was to never underestimate the power of an inside man.

"You're going to have the phone planted?" Roman asked.

"Yes. Go handle the remaining things on your end. Don't fail me again." Before he made any promises, she hung up. Then she dialed Officer Nicholas Foley. "It's me. I need to put you in play."

"Yes, ma'am. How may I be of service?"

"The item I sent for you to hold until I gave further instructions," she said, referring to the burner phone, "needs to be found in Montgomery Powell's locker when it's searched." The phone was Roman's suggestion. Once he explained his rationale behind the idea, she'd wholeheartedly agreed that planting the phone at the right time would be genius.

"You're sure it will be searched?" Foley asked.

If the LPD was doing their job, his locker would definitely be searched. She couldn't give any guarantees, but, if necessary, she'd get Nicholas to whisper a suggestion in the right ear. "I'm sure this must be done."

"It might prove difficult."

"You're not being paid double what you're making wearing the badge because you were going to be asked to do something easy. Get it done. Within the hour."

"I'm on patrol. I can't just leave and waltz into the station."

Excuses were number two on her list of things she hated, right after failure. "Figure it out. Quickly. Or I have no further use for you. Or your wife." Both were her employees. Both would suffer the consequences. "Do you understand what I'm saying?"

"Yes, ma'am. I'll see that it's done."

"You had better. For your wife's sake, if not for your own." She hung up and had one of her guards posted near her office fetch Leo.

He knocked twice.

"Come in," she said.

Leo entered, eyeing the broken mug on the floor. "Would you like me to have someone clean it up?"

"No." The maid would take care of it later. She beckoned him forward.

Dressed in his usual simple, off-the-rack, black suit and white shirt with a skinny necktie, he stopped right in front of her desk, hands clasped behind his back like a good little soldier still in the army. He followed orders so well, sometimes she found it hard to believe he had ever been dishonorably discharged.

"Time to get your hands dirty," Valentina said. "Go to Laramie. Montgomery Powell is in the hospital. Send me updates on his status. I want to know when he's released and who his visitors are. Then I need you to put your sniper skills to use." She removed a folder from her top desk drawer and opened it. Sifting through the photos, she found the one she wanted and slid the glossy 4x6 across the desk to him. "This is your target."

His dark eyes widened. "Really? Him?"

She gave a single nod.

"Do you want him injured or—"

"Dead. A bullet to the stomach would be better than the heart." When he raised an eyebrow, she explained. "Nice slow bleed-out over an instant kill shot." *To give loved ones false hope.* "And I'd prefer you to do it in front of Montgomery, if at all possible. They live on a compound. You'll have to get creative. There'd be a sweet bonus in it for the personal touch provided you can pull it off where Montgomery can see it."

Leo grinned. "I'll head out now."

"Max will go with you," she said, deciding on the guard with the hulking chest and goatee to accompany him. Max would keep an eye on Leo and report back on how he handled himself.

Leo picked up the picture and stared at the target. "What have you got against Montgomery Powell, if you don't mind me asking?"

An eye for an eye. She wanted that man to suffer unimaginably. Before he died, he'd feel the same heart-wrenching pain that she had endured. The thought of her brother, beaten and stabbed in jail, and her father's subsequent stroke had her chest constricting again. She had to concentrate to take a simple breath.

"I do mind," she said. "All you need to know is that you begged for this opportunity to prove yourself. Don't waste it."

Leo slid the picture into his pocket. As he opened the office door, her nephew bolted into the room faster than a rocket. He was holding Legos and a piece fell off, clattering to the floor. A harried nanny ran in after him, and Leo left, closing the door.

"Auntie Val, Auntie Val! Look what I made." The four-year-old leaped into her lap.

"Let's see it."

Julian held up the toy.

She scrutinized it for a moment. "Is it a gun?"

"No, silly." He giggled. "It's an airplane."

"Of course, it is, but it's lost a wing." Not her fault he held it like a gun and a piece was missing. "You're so smart and creative." She ruffled his dark curls and hugged him tight. Every time she held her brother's son, she felt a little closer to Santiago.

"I'm sorry, madam." The nanny wrung her hands as her face creased with worry. "He got away from me."

"I was about to take a break anyway. Julian, how about we have lunch together today?"

"Yippee!" He hopped down. "Can we have pizza and carrots?"

"Of course." Valentina closed the file, covering the pictures of the rest of the Powell family and tucked it back in her desk.

One way or another, Montgomery was going to get what was coming to him.

Of that, she would make certain.

Chapter Five

Amber walked through the lobby of the hospital alongside
Logan and Monty, who sat in a wheelchair, pushed by Nurse
Shelby. Chance had left a couple of hours earlier to go over
the case with the top criminal defense attorney in Cheyenne
and was planning to meet them at the Shooting Star Ranch for
a family meeting.

As they neared the exit, she slowed to a stop. "That vile
reporter, Erica Egan, is waiting outside. She even has a camera guy."

"I thought she was bad before," Logan said, "but her pro-
motion to the KLBR TV station has only emboldened her."

"Are they here because of Mr. Powell?" Shelby asked.

"Yeah, they are." Logan's voice sounded tight and annoyed.
"No way they've been waiting out there in the cold for hours.
Someone must've tipped them off that you were being dis-
charged."

"I can take you to a different exit. Most people don't know
about it. We use it for mothers with newborns, so they don't
have to encounter as many folks."

"That'd be great," Logan said.

Monty nodded. "Much appreciated."

"It's this way." Shelby turned down a hall on the right.

"I'll use the main exit to distract them," Amber said. Her father's death had been big news in the area. Reporters jumped at the opportunity to remind everyone how close the Powell and Reyes families were. She'd caught her picture in the paper and on TV more than once since she'd been home. "I'll meet you at the house."

"See you soon." Logan flashed her a sad smile. "Thanks for everything."

Down the hall, Monty grumbled, "I'm fine to walk on my own. I don't need a wheelchair."

"Sorry, it's policy," Shelby said. "You're free to do as you please once you leave the hospital."

Amber stood still, giving them time to reach the less frequented exit. Once they disappeared from sight, she headed for the sliding doors.

"Ms. Reyes." Erica Egan rushed toward her, holding up a microphone. Her colleague pointed the camera at Amber. "Were you here at the hospital to see Montgomery Powell?"

Although Amber wanted to run to her vehicle, she forced herself to slow down. "I was here for personal reasons." Over the shoulders of Egan and the cameraman, she spotted Logan and Monty hurrying across the parking lot.

"Would those reasons have anything to do with Mr. Powell?" Egan asked.

"As I've already stated, it was personal."

"What to do you think of Monty Powell being the prime suspect in the murder of Pandora Frye?"

Stopping, she gathered her thoughts. "First, the murder is a horrific tragedy. Second, I believe the evidence will eventually show that Monty is innocent."

"Are you saying he isn't capable of murder?" Egan thrust the mic back in Amber's face.

"Yes, I am."

Logan's truck zipped out of the lot and turned onto the road.

"A source has told me that the two were lovers and this was a crime of passion," Egan said. "How long were they sleeping together?"

Amber's cheeks burned, her chest tightening. All she could do was shake her head at the accusation.

"Would you care to comment, Ms. Reyes?"

"Yes. Get better sources. Please excuse me." Amber pushed past them and hustled toward her Jeep. She dug into her purse, rifling through it for her keys. Why hadn't she simply put them in her pocket?

Finally, she found them. She hit the key fob, unlocking the door, and rushed around the rear to get to the driver's-side door.

"Ms. Reyes." Waylon Wright tipped his hat at her. "I have a couple of quick questions for you."

He'd been waiting to ambush her.

She looked around. No sign of Hannah. "I'm sorry, but I need to go. I'm expected somewhere."

"At the Shooting Star Ranch for a big Powell meeting? I figure they'd be keen to circle the wagons since Monty has been discharged."

She swallowed past the lump in her throat. "I don't have time to talk right now." She reached for the door.

But he stepped in the way, blocking the handle. "This won't take long. Make time. Unless you have something to hide. See, I'm starting to get the sneaking suspicion that you might. Considering how you insisted that Monty not talk to me. An innocent person has nothing to fear."

"Monty is innocent, but I believe he has a great deal to fear from you. As for insisting that he wait for his lawyer before answering questions, it was common sense. He wasn't in a good state of mind since he was under the influence of—"

"Ketamine. Yes, I'm aware. His blood work came back." He pulled out a notepad and pen. "Still doesn't explain your reluctance to answer a few questions yourself. Might that have something to do with the terms of your father's trust?"

She stiffened. "What do you mean?"

"It's simple. The land you stand to inherit has a river running through it. A river that is vital to the Shooting Star Ranch because their cattle depend on it. Your father had a neighborly agreement with the Powells, giving them access to the water until his death. If you don't marry Monty Powell in a little less than a month, then you'd lose everything and Pandora Frye stood to inherit it all. It would explain why he was sleeping with her," Waylon said, and the fire in her cheeks spread to her chest. "As an insurance policy in case things didn't work out with you. But maybe things turned sour last night, giving him a motive to kill her."

Amber shook her head. "The amount of ketamine in his system would've been too high."

"He could've killed her and then taken ketamine."

"Why would he do such a thing?"

"To put reasonable doubt in the mind of a jury." He rested his forearm on her 4x4. "A cop planning a murder would think of that kind of thing."

"Not Monty."

"You seem certain. If he's such a great guy, why haven't you married him? Based on your father's will, I'm sure he'd make an eager husband."

Fiddling with her keys, she averted his keen gaze. "Marriage should be based on love. Not money." But she couldn't squeeze blood from stone. She never wanted any man to feel forced to marry her. "Monty is flawed, but he isn't a murderer."

"For the Powells, that river and your land it's on are priceless. Even if he didn't kill her, it still gives every member of his family a motive. Also gives you a pretty big one, too."

Amber staggered back a step, shocked at the redirection of his line of questioning. "Are you accusing me?"

"Why were you at your half sister's house this morning? And if you even think of stonewalling me, I'll cross this parking lot and give Erica Egan the scoop of her life. She'd gladly swallow every crumb I threw her way, particularly the part about you being at the scene of the crime. This can play out in the court of public opinion if you want."

Egan would paint a story that was thirteen shades of ugly, portraying Monty or even her as a cold-blooded, greedy murderer. Amber sighed, her breath crystallizing in the chilly air. "I assume you know that she also inherited my family home."

Waylon gave a single, slow nod. "I do."

"I wanted her to sell it to me and Chance. She agreed to meet me. To discuss it. She texted me last night, telling me to come over this morning."

"May I see the text?"

He already seemed to know so much. What harm could it do?

She pulled out her phone and brought it up.

Waylon took her cell, glanced at it and scrolled through several other messages. "You've had some heated exchanges back and forth."

Lowering her head, she did her best to tamp down the spurt of anger. "I didn't know I had a half sister until the reading of the will. Not the best way to find out. I just lost my father and I didn't want to lose our family home, too."

"The message told you to come at ten. Why did you arrive so early?"

She huffed out a breath. "It was silly. I've been working as a substitute teacher while I'm in town. School starts at nine. I felt like inconveniencing her rather than be the one inconvenienced."

"Are you involved with Monty?"

Blood drained from her face, her entire body growing heavy as stone. "W-w-we aren't a couple."

The corner of his mouth hitched up. "Have you ever been romantically involved?"

She clenched her fingers around her keys. "Years ago."

"What about since you've been home, after the reading of the will and he learned about the trust?"

Everything inside her went numb. She glanced past him at the door. "This is taking too long. I need to go."

"When you arrived early at your sister's place and discovered that Monty was with her, did it anger you?"

"Half sister." She looked up at him. "If you're asking me whether or not I killed her, I didn't. I swear it. The front door wasn't closed all the way. It swung open after I knocked. She was already dead."

"I believe you," he said, quickly, easily.

Relief crept through her. "You do?"

Waylon nodded. "You got there at seven forty-eight. You didn't kill her. But I think you were worried that Monty had. Why else would you call Logan?"

She grimaced. How did he know that?

"This looks bad," Waylon said. "Your phone call could get Logan into a lot of trouble, legally, professionally, but an honest answer could make it better."

The last thing she wanted was to incriminate Logan in some way or make this worse. "I freaked out." She shrugged. "He popped to mind because I realized he would know what to do."

"What did he tell you?"

She hesitated.

"I only want the truth," he said, his tone comforting and sincere, "and you've got nothing to hide, right?"

"He told me that he was at Divine Treats and would come straight over, but to hang up and call 911."

"Logan told you to call right away *before* he got there?"

She nodded. "He insisted on it."

Waylon handed over her phone.

The screen was on her recent calls. He'd toggled over and had already seen how long they'd spoken and that she'd called the authorities right after. "Were you testing me?"

"I prefer to think of it as poking around to get a good sense of a person." He stepped away from her Jeep. "You never answered my question. Have you been romantically involved with Monty since you've been home?"

This man kept finding ways to corner her and squeeze out answers. "You lied, Detective Wright." She opened her door.

He narrowed his eyes. "That's the first time anyone has ever accused me of lying. About what exactly?"

She climbed inside the Jeep. "You said this wasn't going to take long. Now, I'm late for an important meeting."

"Apologies, ma'am. I stand corrected. And that's twice you've dodged the same question about the nature of your relationship with Monty since the reading of the will. Some might consider that an answer."

Amber closed the door, cranked the engine and peeled out of the lot.

Chapter Six

Friday, December 6
4:45 p.m.

A hundred different things crawled through Monty's head with his brain still pounding as he rested his eyes during the drive to the ranch. He was grateful for the silence.

In a few minutes there would be nonstop chatter and strategizing.

"We're here," Logan said far too soon.

Monty opened his eyes. "This is a nightmare."

His brother gave a grunt of assent and put the truck in Park.

"Thanks for having my back, looking out for me."

"Always. You're my brother." Logan pressed his lips in a firm line, his jaw tightening.

Clearly, his brother was weighing his words, deciding if he should give voice to them. "Are you going to spit it out or keep it to yourself?"

"Most of what I have to say should probably wait until we're all together."

"And the rest of it, you want to get off your chest now?"

"This isn't about whether you're guilty. I know you didn't kill anyone."

"Thanks. I'm sensing a *but* there."

"But sleeping with Pandora, the fact that Amber had to

see you with her, like that." Logan shook his head. "Her of all people."

"I don't even know why Amber was there, but that's beside the point. I didn't—"

"I'm not finished," Logan said, cutting him off. "You really hurt her bad with the engagement, scheming with Dad and Mom, lying to her the way you did. When are you going to stop being a source of pain for her?" He clenched his hand into a fist. "Enough is enough. I won't stand by and watch you do it again. So help me, I'll knock your head off myself first. Do you hear me?" Logan jumped out, slamming the door closed behind him.

Monty scrubbed a hand over his face, wanting to disregard Logan's anger. After all, Logan was his least favorite brother and that included Matt in that count. Yet, the brutally honest words rang true in his head.

To many, his history with Amber looked black-and-white. Simple. It was anything but.

He stared up at his family home. His parents had meticulously crafted the house. Floor-to-ceiling windows, ten bedrooms, twelve bathrooms, gourmet kitchen, gym, movie room and state-of-the-art automation. They had designed it to entice their children to stay close. They often talked about their legacy, the importance of the ranch, about all the weddings, holiday celebrations and big birthdays they wanted to have here. With plenty of room for grandkids, extended family, in-laws and friends to stay.

More than a home, more than a ranch, this sanctuary embodied their hopes and dreams. And those of many Powells before them who had sacrificed so much in the hope it would be passed to the next generation.

He'd never wanted the responsibility of that legacy. Fought against it for as long and as hard as he could until that fateful day in the kitchen with his folks.

He could still hear his parents like it was yesterday.

"All I've ever wanted was for my sons to take up the mantle," Dad said. "Do what my father and his father before him has done. Hold tight to the ranch, grow, prosper. I have five boys and a nephew I love like a son. Six of you. I figured at least one of you would surely want to run this place."

"I can't speak for the others," Monty said. "I want to be my own man. Make my own choices. Live my own life. Not one you've decreed." He turned to his mother. "You claim all you want is for us to be happy."

"That's true," she said. "But you seem miserable being a state trooper. Driving around handing out speeding tickets half the time. Like you picked that job just to spite us."

Monty heaved a breath. "You're missing the point. I picked it. It was my choice."

"This land, being a part of the ranch, working with the cattle makes you happy," she said. "It's what you were born to do. I've seen how you thrive." She sighed. "Amber has been in love with you forever and I know that if you open your heart to her, you're bound to fall in love. And unlike most of those fast fillies you usually go after, Amber will stand up to you and not let you treat like her garbage, which is what you need. A woman with a backbone."

Monty chuckled. He'd pay to see that. The reality was Amber doted on him every chance she got. He could do no wrong in her eyes.

He didn't want a doormat. Even if she was perfect for him, which she wasn't, he still wouldn't want her—a woman picked for him by his parents, a bride he was expected to marry.

Like this ranch that he was expected to love and oversee until the day he died.

No, thank you.

"The two of you are opposite sides of the same coin." Mom took his hands in hers and met his eyes. "You could have a

wonderful marriage with Amber. Just give it a chance. Put the work in and really try. You'll see."

Pulling away, he turned his back on her. "No."

"Yes! You, insolent son of a gun!" his father said, his eyes filled with anger and...pain. "I have never asked anything of you. We have never asked. If we don't control that land with the river, anything could happen to it. You don't marry her, the land will go to someone else. A person with no love for our family. Someone who might one day decide to dam it."

"Whoever it is, we could buy from them," Monty said, suggesting a reasonable solution.

"We can't tell you who." His father clenched his jaw. "But trust me. That person won't take our money. Their ears have been poisoned against the idea. They'll sell it, perhaps to someone who wants to build a big, noisy resort. Frightened cattle with no access to water means the end of this ranch. You don't do this, everything we've built will be lost."

Monty grimaced, his heart throbbing like an open wound.

"For once in your spoiled life, you're going to put this family ahead of yourself!" Dad jabbed a finger in his chest. "We need the river and you're the only one who can get it for us. You'll marry that girl. Get yourself a sidepiece if need be."

Mom gasped. "Buck! How dare you. Amber deserves a real husband."

"A cheating husband is still a real one," Dad said.

Monty imagined sex with Amber as vanilla. Boring. She was so young, seven years his junior. He'd never seen her go out with anyone, and she was probably a virgin. He preferred spicy girls with more experience, but he would never humiliate her or any wife by treating her like that. "I'm not the cheating kind."

"Even better." Dad threw his hands up. "We need you to do this, son."

As much as Monty despised the idea, the pressure was un-

relenting, making him consider it. "If I did do this, I'd have to tell her up-front that it's just for convenience only."

"You can't." Mom shook her head, her eyes weary. She looked bone-tired. "Carlos made it very clear. He doesn't want her to know. That's why he's putting things into motion now, long before he dies, and she learns she'll inherit all the land."

Of course, Mr. Reyes wanted this to feel organic for Amber rather than orchestrated. He'd like to give that man a piece of his mind, trying to dictate whom Monty should marry, whom he should love, how he should live. Just as bad and manipulative as his parents.

"Don't tell her. Woo her. Get hitched," Dad said. "Give it a solid go for two years, putting in the work like your mother said. Those are the rules. After that, you can decide about forever and it'll be whatever life you want. Free from the legacy that you're too good to carry on, and may I live long enough to have a grandchild who'll do so."

Monty felt like a block of stone split in two, cracked right down the middle, but keeping the truth from Amber made him sick to his stomach. "No. I won't do it."

A week later his father had a heart attack. At his bedside, his mother begged Monty to agree.

Was it weakness? Fear? Love? Duty? All Monty knew was he'd caved.

He courted Amber and proposed. For the land. For the river. To make everyone, other than himself, happy.

They all thought he'd told Amber some great lie.

But he never said those three little words, *I love you.* Not once. He never painted a rosy picture of happily-ever-after. Never whispered sweet things in her ear. Never wooed her. Never seduced her. He didn't have to do any of that stuff. Plainly asked her out and things went from there. She had been the one to initiate sex. As he'd guessed, she'd been a virgin. He'd underestimated the power of that experience on both sides. To be her first everything—not something he took lightly.

The truth was, he didn't have to put in much effort to get the relationship to bloom. She got caught up in a fantasy of her own making, and he let her.

He let her because it made her happy. He let her because his parents had promised his duty would be done. No more pressure for him to take over the ranch if only he married Amber Reyes. He let her because he reached a point where he believed he could make it work. Make it real. Give her what she needed. Saw she was what he wanted after all. As much as he'd been loath to admit it, his mother had been right about him and Amber. Forced together, a collision of smashing pieces, they fit and became easily entangled.

They had just found their footing as a couple, enjoying the discovery of one another, with him surprisingly excited for the future. A future with her. Instead of feeling he had settled for someone else's choice, he simply felt settled. Delighted by how deeply, madly he'd fallen for her. How she knew him better than he knew himself. Like they were really meant to be.

Then it fell apart. Because he hadn't been honest.

Still, he'd been wrong to do it. After she left, he missed her something awful. A lot more than he ever thought possible. There was a hole in his life, where she had always been. Sometimes he lay awake at night, especially during the past four months—thinking about Amber, about the time they'd spent together, about how right she felt in his arms, about how the sex had been vanilla sweet and spicy hot, the best of both—and he tossed and turned. Sick down in his soul with regret.

Now everyone probably thought history was repeating itself and he'd lured Pandora Frye into some romantic web.

What a fool he'd been to go to her place last night only to talk about a potential deal they could make for the land if Amber didn't marry him. His mountain of mistakes kept growing higher.

He had a sinking feeling that he was playing right into someone's hands. Whoever had killed Pandora was trying to frame him for murder.

But why? Did it have something to do with the Reyes land? The river? Or was there another reason?

Until he had answers, he might have a tough time proving his innocence.

Chapter Seven

Friday, December 6
5:06 p.m.

By the time she pulled up to the sprawling Shooting Star Ranch, which was really a compound, and waited for the grand wrought iron gate to open, she was fuming.

Where was Hannah? How did Waylon find out the details of the trust so fast? Had Detective Delaney told her new partner?

The main house came into sight with a mesmerizing backdrop of the mountains. A modest term for the massive estate that was a haven of luxury.

A lifetime ago, this had been a place that Amber loved. Not for the amenities or upgrades that the Reyes house lacked. Once, in a dream never meant to be, she'd thought this ranch was going to be home.

She pulled into the circular driveway behind a long line of vehicles. The only two people who wouldn't be at the meeting were Jackson and Sawyer. They'd both come to her father's funeral. It had been nice to catch up with them and to discover Sawyer had married his high school sweetheart, Liz. Theirs was a tragic story but one with a happy ending. It would be nice to see them again in a couple of weeks for Christmas.

The rest of the boys lived on the ranch. Holly and Buck had built Monty a cottage farther back from the main house after he had proposed to her. Meant for the two of them. Holden and his wife had their own cottage now, with a fourteen-month-old son and another baby on the way. The kind of life Amber had once fantasized about having with Monty, being his wife, living on this ranch. Even though her dream had crumbled to ash because of his lie, he'd still decided to move into the house that was supposed to be theirs, where they were going to have a family and raise their children.

Climbing the stone steps of the main house, she put her hand on her belly one last time. Once she walked through those doors, she didn't dare call any attention to the life growing inside her.

She didn't bother to knock. They never locked the front door and already expected her.

"You made it," Buck called out to her as he came down the stairs. At sixty-five with salt-and-pepper hair, he exuded the virility and indomitable strength of a man half his age. After his heart attack, he'd cut back on drinking and stopped eating red meat. He was still handsome in the fit and tailored way of the wealthy. In his arms, he carried his first grandchild, Kayce, and his daughter-in-law was beside him.

Grace was a nurse and the nicest person, caring and thoughtful, making sure that Amber had everything she needed the week of her father's funeral, though they barely knew each other. Since then, she called regularly to check on Amber and invite her to lunch.

Not only was Grace easy to like but also a natural beauty. Flawless brown complexion and sparkling eyes. At eight months pregnant, she glowed, her belly round and tight under the empire waist of her dress, hair falling in long, dark curls around her shoulders. All soft curves and fertility. Somehow, she had only gained weight in her stomach. While Amber was practically subsisting on crackers and already packing on the pounds. But Grace's mother was the famous supermodel Selene Beauvais, which was like hitting the genetic lottery.

"They're in the great room talking now." Grace gave her a warm embrace. The best hugger, too. "Kayce was napping in a guest room and woke up. Buck insisted on coming with me to get him."

"I was so focused on ranching when my own were young that I didn't realize how much I missed until this little fellow was born." Beaming, Buck kissed the boy's forehead. "They grow so fast. I don't want to miss a single minute this time around." He stared into the boy's bright brown eyes. "You're going to grow up to be a rancher like your grandpa. Aren't you? Say yes, yes, I am," he said with a smile for the child in his arms. "As soon as you're old enough to ride, I'm buying you a pony."

"You're going to spoil him," Grace said.

"That's what grandfathers are supposed to do."

Kayce was the perfect mix of Holden and Grace. Tan with curly blond hair and a calm temperament, and he'd slept through the night since he was three months old. Amber had only seen him fussy if he was hungry.

"Do you want to hold him?" Buck offered.

Amber loved holding babies, the way they smelled, how their warmth soothed something in her soul, but with her hormones all over the place today she worried touching Kayce might bring tears to her eyes.

"I wouldn't dare deny you the pleasure," Amber said. "I'll get a chance the next time Grace and I have lunch."

"Which I hope will be soon." Grace took her arm and ushered her deeper into the house. "Since I'm on leave from the hospital until this one comes," she said, rubbing her belly, "I have free time. We better make the most of it while we can."

Smiling, Amber nodded. "With two under two, you're going to have your hands full."

Grace flashed her a weary expression. "That's an understatement."

"Your mom is flying out soon from Los Angeles to help, right?"

Buck and Grace laughed in unison.

"My mom is coming, but it'll be like having a third child to take care of. She can be pretty high maintenance."

"Holly is on it," Buck said. "She's already spoken to Selene and is putting her up in the main house this time. She also hired one of the best night nurses in the area to help you and Holden for the first few weeks."

"Wow." Grace put a hand to her chest. "But they're so expensive. I can manage. Women do it all the time."

Buck clasped her shoulder. "What's the money for, sweetie, if not to make your lives easier. It's a Christmas gift. Please don't tell her I spoiled the surprise, or I'll never hear the end of it."

Grace smiled. "I won't. Promise."

Raised voices carried from the great room around the corner.

"Waylon thinks you were sleeping with Pandora to get your hands on the land," Hannah said.

"It wouldn't be the first time you've done something like that." Logan's voice held a bitter note that Amber knew was on her behalf.

"If you were," Holden said, "we'd understand, but we need to know."

"I wasn't." Monty's tone was sharp. "She's not my type."

"Are you sure you weren't lovers?" Chance asked. "We all know you've compromised your integrity before to do your duty to this family, regardless of the woman not being your type or who got hurt in the end."

Another person on her side.

"I made a mistake with your sister. I regret ever laying a finger on her wit—"

Buck let out a loud, whooping cough, drawing everyone's attention to them as they entered. Silence descended like a foul odor.

Humiliation burned Amber's cheeks as her stomach sank. Taking a seat in a chair on the far side of the room, she avoided eye contact with the others. She slipped off her gloves and coat, wanting to disappear into the furniture. Maybe she shouldn't have come. But Pandora's murder affected both their families and the prime suspect was the father of her unborn child.

Tension hung over the room, finally eased by a tiny squeal of pleasure coming from Kayce as he smacked his grandpa's cheeks.

She dared look up and found Monty staring at her with a mix of sadness and something else she couldn't quite name. Maybe pity. She was pitiable right then after his declaration about her to all of them.

He stood and took a step in her direction when Holly waltzed into the room. Her presence had him shuffling back and sitting down.

His mother came from the opposite hall and entrance, accompanied by her assistant, Eddie Porter, and her campaign manager turned chief of staff, Brianne Mallard—a woman who never stopped managing Holly's public image.

"Why are you all so silent and still?" Holly asked. "What happened?" Her gaze scanned the room, landing on Amber, and the new mayor pursed her lips. "Oh. I see everyone has arrived. What did I miss?"

"We're discussing whether Monty was sleeping with Pandora," Logan said. "Because it definitely looks that way."

Amber's stomach lurched.

"And I've already told them that I wasn't." Monty leaned forward and rested his forearms on his thighs. "But they don't believe me."

"It's understandable if you're reluctant to admit to it. We

just need to be sure." Hannah scooted to the edge of her seat beside Matt. "Waylon is going to look for proof that you're lying about this because it makes the most sense in light of the terms of the Reyes trust."

Staring at the detective, Amber fumed all over again. The woman was a newcomer to this inner circle. She and Matt had been together less than a year. Although they were engaged, she didn't wear a ring, there was no talk of marriage, or a wedding or kids, and it was plain to see that his uncle Buck and aunt Holly didn't know what to make of it. Amber had asked Matt about it once while casually chatting and he'd intimated that he didn't want to *push* the detective and was happy simply living together. Another thing that raised eyebrows in this circle.

No telling where Delaney's loyalties rested. Amber couldn't hold her tongue a second longer. "How did Waylon find out the details of the trust so fast? He knew everything and interrogated me about it in the hospital parking lot. He only stopped short of accusing me of murdering her, too. Did you tell him?"

The full force of everyone's scrutiny swung to the traitor in their midst. "We spoke to Fiona Frye. She's in Arizona, visiting family. We had to inform her about her daughter's murder over the phone." She hung her head like that had been the hardest task in the world. "She's flying back sometime late tomorrow. We'll get an official statement from her in person on Sunday, but she didn't hesitate to accuse this family of murdering her daughter. Because of the land." Hannah turned to Monty. "She claims she has proof that you were sleeping together."

Monty turned pale as a ghost and looked like he'd just been slapped upside the head by one. "That's impossible."

"She said Pandora was seeing someone," Hannah said, "but her daughter couldn't talk about it yet until things were official. Legally. That by the time her mother got back from

Arizona it would be and she'd be able to tell her everything. Apparently, Pandora also gave her a flash drive as insurance."

"What's on the drive?" Monty asked.

Hannah shook her head. "She never looked. Fiona says her desktop computer is thirty years old and doesn't even have a USB port on it, but she's confident it'll prove you two were in a relationship."

"I can dig up dirt on Pandora Frye and her mother," Brianne said, with a spark in her eyes. "Feed it to the press. Change the narrative. Get us control of the story."

A horrified look crossed Holly's face. "We're not talking about an opponent in an election. Fiona is grieving the loss of her only child. We won't get dirty by tarnishing Pandora's reputation. Or hers."

"Not even if it helps Monty?" Eddie pushed his glasses up the bridge of his nose and smoothed back his hair. "And in turn the whole family? Guilt by association is a real thing for the constituents." He was a mild-mannered, soft-spoken man, at Holly's beck and call.

"He's right." Brianne typed away with one hand on her tablet. "We need to think of your public image."

"No," Holly said, with a wag of her finger. "Not another word about it."

Everyone was just going to let Hannah Delaney skate by without answering the question. Cops and lawyers were good at that, but Amber was equally good at catching it. "Did you tell Waylon about the trust?" Amber asked. "Yes or no."

The detective's gaze flashed up, meeting hers. "Yes, I did."

Matt sighed with a shake of his head. "We should go."

"No." Hannah turned, angling toward her fiancé. "I'm not scurrying out the door with my tail between my legs. They need to understand I made the right call."

"Explain it, then," Buck demanded. "Why you'd hand Waylon a motive on a silver platter?"

"Because as soon as we spoke to the mother, he was going to find out anyway. Figured it was better to use it to my advantage. Before I told him, he was certain he wanted me removed from this case and now he's not so sure. If I'm not on it, then I can't pass along information."

"Such as?" Buck handed the baby to Grace and put his hands on his hips.

"The direction the case is headed."

"Go on," Amber said. "We're going to need more than that."

The detective narrowed her eyes. "The warrant was approved. Monty's truck, house, even his locker at work is going to be searched. Tomorrow, once they have enough officers available to handle it. Since he lives here, they'll have access to the whole ranch. Waylon is planning to use that full authority."

Buck pivoted on his heel and glanced over his shoulder. "You got anything to hide, son?"

"No, sir."

Amber huffed a breath. "Don't say anything else."

Monty rubbed his temples like his head still ached. "But I don't have anything to hide."

"This information sharing is a two-way street," Amber said. "Everything we say, she's going to report."

"Is that true?" Buck asked the detective.

But Logan answered, "It is."

The traitor nodded. "Yes, I have to. I'm still a cop working this case and Waylon is the lead on it."

"We can't talk freely. She shouldn't stay." Amber jumped to her feet. The room spun. She reached out for the closest thing to steady herself and sent a lamp crashing to the floor. Stumbling, she headed for a face-plant, but Chance and Monty leaped up and were at her side. They each grabbed hold of one of her arms.

"Are you okay?" Monty asked.

A new twinge in her stomach around her belly button stole

her breath. "Fine." Amber shook her head, trying to ward off the dizziness. "Low blood sugar. I haven't eaten today. Shouldn't have moved so fast."

"How does a piece of lasagna and a glass of wine sound?" Holly asked. "I'm sure you could use a drink after the day you've had."

Her stomach roiled. "Crackers and ginger ale would be perfect."

"You need to hydrate," Chance whispered.

Holly crossed the room, took hold of her arm and shooed the others away. "Let's go to the kitchen. Grace, darling, please join us."

"Matt," Buck snapped.

"I know, sir." Matt rose from the love seat. "Come on," he said to the detective. "We're leaving. Now."

Grace passed the baby to her husband and trailed them to the kitchen, along with Brianne and Eddie.

Holly sat Amber in a chair at the long wooden table near the marble island. "Grace, please make sure she's all right." Holly whispered something to Eddie, who ducked inside the walk-in pantry.

Grace poured a glass of water, handed it to her before the nurse took a seat beside her and proceeded to take her pulse.

Clutching her tablet, Brianne leaned against the wall, looking bored.

"Here you go." Holly took something from Eddie and shoved it in Amber's face.

A plate with a peeled banana.

The smell made Amber gag. "I think I'm going to be sick."

Holly handed the plate back to Eddie. "You're pregnant."

"What?" Amber stared up at her, horrified by the emphatic statement.

"You haven't eaten all day, but the only thing you want is

crackers and ginger ale." Holly glanced at Eddie. "Please get that for her and applesauce and lemon wedges."

Pam, the housekeeper and cook, stopped what she was doing at the stove. "I'll handle it."

"When your mother was pregnant with you and Chance," Holly said, "the doctor told her to try eating bananas to quell the nausea, but the smell of them always made her want to retch."

Amber considered concocting a story as to why she was sick.

"Those wheels are spinning so fast in your head that I can practically see smoke coming from your ears." Holly sat across from her. "You always did wear your heart on your sleeve and your thoughts were easy to read in your face. Please don't insult me by denying the pregnancy."

What would be the point? Soon enough they would all know the truth. "I am," Amber said.

"Congratulations," Grace said softly and covered her hand with a warm palm. "I've known for a while. You threw up at our last few lunches and you're starting to show. I figured that's why you began wearing baggy clothes. But I thought it best to let you tell me when you were ready." Grace cast a scolding glance at her mother-in-law.

Holly cut her gaze from Grace, sliding it back to Amber. "Is the child Monty's?"

Amber stiffened at the invasive question. "This is very personal and I'm not ready to discuss it." Especially around people she didn't know well. Everyone in the Powell household might have been used to Brianne and Eddie's constant presence, but she wasn't.

"You don't have to say another word about it," Grace said, with a reassuring squeeze of her fingers.

"Please excuse us," Holly said to her assistant and campaign manager as if reading Amber's thoughts on her face.

"And, Eddie, call Vera, tell her that since I've been out of the office today for personal reasons, and with me being busy in town all day tomorrow, we'll have to work on Sunday. I'll be in after the eight-thirty church service and will need her in the office by then. I've got so much work to catch up on."

Vera was Holly's secretary. Amber had met her a couple of times. Nice, hardworking lady.

"Sure thing," Eddie said. "Should I tell her to expect you there by ten?"

Holly nodded. Once they were gone, she put her clasped hands on the table. "I don't wish to be indelicate, but in less than thirty days, land that we need will go to Pandora's next living relative. Her mother. If the child is Monty's, when he finds out, he'll insist on marrying you. Why drag this out any longer? Is the baby his?"

Amber was really going to be sick now.

This kind of pressure was one reason she didn't want anyone besides her brother to know the truth. She also didn't want further humiliation. Unrequited love, the duped former fiancée, the man who broke her heart sleeping with her again out of pity, the unplanned pregnancy. It was the plot of some melodramatic movie or a soap opera storyline.

"If I wanted Monty to marry me out of obligation, I could've had him as a husband ten years ago. The entire room heard him say that I was a mistake and that he regrets touching me." Unwelcome tears sprang up, blurring her vision. "Yes, the child is his. But *I* will let him know when I'm ready." Her eyes burned and she closed them. Still, more tears escaped, and she quickly dashed them away. She refused to let Holly think this was a moment of weakness that she could exploit. Opening her eyes, she pinned the formidable older woman with an unwavering stare. "If you tell him or get one of your flunkies to let it slip or try to push me in the slightest, so help me, I'll disappear. *Unmarried.* Unconcerned what happens to the land or the river running through it. And there's no telling when you'll see this baby. Understand?"

"All right. Calm down, dear," Holly said in an easy-breezy tone. "I think we understand each other quite well."

Pam set a tray in front of her with crackers, applesauce, lemon wedges, a can of ginger ale and a glass of ice.

"Thank you," Amber said to Pam. "What's the lemon for?"

"Take a wedge." Holly pointed to the slices. "Sniff it."

She did and the refreshing, citrusy scent immediately tempered her nausea.

"Worked like a charm for your mother. The applesauce helped, too. See if it works for you."

Willing to give anything a try, Amber spooned a little into her mouth and was surprised she wanted more.

"Right after you ran away all those years back, everyone blamed me and Buck, and of course Monty. But it was your father's decision to write that will and trust that started it. Truth be told, this entire mess is really your fault," Holly said.

Amber almost choked on the applesauce. "Is that some kind of sick joke?"

"After your mother died, and with Chance living in a different state, on the road to becoming a bigwig lawyer, your father was worried about you being alone once he passed eventually. He wanted to give you your greatest, deepest desire. *Monty.* So he hatched this twisted scheme with the trust, playing games with hearts, like people were pawns. *For you.*"

"I thought he was only thinking about leaving me the land back then. He'd already written the trust, with Pandora in it?" Amber asked.

Holly nodded. "As soon as he finished and made it legal, he couldn't wait to tell us all about it on the back porch over a glass of whiskey. About Pandora, too, using her as leverage in the trust. Of course, he knew we'd steer Monty toward you," she said. Amber believed it more possible they shoved him toward her. "And it blew up in our faces when you ran away."

It blew up when she overheard Monty admitting to one of his brothers, Sawyer, that he was only marrying her to get the land for his family because she'd one day inherit it. She had been nothing more than an obligation. A chore on his to-do list.

"I thought Carlos might change his mind and rip up the trust," Holly said. "He might've if you had ever married or moved on with someone new."

Goodness knows, she had tried hard to do so, but no man ever measured up to Peter Pan.

"When that baby is born, you'll understand the desire to see him or her happy, to give them what their heart wants," Holly said. "Too bad you didn't love Logan instead, huh?"

It would've made things easier for everyone if she had.

Grace patted her hand. "Finish eating, then you should go home, rest and hydrate. Nurse's orders. Chance can fill you in on the meeting."

Starving, Amber stuffed a cracker in her mouth.

"Yes, rest up." Holly stood. "I'll be expecting you at the Holiday Tree Lighting ceremony tomorrow. It's from noon to six. I need you there by four thirty. We're lighting the tree with fireworks promptly at five. Your father was meant to have the honor of pressing the button. You'll do it in his stead."

A command. Not a request. *Typical.* "You can't seriously be planning to go through with attending the ceremony," Amber said while chewing on a second cracker. "The police are coming to execute the search warrant tomorrow."

"All the more reason for the entire family to be out of the way," Holly said. "Besides, this is a town function that everyone from Laramie to Bison Ridge looks forward to each year. We've expanded the activities—a children's craft center, petting zoo, pop-up holiday markets, live music and food trucks.

It's grown into a big deal. As mayor I've organized everything and it's my duty to be there. The show must go on, my dear." She turned to head out of the kitchen.

"Holly," Amber said. "You won't say anything, not even to Buck?" She wasn't concerned about Grace spilling the beans to Holden. They'd become fast friends, and if Grace had already known Amber was pregnant for weeks, she'd more than proven she could be trusted.

"Your secret is not mine to tell. I won't say anything," Holly said. "We meddled once before and look how that turned out." She glanced up at the ceiling with a faraway look for a moment. "I want to be in the lives of my grandchildren. All of them. The boys, the women they love, the grandbabies and their mothers—that's all that really matters in the end."

"Thank you." Amber truly meant that. Holly Powell could've made it much harder.

"If you need anything," Holly said, "absolutely anything, please don't hesitate to let me know."

Amber nodded, wanting to feel relieved at not having to deal with future pressure from Holly. Instead, dread filled her in anticipation of the moment when she would have to tell Monty the truth.

Chapter Eight

Are you at the ceremony with Amber, yet? I need to speak to her.

Hoping he'd finally get a reply, Monty sent a third text to Chance. He stood on the fringe of the crowd, far from his family, sandwiched between a Belgian waffle food truck and another selling doughnuts and warm apple cider. The delectable aroma was enticing but he wasn't in the mood for sweets or revelry, or to put on a show of a united front with the rest of the Powell clan, pretending everything was fine.

Yesterday, the family meeting had turned into an inquisition. Even Hannah had been under fire when she was only doing her best to walk a fine line. Being a part of his big, bossy, overbearing and close-knit family could be a lot for someone unaccustomed to it. Heck, plenty of times it overwhelmed him and was part of the reason he spent so much time off the ranch. He understood the precarious position Matt's fiancée was in and respected her efforts to help. The rest of the family should have done the same since he was innocent. None of them needed to compromise their integrity for his sake.

For some reason, the people closest to him doubted him. Not that it had dampened their staunch support of him.

Sure, he'd made plenty of mistakes, chief among them deciding to talk to Pandora on her terms, but the only thing he was guilty of was being a foolish, insensitive jerk to Amber years ago. Downright reprehensible.

I'm a horrible person.

But he was *not* a murderer.

Looking up from his phone, which still hadn't chimed with a reply from Chance, he caught an elderly couple giving him sidelong glances, whispering and pointing at him. A child leaving a food truck line with a loaded waffle piled high with fruit and Nutella waltzed in front of him. Her mother cringed at the sight of Monty and snatched the little girl away, drawing her close, like he posed a serious threat.

Mrs. Sanders from the Ranch and Feed Supply store noticed him and got out of the line for the doughnut food truck. She'd always been kind to everyone. His family had used their store forever, making them not only loyal customers but substantial ones.

He plastered on a soft smile. "Hello, Mrs. Sanders. How's your husband?"

"You should be ashamed of yourself." She pointed an accusatory finger at his face. "What you did to that girl." Mrs. Sanders reeled back with a disgusted expression, drawing attention from passersby. "I can't believe your mother let you show your face here tonight."

Stiffening, he reminded himself that he wasn't guilty, and the truth would come to light. At least, he hoped it would. "For the record, I haven't been charged because I'm innocent."

"Likely story. Or is the real reason because your mama is mayor?" Her voice rose along with the number of onlookers. Some of whom nodded in agreement. "There are kids around here. This is a family-friendly event. Do the rest of us a favor, go back to your ranch and stay there."

Perhaps standing idle in a spot that drew so much foot traffic, with a uniformed officer babysitting him since he was under surveillance, wasn't the wisest idea after his picture had been splashed across the evening and morning news. All day, he'd dealt with much of the same.

His mother had insisted that he be here with the family to help finish setting up and that his attendance during the remainder of the festivities was mandatory. The least he could do since they were here publicly supporting him. It had been a day of walking around feeling like he wore a scarlet letter branded on his forehead.

Shifting his black Cattleman-style hat forward to shield more of his face, he moved on, deciding it best to circulate. Might be the only way to find Amber before she had to go up for the tree lighting. He was sure she'd disappear after she pushed the button.

With the cop following him, Monty strode by a giant, inflatable snow globe, a line for free horse-drawn hay wagon rides around the town center, a decorated drop box for unwrapped presents to donate to local children in need and the largest Christmas light display in the state with more than a hundred individual pieces. Santa, Mrs. Claus and their elves had arrived by firetruck ten minutes ago and were setting up to hear wishes and take photos in the gazebo. A table beside it offered free cookies and hot chocolate—courtesy of the mayor.

This was the biggest Laramie–Bison Ridge Holiday Tree Lighting celebration ever. His mother had transformed downtown into a winter wonderland fit for a postcard.

He looked over at the stage. His mother stood with his father by her side, both smiling as the women's auxiliary choir sang holiday carols. The children's chorus had already performed and the Cowboy Harmony Group, an all-male singing society, was up later.

His mother was in her element, bringing people together, hosting the ceremony, working the crowd, shoring up Powell defenses by trying to garner public support. Managing anything from a staff to a ranch, to finances, to an entire town, came naturally to her. Hard to believe that at one time she'd wanted to be a federal law enforcement officer like her dad and grandfather. She even had a degree in criminal justice. Then Monty's grandfather got sick, and his parents had decided to take over the ranch. Their duty. Their honor.

He stared at his mother, so proud of her.

Being mayor suited Holly Powell, like she was always meant to have the job. In the same way being a rancher suited his father. The Shooting Star had been a part of his family for six generations.

A legacy Monty still didn't want. One of his other brothers was welcome to have it and run the place. Not that being a state trooper fulfilled him. Quite the opposite in fact. Law enforcement was in his DNA on his mother's side, but every time he put on the uniform, he felt like a fraud living the wrong life.

At least it was a life of his own choosing. A man should have the right to that, even if he messed it up.

Moving through the crowd, he spotted Amber. Chance was on one side of her and Logan on the other, his arm slung around her shoulder.

Gritting his teeth, Monty took out his phone and sent another text to her brother.

Chance dug out his cell, looked at the screen and shoved the phone back in his pocket.

He was being deliberately ignored. First by Amber and now her brother.

Giving her space, allowing her to decide when and where they spoke, hadn't worked for months. He was done using that tactic. Ever since he woke up in the hospital yesterday, a clock ticked in his soul, making him feel time was running out. He couldn't afford to wait any longer.

Monty cut through the crowd, weaving around people. "Excuse me," he said several times, drawing closer to the front near the stage, where Amber was headed. He pushed through gently, ignoring the wary glances he drew once people recognized him.

Under normal circumstances, he loved living in a small town where everyone knew each other, but once he was suspected of murder, those friendly neighbors, some of whom had known him since he was a child, had turned on him quicker than a pack of wolves on a wounded stag.

For a second he lost them, but then he homed in on the group standing a bit taller than most. Matt, Holden, Logan and Chance stood out clustered together. He made his way over to them.

Grace was next to Holden, who held Kayce. Matt was singing along with the choir to the baby and making funny hand gestures that had the little one giggling. Hannah was off at the ranch, searching it from top to bottom with Waylon and as many officers as they could muster.

Narrowing his eyes at Chance, he slipped an arm past him and caught Amber's elbow, drawing her gaze. "Hey, can we talk? I really need to speak with you."

Logan flashed him a surly expression that he wanted to knock off his face, but his brother was only being protective of Amber. How could he not respect him for that?

"Talk about what?" she asked, like she didn't have the foggiest idea.

"Everything. Yesterday morning and the way it looked." Monty glanced around, needing to be discreet, but the crowd made it a challenge. "What's happening to me," he said, in code for the fact he was accused of murder. But they also had other things to discuss. "About us. That thing after your father's funeral." Namely, the hot sex they'd had and how the thought of it, of her, had been torturing him for months until he woke up with a dead body yesterday morning, changing the priority of his concerns. "Just give me a minute."

She didn't look amenable.

Then Logan dared to add, "You don't owe him anything. In fact, it's the other way around."

Fighting hard to ignore his brother, he stayed focused on the person who mattered right now. "Please. I'm begging." Something he never did.

She held up a finger. "One minute."

Cupping her arm, he glared at his brother before he led her to the side of the stage by the stairs she would have to use in a few minutes when his mother called her up.

It wasn't ideal. Brianne and Eddie were standing close. The chief of staff mooned over his mom's assistant. She fed him a piece of a doughnut and brushed crumbs from his mustache. He thanked her with a peck on the lips.

"Would you mind giving us a minute?" he asked them.

Brianne pursed her lips at the intrusion into the space they had occupied first, but Eddie smiled and ushered her off in the direction of the food trucks.

"I'm not sure what you could possibly have to say about sleeping with Pandora," Amber said, "but I know you didn't kill her."

"But there was nothing between me and Pandora. I've never slept with her. I need you to know that."

"Really? You expect me to believe that?" Amber shook her head, pursing her rosy, bow-shaped lips. "Please don't try to spoon-feed me the same hogwash you used with your family about her not being your type. I know better. Svelte blondes and redheads, who only need you to look their way and smile to spread their legs, is precisely what you like."

He loved the fire in her, even when it burned in his direction hot enough to scorch, especially when it burned in his direction.

"Sleeping with her would've hurt you. That's why she wasn't my type," he said. Her gulp was audible. Maybe he was getting through to her. "I'd never do that to you. Never. I promise."

Those striking hazel eyes that were an intriguing mix of brown, green and amber framed by inky, thick lashes widened, boring into his. Her tongue darted out, wetting her pink lips.

And he was struck by how pretty she was. Not drop-dead gorgeous, but the kind of face that only got better with age. That caught and held his attention. Always had. A head full of dark curly hair that she kept wild and free. A soft brown complexion, dimples when she smiled, and when she did, her face glowed with an intoxicating enthusiasm that made him grin, too.

Averting her gaze, she shoved hair behind her ear with a trembling hand. Was her blood sugar low again? Or was he to blame, making her nervous?

But that look of vulnerability, the complete lack of guile in her, the dichotomy of sweet and sassy, had won him over.

"Please, Amber. I need you." Now more than ever and he wasn't going to get her, not really, not the in the way he wanted until they hashed things out.

"Need me for what?" She stared at her boots. "You've got your family. And Chance found one of the best criminal attorneys for you."

He wanted her friendship. Her support. Her affection. And so much more. "It's difficult to explain."

"Now isn't the right time to talk."

The choir finished their song.

His mother went up to the microphone at the podium. "Everyone, let's show the women's auxiliary choir how much we enjoyed their performance."

The crowd broke into a raucous round of applause.

"I agree," he said to Amber, unable to disregard the stares he garnered, ranging from leery to hateful. "We should speak somewhere quiet. In private." Without the prying eyes of the entire town. "But you've ghosted me for weeks. Months. When I called you last night, you sent it straight to voice mail. How about after you light the tree we go somewhere together?"

She looked around. "I can't. I'm exhausted and not feeling well," she said, still not meeting his eyes. "I need to go home and get some sleep."

"Then when?"

Amber shrugged. "I don't know." The fear in her voice was clear.

She was scared he would hurt her again and she had every reason to be guarded, but he had grown up while she was gone. Made changes. The old him was a bull in a china shop when it came to going after something or someone he wanted.

Maybe she was expecting that from him.

With her, he didn't want to come on too strong and have her thinking it was because of the land. He'd learned from his mistakes and would never mislead her, never let her believe something that wasn't true ever again.

"Listen, I've been a very patient man." Too patient. Too passive.

"Good for you. Would you like a trophy with your name engraved on it?"

He swallowed back a groan.

His mother was talking about Christmas, gearing up to bring Amber onto the stage.

"Your son is a murderer!" a man called out from somewhere in the crowd. "He should be in jail! Why hasn't he been arrested?"

Monty spotted the guy. Barrel-chested. Goatee. Stood out like a sore thumb. But several in the crowd echoed the man's sentiments.

"My son has not been charged with any crime," his mother said. "Every single person is innocent until *proven guilty.* Let's get back to the festivities and the reason we've all gathered here as neighbors, friends, a community that stands strong together, united in any adversity."

Needing to get out of the public eye, he turned back to Amber to pin her down on a place and time. "This is important. Come on. You can't avoid me forever, Tinker."

Her head whipped up at him, her angry eyes locking with his. "That's how you still see me, isn't it? An overly emotional fairy, stuck in never-never land, in love with Peter Pan, destined to only be his sidekick. Well, I have news for you. I have a life waiting for me back in Texas, and I deserve more, I deserve better, than the likes of you, Montgomery Beaumont Powell," she said, knocking the wind from his lungs.

"Now it's time for the moment you've all been waiting for," his mother announced over the mic. "The lighting of the holiday tree. Amber Sofia Reyes, the daughter of Carlos Reyes, a pillar of the community who recently lost his long battle with cancer, will do the honor. Come on up here, honey."

Amber spun away from him, hurried up the stairs and joined his mother at the podium.

Monty turned, scanning the crowd for the man who had shouted accusations and riled up the crowd, but he was gone.

"Three!" His mother began the countdown as Amber's hand hovered over the big red button, ready to push it. "Two. One."

Amber pressed the button.

The tree lit up in a dazzling blaze of color in tandem with fireworks going off. But over the "oohs" and "aahs" a sharp crack punctured the air. Monty's mind registered the danger as reflex took over.

A gunshot.

"Get down! Gunfire!" Monty was already up the stairs, bolting across the stage.

His father grabbed his mother, rushing her to safety. From the corner of his eye, he spotted the rest of his family, scrambling for cover as the crowd dispersed in screaming chaos.

Pop! Pop!

Monty lunged for Amber and threw her to the ground behind the podium, pinning her underneath him to protect her.

The sound of the shots echoed in his head. He remained in that position, shielding her, waiting, listening.

"Monty, I need to move," she said in a strained breath, like he was crushing her.

He hadn't realized he'd put so much of his weight on her, and rolled off. "Stay down." He peered out from behind the podium, looking to see if the gunman was still out there.

Then it occurred to him that with all the accusations and hateful glares, whoever had opened fire had probably been targeting him. Maybe by trying to protect Amber, he was the one endangering her. He scanned the area to make sure it was safe for her to get up.

Police were fanning out. His family were all okay. Grace, the baby, his brothers, Chance—no one appeared injured. *Thank goodness.*

It looked all clear.

His mother broke free from his father and dashed out from behind a position of safety, rushing toward him. He was about to tell her that he was fine, but she ran right past him and dropped to her knees beside Amber.

"Are you all right?" his mother asked.

"I think so," Amber said, but her voice sounded pained and exhausted to the point of tears.

Monty knelt to help her up, taking her hand.

Wincing, Amber groaned.

"What's wrong?" He checked her visually, making sure she hadn't been hit.

"She needs to go to the hospital," his mother said.

Amber shook her head. "No." She glanced at Monty before looking back at his mother. "I'm fine." She stood, using his assistance. Once she got upright, she doubled over with another grimace and held her stomach.

"Oh, God. Buck! Get the car!" his mother called out. "We'll go to the hospital and get you checked out. Just the two of us, honey, okay?"

"What's wrong?" Monty asked. "Were you hit?" He didn't see any blood. "Where were you shot?"

"I don't feel well." Amber grimaced. "Something's wrong."

"I'll go with you," Monty said.

Her eyes widened in alarm.

"No, no," his mother said, waving him off. "She's sick with a woman thing. We'll go without you. Buck! Where's your father with the car?"

As if she'd willed it, his father sped up in his mother's Hummer and screeched to halt near the curb. Thankfully, as mayor, she had a reserved spot close by.

Pain wrenched across Amber's face, and she squeezed his hand hard. "On second thought, you should come to the hospital."

"Are you sure?" he asked, panic gripping him.

She nodded. "Just in case everything isn't okay." She curled her arm around her stomach. "I'm not sick. I'm pregnant."

"Pregnant?" Monty stared at her in stunned surprise. But they hadn't slept together in months. Was she that far along? Four months?

His mother smacked the back of his head, nearly knocking off his hat. "Get her to the car."

A protective rush seized Monty's chest like a vise. He bent over and, sweeping an arm under Amber's legs, lifted her up from the stage. Then, holding her tight against him, he ran to the waiting vehicle.

Chapter Nine

Saturday, December 7
5:55 p.m.

Lying on a hospital bed in the Laramie emergency room, Amber groaned as another sharp pain sliced through her pelvic area.

Please, let the baby be all right. Please.

Monty was at her side, holding her hand.

"Is it still the same?" Holly asked, pacing back and forth. "Changed any? Worse or better?"

"It's the same. Something is wrong." Tears welled in Amber's eyes, blurring her vision. "I'm scared."

Amber had lost her mother, her father, and even Monty once. Losing this baby, too, would be more than she could be bear.

Monty brushed hair back from her face and kissed her forehead. "It's going to be all right."

"Now is not the time for empty platitudes, son, as well-meaning as they may be. We need a doctor. Right now." Holly yanked aside the curtain that afforded her a modicum of privacy in the ER bay. "I'm going to find one." She closed it and padded off.

"My mom is about to get scary and make a scene," Monty said.

Amber expected no less from Holly Powell. The woman

was a force to be reckoned with. "She has my blessing. How long have we been waiting?"

He glanced at his watch. "Twenty minutes." He peered down at her and flashed a sad smile. "Don't worry, she's going to get someone in here lickety-split." His tone was off somehow. He sounded distant, filtered.

She couldn't quite put it into words, but she didn't like it. "Monty, I want you to be here with me through this, but you're acting weird. It's making it worse."

He frowned. "Do you want me to leave?"

"No." Another pain lanced her and she hissed, breathing through it.

He kissed the back of her hand. "Is there anything I can do?" he asked, tightening his grip on her.

"I'm scared, terrified I might lose this baby. I need *you*. To act normal. To sound like you."

"I'm sorry." His brow furrowed, his face taking on the expression he got when he was thinking hard, trying to work out a problem, solve some puzzle.

"What are you thinking?" she asked. He hadn't uttered a word about the baby or the fact that she'd hidden it. Hadn't asked her a single question. "I need you to be honest." For once. "Please."

He hesitated, staring at her, looking completely lost.

"If you're angry I didn't tell you or disappointed that I'm pregnant, I'd understand." She stared down at her belly bump.

Once she discovered she was pregnant and got over the initial surprise, there had never been any doubt in her mind that she would keep this child. Raise it. Cherish it. She'd loved Monty since she was twelve, dreamed of marrying him, but after he'd conspired with her father to trick her into marriage so the Powells could have the land they always coveted, she hated him in equal measure. But if she were to ever have a child, it might as well be Monty's. That didn't mean he wanted this baby.

"I'm not angry. I'm not disappointed." He hesitated again.

"Then what is it? What aren't you saying? What are you thinking?" She squeezed his hand so hard he probably thought she wanted to break it. "You need to tell me the truth. Or I'll imagine the worst."

"I'm freaking out. Okay? I know that's not what you want to hear. It sure isn't what you need. Give me gunfire and deranged criminals and I'm fine. Give me fifteen thousand cattle to brand and herd and I'm great. But I woke up drugged with Pandora dead on the floor yesterday. I came this close to getting arrested. We were shot at tonight. Now I find out that I'm going to be a father. Possibly. Because I don't know what's happening with you, if the baby, my baby, *our baby*, is all right. I'm worried I hurt the two of you when I was trying to get you down behind some cover. Maybe I hit your stomach by accident." He scrubbed a hand over his face. "So I've been trying to be quiet, to be supportive, to give you what you need, not that I know what that is, and not make this about me when it has to be all about you and…" He pressed a tentative hand to her belly. "Why didn't you tell me?"

"You know why." She looked away from him and at the pale yellow curtain.

Fluorescent bulbs flickered overhead. The smell of antiseptic made her nausea flare.

"My daughter-in-law needs to be seen right this second!" Holly yelled at someone in the hall. "I know every single person sitting on the board of directors at this hospital. If a doctor isn't in bay four in the next two minutes, examining her and making sure that my unborn grandchild is okay, after we were just shot at, I'm going to start making some unpleasant phone calls."

Monty sighed. "You should've told me about the baby," he

said, his tone gentle, his voice soft. "From the way my mom acted on the stage, she already knew. Didn't you think I had a right to know, too?"

"I was going to tell you. And your mom only found out at the house yesterday."

"I get that you needed time and space." He kept using that tone of gentle compassion that made her want to dissolve into a puddle of emotion. "But I've been calling, texting, leaving notes on your front door, and you've been ghosting me for four months, using Chance as an intermediary. When were you going to tell me?"

She couldn't trust the sweet things he said. Couldn't trust his affection. Most importantly, she couldn't trust herself around him. "When the time was right."

The curtain was drawn aside. Holly stood there, letting someone pass her.

A man wearing green scrubs and a white lab coat entered the bay. He had light brown hair that was receding. Busy chewing, he held a sandwich in one hand and raised a finger from the other, indicating he needed a moment. "Sorry for the delay," he said around the food in his mouth. "The ER doctor heard the mayor's frustration and was afraid to examine you. Dr. Plinsky thought it best for an expert to come down. I'm Dr. Kevin. Like to keep it informal. I'm the head of OB-GYN."

Amber glanced at the partially eaten sandwich in his hand. "Do you need to finish eating?"

With a shake of his head, Dr. Kevin stuffed the rest of the food in his mouth and went to the sink to wash his hands. "I just finished delivering two babies back-to-back. This was my first chance to grab a bite to eat." He dried his hands, pulled on latex gloves and turned to her. "What seems to be the problem, Mrs. Powell?"

Her cheeks were suddenly on fire. "We're not married. I'm Amber Reyes."

"Oh, I see. I must've misunderstood. Everyone else can step outside and go to the waiting room if you'd like."

"I'm staying," Monty said.

Holly nodded. "Me, too."

The doctor frowned. "That's up to Ms. Reyes to decide, sir, and Mayor. We're sticklers about privacy here at the hospital. Amber, it's important that you feel free to speak openly during the examination. Clearing the bay of everyone else might be in the best interest of your health and that of your baby."

Now that Monty knew about the baby and was here beside her, she didn't want him to leave. "No, no." She shook her head. "It's okay." She tightened her grip on Monty. "If they stay, it'll save me the hassle of updating them on everything."

They might as well hear it firsthand.

"I'm afraid only one of you can stay," the doctor said.

Amber looked at Monty.

The corner of his mouth hitched in a small grin. "I'm not going anywhere."

"Mayor." Dr. Kevin turned to Holly. "You can step out to the waiting room." He drew the curtain closed. "Tell me what's going on, Amber."

"I've been having sharp pains, some dull ones, too, right around my pelvic area and belly button. At times it feels like stabbing and other moments like a tight pull."

Dr. Kevin put a blood pressure cuff on her and started the machine. "How long has this been going on?"

"There was a shooting at the tree lighting ceremony," Monty said. "I knocked her to the ground, trying to protect her, and then she was in pain." The guilt in his voice tugged at her heart.

"It actually started yesterday. I got lightheaded at the house. The room spun. And I felt a new twinge, a sort of pulling, in the lower part of my belly here." She showed him the location of the pain. "As the day wore on, it's gotten worse and

I've still been a bit dizzy. I thought it was low blood sugar. I nibbled on something, but the twinge turned into a slight stabbing. Then when I fell—"

"When I knocked you down." His voice rumbled with something that sounded like fear.

"When Monty saved me from getting shot, I protected my belly and fell on my back. But the stabbing pain has gotten bad. So has the pulling sensation. Feels like I'm having contractions."

It was far too soon for that. The baby didn't have a chance of survival outside the womb until she was at least six months.

Amber rubbed her belly. *You have to be all right, peanut.*

She wanted this child more than anything. Not for a second had it been unwelcome. She would never think of this baby as a mistake even if loving its father might have been. The conception had been completely unplanned, but a blessing in disguise. Endometriosis and surgery for it had caused scarring that blocked one of her fallopian tubes. Doctors had told her it might be extremely difficult if not next to impossible to conceive when she was ready.

In a way, the child growing inside her was really a miracle.

"Your blood pressure is elevated." Dr. Kevin removed the cuff from her arm. "Along with your heart rate. But you've just been through something stressful. How far along are you?"

"Seventeen weeks, four days."

"Any vaginal bleeding?" the doctor asked.

"No," she said, thankful for that. "I checked again when we got to the ER."

"Mind if I take a look?" He indicated her belly.

"Please do."

Dr. Kevin lifted her oversize sweater and started prodding her stomach, working clockwise.

"You've gotten so big," Monty said. "That's why you wouldn't see me."

"I honestly didn't think you'd notice," she said. "Figured you'd assume I was simply getting fatter."

"You're not fat. You're voluptuous." He flashed her a warm smile. "I like your curves."

She twisted her mouth, swallowing the word *liar.*

"It's true." Monty leaned over and brought his lips close to her ear. "Believe it or not, a man likes a woman with some meat on her bones," he whispered. "I didn't become attracted to you until you filled out in all the right places. I remember the day I first noticed. We went to the town's spring dance. You wore that skimpy sundress that revealed far too much leg and cleavage. With straps so thin I was tempted to pluck them with a finger to see if they'd snap. And that dress had bright red, plump cherries all over it. Fitted like a second skin. You didn't even wear a bra underneath. Teetered on indecent." He purred in her ear, sending tingles dancing over her skin. "Paired it with cowboy boots and a straw hat. You looked ripe enough to eat, even though you were jailbait," he drawled, his voice dipping low, making her toes curl. "I remember like it was yesterday."

This time her cheeks heated for a different reason. She'd worn it just for him. Her mother had called the dress *scandalous* and *inappropriate*, worried it would set tongues wagging in the small town, and forbade her going to the dance with it on. But her father had intervened, having the final word. He'd even sent Chance on ahead dreadfully early and called Buck, asking him if Monty could give her a ride.

She had been on cloud nine, squealing her thanks to her dad, hugging him tight, so excited to ride alone with Monty Powell in his truck. Until he showed up. Along with all his brothers—the lost boys. The guys whooped and whistled. Except for Monty. He was stone-faced, not cracking a smile, eyes hidden behind dark sunglasses, not uttering a word about the dress, barely giving her a second glance.

"Nice boots, Tinker," was all Monty had said.

And only Logan wanted to dance with her.

A stab of pain had her gripping her lower belly.

Concern etched Monty's face. He pressed a palm to her cheek, and she couldn't help but turn into his touch. What she wouldn't have given for a hug.

"Tell me, Amber, have you had much to eat or drink today?" Dr. Kevin pulled her sweater down, covering her belly.

"Crackers. A little applesauce. Lots of ginger ale. Soup for lunch."

Dr. Kevin nodded as though he was thinking. His face was inscrutable. "I have good news and bad news."

Fear jolted through her. She exchanged a worried glance with Monty.

She braced for the worst and Monty moved his palm from her cheek to grip her shoulder as if to steady her.

Dr. Kevin peeled off his gloves and tossed them in the trash. "The good news is I think it's only dehydration and the usual discomfort that comes as your uterus grows and stretches the supporting ligaments."

A breath of relief punched from her lips. Her little peanut was going to be okay. Monty smiled down at her and kissed the top of her head.

"Thank goodness," Holly said from the other side of the curtain.

Dr. Kevin raised an eyebrow. "I can't believe she's still here," he whispered.

"That's because you don't know my mother."

"Dehydration can be problematic any time, but it's especially concerning during pregnancy," the doctor said. "Not only do you need more water than usual, but your baby needs water, too. Not staying properly hydrated can lead to serious complications. Neural tube defects. Low amniotic fluid. Premature labor. Poor production of breast milk. But even something as mild as dizziness can be an issue if you were to faint."

The number of things that could go wrong was staggering. She should have known better. Three different baby books were on her nightstand, and she had read through two of them. She'd found an OB-GYN in Cheyenne to keep it quiet, and was taking prenatal vitamins, going on long walks for exercise, and had cut out fatty foods and desserts. Well, most desserts. When she could tolerate them, she was guilty of indulging.

"What's the bad news?" Holly asked from the hall.

Dr. Kevin shook his head and mouthed, *unbelievable.* "The bad news is you need to carry a water bottle around and constantly sip on it. That means you're going to run to the bathroom a lot. Especially as the baby gets bigger and presses down on your bladder."

A small price to pay for a healthy child. "Okay. I'll buy one tomorrow." She would do whatever was necessary.

"No need, honey," Holly said. "I'm texting Buck now to go get one before the store closes. Thirty-two ounces with time markers to help you remember."

Dr. Kevin blew out a breath. "The time markers are a good idea to help you remember," he said with a thread of annoyance. "I also want you to try to eat more. Get in some protein, plenty of veggies and fruit. If you don't, a baby will suck its mother dry of nutrients in order to survive."

He made an unborn child sound like a vampire.

"Does she need to be on bed rest?" Monty asked.

"No. I don't see any reason for that. But stress should be kept to an absolute minimum. I would like to take a look at the baby because of your fall. To be certain everything is okay and that there's no placenta abruption. I'll get you started on an IV to replenish your system. Then we can do an ultrasound, if you'd like."

"Yes," she and Monty said in unison.

The doctor got to work setting up the IV drip.

She met Monty's gaze and swore more than affection was reflected in his eyes.

He would finally get to see the baby growing inside her. A joy she had denied him by not telling him.

All she wanted was to protect herself and this child, but maybe she had done more harm than good by giving him the cold shoulder. No matter what happened between them, they were going to be parents, and she wanted him to start bonding with and loving this baby as soon as possible.

But she couldn't help but wonder whether a part of him might resent her for getting pregnant.

"This should help you start to feel better quickly, in a manner of minutes. I'll go get the ultrasound machine." Dr. Kevin left.

In the hall, Holly said to the doctor, "I have some questions for you." Her voice faded as she followed him away.

"I need to ask you something," she said, not quite sure how to put the words together. Typical questions like if he wanted to be a father, to have a baby with her, wouldn't work.

The man was a paradox. Half of him driven by duty and honor. In that regard, he'd give the right answers to conventional questions. Declare he was going to marry her. Do right by the child. But the other half of him was compelled to act in the opposite manner of what was expected of him.

If he felt forced, he'd only be miserable.

She wanted this child to be a source of happiness for both its parents. Not one of obligation. And certainly not a convenient way for the Powells to get their hands on the Reyes land.

"Ask me anything," he said, his voice soft, his expression open, his eyes warm.

"Why did you sleep me with after the funeral? Don't worry, you can be honest. You won't hurt my feelings." Not any more than he already had.

He looked taken aback. "Nature, I guess."

Her throat went tight, and she cursed how wrong she was about the depths to which he was capable of wounding her. The nonchalance of his three-word response broke her heart.

This was torture. Loving someone, desperate to have him love her back and want the life she desired when he didn't.

"Nature?" she asked. Like she had been a mare in heat and him a stallion, following instinct.

Monty shrugged. "Yeah. What are you getting at? If this is about the land, it had nothing to do with that."

"Because it was nature." Sounded so much better. Frustration welled. She shook her head and clenched her hands. "Just say it. You were only comforting me that night." She struggled to hold back tears. "It was pity sex. Yes, you do want the land, for your family, but you didn't sign up for a kid." The terms of the trust were that the marriage had to last two years, no children required. Then he could bail. "You didn't want to be tied to me for the rest of your life. I know you regret sleeping with me."

"What?" A low chuckle rolled from him. "That's not true."

"Stop lying to me. I heard you at the house. You specifically used the words *mistake* and *regret* in the context of having sex with me." *In front of everyone!*

The wound in her heart opened anew at the same time another pang jabbed her pelvis, but the intensity was less than earlier.

Monty sat on the edge of the bed, pressed a palm to her cheek and cupped her jaw, drawing her gaze to his. "I never got to finish what was on my mind because someone interrupted me. I did make a mistake with you. A big one. I regret ever laying a finger on you without telling you the truth first. It was one thing to take you out and spend time with you, but quite another to get intimate. I should've been honest before we made love much less before I proposed. I'm sorry I hurt

you. I ruined everything. Blew up the life we could've had."
He heaved a breath. "You've got a right to believe what you
want. Except for one thing. I didn't sleep with you after your
father's funeral out of pity."

She squeezed her eyes shut to keep tears from falling.
"Then you did it because of his will." She hated that land and
the river on it.

"I am not a manipulator."

"Oh, no?" Tightness pulled at her belly. Wincing, she rubbed
the bump. "Could've fooled me. Ten years ago, you made me
believe that you loved me. That you wanted to marry me."

"Made you believe?" he asked. "Or let you?"

She glared at him. "Are you trying to spin this back onto
me somehow?"

"It takes two, sweetie. You have some culpability in what
happened. Not much. Maybe the size of a mustard seed while
I'm responsible for the bushel, but it's there."

Amber rolled her eyes. "You misled me. How is that my
fault?"

"Did I ever tell you I loved you?"

She thought about it and squirmed. "Well, no."

"Did you ever ask yourself, or me, why would a man who's
never said those words propose to you?"

She'd gotten so caught up in the butterflies and the romance
and the fairy tale she'd dreamed of finally coming true that she
didn't want to ask. "But you made me feel like you loved me."

"I've always had deep feelings for you." He brushed her
jaw with his knuckles. "I only hid it well."

"Why? If that's true, why would you hide how you felt?"

He took off his hat and sat it on a table, which meant this
was going to get serious. Real.

"Two reasons," he said. "First, Logan was in love with you.
I was the eldest. The one who gave up toys, clothes, the extra
dessert, who took tasks that the younger ones didn't want to

do. If there was something we both wanted, I let whichever brother who desired it have it. No way, no how, was I going to flirt with you or date you and rub his nose in it. No, sirree. That might not make sense to you because you're the youngest and a girl, the apple of Carlos Reyes's eye, and always got everything you wanted."

Except for you.

"It makes sense, in a weird way," she said grudgingly. "What's the second reason?"

"That one's personal."

The only thing stopping her from screaming her frustration was this baby. Her lungs burned as she inhaled. "Hiding things from me is how you ruined everything before. I need the truth."

"This is true." He leaned in, gently gripping her chin between his thumb and forefinger. "Back then, when we were going out, the more time we spent alone, talking, having fun, *having sex*, taking long drives with no destination and enjoying the journey together, the more I felt for you until I loved you, so deeply. More than anything. But then I lost you."

She dropped her head back on the pillow, wanting to believe him. But how could she? Only someone glutton for punishment would. "Fool me once shame on you. Fool me twice shame on me."

Monty sighed. "After your father's funeral, I found you in the barn, brushing his horse." He put a palm on her wrist and leaned in close, sending a rush of warmth spreading through her chest. "I hugged you and you started crying. I was wiping away your tears, feeling sorry for your loss."

So it was *pity.* The man was an incorrigible liar.

"But..." His voice trailed off. "This is going to sound selfish—I felt more sorry for myself because I'd let you go and didn't run after you. I've regretted it every day, every single second, of these past ten years. When we were in the barn, alone, I held you and looked down into your face and I wanted you. The way a man wants a woman. *Nature*. Wanted to kiss you, to hold you, to be inside you again," he said, and her stomach swooped.

She swallowed, blinking through a shimmer of tears. Why was he doing this? Saying everything she wanted to hear? Reeling her in when she was vulnerable? She didn't know if she could go down this path again. It had taken years of therapy to recover from the betrayal. She wanted to trust the father of her child, the man she desperately loved, but she didn't want to get hurt again.

Meeting his gaze, she was thunderstruck by what she saw in his eyes. Regret. Anguish. Desire.

"Amber." He cupped her face with his hands. "That night I needed to show you what you meant to me and how much I still love you."

And then he kissed her.

She squeezed her thighs together to ease the ache of longing that spread in an instant.

His lips were hot and firm and certain. A mix of fire and hunger. He kissed her like he was starving. Drinking her in with each stroke of his tongue that plunged deeper, sliding against hers in the sweetest heat, melting her to pieces.

Chapter Ten

Saturday, December 7
6:45 p.m.

This was his woman. His future wife. The mother of his unborn child. And Monty let her know it the only way he could. With this kiss, he told her all the things he couldn't say because she wouldn't believe him. All the things he wanted—to devour her, to take her to his bed, to have her body beneath his. To lose himself in her. To hear her cry out his name.

To hold her. To love her.

To have a second chance.

A chance to get it right.

The sound of the curtain being drawn had them jerking apart.

The doctor cleared his throat as he wheeled the ultrasound machine into the bay. Based on the wide grin on his mother's face, she had also seen them.

He looked down at Amber and swallowed, his mouth going dry again. In her eyes, he saw lust and desire and possibly the spark of forgiveness. Everything he'd hoped to see.

Hell, that kiss should have taken away some of her doubts. The chemistry they had—he'd never experienced anything like it. And right then, he'd never wanted anything so much in his life as he wanted to kiss her again.

"How are you feeling?" Dr. Kevin closed the curtain in Holly's face. "Any better?"

"Much better actually. The twinges and pangs are less frequent. The intensity decreased, too."

"Good. That's exactly what I was hoping to hear. Are we ready to do an ultrasound?"

She nodded.

"Yes," Monty said. He needed to make sure Amber and the baby were okay.

The doctor turned on the machine and washed his hands again.

"I'm sorry you missed the first one," she said, looking up at him. "You had a right to be there. It's your baby, too."

"It's okay." He understood why she'd kept the truth from him. "When did you do it?"

"The doctor recommended at seven weeks. The baby is due May sixteenth."

A May baby. "Did you go alone?"

"Chance came with me."

Of course, her brother had the whole time. It explained why he had agreed to act as a go-between, not letting him in the house, but passing on his messages. Normally, Chance didn't like to get involved in other people's affairs. Not that Monty could be angry with him for supporting his sister. She had needed someone to be there for her when she probably worried she'd have to contend with the full force of the Powell clan.

"Well, I'm here now." He took her hand in his. From here on out, they were going to do this together. He couldn't wait to see his baby for the first time.

Dr. Kevin put on gloves. "Pull your sweater up for me and lower your waistband. Sorry, the gel is going to be cold."

As Amber adjusted her clothes, Monty noticed her hands trembling slightly. "Are you hungry?"

"Yeah. I find it easier to eat a little bit at a time."

"Craving anything?" he asked, knowing his mother was still eavesdropping.

"This IV must be doing the trick because I'm craving a hamburger smothered in ketchup. And ice cream. A chocolate milkshake. But I know I shouldn't have it."

Dr. Kevin picked up the gel. "Sounds like you haven't been eating much lately. A burger is perfect. Full of protein, iron, zinc and several B vitamins. And there is nothing wrong with a milkshake as long as you're not drinking one every day. You and the baby both need the calcium."

Monty leaned in close to her ear. "How much do you want to bet that a burger and chocolate shake will be waiting for you once you're done here?" He gestured to the curtain with his head.

She smiled bright and warm, full of pure joy, and his heart danced in his chest as he grinned back at her.

The doctor moved the sweater higher and her waistband even lower.

Monty hadn't been lying about loving her figure. Full curves in all the right places that he couldn't get enough of. He wondered what she would look like with her belly big and round, heavy with his child and her breasts too full for his hands. Even sexier was his guess.

He stroked her hair, running his fingers through the lustrous, soft strands.

Dr. Kevin squirted goo on her abdomen. Amber gasped.

"Sorry, I know it's cold," he said.

"It's all right. You did warn me. I just hadn't been prepared for how cold. The gel my OB uses is warm."

"Who's your doctor?"

"Jennie Jankowski."

"Out in Cheyenne?" Dr. Kevin asked, and Amber nodded. "She's great, but if you're planning to have this baby around here, you should find someone local. Otherwise, although you may develop a good, trusting relationship with Jennie, she probably won't be the one to deliver the baby. Having a stranger help you bring your child into the world can be disconcerting."

"I guess I'm not sure where I'll be when this peanut is born."

She wasn't thinking of going back to Texas, was she?

Not pregnant with his kid and alone.

The doctor pressed the probe to her belly and moved it around while staring at the screen until a weird throbbing noise echoed in the room as a grainy image flickered on the screen.

"Looks good so far," Dr. Kevin said. "Nice, strong heartbeat, this one. No worries there."

"Is it supposed to be that fast?" Monty wondered.

"One hundred forty-five beats per minute is perfectly normal." The doctor grinned. "Should be almost twice the mother's heart rate."

"Is everything else okay?" Amber asked.

Dr. Kevin moved the probe around her belly, staring at the screen. "There's the head, the arms, legs," he said.

It looked like a baby. Not just some peanut-shaped blob the way he'd expected.

A perfectly shaped, tiny hand came into view. Monty leaned in toward the screen, his chest coming close to Amber's head. If his mother peered in now to catch a glimpse of the scene, she might naturally assume there was no question this would work out, the two of them as a happy couple, and for a wild, hopeful moment he wished with all his heart it would be that easy.

Even though her father had thought his last legal wishes would bring them together, and it had ten years ago, it kept them apart now.

"Everything looks normal. Very healthy. I'm not seeing any issues with the placenta," Dr. Kevin said, and Monty heard his mother exhale in relief. "Your baby is a little over five and a half inches long and almost seven ounces. Hey, fun fact, your baby's fingerprints are now formed."

Amber grinned from ear to ear, and Monty lit up. They were going to have a baby. The specifics still had to be worked out, but they were a family. Despite everything else going on, this was something to be celebrated.

"Would you like to know the baby's gender?"

Tipping her head back, she smiled at him and shrugged. "I don't know. This could be a once-in-a-lifetime surprise. Maybe we should wait. What do you think?"

He was chomping at the bit to know, but it was Amber's decision. "Whatever you want to do, that's what I want. A once-in-a-lifetime surprise sounds nice."

"You're disappointed," she said. "I can hear it in your voice. You want to know."

"This isn't about me. I'm happy to wait."

"Be honest. Please." She studied his face. "What do you want?"

This was a test. In his gut, he knew it. He had to be honest in all things. "Whether it's a boy or girl doesn't matter. Either way, I'll be thrilled, but I do want to know. I just don't want to spoil a surprise for you. Ruin it for you."

"This baby is healthy. As long as he or she stays that way, nothing is ruined." She looked at the doctor. "Tell us."

Dr. Kevin moved the probe again, making some adjustments. "Sure you want to know? You can always wait for a later appointment."

"I'm sure. We're together now. I don't know about the next ultrasound," she said, and something in his chest pinched.

She still doubted him. Much more than he thought.

The doctor pointed to the screen. "There you go. Can you see the package?"

"Do you mean…" Excitement competed with anticipation, leaving him speechless. He waited for confirmation.

Dr. Kevin nodded.

Monty's eyes watered. "A boy." His voice was choked. "Amber, we're going to have a son."

Her bottom lip trembled and tears welled in her eyes. "A son," she echoed, in amazement or disbelief, or perhaps a bit of both. Pressing her hands to her chest, she stared at the monitor before turning back to him. She sent him a tremulous smile.

Monty didn't hesitate to bend over and give her a gentle kiss on her lips.

"Buck, it's a boy!" his mother squealed. She must've called his father on the phone.

Monty pulled away, beaming at Amber, and they both laughed.

The doctor raised his eyebrows. "I forgot she was there," he whispered.

Staring deep into her eyes, Monty wished he could name all the emotions flooding his heart. He looked back at the screen, awestruck. The baby was so tiny. So fragile.

And someone had fired a gun several times, endangering Amber and his little one.

He needed to figure out what was going on and fast. It was the only way to keep them safe.

"Would you like me to print a picture?" Dr. Kevin asked.

"Yes," they said in unison.

"One for each of us," Amber clarified. "We're not together."

Dr. Kevin's smile deflated right along with Monty's hope. He had more work to do than he realized. Regret siphoned some of his elation, but he hid it well, not wanting to dampen Amber's spirits.

"Please print an extra one for me," his mother called out.

The doctor handed one to each of them along with some paper towels for Amber. "The IV should be finished in another fifteen to twenty minutes. I'll have Dr. Plinsky get your discharge paperwork ready for you."

"Thank you." Amber wiped the gel from her belly. "We appreciate you rushing through your late dinner."

"I'm happy to assuage your worries. Be sure to eat, drink lots of water and get plenty of rest."

"I will."

Smiling, the doctor handed his mother an ultrasound picture on the way out.

Monty took the paper towels from Amber and tossed them in the trash. "Go to the waiting room, Mom." His tone brooked no argument. "I'm serious."

"I'm going," she said, with a smile and a nod. "We got you a burger and milkshake, honey. Do you want me to bring it to you?"

"Thank you," Amber said. "But I'll wait to eat on the way home."

"Okay. If you change your mind, text me." His mom waved and shut the curtain.

Monty sat back down on the bed next to her. "I want us to be together," he said, plainly.

Cringing, she squeezed her eyes shut. "Don't. Please don't." She huffed a breath. "Monty, don't do this—talk about marriage. I should've known better. You can't just be happy that the baby is healthy. That's it's going to be a boy. Can you? You're never satisfied with halfway. You always want it all. This is why I've dreaded telling you, because I knew you'd go caveman on me when I can't trust a single word that comes out of your lying mouth."

"I love you, Amber Reyes."

Her wary gaze flashed up to him and she looked as though she was holding her breath.

His timing was wrong. No, it sucked. But he'd put it out there and now he had to double down. "Did you hear me? I've never said that before to anyone."

"I heard you." Her voice was soft, her tone skeptical. "Want a trophy for that, too, *Peter Pan*?"

Frustration bubbled in Monty's gut. Enough was enough. "Listen, woman, this stops right here. You're not Tinker Bell. I'm not Peter Pan and I'm not some crude Neanderthal from the Stone Age either." He was a cowboy who'd finally gotten his head screwed on straight. "This isn't a fairy tale. It's messy. It's ugly. People make mistakes. Goodness knows I've made a lot of them. But this is also beautiful. And it's real. This is us, for better or for worse. We're going to have a baby. That makes us family. For life. Whether we get married or not. But I *want* to marry you. And not out of duty or honor or to get the land."

"Then why? Why do you love me? Why do you want to marry me?"

He had an answer at the ready because he'd spent many a night, tossing and turning, pondering the same thing. "I think of my life in terms of B.A.R. and A.A.R. Before Amber Reyes and after Amber Reyes. Before we got together, I was fine. Thought I was, anyway, content with my life just as it was. After you left, there was a gaping hole. Like a sucking chest wound. I became painfully aware that I was lonely. Miserable, if I'm being honest."

Raw emotion gleamed in her eyes, but she still looked dubious.

Silence stretched between them.

Taking a breath, he resolved to try harder. "It was kind of like watching the *Wizard of Oz*. Everything is black-and-white and looks pretty good until it changes to Technicolor. That's what you are for me. Every color of the spectrum in high definition, brightening and enriching my life. I'd be lying if I said I tried to move on. I didn't even bother. In my gut, I knew it'd be futile. I've just been existing. Passing time. Waiting for you. Now you're back." He put a hand to her belly. "Pregnant with my son. I need you, sweetheart. I'm miserable, sick down in my soul, without you."

Tears streamed from her eyes and her bottom lip trembled once more. "Before my father made the land become an issue and you asked me out, you claim you had feelings for me."

He nodded. "I did. Took a while for me to realize it was more than lust. It was in the way I tried to look after you. Protect you. Help you with anything that you needed. Just wanting to be near you. It was coming from a place of me loving you for years." All along. Way before their parents meddled.

"Then what's the second reason, besides Logan, why you never acted on those feelings? No more secrets. No hiding anything from me."

For her to believe, he was going to have to open up and lay himself bare. He got to his feet and peeked through the curtain into the hall, checking to make sure his mother was gone.

Satisfied she wasn't lurking within earshot, he sat back down beside Amber.

He wasn't proud of his reason, which wasn't anything noble, and that was why he classified it as personal.

Lowering his head, he pinched the bridge of his nose. "Since I was little, I was told who I was and what I was going to be. Buck and Holly Powell's eldest. Born to be a rancher. Destined to carry on the legacy. I'm sure you've noticed I don't like to be told what to do."

"I have. Kind of hard not to."

He took her hand. "I had an eye for you something fierce since you wore that cherry sundress, but Logan's interest forced me to keep my cool and my distance, like I said. But one day I overheard our parents talking about how you fancied me and how good we'd be together. How wonderful it would be if we got married and had kids. The Reyes and Powell land becoming one since neither you nor Chance wanted to be ranchers. They had my whole life mapped out for me.

Choosing my vocation, choosing my wife. Then I found myself pushing against that, too. *Real hard.*" From an early age, since he could ride a horse, he'd decided for himself who he was going to be. What he was going to do. "I set my mind against being with you. Told myself all sorts of lies, like you were too young, sex with you would be boring." His eyes flew up and he stared at her, horrified to see hurt in her gaze. "Idiotic nonsense I tried to believe to stay away from you. Making love with you is perfect. Sometimes sweet and slow. Sometimes dirty, hot and wild." She brought him such pleasure, opening herself, holding nothing back, and he endeavored to do likewise. "I dream about it. A lot. Anyway, I couldn't see past those two reasons—Logan's feelings and being told I should be with you—until we were actually forced together. Sounds foolish, I know."

"It doesn't." She whisked the tears from her eyes. "Simply sounds like you."

Drawing in a breath of relief, he was glad she knew him so well. "You believe me?"

"I want to. Really, I do. More than you know. But..." She shook her head. "How can I?"

The land. The river. *The trust.*

Pain lodged in his chest. He would do anything to reassure her. "I can prove it to you. In less than thirty days, if we're not married, the land will go to Pandora's next of kin. Her mother. We let it happen. Then when you believe in my feelings, when you're ready to say yes, I'll propose again. Whether that's in two months, two years, or twenty."

Her mouth fell open, and she reeled back. "You can't be serious. You wouldn't give up everything for me. You love that land. And it means so much to your family. It would devastate your parents."

The land he'd grown up on was like gravity for him. Grounding him. Keeping him steady. Calling him always. Being out there on horseback, wrangling cattle, gave him a sense of satisfaction, of purpose, like nothing else ever had. "I love my parents. I love that ranch. But I love you more. You and this baby are everything to me. All that matters."

Staring at him, she looked stunned. "They'd never allow it. Buck and Holly would coerce and push and plead until we got married just to keep that land from going to Fiona and you know it."

A valid point. Buck and Holly were resourceful. Persuasive, too.

An idea came to him. His parents would hate him for it, but it might be the only solution. "Once we figure out what's going on and clear my name of any suspicion of murder, we leave town together. Go to Texas. Without telling anyone anything. I mean no one. Not even Chance." If word got out, they'd be in a pressure cooker. "Simply pack our bags and leave one night. And if you think that they'd follow us and harass us, then we go somewhere else until the deadline passes and it's too late."

"Monty." Amber stiffened. "I can't ask you to make that kind of sacrifice."

"You didn't ask. I need to do this to prove to you this is real and how much I love you."

"They'll never understand. They'll never forgive us. Forgive me."

He gave her a sad smile. "Yes, they will."

She shook her head slowly, unconvinced.

"Once the dust settles, after they've sold the cattle, and thousands of acres of our land since they won't need it, they will forgive us. Because of the baby you're carrying." He rubbed her belly. "They'll want to see him. They can only do that if they're nice to both of us." Might be asking a bit much. "At least civil. I won't have them giving you the stink eye or saying a cross word about you." They could curse his name if it made them feel any better.

She tore her gaze from him. Wringing her hands, she considered it.

"Give me this chance and I won't let you down." He cupped her face. "Not ever again. Take this leap with me. What do you say?"

Her swallow was audible, her cheeks going rosy, her eyes luminous. "Yes."

"Yes?"

She nodded. "I love you. I want us to be family."

Growling with soul-deep satisfaction and relief, he pulled her close and crushed his mouth to hers. He closed his eyes and reveled in the kiss, in the sultry jasmine scent of her, in the feel of her rounded baby bump pressed against his abdomen. Luxuriated in the moment. This was bliss—the quiet connection to the one woman who'd always been meant for him.

His heart drummed a frenzied rhythm against his ribs. Every muscle in his body went taut, vibrating with anticipation, straining with need so strong he ached down to his bones.

But thoughts of Pandora and the shots fired sprang to mind. He clung tighter to Amber, unable to fight the sense of helplessness rolling through him. In the pit of his stomach, he felt this might be the calm before the storm.

Chapter Eleven

Saturday, December 7
8:08 p.m.

The Shooting Star Ranch had been turned upside down and inside out and Waylon had nothing to show for it. He climbed behind the steering wheel of his truck. Hannah jumped into the passenger seat. They'd driven over together since they had to go back to the station to fill out paperwork.

He pulled out, leading the caravan of LPD cops off the ranch.

"That was a complete waste of time," Hannah said.

The hint of smugness in her tone irked him. "Maybe the flip phone the state police found in his locker and delivered to us will have something on it."

"And maybe it's just a spare phone." Hannah shook her head. "The guys didn't have to leave such a mess back there. Looks like a tornado ripped through every residence."

"I'm sure they have people to clean things up. Right? Staff? Servants?"

"No, they don't. Not in the way you mean."

He scoffed. "You expect me to believe that Holly Powell is scrubbing toilets?" he asked with a chuckle.

"There was a time when she did, but Buck and Holly have help now that they're older. Monty is going to have to clean his own cottage."

"Boo-hoo. Cry me a river."

She shifted toward him. "What about Holden and Grace? They'll have to clean their place, too, since you insisted on executing the full scope of the warrant. She's eight, almost nine months pregnant and they have a fourteen-month-old baby."

"Put your violin away, Delaney. The lawful search was a part of the job, and the mess came with the territory. You were standing right next to me when I issued the orders. I didn't tell anyone to get nasty about it." Though he did feel bad for Grace, who was pregnant and had a toddler to contend with, and Holden, whom he liked.

Holden lacked pretense and didn't have the same egotistical swagger as Monty.

"True, but you did seem to pick every available officer with a grudge against the Powells," she said. "You knew what was going to happen."

"I think they'll survive." He switched the radio on low. "You didn't happen to give them a heads-up about the search, did you?" He quirked an eyebrow at her.

"Monty was found with a dead body. A reasonable, rational expectation would be for a search warrant to be executed. Do you really think they needed me to do the math, two plus two equals four? Simple enough without my help."

Popping a piece of gum in his mouth, he restrained a chuckle at her continued avoidance of answering his questions regarding that family. "Do you want to know what I think?"

"Of course, I do, partner."

Sarcasm duly noted. "I think you told them that the search was going to happen before they gave you the heave-ho from the family meeting yesterday." He would've moved the timeline up if he'd had the necessary personnel available.

Delaney had extended the courtesy of giving him a heads-up about the meeting, which he appreciated, but he wasn't a fool.

"If I was so helpful to them, why do you suppose they kicked me out?"

"Because you're conflicted. They can smell it on you, the same way I can."

She straightened in her seat and opened another energy drink. "I know where I stand."

"Want to enlighten me as to which side that's on?"

"The side of truth." Her phone chimed. She took it out. "Monty's financials are in."

He gave her time to scroll through it. The silence was welcome. Trading barbs with her was exhausting.

"Anything of interest?" Regardless of her answer, he'd comb through it himself later.

"Possibly." She looked over at him. "What time did the outdoor security camera at Pandora's show her and Monty arriving?"

"Ten thirty."

"He used his debit card to pay at the Howling Wolf Roadhouse just before that."

"Time?"

"Four minutes past ten."

"We've got ourselves a lead. Get on the radio and let the others know we're going to peel off." The turn for the street that led to the roadhouse was about to come up soon.

Hannah passed along the message.

Once they made their turn, the others continued to the police station. The parking lot at the Howling Wolf was half-full. Security cameras mounted on the outside covered the lot and probably the road in front as well.

They climbed out and headed inside. Typical dive bar. Dim lighting. Shabby decor. Darts. Pool. Food and drink. He preferred to grab beer outside of town in Wayward Bluffs where he lived.

He wouldn't call the place seedy but wouldn't be surprised if drugs were sold out of it either.

They approached the bartender. A lanky guy covered in tattoos drying a glass.

"I'm Detective Wright. This is Detective Delaney. Were you working Thursday night?" he asked, and the guy nodded. "What's your name?"

"Finn."

"Was this guy in here that evening?" Hannah whipped out a photo of Monty on her phone.

"Yeah. Monty is in here every Thursday like clockwork."

"Oh, yeah." Waylon leaned against the bar. "Describe a regular Thursday night for him. What time does he arrive and leave? What does he do while he's here?"

"Gets in around nine. After his shift ends at eight." Finn put a tall glass under a spout and filled it with beer. "Orders dinner. Eats. Usually leaves with a woman. Rarely the same one."

Sounded like one of Waylon's Friday nights.

"Or I should say he used to leave with someone," Finn said.

"What do you mean used to?" Hannah asked.

"He stared eating alone and leaving alone."

Waylon scratched his chin. "When did the change start?"

"I don't know," the bartender said with a shrug. "Been a while. A few months back I guess. Maybe in August."

When Amber Reyes came back to town for her father's funeral. "And he only comes in on Thursdays?"

"Yep. Like clockwork."

"What about last Thursday?" Hannah asked. "Was he by himself?"

Finn laughed and set the beer down in front of a customer. "Nah, he wasn't alone. A hot redhead came in as he was finishing dinner. She was draped all over him, coming on strong."

"And how did he respond?" Waylon asked.

"Oh, he was into it. Feeling her up, stroking her leg. Smiling at her. Looked like those two were ready to get a room."

Hannah narrowed her eyes. "Really?"

That was the same question on Waylon's lips. The footage at Pandora's had showed a different sort of interplay in which Monty wasn't a happy camper. Maybe something had soured between them by the time they got to her place.

"Yeah," Finn said. "I guess he was looking for some action the other night and she was ready to show him a good time."

Hannah turned in a slow circle, scanning the place before looking back at the bartender. "We'd like to see the security footage from that night."

Finn ran a hand through his greasy-looking hair. "I wish I could show it to you, but we've been having problems with the system. It's on the fritz."

"That's convenient." Waylon exchanged a furtive glance with Hannah. "How about the cameras outside? Those aren't working either?"

After a moment of hesitation, Finn shook his head. "Nope. The whole system is down." He rubbed the back of his neck.

"Let me show you something." Waylon beckoned to him with a finger. The guy leaned across the bar and Waylon pointed to one of the cameras. "You see that little green light at the bottom? That says different. Tells us the cameras are operational and that you're lying."

The question was why.

Finn reeled back. "Nah. I'm not lying. You misunderstood me. They're working now. But they weren't Thursday."

Hannah raised an eyebrow. "Just got them fixed?"

"Yep. Sure did. Friday."

"Do you have a work order? A receipt?" Waylon folded his arms across his chest. "What company repaired the system?"

"My cousin fixed it," Finn said, easily. "He tinkers with electrical stuff. Really handy."

Hannah smiled. "If you're not lying, then you won't have any problem taking us to the office and showing us the footage that doesn't exist. Come on, sport." She hiked a thumb toward the hall.

"I've got customers. I can't just leave the bar and register unattended."

"Get moving," Waylon said. "Or I'll get you moving."

Hannah grimaced at the bartender. "Trust me, you don't want that."

"All right." Finn wiped his hands on a dish towel and led the way to the office in the back. He sat down behind a desk and logged into the computer.

Waylon and Hannah stood on either side of him, peering over his shoulder at the screen. He toggled over to the folder for the indoor cameras. Clicked one labeled Main Bar. Then December.

Footage for Thursday, December 5, was missing.

"Get up." Hannah tugged on his collar and the guy moved, letting her sit down. She got out of that folder and went to the recycle bin—a temporary storage location for items recently deleted, whether by mistake or purposefully. People often forgot to clear it.

The recycle bin was empty.

Her shoulders tensed but her face was deadpan.

Finn grinned. "See. I told you. This proves I wasn't lying."

Waylon shook his head. It was the exact opposite.

If the surveillance camera had been experiencing glitches, there would be footage that showed some problems throughout the day. Pieces missing. This proved the entire day had simply been deleted.

"Check the footage for the outside cameras," he said, and Finn stiffened, his premature smile falling from his face.

Hannah moved the mouse, sliding the cursor to the folder for the outside cameras. There were two. He pointed to the one that he thought offered the best view of the parking lot. She opened it and went to the night in question.

There was footage available. Waylon smiled.

Finn didn't move a step, but his gaze kept flying to the door like he wanted to run.

Waylon pinned him with a look and pointed a finger at him. "I hope you're not thinking of going anywhere."

"I'm just worried about my customers, that's all."

Hannah brought up the footage, sped to the point where Monty arrived and parked.

Shortly before ten a red Alfa Romeo Stelvio pulled into the lot. Pandora hopped out of her sporty SUV, wearing a short dress, leather boots and a fur jacket. The young woman put on lipstick and fluffed her hair before strutting inside the bar.

Carefully easing the footage forward, Hannah took the video to three minutes after ten. She let it play.

Waylon leaned in and watched alongside her.

Minutes later, Pandora sauntered out alone. She sashayed over to her vehicle and leaned against the hood, waiting. It wasn't long, a few seconds, until Monty left the bar, too. With his hands stuffed in his pockets, he strode up to her. He nodded as he said something.

A bright smile spread across Pandora's face. She stepped closer and ran her hand up his chest, but he backed away, ending the physical contact, and got in his truck. She pulled out of the lot first and he followed behind her.

Hannah sighed, her disappointment palpable.

This didn't confirm Finn's version of events. It also didn't prove that they weren't romantically involved either.

"Why did you lie about the security cameras glitching?" Waylon asked Finn.

"I don't know what you're talking about." The guy rubbed his arm, his gaze shifting. "There was no footage inside the bar. I guess I got it wrong about outside."

"The redhead who was in here the other night is dead. This is a murder investigation, understand?" Waylon stalked over to him, and Finn's eyes grew big as hubcaps. "I'm going to give you a choice. You can give us honest answers and we'll leave you alone. Or we get one of our techies in here and it'll be easy enough to prove you deleted the file. That's obstruction of justice, buddy. Continue to lie and it'll only make this worse. Also, it'll just tick me off. Means I'm going haul you in. Did you know you could get up to a year in jail?"

Hannah stood and went around the desk. "And because we don't appreciate having our time wasted, this place is going to be raided, regularly. We'll be sure to use a narcotics detection canine."

"So, I'm going to ask you one more time." Waylon got up close and had to peer down in his face since the bartender was a head shorter than him. "Why did you lie?"

Finn's gaze fell for a long a moment, then he looked back up at them. A fixed gleam in his eyes. "I didn't lie. Monty was hot and heavy with that woman."

"Lied about deleting the footage," Delaney said, clarifying for him. "*That woman* is dead, remember?"

"Sorry she's dead but it's not my fault," Finn snapped.

"Watch your tone." Waylon pointed a finger at him. "That's no way to talk to a lady."

"Thanks. But I'm no lady. I'm a detective."

A thought occurred to Waylon. "Maybe you deleted the video footage because it shows you slipping a roofie into Monty's drink. Maybe the redhead paid you to do it. Maybe you were in cahoots together and now that she's dead you're worried we'll think you killed her."

Finn's eyes grew big and he shook his head. "No. No way."

Hannah's face hardened. "Are you sure? If we find out that you're lying, you're going to regret it."

"I'm sure. It wouldn't have worked anyway. No way to slip

him a roofie. Monty only orders bottled beer while sitting at the bar. Always wants to open it himself. Never leaves his drink unattended. He'll chug it before going to the bathroom."

Sounded paranoid. But with everything going on, maybe the man had justified cause. If he was so cautious, it begged the question of whether he was indeed roofied or took the drug himself to cast reasonable doubt. "What about the redhead, was she ever in here before?"

"I'd never seen in here until last Thursday."

How did Pandora know to find Monty at the Howling Wolf on Thursday night at the right time?

"The file. Why did you really erase it?" Hannah demanded.

"I deleted the file because it was useless from going in and out. Real glitchy. You couldn't see anything. I've only got so much storage space on the drive. It made sense to get rid of it."

That was his *story,* and he was sticking to it for now.

"If something comes back to you and you remember things differently, let us know." Waylon handed him a business card, itching to take another go at this guy. But not now. Later, when they had more information. Use a lot more pressure and put the fear of God in the man.

Finn snatched the card. "Sure. I'll do that."

They went back out through the bar and left.

After they got in his truck, Hannah turned to him. "What do you make of it?"

"He's lying. About deleting the file for certain. Not so sure about his replay of how things went between Monty and Pandora inside the bar, though."

"I agree about the footage." Hannah nodded. "But do you still think Monty was sleeping with Pandora?"

He gave a one-shoulder shrug. The more he learned, the more he suspected Monty might not be guilty of murder. Didn't mean he wasn't sleeping with her. "I wouldn't put it past him." Monty was selfish, arrogant and tended to take what he wanted. "Do you have any idea what that ranch is worth with the cattle and access to the river?"

"No idea."

"Millions. Tens of millions. I've known men who have slept with two women at the same time for a heck of a lot less. And if he was bedding both of them, it would explain why he'd want it to keep it secret. So it doesn't upset the one who is still alive. He had to be extremely careful with Amber, didn't he? I mean with the engagement falling through ten years ago. Him using her to get the land way back then and now once again."

"I don't think it's that straightforward. He lied to her and proposed to get the land, but I think he's always truly cared about her. Monty isn't a typical user. He's not a womanizing manipulator. Not the way you want to believe."

The whole town had heard about the engagement. Two powerful, wealthy families about to be united. Then Amber Reyes fled in the night. Never to be seen again until her father's funeral. Waylon had no idea why it had fallen apart.

Or that Monty had lied, seduced her and proposed only to get the land for his family. It simply had been a connect-the-dots suspicion of his.

But thanks to Hannah Delaney's little slipup, he knew for certain now.

His phone rang. "It's the medical examiner." He put it on the Bluetooth speaker in the truck. "Hey, Roger. Delaney is with me. What do you have for us?"

"You'll have my full report in the morning, but I wanted to give you a quick update. I've narrowed the time of death to between six and seven in the morning. And she didn't die from exsanguination. The victim was strangled to death first. The perp waited before slitting her throat. Based on the low amount of blood flow I'd estimate twenty minutes."

"Maybe he was busy setting the scene," Hannah said, "and

saved cutting her throat for last to keep from tracking blood around."

"I was thinking the same possibility. Anything else, Roger?"

"The victim recently had intercourse. My guess is fairly close to the time of death."

"Consensual," Hannah said, "not rape, right, Doc?"

"Yes. But he didn't leave behind any bodily fluids. That's about it. Wanted you to know straight away. The rest will be in my report."

"Thanks, Roger." Waylon disconnected. "We need more answers. Fiona Frye is supposed to come at nine. Something she said keeps bothering me."

"About the proof that Pandora was seeing Monty?"

"No, not that, but it is odd. Right? I mean if she was seeing Monty or someone she trusted, why would she need insurance? The part that bugs me is when she told us her daughter was waiting until things were 'official' before she could tell anyone." The word kept turning over in his head.

"Like a deal for the land?"

Rubbing his eyes, Waylon fought a yawn. "Maybe. There's a whole lot about this case that I don't like." Things niggling at the back of his mind. "A puzzle with too many missing pieces." He started the engine. "Too many things just don't add up. The missing micro SD card in the security camera at Pandora's. The techies cracked into her hub and everything before that night was deleted. Her entire place was wiped clean of prints, except for the studio where she and Monty were found. The ketamine in his system. This story from the bartender about deleting a bad file to save on storage space. Now no bodily fluids left in the victim."

"What's odd about the last part Roger told us?"

He pulled out of the lot and hit the road. "There were no used condoms found in her home. If Monty slept with her, he didn't run out to dispose of it, only to go back, drug himself and wait to be found. Whoever she did sleep with right before she was murdered was careful." Waylon shook his head. "We can't discount what the bartender told us either about Monty and Pandora getting hot and heavy in the bar. What reason would he have to make up something like that?"

Delaney sighed.

A similar frustration pounded in Waylon's temples. "It's time Monty filled in some of the blanks for us. Talking to him after we speak to Ms. Frye would be best. Can you arrange for him to come in, with his lawyer if he insists, for a chat at eleven?" Plenty of time. There shouldn't be any excuses.

"Sure." She took out her cell and fired off a text. "I'll follow up with a phone call and convince him it's in his best interest to cooperate and simply talk to us already. Stonewalling is not helping him."

Although Waylon was starting to suspect that Monty wasn't the murderer, he still expected the eldest Powell son to be tight-lipped and lawyered up.

Sometimes he had to rattle a cage and poke the bear, get it angry to get progress. And one thing he knew about Montgomery Powell was that when he was angry, he ranted, at times even saying things that he shouldn't.

Tomorrow, Waylon would see if it'd work.

Chapter Twelve

Saturday, December 7
11:00 p.m.

The text message was unexpected.

Tapping her fingernails on her desk, Valentina wasn't sure what to do with the news she had just received. Tying up loose ends was always a good thing. But there was a bigger opportunity here. She simply had to see how to use it.

A knock on her office door pulled her from her thoughts. "Enter."

Max and Leo shuffled inside the room. From their hung heads and wary expressions, they'd failed.

Valentina crossed her legs and leaned back in her chair. "I'm going to ask you something, Leo, in a way that you can understand. What is the maximum effective range of an excuse?" The US Army was fond of that question, or so Roman had told her when she hired Leo. Back then she'd seen such potential in the young man, to prove himself, rise through the ranks of her drug empire. Staring at him now, she was no longer so sure. If he couldn't kill one man, how could he be trusted with the inner workings of the cartel?

"Zero meters is the maximum effective range of an excuse, ma'am," Leo said, hands clasped behind his back, standing at attention.

"Remember that and think carefully before you answer my next question. Why isn't Holden Powell dead?"

He looked up at her. "The family was finally out in the open at the tree lighting ceremony in the center of town. I had him in my sights. But he was holding a baby the entire time and had his pregnant wife next to him."

Valentina wrinkled her brow. "I'm not hearing a reason."

Confusion took over Leo's face. "I couldn't get a clear, clean shot. He—he had a baby in his arms."

"I understood the words the first time."

Anger sparked in his eyes. "I could've hit the kid by accident. If I took a head shot, the child would've fallen. Might've cracked his skull on the pavement. They're fragile as eggs when they're that little. Did you want me to hurt a baby?"

Her thoughts careened to Julian. His laughter. His smile. His warmth. "No. I only wanted the brother dead. Him first. The one with a kid." Like her own brother, who had to leave his son fatherless.

Because of Montgomery Powell.

Seemed fair.

"First, ma'am? Who would you like me to kill second?"

"Buck," she said, the name spilling from her lips with bitterness. "The leader of that clan. But I want the dominoes to fall in the proper order until I've destroyed everything Montgomery holds dear. Not that you've proven yourself capable of helping me." She slid her gaze to her burly guard. "And what did you do, Max? Simply stand there and watch this failure unfold?"

"No, *jefa*. Leo asked me to stir up the crowd. That way after there were gunshots, it would appear random. Unplanned. In-the-heat-of-the-moment kind of thing and not like an assassination."

She hadn't considered that. "Smart. Still doesn't change the fact that an opportunity was wasted."

Leo dared to step forward. "But it wasn't, ma'am," he said, his voice rippling with confidence.

Maybe she wouldn't kill him today if he redeemed himself. "Explain."

"After the gunshots, Montgomery Powell picked up a woman and rushed her to a vehicle. The entire family raced to the hospital. We followed them over. I slipped inside and hung around in the waiting room, eavesdropping. The woman, Amber Reyes, is pregnant. And the baby is Monty's. It's going to be a boy. They were all overjoyed."

A sweet smile spread across her face. Now she knew precisely what to do with the information she'd received in the text message. "There's something I want you both to do."

Leo straightened. "Anything, ma'am."

She grabbed a notepad, pen and the folder from her top desk drawer. "First, I want you to go to this address." She copied it from the text that had been sent to her. "You'll find a dead body in the house. I want you to take it and put it in the trunk of another vehicle." She wrote down the second address, along with the make, model and license of the car. "Stealth will be required. People will be at home and asleep at the second house." She handed him the paper. "You're not to be noticed."

"That's it?" Leo asked. "You don't want me to kill anyone?"

"Well, I did, but you messed that up, didn't you? For this task, the blood has already been spilled. Get this errand right. No mistakes."

Both Leo and Max nodded.

"You may go." She waved them out, picked up her phone and dialed Officer Nicholas Foley.

He answered on the fourth ring. "Yes, ma'am. The Laramie PD has the cell phone that was *found* in Montgomery's locker."

"Good boy," she said, like he was a dog. "I have another mission for you. Tomorrow morning, I need you to do your job and make a traffic stop."

"Who am I pulling over?" he asked.

"Amber Reyes. She lives on the big ranch on Longhorn River Road. She will have an appointment in town at ten. There's only one route for her to take. Expect her to leave her home sometime between nine fifteen and nine thirty. She likes to arrive early. During the traffic stop, you need to search her trunk."

"Want to tell me what I'm looking for?"

Valentina grinned. "Don't you like surprises?"

"No, ma'am. Not when I'm working for you."

She chuckled. "Once the trunk is open it'll be obvious. Trust me on that."

"Are you sure she'll be going that way around that time? I can't sit out on the road forever. Someone will notice me. This appointment is set, and she'll keep it?"

"No, not yet. But if you pass the phone to your wife, she can help me arrange that part."

"Sure. One second."

There was a rustling sound. "Hello, Ms. Sandoval. What do you need from me?" the wife asked.

"Two things. Both are equally important. Contact Amber Reyes. Set up some kind of urgent meeting in the morning somewhere in town. Tell her she needs to be there by ten. You will not accept 'no' for answer. Ensure Ms. Reyes is in the right place at the right time."

"What else?"

"The project you worked on regarding Holly Powell. Activate it as soon as possible."

"I could reach out to Erica Egan tonight. Get the ball rolling. That woman will answer the phone no matter what time it is. But she'll want the proof tonight as well. Or would you like me to wait until tomorrow morning?"

"Which one is as soon as possible? Tonight? Or tomorrow?"

"Okay. I understand. I'll call her right now and arrange everything tonight. You should see it on the news about Holly before lunch."

Valentina ended the call.

Never underestimate the power of an inside man. Or woman.

Chapter Thirteen

Sunday, December 8
9:40 a.m.

The next morning, Amber stared absently through the windshield of her Jeep, feeling unsettled as she drove into town. Vera, Holly's secretary, had called, insisting that she come down to the mayor's office by nine. To talk with Holly away from the house in private.

She cringed on the inside over how that discussion was going to go.

Hold your ground. Create boundaries. It'll be fine.

She'd already decided there would be no talk of marriage or the status of her relationship with Monty at all. Baby talk was fine. Nothing more.

The one bright spot was that Vera promised to have a wide selection of munchies from Divine Treats. A boiled egg, applesauce and toast for a quick breakfast wouldn't hold her long. She was ready for a mouthwatering, sugary treat. Then she crossed her fingers her appetite would last.

She took a sip from the new water bottle Holly had gotten Buck to purchase last night. Already it had made a huge difference in her water consumption. Monty's family was overbearing and intrusive, but they meant well and looked out for those in their inner circle.

Rubbing her belly, with one hand on the steering wheel, she thought she'd be overjoyed to know that Monty loved her, to have proof she mattered more than the land and the river. And a big part of her was, but the only way to know for sure was to let him lose it all.

The idea of taking away the ranch, the land, generations of hard work from him, from her unborn son, from Kayce, from the child Grace was carrying now, made her heart weep.

As much as Monty didn't want to admit it, he was born to be a rancher. One day he'd come to realize it. But she couldn't let that happen with him working on someone else's land.

The next generation of Powells being born might have a love for ranching in their souls. Wouldn't that be something? The operation was large enough to share among so many, especially once it was combined with the Reyes land, and Matt was expanding the business further. Offering wild game hunting for tourists. Cabins were being built on the Little Shooting Star. She'd heard all the boys had pitched in, helping to build the cabins that would be rented out.

She made a right onto Route 207, which turned into Third Street, the main road into town.

Who was she to steal such a thing from everyone just to be 100 percent positive Monty's feelings for her were real? That she mattered more?

In the end, would he resent her? Would her son, after he learned about the incredible legacy that should've been passed to him?

A siren whooped once behind her.

Amber looked up in the rearview mirror. Red and blue lights flashed on a state police cruiser. Sighing, she pulled over, came to a stop and put the SUV in Park.

An officer strolled up to the driver's side and gestured for her to roll down the window with a gloved hand.

"I'm sorry, Officer. Was I speeding?" She had a tendency to do that. A bad habit she needed to break.

No more speeding with baby on board.

"License and registration." A rough voice rumbled in that authoritative way cops had. He hooked his thumbs on his utility belt and waited.

"Oh." She reached over to her glove compartment. Found the registration and handed it to him.

"License."

She opened her purse and stared at the envelope she still hadn't opened. Her father's letter. Bypassing it, she grabbed her wallet and gave him her license. "I know I was going too fast. If you let me off with a warning, I promise not to do it anymore."

He looked over her documentation. "Your registration from Texas expired last month."

She cringed. "My father died in August. I came here for his funeral and after the reading of his will things got topsy-turvy. I wasn't expecting to stay this long, but then I did. I didn't forward my mail and didn't realize the expiration was coming up. Once my brother pointed out to me that it had in fact expired, I didn't know if I should renew the registration in Texas or get a new one here. Everything in my life is changing so fast. It's so complicated and messy. I might stay. I might go. But I'll know for sure in a couple of weeks and figured I would take care of it then. In January. Once I knew if I was getting married or not. Or staying here. Or going back to Texas. Do you see what I'm saying?"

The cop grimaced.

"That was long-winded. I apologize…" She looked at his name tag. "Officer Foley." She looked over his state police uniform and made the connection. "Do you know Monty Powell? You two probably work together. We're very close."

"Ma'am, please step out of the vehicle."

"Come again?"

He put his hand on the hilt of his weapon. "Please step out of the vehicle."

She stiffened. "Yes, Officer." She did as he instructed, and her legs shook. Something like this had never happened to her before. Sure, she'd gotten a ticket before. Okay, lots of speeding tickets, but the police had never asked her to get out like she was a criminal.

He peered inside her vehicle and looked around. "Ma'am, please open your trunk."

"Is this really necessary?" she asked, incredulously. A bit excessive, wasn't it?

His features tightened to stone. His jaw set as he put his hand back on the hilt of his gun.

A flutter zipped through her chest. "Of course." Amber tapped her coat pocket, checking to make sure the key fob was inside, raised her palms and walked around to the rear of the Jeep. "This seems silly, if you ask me. I only have an emergency kit in there. Flares. Jumper cables. And a spare tire." Since the key fob was on her, she just moved her foot under the rear bumper in a straight kicking motion, activating the hands-free sensor.

The hazard lights flashed and the liftgate opened.

Her heart dropped to her stomach and the ground beneath her feet seemed to crumble away like the earth had split open wide. She staggered back. "No," she choked out.

Fiona Frye was dead. In her trunk.

"Ma'am, put your hands on your head. You're under arrest." The officer wrenched her wrists behind her back and slapped handcuffs on her while reciting her Miranda rights. He steered her to his vehicle and put a hand on the top of her head, helping her inside.

Her pulse was pounding a mile of minute, but a weird calm

stole over her. "Can you please grab my purse and water bottle? I'm pregnant. The doctor said I had to stay hydrated."

The officer hesitated a second. "Sure. But you've got to wait until after you're booked to get the water bottle."

"Can I be booked at the sheriff's department?" she asked. The sheriff was in California helping his and Grace's mother with something, leaving Holden in charge.

Holden would sort this out. She'd be okay there.

At the Laramie Police Department, with Waylon Wright eager to believe in this dreadful conspiracy spreading like a disease, there was no telling what would happen to her.

"I do know Monty, ma'am," the officer said. "His brother is chief deputy at the sheriff's. Sorry, but I'll be taking you to LPD." He slammed the door shut.

Oh, my God. Fiona, the next person who stood to inherit the land, was dead, and she was about to be booked for her murder. If she hadn't been sitting, she would've collapsed.

First Monty.

Now her.

Who would be the next person to die? And who would be blamed?

Chapter Fourteen

Sunday, December 8
10:55 a.m.

Done prepping for his upcoming interview with Monty, Waylon closed the folder he planned to bring inside the room with him. He couldn't believe what they'd found on Monty's flip phone that had been seized from his work locker.

Montgomery Powell had a lot of explaining to do, and Hannah Delaney wasn't going to be there to help him. When Fiona Frye never showed up for their appointment, he'd sent her to go check on Ms. Frye and to take another crack at questioning Pandora's neighbors. Neither who lived on either side of the young woman had been at home when they'd tried before. They could get lucky. A neighbor might have seen Pandora with Monty or with some other man.

"Hey, Wright." One of the officers who had participated in the execution of the search warrant last night came over to him. "Maybe we searched the wrong ranch last night?"

He sipped his coffee. "What are you talking about?"

"I guess you haven't heard. Amber Reyes was just booked for the murder of Fiona Frye and is sitting in a holding cell right now."

That caught his attention. "Do you mean for the murder of Pandora Frye?" he asked, but that still didn't make a lick of sense. Instinct told him that she wasn't a murderer. Besides, based on the security camera footage, she wasn't guilty.

"No. The mother. Fiona Frye."

His gut twisted. Waylon shot him a confused look. "Who was the arresting officer?"

"A guy with the state police. He's still here doing the paperwork." The cop pointed to him.

Familiar face. "Thanks," Waylon said to the cop. Grabbing the folder for his interview, he got out of his chair and waltzed over to the state trooper. "Officer Foley. Two times in two days that you're here. First, you dropped off the phone from Powell's locker."

"Yeah, they figured it made sense for me to run it by since I live in the area."

"What brings you here today?"

"Routine traffic stop turned into something more. There was a dead body in the trunk."

In mock surprise, Waylon raised both brows. "Wow, you don't see that every day. Especially not around here in our small town."

Foley flashed an easy smile. "I know, right?"

Waylon sat on the edge of the desk the guy was using. "Walk me through how it happened. The specifics."

"I was on my way to work when my wife called. So I pulled over to see what the Mrs. needed."

"Where were you?"

"Oh, I was on Route 207 near the intersection of Longhorn River Road. Anyway, this woman—"

"Name?"

"Amber Reyes. She failed to come to a complete stop at the intersection where there was a red light and didn't use her signal when you make a right turn. Turns out her registration has been expired for weeks. Then she started rambling incoherently. I asked her to step out of the vehicle. She didn't want to do it. Tried to talk her way out of it, still not making any sense. I got a weird feeling, you know, a cop's sixth sense," he said, and Waylon nodded. "With all those violations and how suspicious she was acting. So I asked to see the inside of her trunk. Bingo! Dead body."

"Golly. That's some story." A lot of stories were flying around lately. Waylon stood. "Hey, tell me something. Where do you live?"

Foley spouted out his address. The trooper lived on the western outskirts of town while the Reyes ranch was in the northeast, nowhere near town.

"Huh? That's clear on the other side. Do you drive past Longhorn River Road every day?"

"No. I was craving one of those Cronuts from Divine Treats and decided to take the scenic route to enjoy it on the drive. Pure coincidence what happened."

"Yeah, three things I love. Scenic routes. Perfect timing. And coincidence." Waylon clapped the trooper on the back. "You keep up the fine work."

Foley's smile brightened. "Will do, sir."

Waylon made his way back to the holding cells, where he found Amber Reyes looking pale, rigid and unwell. "Ms. Reyes."

She met his gaze with tired eyes. "Detective Wright. Are you here to gloat?"

"No, ma'am. I admit I'm guilty of schadenfreude when it comes to the Powells, but please believe that I take no enjoyment from the troubles of anyone else outside that family. Especially when it involves another murder."

"I didn't do it. I don't know how Fiona's body got into the trunk of my car."

"You're entitled to have a lawyer present."

"They told me I had to wait to make my phone call. But I'd tell you the same thing with an attorney present. I didn't like Fiona or Pandora. But I didn't hate either woman. I didn't wish them ill. I certainly didn't kill them."

He believed her. "Speaking of ill, that's how you look. Can I get you anything?"

"The officer who arrested me brought my water bottle and my purse. Can I have them and something to eat?" She put a hand to her stomach and rubbed it. It almost seemed an unconscious movement. "I had to go the ER last night. The doctor said I need to stay hydrated and eat. I missed breakfast."

The way she sat, hunched like the weight of the world rested on her shoulders, highlighted the outline of her belly bump. "Are you pregnant?"

Her eyes widened, but she nodded.

"Is it Monty's?"

She licked her lips and bit the inside of her cheek. "Yes."

"I'll make sure you get your phone call, the water bottle and something to eat. I can't give you your purse. Was there something inside you wanted?" Maybe she had prenatal vitamins or something for nausea.

"There's a sealed letter. From my father. I think I'm finally ready to read it."

"I'll get you taken care of, ma'am." He turned to leave, but then looked back at her. "Don't worry, Ms. Reyes. You won't be in here long. Just be patient. I don't think you killed Fiona Frye any more than you did Pandora."

"As you've already pointed out, I stand to gain if those two are gone. Why do you think I'm innocent?"

"Because I don't believe in coincidence. No such thing. And when people start using it to explain something that doesn't add up, it sets my teeth on edge. I'm going to get to the bottom of this. You can trust that."

On his way to the interrogation rooms, another officer stopped him.

"Montgomery Powell is in room one with his lawyer waiting for you."

"Thanks. Do me a favor. Ms. Reyes is in holding. Let her make her phone call ASAP. Also, see that she gets plenty of water, let her order whatever she wants to eat from Delgado's Bar and Grill—I'll cover the charge—and find her purse. There's a sealed envelope inside. Supposedly a letter. Check it to be sure and then let her have it."

"No problem."

Waylon went to room one and grabbed the handle. Taking a breath, he considered how to play this. *Poke the bear or good cop?*

Today felt like the perfect day to rattle a cage. "Poke the bear it is," he whispered to himself.

He entered the room and sat down.

Across the metal table was Monty, wearing a button-down under his shearling jacket, jeans and his black cowboy hat. His lawyer sat stiff as a board in a suit, sipping a coffee.

Waylon slapped the folder down and put his hand on top of it. "I see someone has already offered you something to drink."

"Let's get on with it," Monty said.

"I'm Tim Lemke, Mr. Powell's attorney. He has graciously agreed to cooperate with you today. We only ask that you be respectful of his time."

"Certainly." Waylon nodded. "Walk me through the events of Thursday evening."

Monty opened his mouth, but Lemke put a hand on his forearm, stopping him.

"Could you please be more specific?" the attorney asked.

"Sure." Waylon shrugged. "Where were you at nine p.m. on Thursday night?"

"The Howling Wolf Roadhouse. I have dinner there—"

Lemke leaned over to his client. "Only answer the question asked. Don't offer any additional information."

"Look," Waylon said, "this will take all day unless he fills in the blanks by offering additional information, which is the reason he's here. I thought you wanted me to be respectful of his time. Either you killed Pandora Frye or you didn't. So, if you want to get on with it, start talking."

"I have dinner there on Thursdays," Monty said.

"Why Thursdays?" Waylon wondered. "Why not Fridays?"

"I have seniority. I only work Monday through Thursday. That's my Friday, the night I want to unwind. The other three days I spend working on the ranch. Long, hard hours and I don't feel like driving to a bar afterward."

Satisfied, Waylon nodded. "Do you only eat dinner there? Do you ever pick up women?"

Monty clenched his jaw. "I used to."

"What changed?"

Monty looked at his attorney.

"I don't see the relevance," Lemke said. "How does this pertain to last Thursday? Why don't we stick to that?"

Everyone had secrets, the guilty and innocent alike. But Waylon needed to know why Monty wanted to hide his relationship with Amber if he wasn't sleeping with Pandora.

"Okay. Did you see and speak with Pandora Frye at the Howling Wolf that evening?" Waylon asked.

"I did."

"And?"

Monty looked to his attorney and got the okay before going on. "She approached me as I was finishing dinner."

"Did she make any amorous overtures that you welcomed or encouraged?"

"She tried to touch me a couple of times. Pandora is— *was*—a handsy person. I didn't take it as her hitting on me or anything, but I also let her know that I didn't like it."

"Let her know how?"

"I removed her hands from my body."

"Interesting. The bartender at the Howling Wolf, Finn, told us that you two were all over each other and looked like you—and I quote—'needed to get a room.' Any idea why he would tell us that if wasn't true?"

"None at all. I think you should go back and ask him again."

That was on Waylon's list of things to do for this afternoon. They needed to squeeze the bartender and get to the bottom of why his story felt off. "Why did Pandora approach you?"

"Told me she didn't think Amber was going to marry me. But once Pandora inherited the land, that we could strike a deal where I could get it."

"What were the terms of this deal?"

"She refused to talk about it at the Howling Wolf. Told me that I had to do it at her place over a drink or there would be no deal. Then she left."

"What happened next?"

"I paid the bill. Went outside to find her waiting. I agreed since I didn't see the harm in hearing what she had to say."

"You drove yourself to her place?"

Monty nodded. "I followed her over. She let me in and showed me into her studio, where she worked. I took a seat. She poured me a drink. Then she made small talk for a bit. The conversation turned to Amber and Chance. Pandora told me that she would never give up the Reyes family home, but she didn't want that to put her at odds with her half siblings. She wanted to get to know them. And then." He shook his head. "I don't remember anything clearly until I woke up in the hospital."

"Did you watch Pandora pour your drink?"

Lowering his head, Monty looked like he was thinking about it. "No. She handed me one of her portfolio books and asked me what I thought of her work while she poured the drinks."

Maybe he had let his guard down around her. What danger would he have assumed a woman weighing one hundred twenty pounds would've posed to him? How was he supposed to know where the night was headed?

One possible theory.

But there were others and they all needed to be explored. "The portion of the Reyes land that might've gone to Pandora is extremely valuable to your family, isn't it?"

"It is."

"Valuable enough for you to have started a romantic relationship with Pandora. To have seduced her. Perhaps promised marriage to her."

Monty's eyes hardened. "No."

"That's impossible?" Waylon gave a light, incredulous chuckle. "You wouldn't seduce a woman for the land? Or should I say once more. The way you seduced a young and vulnerable Amber Reyes when she was only nineteen years old shortly after losing her mother."

"Watch it," Monty said, through gritted teeth.

"Did I strike a nerve?" *Good.* Waylon was only getting started. "In your locker at work, a burner phone was found. I printed out screenshots of some of the texts." He pulled a couple of sheets from the folder and slid them across the table.

Monty picked up the papers. He and his lawyer read through them. Alarm washed over Monty's face.

"Steamy stuff in there," Waylon said. "Kinky, too. A lot of talk about what you liked and how much she enjoyed giving it to you. How much she loved you. How she couldn't wait to marry you."

"I've never seen these texts." Monty finally looked scared. "I didn't write them or receive them."

"My client's name is never mentioned," Lemke said, stabbing the paper. "Nor that of Ms. Frye. Only McDreamy, Lover, Bubba and Cupcake. These texts could be between any two people."

Waylon frowned. "The problem is that the phone was found in your client's locker and the number he texted did in fact belong to Pandora Frye. There were also some racy photos that you took of Pandora that were found on the phone." He took blown-up copies of the pictures from the folder and slid those over next.

Monty peered down at them and his jaw dropped.

"Looks like you're into bondage," Waylon said, his stomach turning. That was not his thing. "And asphyxiation during sex." There were photos of Pandora tied up, nude, someone with a gloved hand choking her. The person had worn long sleeves. In some of the photos pleasure was on her face, either real or feigned. But in the rest the fear in her eyes was clear. All the pictures and texts were from last month. "Maybe you got too rough during sex on Thursday night. Choked her to death by accident." Most crimes of passion were violent, such as strangulation or a stabbing, a hands-on act done in the heat of the moment. "Then you got desperate and needed to cover it up." He shoved a picture of Pandora, lying on the floor, naked and murdered, in his face.

"Go to hell!" Monty threw the photos at him and jumped to his feet. "We're done here!"

"You're going to sit back down," Waylon said calmly.

Monty narrowed his eyes and clenched his hands. "Or else what?"

"Or else I'm going to have a little chat with Amber Reyes. Who, by the way, is sitting in a holding cell right now because a dead body was found in her trunk this morning."

"What?" Monty reeled back. "Whose body?" he demanded.

But Waylon was on a roll and ignored the question. "And when I talk to the mother of your unborn child, I'm going to show her those racy photos and tell her my theory about your kinky side."

A ferocious expression darkened Monty's face, and he cocked back his fist, ready to pound into Waylon.

His attorney jumped between him and the table. "Don't do it. You can't."

"No, let him," Waylon said with a grin. Gone were their high school days where he'd been smaller than Monty. Now he was two inches taller, outweighed him by about twenty pounds of solid muscle and still had sharp reflexes. He could've stopped him if he wanted, but he welcomed the punch. "I'd love to charge him with assault of a police officer. I can put you in a cell next to Amber's."

"You sick son of a—"

"Stop and get control of yourself," his lawyer warned. "This is what he wants. You acting like a crazed animal with anger management issues." The lawyer faced Waylon. "My client's face was not in any of the photos. You can't prove it was him."

"The phone they found isn't mine," Monty said.

"Then how did it get in your locker?"

"I don't know, but the only reason you're doing this is because of what happened in high school." Monty lowered his fist. "I'm sorry, okay? I didn't know Tara was your girlfriend when I asked her to homecoming."

This wasn't about some gripe from high school, but since Monty had brought it up, he was willing to discuss it. "I told you she was and that the only reason she said yes to you was because your father and hers were in business. That she thought she had to agree."

"And I thought you were a lying, sore loser! It wasn't until I didn't end up going to homecoming and she confessed to me that she was relieved not to go with me that I learned the truth."

"Take what you want, regardless of who gets hurt," Waylon said. "That's your motto. That's the code you live by. And as if that wasn't enough, you had to break my hand."

Indignation twisted Monty's features, reddening his cheeks

as he shook his head. "You picked a fight after football practice. I was holding my helmet and used it to block your fist. I didn't mean to break your hand and end your football season."

"I guess you didn't mean to throw me into the trophy display case either, shredding my face with glass." He had fallen face-first. Took thirty stitches. Not to mention the pain. For the rest of his senior year, everyone called him *Scarface*.

"It was an accident. I never intended for you to get hurt. Not like that. And I came to your home and apologized."

"Only because your father made you." The gall. Monty could've shoved that artificial, hollow apology where the sun didn't shine for all Waylon had cared. "What really burns me to the core is that after the stitches and getting a cast, I was the one sentenced to detention for fighting. Not you. Oh, no, a Powell was too good for detention. That was beneath the son of the almighty Buck and Holly."

A roar of angry laughter rolled out of Monty. "You're right, I didn't get detention because I'm a Powell. But what you don't know is that my father whipped me with a leather strap until I bled because you were smaller than me at that time and got hurt so badly. I didn't get to go to homecoming. I didn't get to finish the football season either. My father pulled me from the team. And I'm the one who had to pay for a new display case by working on the ranch well before dawn prior to school and after until midnight. Every day for months. He came down on me particularly hard because I was to be made the example for my brothers. The cautionary tale of what not to do. So, yeah, I'm sorry I didn't get two weeks of detention, but there was ranch justice exacted on your behalf. Take some consolation in that."

Waylon had no idea his father had been so harsh on him. If he had known, it would've been water under the bridge eons ago.

"No matter what you think of me," Monty said, "I'm not

a murderer and I have never slept with Pandora. And I won't tolerate you hurting Amber to get to me."

"Then why were you hiding your relationship with Amber?"

"It all looks bad! Having a relationship with her makes it look worse, especially if you think I was sleeping with Pandora, too. But I wasn't and never would."

Waylon spotted another opening and pushed. "Why *never*? Why such an impossibility? She was a very pretty girl and you had a lot to gain by doing so."

"Sleeping with Pandora Frye, hell, looking at her the wrong way would have hurt Amber. I broke her heart once. I love her. I want to win her back. Last night I told her the land doesn't matter. We can wait to get married to prove it to her. Fiona Frye can have it for all I care. Even if it means my family's legacy has to die. Amber, our baby, that's all that matters."

Waylon leaned back in his chair. "The dead body in Amber's trunk was Fiona Frye."

Monty spit out a curse. "I don't believe this." Heaving a ragged breath, he scrubbed his face with his hands. "This can't be happening. Amber didn't do it. You probably figure the same. Why would she drive around with a dead body in the trunk? Unless you think I did it and asked her to take the body somewhere?"

"I don't think you did it." Waylon stood. "There's a bigger game at play here. I needed you to be honest. I'm talking bare-your-soul-in-a-confessional kind of honest to fill in some of the blanks. I need to get to the bottom of this before any more dead bodies turn up. No hard feelings. Right?"

"To clarify," Lemke said, "you're not charging my client?"

Waylon took a deep cleansing breath. "No, I'm not charging him."

"You're going to release Amber?" Monty asked.

"She will be. There's a procedure. I need to talk to the chief and explain."

"I want to see her," Monty said. "Make sure she's all right. She needs to eat and drink water."

"I made sure she's being taken care of."

An urgent rap on the door interrupted them before a cop poked his head inside. "Assistant District Attorney Melanie Merritt is on the phone for you. Says it can't wait. You can pick up line two in the next room."

A tingle zipped down Waylon's spine. "I'll be right back." He hurried next door and answered the phone. "Howdy, darling, please tell me this call is of a personal nature."

Two and a half years ago, when Melanie moved to the area, before he knew she was going to be the new ADA, they'd run into each other at a bar in Wayward Bluffs. One thing had led to another, and they'd slept together.

Since then, they'd been in a quasi-relationship. Unofficially and under wraps. Always on her terms. They usually met at his place or hers three to four times a week. Sometimes in the middle of the day for a hot quickie. Strictly sex had become sentimental and even sweet. But he was ready to take things to the next level. Exclusivity in secret was no longer enough. He wanted to go from quasi to serious. Surprising her with tickets to the Caribbean for Christmas was either going to get him what he wanted or scare her off.

"Sorry to disappoint you, cowboy," she said, her tone all business, and the spark of anticipatory joy in him fizzled. "Next time watch it, I could've had you on speaker."

The line between personal and professional were critical to her. He got it and had to if he wanted to see her whenever she fancied herself in the mood.

"Are you not alone?" he asked.

"Yes and no. Someone unexpected is paying me a visit. I waited until he went to get coffee to call you because you tend to be unpredictable on the phone. I never know what filthy thing might come out of your mouth. I need to see you, Delaney and Montgomery Powell right now."

"Delaney is wrapped up at the moment, but I'm with Powell. I've got him in the next room."

"Good. I'm sure you've been scratching your head over the Pandora Frye case."

"As a matter of fact, I have. The pieces don't add up." He had the feeling Monty was being framed.

"I think I have some answers for you. Get him over to my office on the double. This can't wait for any reason." She hung up before he could respond.

"Yes, ma'am," he said to himself. He pulled out his phone and called Delaney. "Hey, Fiona Frye is dead."

"I figured as much. I'm at her place now. Looks like a tornado went through here."

"The body was found in Amber Reyes's vehicle."

"You've got to be kidding me."

"Wish I was. Hey, Monty claims he wasn't sleeping with Pandora and that their discussion at the bar was all business. Funny thing is, I believe him. Which means the bartender is lying. Go back and talk to him again. Find out why. Tell him we've got a witness who was in the bar that night contradicting his story. Lean hard on him."

"Are you mansplaining to me how to do my job, Lieutenant?"

Waylon cleared his throat. "Apologies. You've got this. I'm heading to the ADA's office with Monty."

"Why?"

"Don't know. She wants to see us about the case. I'll text you with an update when I know more."

"Okay." They hung up, and he ducked back into the interrogation room. "The ADA has information about this case. She needs to see us in her office immediately."

"But I need to see Amber."

"That'll have to wait. Trust me, she's fine." Waylon hurried Monty and his attorney out of the room and down the hall. "Hey, do you know a state trooper by the name of Foley?"

"Yeah. Nick."

"Does he have a grudge against you? Any reason to have it in for you?"

"None that I can think of. Why?"

Waylon shook his head, not ready to get into it any deeper. "Only wondering."

As they crossed through the bullpen, Detective Kent Kramer was ushering in Holly Powell in handcuffs. Her assistant, Eddie Something, was following them, carrying her purse.

"Mom!" Monty rushed over to her. "What's going on?"

"I've been arrested." She held up her hands, wrists cuffed in front of her.

"For what?" her son asked.

"Embezzlement."

The Powell family house of cards was tumbling down today. Waylon approached the other detective. "What's going on, Kent?"

"Erica Egan stopped by to see me earlier as a *courtesy* and handed over proof that Mrs. Powell has been embezzling money from the mayor's office. Twenty-five thousand dollars."

"That's absurd," Monty said. "She doesn't have a need to steal any money."

"I had Eddie call Buck to get our attorney, Corthell," Holly said.

"He's on the way, along with your husband." Eddie stepped forward. "I also asked Brianne to get out in front of this."

"Not Corthell, Mom." Monty shook his head. "You need a criminal attorney." He grabbed Lemke by the arm and shoved him toward his mother. "Use mine."

"Anyway," Kent said, "I think Egan was so generous sharing the information before she broke the story because she wanted to catch us arresting Mrs. Powell on camera. I'm sure it's all over the news by now."

"The world is going to hell in a handbasket, Mom," Monty said. "Amber was arrested, too."

"Oh no! That poor thing," Holly paled, pressing her hands to her chest. "Is she all right?"

"Have them put Mrs. Powell in the cell next to Ms. Reyes," Waylon said to Kent. "We need to go see the ADA. She said it can't wait for any reason." He took Monty by the arm, and the man jerked free of his grip. *Guess there are hard feelings.* "Let's go."

Chapter Fifteen

Sunday, December 8
12:20 p.m.

"What's this all about?" Monty asked, walking into the assistant district attorney's office. Best for them to get straight to it. The sooner they did, the sooner he could see Amber.

"Take a seat," Melanie Merritt said, seated behind her desk. She turned toward a man who was standing in the corner, staring out the window. "This is Agent Welliver. He's with the Drug Enforcement Agency. This is Montgomery Powell and Detective Lieutenant Waylon Wright." The ADA used Waylon's full pompous title that everyone else simply shortened to detective.

The man strolled over to the desk, holding a cup of coffee. Looked to be in his late fifties. Weathered. He wore a crisp black blazer and jeans. He offered a tight smile. "I'd say it's a pleasure to meet you, but I come as the bearer of bad news."

"Related to the homicide case of Pandora Frye?" Waylon asked.

Monty cut his gaze to the detective. He was still simmering over the interrogation but he now had a better understanding of Waylon and was trying to not take the harsh tactics so personally.

But it felt brutally personal.

"I believe so," Agent Welliver said. "We've been working on a case for a long time. Years really. Trying to bring down the Sandoval cartel. Earlier this year, we finally infiltrated them. Got our guy recruited. He's been working as a driver. Feeds us information."

"Some of that information helped us with a local case," Melanie said, "that led to the takedown of Todd Burk and a few Hellhound bikers. We were worried that Rip Lockwood and Ashley Russo had popped up on the Sandoval radar. Consequently, they had to go into hiding."

Monty knew them both. Ashley had worked for the sheriff's department. Her brother had been Holden's best friend in high school, before he was killed. They'd all suspected that Burk had been behind it. Monty had been thrilled when he'd learned of Burk's arrest. Justice finally served. "Yeah, I heard they picked up and disappeared. What does this have to do with me or the murder of Pandora Frye?"

"Welliver contacted me earlier," Melanie said. "Gave me the heads-up he was coming and why."

"Our inside man called me at two this morning. He's been trying to reach me for a couple of days, but he's being watched closely." Welliver sat on the edge of the desk, his expression grim, his eyes predatory, and Monty supposed one had to be a predator when hunting monsters. "Valentina Sandoval, the head of the cartel, has you in her crosshairs." He pointed at Montgomery.

"Me?" He stiffened. "Why?"

"After we talked a few hours ago," Melanie said, "I rushed into the office to see if I could figure out why. I cross-referenced your name with any cases related to the cartel. I got a hit on a big one." She offered the file and Monty took it. "Does the name Santiago Sandoval ring a bell?"

"Not really." He opened the folder. As soon as he saw the picture, it hit him. Dark eyes, slicked back hair, cocksure attitude. "I do remember him. He was speeding in a Mercedes-Benz G-Class. A two-hundred-thousand-dollar car. I expected a hard time. A smooth talker who wouldn't care about a hundred-dollar ticket. You know the type, it's more about the inconvenience. But this guy was different. A nasty piece of work. Real ballsy. He had a woman in the passenger seat, performing a sex act on him. She stopped at the last minute. He had white powder on his nose. There was more on the dash. When I questioned him about it, he offered me money. A lot of money. In cash. Boasted about how it was more than I make in a month. Told me to shut up, take it, get back in my vehicle and forget I ever saw him. Or there would be consequences. Life-and-death consequences."

"Of course you arrested the jerk," Waylon said.

"Of course." Monty nodded. "I did so with great pleasure, too. Turns out he had ten kilos of cocaine and one gram of fentanyl in the trunk. Along with a lot more cash."

"He was the son of Alejandro Sandoval," Melanie said. "Who used to run the cartel. Santiago was sentenced for possession with intent to distribute and received seven years in prison. His wife, who was in the passenger seat, got three years."

"Okay." Monty shrugged. "You do the crime, you do the time."

Welliver grimaced. "Not so simple. In prison there's a system, a code, a manner in which things are handled. Someone inside broke that code. A guard was probably paid off to move Santiago to a cell block where he didn't have protection. He died a very brutal, very violent death. It was slow. Painful. Real ugly. His father suffered a heart attack shortly thereafter, leaving Valentina in charge of the cartel and as guardian of her nephew, Santiago's son."

Ice ran through Monty's veins. "I take it she blames me. Because I didn't take the bribe and let him get away."

"Pretty much, yeah." Welliver sipped his coffee. "The reality is that she could blame Santiago's lawyer. The prosecutor on the case. The judge who sentenced her brother. The guard who was paid off. But you make an easy, simple source for her vehemence because probably in her twisted, dark mind it started with you. Makes it all your fault."

"Did your inside man give you anything else to go on?" Waylon asked. "Specifics?"

Welliver nodded. "Valentina asked him to assassinate your brother Holden. He made it look like he tried during the holiday tree lighting ceremony."

A hot blade of agony stabbed his chest. "She tried to have my brother murdered. But why?"

Welliver shrugged. "Because her brother is dead."

"But I've got a lot of brothers. Why would she single out Holden?"

"We've asked ourselves the same question. Best guess? He's the only one with a child," Melanie said. "I think that might be the reason, as disturbing as it sounds."

He swallowed down the raw bitterness rising in his throat.

"She also told my guy that she wanted him to do it in front of you, where you could watch. Valentina is a sadist. Next, she wants your father, Buck, to be executed. Her plan is to destroy everything you care about. Piece by piece."

Rage prickled his skin. "You think she's responsible for Pandora's murder."

Welliver tipped his head from side to side. "Stands to reason, considering I know she's behind Fiona Frye's death. She had my guy and one of her guards move the body and plant it in Amber Reyes's trunk."

Monty swore. "Why did she have to hurt so many other people? Why not just put a bullet in me and be done with it?"

"Too easy." Welliver smiled. "To her, you probably don't deserve a quick death since her brother didn't have one."

"But why kill Fiona?" Melanie asked. "To compound your guilt and implicate Amber?"

"I think there's more to it." Waylon moved to the edge of his seat. "Pandora was seeing a man. She had intercourse less than an hour before she died. My guess right there in her house, where you were blacked out. I think Pandora didn't fully trust this guy. Rightfully so. She gave her mother a flash drive with proof of who this man is and the nature of their relationship. Proof I'm sure we'll never find now."

"This guy is out there somewhere. In town." Monty stood. "My family isn't safe. None of them."

"I suggest you all go on lockdown at your ranch," the ADA said. "Lie low and wait it out."

"Wait? For how long?" Growing unease curled through his body. "Are you going to arrest Valentina?"

"For this?" Welliver asked.

"Yes!" Monty took a breath, doing his best to control his temper.

"Look, buddy, these are the facts." Welliver crossed his arms over his chest. "We have no proof that she's responsible for Pandora Frye's death. We have no proof that she ordered the murder of Fiona. Only that she had a body moved."

"What about my brother?" Monty asked in disbelief.

"Attempted murder for hire," Melanie said. "Solicitation carries the same potential penalty as the underlying crime. In this case, a conviction would carry a life sentence."

"There we go." He clapped his hands together once. "Make the arrest."

Welliver shook his head.

The ADA sighed. "This is her first offense. The judge will set bail. Probably somewhere between one hundred thousand and a quarter million."

"Chump change for her," Welliver said. "And what do you think she's going to do in the meantime? No need for suspense,

I'll tell you. Send the full force of her cartel to slaughter your entire family. And my guy will have been burned by then, so no more information from him. You won't see it coming. Not to mention she'll also put a hit out on my informant so he can't ever testify."

"What are you saying?" Monty asked. "There's nothing I can do?"

"We have to do more than arrest her," Agent Welliver said. "We need to cripple her business. Isolate her. And take down her crew as well."

"My family won't hide out at home indefinitely." Monty shook his head, sick with worry. "My mother is the mayor. My brothers are in law enforcement. They will feel obligated to do their jobs."

"Speaking of your mother," Waylon said. "I guess we should assume the embezzlement case that coincidentally popped up against her today is bogus."

"Based on the timing," the agent said, "in all likelihood."

"Listen, your ranch is a compound." The ADA met his gaze. "Call your family and have them muster there. Lock it down."

Monty nodded. He hated it, but she was right. "I need you to get my mother and Amber released from jail," he said to Waylon. "I'll call my father. He'll make sure they get to the ranch safely and he'll give everyone else a heads-up about what's going on."

"I'm on it. I'll call Chief Nelson. I can see if we can spare any officers to safeguard you guys at the ranch." Waylon took out his phone. "I also need to text Hannah about this."

"Don't ask for any police assistance," the DEA agent said. "We don't know who is in her pocket."

"You make a valid point." Waylon nodded. "Remember when I asked you about Officer Foley," he said to Monty.

"Yeah."

"He's the one who brought us the phone that was found

in your locker at work. He was also the one who pulled over Amber on a traffic stop and searched her trunk, where Fiona Frye had conveniently been dumped."

"I know him. I work with him," Monty said, exasperated. "He seemed like a good guy."

"They all do until they don't." The DEA agent strolled back to the window. "That's how it works in the underworld."

"The four of us need to put our heads together and map out how Valentina has done all of this," the ADA said. "She has more than Agent Welliver's inside guy helping her. Officer Foley is a possibility that we need to verify. He could be the tip of the iceberg. Until we figure out how deep this goes and who is involved, we don't know how much danger you or your family are truly in."

"You're right," Monty said. "Without knowing, my family and I are vulnerable, exposed, essentially operating blind." His gut burned.

If he didn't know the extent of the danger, how could he ever hope to keep his family safe?

Chapter Sixteen

To Amber, it was all a vicious blur. Seeing Fiona Frye in the trunk of her car. Being arrested. The mug shot. Having her fingerprints taken. Hauled to this awful cell and locked up.

She couldn't believe that having Holly in the cell next to her was comforting. Even though the accusation of embezzlement was unnerving. It seemed they were all being systematically targeted. But why and to what awful end?

"Honey, you can't keep stalling, sitting there simply holding your father's letter," Holly said.

Amber glanced down at the envelope in her hands. "I'm afraid."

"Of what?"

"I've been mad at him for so long, needing..." Her voice trailed off. She wasn't actually sure of what. "Something." An apology. An explanation that made her feel better. "And I'm scared that he won't give it to me in this letter. That I'll still be angry with him."

"Anger is the second stage of grief. As I see it, you've been grieving the loss of your relationship with him since you left. It's time to work through the other stages."

Amber shook her head. It couldn't possibly be that simple. Read a letter and work through the stages. Could it? "He should have told me that he was sick and given me a chance to fix this broken thing between us. Why would he deny me that closure?"

"Maybe it's in the letter. There's only way to find out." Holly leaned back against the wall. "My dad died on the job. Shot in the line of duty. He was healthy. In his prime. I never got to say goodbye to him either. But I would've given anything to have the kind of letter that you're holding now. It's a rare gift."

Amber swallowed hard. No matter how she felt after reading it, this was her father's final attempt at speaking to her. She owed him the respect of finding out what he had to say. She took a sip from her water bottle and opened the envelope.

Slowly, she removed the handcrafted white wove paper with the Longhorn Ranch logo embossed at the top and read the *handwritten* letter that she'd been carrying four months.

My Dearest Amber Sofia,

If you're reading this, then I have passed and, hopefully, I'm reunited with your mother. She was the love of my life. After hearing my last will and testament and the full terms of the trust, I'm sure you question that. Yes, I had an indiscretion many years ago. I have no excuse for it. Your mother was perfect, far too good for me, while I was a deeply flawed man who gave in to a stupid moment of weakness. The affair was short-lived because I realized that if Sofia ever found out it would break her heart. By that point, Fiona was pregnant and wanted to keep the child.

I provided for them, with the understanding that Sofia would never know the truth and Pandora would only learn I was her father when I was ready. Fiona agreed and waited for years. When your mother died, I was lost. Scared. Terrified about what would happen to you.

I didn't want you to be alone and I didn't want you to settle for less than you deserved.

You were my princess. I wanted to give you the world. I thought I could give you Monty. You loved him and I knew that he would love you in return one day. That he would make a strong, caring husband who would be a true partner through life. Also, through your union, our ranches could also be united. I never wanted to push either of you into ranching the way Buck did him. The boy only rebelled.

Buck treated him like he was a wild horse that needed to be broken. Tamed. But I saw something different. Monty is no horse. He's a mule. For one thing, they're smarter and can't be bullied. They need a legitimate reason to do what you want. "Because I said so" isn't good enough reason for them. You can't push them the way you can a horse and you have to have a ton more patience. Instead of using a whip, one must use love, understanding and a good reward system.

That's why I created the terms of the trust, as Machiavellian as it might have seemed. And it worked, too. Only weeks after you two became a couple, he was ready to marry you with a heart full of love, to be a faithful husband, a dedicated father to your children. But you found out about my machinations and split.

I can't say I blame you, my dearest. You have your mother's fire, her pride, her fighting spirit. I respect you for leaving and for turning your back on me.

My one regret is that I didn't apologize. It was the only way to get you to come back home. That or die. Ha ha! You see, I couldn't give you the apology you wanted, some heartfelt "sorry" because, well, I wasn't truly sorry. How could I be if I was willing to do it again?

And a million times over, I would do it.

You wanted Monty and I aimed to get him for you. Hence the reason I kept the trust as is. You never married. Monty never married. I must have faith in the belief that I have done the right thing and that you shall reap the reward even as I endured the price at not having you by my side in my final days.

Which brings me to Pandora. My child who suffered in my absence from her life, not having a father growing up though I lived in the very same town. She never had the memories and the birthdays, the celebrations, and the words of adoration from me. The hugs and kisses. My support or encouragement. To see the sparkle in my eye the way you did every time I looked at you. I can't ever give her those things. But I can give her the Reyes family home.

I know that one day you will call the Shooting Star Ranch your home. And Chance has moved on from Wyoming, and he doesn't care about the house.

Let Pandy have it with peace in your heart. Call her sister. Embrace her. Welcome her. If you don't, Chance never will.

Do this for me, though I have no right to ask anything of you. Please. I bet you can count on one hand how many times I've used that six-letter word with you and have fingers left over. Don't be angry with me anymore. Let it go.

Remember me. Toast me. Don't put flowers on my grave. Save those for your mother's. Pour a little whiskey on mine instead. The good stuff.

You are now and will forever be my sunshine.
Your Loving Father

Amber wiped the tears streaming down her face, but she couldn't stop crying. She was a total sobbing mess.

"Oh, honey, I wish I had some tissues for you," Holly said. "How was the letter?"

"You were right," she said, choked up. "A rare gift."

She suddenly missed her father so much and wished she could hug him. Hug him tight and tell him how much she loved him. That she was the one sorry and he was right about Monty. How he'd love to hear that. "You were right, Daddy," she whispered. "You were so right."

If only she had read the letter sooner. Before Pandora was murdered. She could've done as he requested. Maybe it would've made a difference somehow.

An officer came down the hall and stopped at their cells. "You're both free to go."

"Really, why?" Holly asked.

The cop shrugged and unlocked Amber's cell. "Orders from the chief."

Rubbing her swollen eyes, she rose to her feet and stretched her legs.

Next, he let Holly out. "Mr. Powell is waiting for you two."

Which Mr. Powell? Amber wanted to ask. There were so many of them.

Outside of the cells, Holly pulled her close, wrapping her in a warm hug. "You looked like you could use one of those."

She hugged her back, grateful for the affection. Having Holly and Buck as in-laws would be a mixed blessing. The best part was that they could tell her stories about her parents, things she didn't know, like the stuff about the bananas and lemon wedges. Stories that she'd be able to pass on to her own children even though her parents were gone. Their memories would live on.

"Thank you." Amber gave her a sad smile. "Let's get out of here and see who's waiting for us."

"My money is on my husband," Holly said.

Amber was relieved to leave the holding cell area and step into the hall on their way to freedom. "Even though we didn't get a chance to have the morning meeting you wanted, we still got to talk." It had been nice to have Holly there, for support, for comfort, for a friendly ear with no pressurizing discussion of the future and marriage.

"What meeting, honey?"

Amber furrowed her brow. "The one Vera called me about. She said you wanted to talk to me privately, away from the house."

"I didn't ask her to do that. There must be a misunderstanding. Maybe I made an offhand remark about wanting to speak with you and she took the initiative. She's helpful that way. Reading my mind, anticipating my needs."

"Must be nice to have such a helpful staff."

"I couldn't do this job as mayor without my team."

They passed the bullpen and could see the lobby. She spotted Buck and Eddie waiting for them.

As soon as they pushed through the double doors, Buck enveloped Holly in a bear hug and kissed the top of her head. She was a petite woman but looked even smaller and more fragile in her husband's arms.

"Why did they release us?" Holly asked. "Not that I'm complaining."

"Something to do with the Sandoval cartel and a woman named Valentina," Buck said. "Apparently, she's been targeting Monty. Wants to make him pay. All this misery we've been through over the past couple of days has been about a vendetta. She even tried to have Holden killed."

Holly gasped. "No."

Shock filled Amber's chest.

"That's what those shots fired at the tree lighting ceremony were all about," Buck said. "Goons from the cartel trying to take out our boy, Holden. I guess to punish Monty. We need to go to the Shooting Star. Arm up. Get the ranch hands in the bunkhouse to stand guard. And we'll wait for Monty. Once he has more information, we'll decide what to do."

"Where is Monty?" Amber asked. Why wasn't he here?

"He's working with Waylon, the assistant district attorney and a DEA agent. They're trying to figure out how deep this goes and who in town might be involved."

"Why is a DEA agent here?" Eddie asked. "Is it simply because it's about the cartel or are drugs a part of this?"

Buck shook his head. "I'm not entirely sure. Come on. We should get going."

"What about Grace?" Eddie pushed his glasses up his nose. "She and the baby are at the church. She was staying after service to help sort the donated toys for children in need. I hate to think about something horrible happening to her or poor little Kayce."

Holly pressed a hand to her chest. "Oh, no. Buck, we need to pick them up right away. I don't want her on the road alone. Unlike you and me she refuses to carry a gun."

"By the way," Buck said. "Here's your purse." He also handed Amber hers.

Holly took the handbag and checked the contents. "I need to buy her and you," she said, pointing to Amber, "a Beretta like the one I have. Small, but packs a deadly punch. Let's go to the church."

"Why don't you two go and get Grace and Kayce and I can take Amber to the ranch," Eddie said. "It's not best to have everyone clustered and so exposed. Two pregnant women and a baby all together? Makes for a tempting target. These cartel folks could have hired men lurking in every corner of the town."

"That's true." Holly put her purse under her arm. "But they're messing with the wrong family."

"Are you carrying?" Buck asked.

"Always." Eddie flashed the gun in his shoulder holster under his jacket.

"All right." Buck gave a firm nod. "You two go straight to the ranch. We'll be along shortly."

They hustled outside and separated, going toward different vehicles.

"Do you mind if we swing by my house first?" Amber asked. "I need to pick up some things. Clothes. My prenatal vitamins."

Eddie frowned. "Buck told us to go straight to the Shooting Star. We should listen to him."

"But there's no telling how long we'll be on that ranch." It wasn't like she could borrow stuff to wear from Holly or Grace. Neither would have anything that would fit her. Even Grace at almost nine months probably wore a size small in maternity clothing. "Please. I promise I'll be quick."

"Okay. Do you mind driving?" Eddie asked. "I've never been out to your place. That way instead of me focusing on directions, I can keep an eye out for anything suspicious. Worst-case scenario, if we were under attack, it would be hard to shoot at someone while driving."

"As long as it's not a stick. I'm not good with a manual."

"You've got nothing to worry about." He handed her his keys, and they climbed into his Chevy Tahoe.

Watching Buck and Holly speed in the direction of the church, she signaled and pulled out. At the corner, she turned onto Third Street and headed home.

Eddie was vigilant. Checking the rearview and side mirrors. Turning around and looking over his shoulder. Once they made it out of the busy part of town, he settled down.

It was easier to see someone trailing them or racing up behind the vehicle on Route 207.

"I have a small confession to make." A sheepish grin tugged at the corners of his mouth, and his brown eyes sparkled briefly.

"Please don't tell me you don't know how to fire a gun or aren't a very good shot," she said, half joking. She wouldn't have been surprised if that was the case, since he was such a gentle man with a quiet voice, disinterested in typical cowboy things like riding and shooting, but the odds were low. Most people raised in these parts or had lived here for a substantial amount of time learned to shoot and understood gun safety.

"Oh, no, it isn't that," he said. "I'm a rather good shot."

"Then what is it?"

"I wasn't entirely honest."

Longhorn River Road was coming up soon. "About what?"

"That you have nothing to worry about."

She glanced at him, trying to understand what he meant.

Eddie pulled his gun from the holster and aimed it at her.

Panic shuddered through her as her mouth fell open. "What are you doing?"

"Incentivizing you to do as I say. You're going to pass Longhorn River Road and make a left onto Big Canyon Way instead. Then we're taking Interstate 80 to I-25 South."

Her heart pounded, and her brain raced a million miles a second. "But why?"

"We need to go to Boulder."

She looked at him in shock, unable to keep her full focus on the road. "What's in Colorado? Why do we need to go there, Eddie?"

Taking a deep breath, he removed his glasses, setting them on the console between the seats. He peeled off his mustache, giving it a little yank that seemed to hurt. With a good, solid tug, he pulled the wig back, revealing a bald head. "Call me Roman. My boss is there," he said, his voice changing, deepening, hardening. His demeanor shifted, too, transforming before her eyes from unassuming into terrifying. "Valentina Sandoval. She's the head of the Sandoval cartel. One of the most powerful and ruthless individuals on the face of the planet." He spoke honestly without any affectation, and every muscle in her body vibrated with fear. "She's also the woman who wants to make Montgomery Powell suffer. Hence the need for you, the mother of his unborn child."

Chapter Seventeen

Sunday, December 8
2:50 p.m.

"Thank you. I appreciate the information." Monty hung up the phone. "My captain said that Nicholas Foley came in off patrol early on Friday afternoon. Claimed he wasn't feeling well. The camera showed him entering the locker room between shifts, when it wasn't busy and most likely empty, where he remained for less than five minutes and then left. But since we don't have cameras inside the locker room, we can't prove that he planted the phone."

"The flip phone had been wiped clean of any prints," Waylon said. "And there's no way it was coincidence that Foley was the same officer to pull over Amber. His story doesn't make sense. The guy lives way on the other side of town."

Monty grabbed one of the steaming hot coffees that had been brought in on a tray. "If Foley is a part of this, then his wife might be, too."

"Who's the wife?" the DEA agent asked.

"Vera. She's my mother's secretary in the mayor's office."

The ADA snapped her fingers. "Explains the neat packet of evidence that landed in Erica Egan's lap and made its way to the LPD. I'm sure that if we explain to her the extenuating circumstances, she might be willing to make an exception to her rule as a reporter and reveal her source for the story on your mother."

"I can light a fire under her," Waylon volunteered.

Monty gave a nod of gratitude. It was so much nicer to have this guy on his side rather than working against him.

There was a brief knock on the door before it opened. Hannah stalked in, shutting it behind her. "The bartender was lying. A guy came to see him on Friday morning after the murder. Broke into his house and woke up from a deep sleep. Terrified him. Paid him a thousand bucks to feed any cops that came sniffing around, asking questions, the story he told us and gave instructions to delete the footage. Threatened to kill him if he didn't."

"Did he give you a name?" Waylon asked.

"No, but he described the guy. Tan. Muscular. Not like a bodybuilder. But someone who works out. The guy could handle himself. Bald. Extremely scary. I showed him a picture of someone and it was the same guy."

"I don't understand," Monty said. "How do you have the guy's picture?"

"I was at Fiona Frye's house. It was ransacked. Someone was clearly looking for something and turned the place over good."

"He was looking for the flash drive." Waylon stood and stretched.

Monty happened to glance at the ADA and caught her watching the detective quite intently with unmistakable interest. Waylon's gaze flickered to Merritt's and a sly grin tugged at the corner of the detective's mouth a split second before the two looked away from each other.

The ADA and Waylon shared a mutual attraction, or they were discreetly involved. Either way, Monty saw the potential for problems.

"But he didn't find it," Hannah said with a smirk. She

pulled out an evidence bag from her pocket. Inside was a flash drive. "I did. Found it hidden in the bottom of a can of vegetable shortening in the pantry. Fiona was careful, too. When I popped the lid, it looked perfect. Brand-new. But something told me to dig."

"And our guy is on there," Waylon said.

"He is. Along with proof that the mystery man and Pandora were involved in a hot and heavy relationship."

"Let's see it." The ADA extended her palm. "We need to take a look at him."

"I can do you one better." She took out a folded-up paper from her jacket pocket and opened it. "I checked out the drive on one of the laptops Forensics had. Found a clear shot of his face and printed it." She slapped the eight-by-eleven-inch photo down. "It's him. That bald head is distinct, and Finn confirmed he was the one who paid him to lie and delete the security footage. The bartender was more afraid of this guy than of going to prison for obstruction of justice."

They all gathered around and peered at the picture.

Agent Welliver groaned. "That's Roman Cardoso. An enforcer turned lieutenant, holding the second highest position in the Sandoval cartel. He was Alejandro's right-hand man and is now Valentina's. If that man is in town," the DEA agent said, pointing to the picture, "then your family is in grave danger. I can't impress upon you how deadly this man is. He's not just a killer. He's clever. A seducer, snake charmer. A chameleon."

Chameleon. Monty stared at the picture. The eyes were familiar. Yet different. And there was something about the shape of the face that he recognized. "Give me a pencil."

Someone handed him one. He drew a pair of classic rectangular frames around the eyes, added a mustache and began filling in hair. A sledgehammer of horror slammed into Monty's chest.

"Dear God," Hannah said in a low voice, seeing exactly what he saw. "That's Eddie Porter. Your mother's assistant."

Eddie was always with his mother, attached at the hip. In the office. At the house. The man had unfettered access. "He's with my family right now." He whipped out his cell phone and hit the first speed dial—his father was number one, at the very top of his contacts. He was barely able to hear the numbers beep over the pounding of his heart in his ears.

"Thank goodness. I was about to call you," his dad said.

"Why? What's happened?"

"I—I—I don't even know how to say it. Monty…" His father's husky voice trailed off, only heightening his alarm.

His pulse quickened as he stared at the carpet. "Tell me what's wrong," he ordered, pressing his suddenly damp palm to his side. He'd never heard his dad, a man who was a stone pillar, unshakable, sound despondent. *"Tell me."*

"Amber's gone."

Monty drew in a sharp breath, his chest squeezing tightly. "What in the hell do you mean she's gone?"

"She left the police station with Eddie and they were supposed to go straight to the ranch, but they never made it here, Monty. I thought the cartel might've gotten to them on the road. But there's no sign of them of them anywhere. I've checked and her phone goes right to voice mail."

Rage churned in his stomach. "How could you let this happen?"

Silence. Sheer deafening silence over the phone.

"Son," his father croaked, with such despair echoing in the single word. "Monty… I'm so sorry."

Monty couldn't remember ever feeling this way, powerless, scared, spiraling out of control. But causing his father pain by blaming him wasn't going to solve anything. Eddie, that cunning viper, had fooled them all.

Focus. For Amber's sake, for the sake of our son. Focus!

He looked at the others in the room. "Eddie—Roman Cardoso—has Amber." He spoke through unbearable pressure swelling in his chest. "She's missing." The thought of her at the mercy of some sadistic kidnapper with a vendetta against him made his heart clench like a fist.

Agent Welliver let out a soft curse. "He's probably taking her to Colorado."

"You know where?" Monty asked.

"I don't know, son," his father said. "I'm so sorry."

"No, Dad. Not you. Hold on."

The DEA agent nodded. "Valentina has several places. My inside guy told me that Sandoval is in Boulder. I know the property."

Hope fired in his chest. "Then I'm going. With my brothers. We'll get her back."

Welliver shook his head. "You should let us at the DEA handle it."

No way was he waiting for approval and red tape to clear. "She might not have that kind of time. Boulder is a two-hour drive. We can arm up and strategize on the ride. Where is it?"

Welliver raked a hand through his thinning hair. "You and your brothers have no authority across state lines. I'll go with you. I can have some other agents meet us there. Trust me, you'll need every able body you can get. Valentina travels with an armed team. They are as capable as any paramilitary unit."

More manpower and more experience. He'd take it if didn't mean unnecessary delays. There wasn't a minute to spare. "No red tape?" Monty asked, wanting to be sure they were clear.

The corner of Welliver's mouth quirked up in a wicked grin. "I color outside the lines. A lot." His eyes flashed a predatory gleam. "I'll go hunting with you. No red tape."

Monty put the phone back to his ear. "Dad, tell my brothers we're going to get Amber. And ask Matt to bring his special toys." When Matt left the military, he took some Special Ops equipment with him. "It might come in handy since we're not entirely sure what we're going to be up against."

"We can cover you with almost anything you'll need, weapons, equipment," Welliver said. "We're used to this kind of thing. Trust me, we're prepared."

Monty gave a nod of thanks.

"I'll let the boys know," his dad said, "and I'm coming, too."

"Nope. You're not coming. You and Chance need to stay with Mom, Grace and the baby. Make sure you keep them safe."

"Chance won't like this anymore than I do," his father grumbled.

"He's the last Reyes male, the one expected to carry on his family name. If anything happened to him, I'd never forgive myself. Do what you can to make him see reason."

"Easy if I go with you and he does the babysitting."

"Mom would have a conniption. You're not going, Dad. You're needed at the ranch. That's final. Got to go." He hung up before his father could argue.

"Got room for one more?" Waylon asked.

Hannah clasped Monty's shoulder. "Make that two."

Monty nodded, the tightness in his chest easing a fraction at the show of support. "The more help the better."

4:35 p.m.

Amber's pulse skittered in her veins. She was in a warehouse filled with drugs and a small army of scary-looking men armed to the teeth. This was bad. Even if Monty was able to figure out where they were holding her, it would make a rescue problematic.

She stumbled into a small room on the second story, pushed by Roman. He shoved her down into a heavy metal chair bolted to the floor and restrained her to it using zip ties. Her gut knotted.

The fact he hadn't blindfolded her once during the trip and allowed her to see the abundance of drugs stored on the lower level didn't bode well at all.

"What do you hope to gain by this?" she asked him.

He sneered at her, and she ached to kick him between the legs, but she was bound and helpless.

"Gain isn't my goal," he said. "It's my pleasure and privilege to be of service. To Sandoval."

High heels click-clacked across the floor, close by, and an elegant woman appeared in the doorway. She wore varying shades of purple, from her silk top to her designer shoes. "You should understand, Ms. Reyes. Roman is talking about loyalty. To family. You're loyal, aren't you? To your brother. To the Powells. To Montgomery, no matter what he does."

"That's not true," she said, wanting to sound brave, but the tremble in her voice gave her away. "Monty hurt me once. I didn't stay with him. I didn't trust him, and I left. Because I deserved better."

"And now you think that's what he is. *Better.* Is that why you climbed back into bed with him? Had unprotected sex? Which requires a high degree of trust in my book. Why you're so excited to have to his child?"

Amber lowered her head. She didn't know how to answer. The truth would only confirm how much she loved him, putting her in more danger, and a lie would backfire since she wasn't good at pretenses. There was no winning if she played this woman's game.

"I get that you have a vendetta against him," Amber said. "That you want to hurt him. But why did you have to kill Pandora Frye?"

After reading her father's letter, she wished she'd had a chance to fulfill his wishes. To welcome and embrace the woman she had once unjustly hated.

"I didn't kill her." Valentina flashed a smile sweet as saccharine. "Roman did. As to why, well, her murder accomplished two objectives at once."

"First." She raised a single slender finger with a nail long as a talon. "Framing Monty for a crime that would land him behind bars for a considerable amount of time. And second…" Another finger lifted. "Gaining the power to destroy his family's legacy."

The land with the river. "But you lost that power when you killed Pandora."

Valentina quirked a brow. "Did I?"

"If I don't marry Monty—"

"Believe me, you won't live long enough to do that," Valentina said, cruelty radiating from every pore.

Amber drew a shuddering breath. She was scared. For her unborn child. She didn't want this precious life to be collateral damage in this woman's bloodthirsty quest for vengeance. "The land would've gone to Pandora," she continued, steeling her voice. "After you killed her, then it would've gone to her next of kin. Fiona. But for some sick, awful reason, you murdered her, too. Now the land will go to my brother." She thanked God that Chance was safe, far from the clutches of this vile woman. "He'll gladly give it to the Powells. So, you see, no matter what you do to me, the legacy of Monty's family will live on. It will thrive. It will grow. And there's nothing you can do about it."

Tapping a finger at the corner of her mouth, Valentina gave a mock frown. "Poor thing. You're two steps behind. Your little line of succession would be correct if Fiona had been Pandora's next of kin."

"I don't understand."

"Clearly. I'll spell it out for you." A Cheshire-cat grin spread over her face as she circled closer. "Fiona wasn't Pandora's next of kin. Roman is." She strutted up behind him and rubbed his shoulders.

"We were married last week," he said. "Our secret from everyone. Except *la jefa*."

This couldn't be happening. "You have a marriage license and had a ceremony?"

He nodded. "The whole shebang."

"A marriage to a fake person, to Eddie Porter, won't count." Monty and the rest of the Powells would piece it together.

He smiled, making him look even more terrifying somehow. "She married the real me. Roman Cardoso. A valid license. A legally binding marriage before her tragic and untimely death."

Amber reeled from the duplicity, the depths of evil. "But then why did you kill Fiona if she wasn't the next of kin?"

"She had evidence I was involved with Pandora. The mother might've been able to identify me."

"Why put her dead body in my trunk?"

"To wreak more havoc in Montgomery's life by framing you for murder and his mother for embezzlement. Next, I have wonderfully creative plans for the land," Valentina said, "none of which include the Powells ever getting their hands on it. Maybe I'll start with poisoning the river. Kill fifteen thousand head of cattle. That'll hurt. But I have so much more planned."

Dread burned up Amber's throat, lodging into a painful lump. "Please don't hurt me. Think of my unborn child. It's innocent in this."

"*He's* innocent," Valentina clarified. "Right? It's a boy. All the Powells are overjoyed."

This monstrous woman knew everything. Amber needed to think of a way out of this or she would be as good as dead. "You could just keep me hostage until January. Then it won't matter. I won't matter. The land will be Roman's."

Valentina tilted her head to the side and gave her a pitiable look that didn't reach her ice-cold eyes. "Aww, but you will matter. Montgomery Powell loves you. Hurting you will hurt him. That makes you a powerful bargaining chip. Whether you live or die will be up to him. I'm going to wait until you're dehydrated, hungry, writhing in pain. Then we're going to make a video. You're going to beg Montgomery to save your life. To save his son. All he has to do is kill an innocent person in public, in broad daylight, and turn himself in for the murder. Afterward you'll be released." Her tone was sincere but, in Amber's gut, she knew she was lying.

A slow, sick misery pooled in her stomach like raw sewage she wanted to expel.

This woman had no honor. And no heart. No matter what she did, Valentina Sandoval was not going to let her live. Fighting a jolt of panic, she took a deep breath. Becoming hysterical wasn't going to help. She had to stay strong.

When it came time for her to make the video, she wouldn't beg Monty to save her. She'd do the unexpected. She'd tell him to survive—that would be the sweetest victory.

If she was going to die, she'd do so without pleading. Fearless. On the outside, if not inside.

The only real chance she had of getting through this by some miracle was if Monty managed to find her before it was too late and came to the rescue.

She ached to wrap her arms around her belly, to protect her child. Shield him from any danger.

Hurry, Monty.

Please!

He had to save them both. It was her only chance.

Chapter Eighteen

Geared for battle, Monty and most of the team stormed the side of the hill overlooking the warehouse in Boulder, where they suspected Valentina Sandoval held Amber captive.

In total, they were ten, including Agent Welliver and three more guys from the DEA.

Two of Welliver's men and Waylon—the Bravo team—were covering the nearby residence, where Valentina was currently located. The inside man had eyes on her and had confirmed her presence as well as chatter about Amber being somewhere on the property. The warehouse looked like the most likely spot since the insider hadn't seen her or heard any mention of her being in the house. If the large building proved to be pay dirt for the DEA, with a cache of drugs, they'd arrest Valentina.

A massive seizure and the arrest of her crew would cripple her operation while she was behind bars. This was a golden opportunity to not only incarcerate her but neutralize her.

That woman had framed him for murder, gone after his brother, set up his mother, planned to kill his father and kidnapped the woman he loved, also endangering his unborn child. Monty needed to put an end to this to protect his entire family.

"Bravo team, this is Alpha. We're getting into position," Welliver said over the Bluetooth comms in their ears to the others waiting near the Sandoval residence, ready to take down Valentina.

Adjacent to the Eldorado Mountains, the grassy ridge was steep and the earth muddy, but they ate up the terrain in steady strides. He needed to clear his mind and focus his energy, but worry for Amber clouded everything.

Monty flattened against the tactical crest of the hill, below the actual peak where they had maximum visibility without advertising their position. Peering through the Eagle Eye scope, he swept the three stories of the warehouse. Cartel foot soldiers in tactical gear crawled throughout each floor. A fleet of black SUVs was parked outside.

"A freaking army down there," Logan said, lying in a prone position.

"We've got this." Matt's confident tone was to be expected.

He used to be Special Forces for years before he had enough of the bloodshed and came back home. This sort of thing had been routine for him.

The only other person with combat experience, DEA aside, was Waylon, but Monty had no idea what the scope and breadth of his skills were, only that he appeared just as at ease as Matt before they had separated.

Holden nudged Agent Welliver. "The size of that crew down there is a little intimidating. We're outnumbered and outmanned. Any chance of getting us some additional backup?"

The seasoned DEA agent chuckled, the sound sharp-edged and almost homicidal. "Nope. Afraid not. This is the best I could do on short notice with no red tape."

Popping cinnamon gum in his mouth, Matt said, "I only see guns and knives down there. We have a force multiplier." He indicated the grenades the DEA had passed out.

They had three varieties, the primary being smoke. Flash

and stun were the other two. The former would act as a great distraction, issuing three to seven loud reports—explosions— each accompanied with a flash. The latter had a more devastating effect. A stun grenade had one huge explosion of up to 185 decibels and an eleven million candlepower flash. Used in a small room it would rupture eardrums and cause temporary blindness.

In a warehouse environment, a stun grenade could buy them anywhere from eight to twelve seconds. Not much time but enough to disarm and incapacitate a gunman if they didn't hesitate.

Welliver had also provided them with top-of-the-line comms, bulletproof vests, helmets and other equipment they needed to help locate Amber. He gave the signal to a younger agent, Jasper Pearse, who deployed the drone fitted with a thermal camera. They were particularly useful for finding a missing person because of their ability to detect heat and temperature differences.

The drone circled the building going one floor at a time from top to bottom until Pearse isolated her probable location. "Look here." Pearse pointed out clusters of men in various sections. Then he brought the drone back around to the second floor, over to a back corner. A solitary heat signature was seated in a small room. "I think that's her."

"Our best bet," Monty said, agreeing with the assessment.

"Let's get this party started." Welliver slung the strap of a grenade launcher over his shoulder. "Once we get close to the building, we should split up. Some go high and some go low. Sweep the building from the bottom up and top down in tandem."

"High," Matt said.

"I'll go with him," Logan volunteered.

Monty flicked off the safety on his personal 9mm, and they swept down the hill in a V-formation with Welliver leading the way. Anxious energy wired him tight.

Off on Monty's left flank, Matt and Logan took out the gunmen on the east side of the building in a controlled sweep of muzzle-suppressed fire.

Once they came within spitting distance, Welliver held up a fist, bringing them to a halt. The team flattened up against the east side of the building while Pearse whipped out two grenades of white phosphorous. Slipping on gas masks, they prepped to breach the building and pop smoke.

Matt and Logan needed time to cut around to the north side of the building to a fire escape before the rest of them entered the building.

Pearse was tracking a countdown on his watch. He gave a vigorous nod once it was time, pulled the pins on two grenades from his pack, yanked open the door and pitched them inside.

A barrage of bullets sprayed the steel door. In ten seconds, thick white smoke would conceal their ingress and throw the Sandoval soldiers off balance.

Pearse gave the go-signal with another sharp nod and opened the door. They rushed inside, peeling off in different directions.

Dense smoke wafted throughout the entry of the industrial space, not quite reaching the high ceiling where metal ductwork ran in heavy rows. On the first level old machinery served as excellent cover for the enemy. Dark figures darted in between concrete pillars and rectangular objects—cases or boxes—digging in for the fight.

The Alpha team fanned out and moved in. Monty was keeping a close watch-out for hostiles in any sniper positions as he maneuvered across the wide warehouse floor. But there was no telling how many of the cartel's foot soldiers lurked. He eased to the far wall, looking for a different angle to exploit.

Wearing a bulletproof vest and sleek tactical helmet, he followed the path of huge ductwork along the ceiling to a wall and series of pipes.

Gunfire came from the far side of the space. Controlled bursts from armed men sweeping in toward the entrance where he'd last spotted Hannah and Holden. They were no doubt picking off targets.

With the chaos and noise of the gunfire, they were operating with limited communication. The one equalizer: the cartel soldiers were functioning under the same conditions.

Monty skirted the wall, scanning for hostile movement, until he hit a barrier. A half wall, maybe an office or, from the heavy industrial look of the space, an old clean-air room used to house special AC equipment.

Testing the stability of a pipe connected to the wall, he shook it. Solid. Risking exposure by climbing up was necessary to find an avenue to gain the upper hand. He holstered his gun and scrabbled up, using the bolted brackets for footholds and handles. Sweat dripped from his forehead under the gas mask, rolled down his temples and pooled under his chin.

His hands found a three-foot-wide gap between the pipe and office-type structure. He pushed off the pipe, gripping onto the top of the self-contained space. Hoisting himself onto the roof, he didn't make a sound. Ten feet of clearance to the ceiling and high above the layer of phosphorous.

Crouching, he stayed low and removed his mask. The smoky air below was dense and heavy in pockets where the grenades had gone off. He scanned the area. Open crates of drugs packaged for possible shipment were lined up in rows.

They had confirmation of drugs. "We've got thousands of kilos in here," he said to Welliver.

Six dark-clad figures circled closer to Hannah and his brother Holden.

An electric energy pumped hot through him. He locked sights on the two closest to them. A couple of soft squeezes on the trigger, and the men dropped. More stun grenades were used. Systematically, they either eliminated or incapacitated the rest of the cartel men on the first floor. Waylon was making his way to a staircase and signaled for them all to advance while Pearse covered the rear.

Confident no more hostiles remained on this floor, Monty jumped from the office structure, landing on the balls of his feet. Pain torpedoed his knees, but he blinked it away, hustling to join the others at the stairs.

They tried to take a furtive peek to see what waited for them on the next floor.

A wave of bullets rang out in a striking clang. Suppressive fire swept over the metal staircase to keep them from ascending.

Backs against the wall, Welliver pointed to his own eyes, then the stairwell. Pulling out a telescoping-wand camera that allowed tactical viewing without getting your head blown off, he ventured to the edge of the staircase to determine the location of the gunmen.

Welliver shifted the wand around the corner for a complete picture. He slipped back beside Monty. "Two shooters. One at the top of the stairs. The second is leaning over the railing. They're taking turns with bursts of fire."

It would require someone to drop to the ground on their back to take the shot. Someone precise. Decisive. Sharp.

"From what you told me," Welliver said to Monty, "you might be better suited for this. Young back and all." He grinned.

On the ride to Boulder, Monty had told him about the marksmanship training he'd had growing up. He loved ranching and shooting. The more his father had hounded him about legacy, the more Monty had focused on handgun and long-range rifle shooting. As a state police officer, he'd aced marksman sniper training.

No doubt the older agent had a ton of field experience, but Monty was probably a better shot.

Now that they knew the setup of the shooters, he listened.

For the pattern and rate of fire. The one at the top, leaning over with a sweeping view of the steps, was the most dangerous and needed to be eliminated first.

Waiting for his blink-of-an-eye window to open, Monty removed his tactical helmet. Not a reckless choice. A calculated one. He couldn't chance the gear getting in his way, throwing him off a centimeter.

The bottom stairs cleared of gunfire for a breath, the shooters prepping to reload. Monty dove, sensing where to aim as much as sighting the targets. He fired, rolled, readjusted and squeezed the trigger again. The first man hit the staircase with a bullet to the head. The second took a slug to the chest.

Monty climbed to his feet. "Did you see all the drugs they've got in crates?" he asked Welliver.

"Yeah. Better than what we could've expected."

"Give the order. Before someone tells Valentina that we're here and she gets away." He couldn't let that happen. "Do it now. There's no reason to wait."

"Bravo team," Welliver said over comms, "you're cleared hot to take the queen. We've got powder. Lots of powder."

"Roger that," another agent responded. "We're going in."

Monty hoped Waylon and the other agents apprehended Valentina Sandoval fast.

Turning his focus back to finding Amber, he bounded up the steps. Quick. Quiet. The others were right behind him.

The landing opened onto the second floor. No corners, no walls to hide behind immediately. That meant exposure at the top of the stairs. Whatever was waiting could hit them full force.

Bracing against the railing, Monty slipped his helmet on. "Be ready to use flash grenades," he said to the rest of the team. "I don't want Amber getting hurt if we use something more aggressive or her getting caught in the middle of a shoot-out."

Welliver held up a stun grenade. "Bigger impact. It would be better."

"You're probably right," Monty said, understanding the disadvantage it would put them at, "but Amber is pregnant. Flash only around her. I won't take the risk. Got it?"

Everyone nodded.

Pounding footsteps resounded on the first floor, drawing closer. Someone must've called for reinforcements to circle around behind them.

"We'll go hold them off," Hannah said, referring to herself and Holden.

Pearse tapped her on the shoulder. "I'm with you guys."

The three of them took off back down the stairs.

Poised near the top of the landing, Monty was ready to bolt up and try to get to cover. He glanced back at the senior agent.

"I'll cover you from here," Welliver said. "And make sure no one gets past those three downstairs and sneaks up on your rear." The agent took a defensive posture on the stairs, the only position affording cover.

Glass shattered on the floor above them. A flurry of activity up there followed. Guns were chambered followed by a riot of gunfire. Logan and Matt must've breached the third floor.

Now or never. Monty raced up the last few steps, rushing onto the second-floor landing. Quickly, he got a look, spotting Amber, and ducked to the left, taking cover behind a wall.

The man he had known as Eddie Porter, kind and agreeable and soft-spoken, was gone. In his place was the cruellooking Roman Cardoso, holding a gun pointed at Amber's head, using her as a shield.

Relief trickled through him. She was alive. Possibly fatigued and dehydrated, but otherwise she didn't appear hurt.

If this got to the point of some feigned negotiation, Monty realized he could lose the woman he loved along with his unborn child. He needed to act first and seize the advantage.

"Come on out, with your hands up!" Roman said. "Or I'll shoot her!"

Monty steeled himself for what he had to do next. He grabbed two flash grenades. Pulled the pins with his teeth. Released the spoons. Counted to two and tossed them into the wide-open space littered with ratty furniture and large crates.

The grenades clanged to the floor. Rolled and detonated.

With the first two pops, he drew his weapon and stormed inside. Roman had released her and was trying to get to cover. Amber had her hands over her ears, with her eyes shut as she crouched beside a stone pillar.

Monty hustled inside and grabbed her by the arm. Shuffling backward, keeping his eyes trained on the room, he ushered her toward the stairs.

Welliver lunged forward, taking hold of her arm. He got her down out of the line of any possible incoming fire.

This wasn't over. No way was he going to leave Roman Cardoso in there to come after his family.

Monty swooped back into the room. He slipped up behind a pillar and then dashed to the next. A figure ran behind one of the crates near the sofa. *Gotcha!* Monty stalked closer to the crate, his weapon up and at the ready.

A man leaped up, holding an AR-15 rifle, and Monty fired, hitting him square in the chest. Just a nameless soldier. As the guy dropped to the floor, another man—packed with lean muscle—lunged, tackling Monty and knocking his gun loose.

Monty let the momentum carry him, flowing into the fall. He drove his knees into Roman's torso, flipping him overhead. Moving fast, Monty spun and sprang upright, sending a blow to the man's forearm, dislodging the weapon. But Roman followed up, throwing a punch toward him. Monty twisted sideways. The fist barely missed his face and rammed into his shoulder, knocking him into a forty-five-degree spin.

Staggering backward, Monty struggled to right himself.

Roman bent down, reaching for something on his ankle. Another gun appeared in his hand.

Adrenaline flaring through him, Monty didn't hesitate. He threw a sideways kick into Roman's wrist. The pistol discharged before it flew from his hand, skittering out of reach.

The slug slammed into the concrete pillar beside Monty. Close. Too close. Another inch or two and the bullet would've hit his abdomen. Not slowing for a beat, Monty kept moving. But Roman was ready for him. Vicious kicks and punches were exchanged back and forth. But Monty couldn't afford to lose, couldn't give this man the slightest advantage.

A brutal punch struck Monty's cheek, another in his ribs, pounding the air from his lungs. The taste of metallic salt hit his tongue.

Monty butted his skull into Roman's head and jabbed a fist into his exposed throat, bringing the guy to his knees. *I've got him!* Now he needed to end this.

A flash of metal glinted.

By the time Monty registered the knife, it was too late. Roman stabbed the large blade into his thigh and twisted it. White-hot agony tore a scream from his lips.

Roman lowered his shoulder and slammed it up into Monty's chest with the force of a battering ram, taking them both to the floor.

A desperate, violent need to shut this man down eclipsed everything else. Monty sent his elbow crashing into the head of the dangerous man who had infiltrated his home and threatened his family. He knocked Roman to the side, but the guy scrambled quicker than lightning. Roman made it up, spotted something on the floor—a gun—and grabbed the pistol.

Breathless and face bleeding, Roman aimed the 9mm at Monty's chest.

His blood chilled at the split-second thought of failing Amber. Of losing her and his baby. Blinking it away, he vaulted at the guy, unarmed, screaming through the gut-wrenching pain in his leg, determined to protect his family. Even if he had to die to do it.

A distinct pop punctured the air, and a shudder ripped through Monty.

The hot slug made Roman's head jerk back on impact. He staggered a step and dropped to his knees and keeled over, dead.

Monty glanced over his shoulder.

Logan stood holding a gun.

The stark fear gripping Monty in a fist-tight hold dissolved as a rush of peace filled him. "I've never been happier to see you."

Logan grinned. "I've got your back. Always."

Yeah, his little brother did. Lucky thing, too, otherwise he'd be the one dead on the floor.

Logan glanced down at Monty's leg, noticing the injury. He hurried to his side.

Monty slung his arm over his brother's shoulder. Matt met them at the landing of the stairs and came up on the other side of him. The two supported Monty, helping him hop down the stairs.

"The queen is dead," Waylon said over comms. "She opened fire. We had to take her out. All of Bravo is fine."

It was over. The nightmare was finally finished. Roman and Valentina were dead. The threats to his family had been eliminated.

His brothers helped Monty limp through the warehouse and outside into the fresh air. Hannah, Pearse and Holden were right behind them. They made their way back to the other side of the hill.

Welliver had gotten Amber to safety and secured inside one of the vehicles they had driven. She spotted him and bolted from the SUV.

He didn't want her to run, but also couldn't wait to hold her in his arms.

She rushed to him, wrapping him in a tight hug, her trembling body crushed to his, and nothing in the world had ever felt better.

Amber pulled back and stared at his leg. "Oh my God. Are you all right?"

"I think I will be." It hurt like hell, but he had Amber, he was on his feet, breathing, and they hadn't sustained any casualties. He couldn't complain.

"We've got to remove it," she said.

"No," several voices said in unison.

He met her frantic gaze. "I could bleed out," he said, with a sad smile. "Best to let a doctor do it."

She threw herself into his arms again, and he basked in the warmth of her embrace, the surety of her touch. No more skepticism. No more hesitation. No more fear.

Raw emotion flooded him, replacing the adrenaline high. He bent down to look into her eyes and smiled at the love shining on her face.

"We need to get him in the vehicle," she said to his brothers.

They helped him hobble over and got him inside. She found a medical kit and climbed in on the other side. The others hung back, giving them a moment alone together.

"Are you all right?" he asked, looking her over.

She nodded as she took gauze out of the kit. "Once I get your leg wrapped to slow the bleeding, I'll grab a bottle of water." She bandaged his thigh as best she could around the Bowie knife lodged in it.

The pain was intense. He'd never felt such agony.

But Amber was all right. His son was all right.

He pressed a palm to her cheek. "I'm so thankful you're not hurt. I imagined horrible things. What they could've been doing to you. I couldn't bear the thought of losing you. Either of you."

She placed her index finger against his lips. "No more imagining the worst. No more regrets. No more looking backward. From this day forward, we're together. A family. No matter what. I love you, Montgomery Beaumont Powell, and I want to marry you as soon as possible."

The words curled around his heart like a warm embrace. He cupped her jaw and gave her a soft kiss. "Are you sure?"

"I'm one hundred percent positive about everything. That I want to marry you. That you truly love me, with or without the land."

"You just went through something horrendous. You might not be thinking straight. We can wait. Stick to the plan. I don't mind."

"We can't stick to that plan because I do mind. It's selfish and rooted in fears that I no longer have." She took his free hand and put it on her rounded belly. "Our son, your brother's children, Kayce and the baby coming in weeks, and all the other little ones on the way deserve their birthright. The Powell and Reyes legacy. We need to protect it, fight for it, not take it away from them."

Joy ballooned in his chest until he could barely breathe. He was in so much pain but had never been happier. "How did I get so lucky to have you?"

"Fate." She shrugged. "Or a wise father's keen insight and persistent machinations."

Smiling, he pulled Amber into his arms and then gave her a heart-pounding kiss that rocked him to his core. "Whether it was fate or your father or both, I know that we were always meant to be together. Joined as one."

Epilogue

Three months later
5:50 p.m.

"What do you think about Beaumont, my grandfather's name?" Monty asked, his voice rough and husky, making her bare skin tingle.

She turned over onto her back, lying in their bed in the cottage that had been built for them a decade ago, and stared at him. "Beau," she whispered, a soft smile surfacing on her face, and nodded. "Could we name him Beaumont Carlos?"

He kissed her on the lips. "Has a great ring to it, but it could be whatever you want. We could name him Peanut if it makes you happy. Peanut Powell has a ring to it also." Then he kissed her full belly and the baby kicked hard. "Oh, I felt that one. A good pop to my mouth. I guess baby says no to being officially named Peanut."

They laughed.

Fully naked, he rolled out of bed and crossed the room, grabbing his boxer briefs from the chair. He still had a slight limp from the knife wound in his thigh and the doctors told him he always would. That made him unfit to continue with the state police, but when he heard the news, a weight lifted from him, and he acted at peace with giving up the badge.

Now he was a full-time rancher in charge of the Shooting

Star-Longhorn. His choice. He woke early with a sense of purpose and pride. He went to bed after loving her and cuddling, a happy kind of tired from the work, without a care in the world. Slept blissfully, soundly, with his arm draped over her.

Things on the ranch were delightfully dull. No danger. No dead bodies. After the reporter Erica Egan gave up Vera Foley as her source on the embezzlement case against Holly, Waylon had managed to squeeze a confession out of her. She admitted to forgery, being the one to embezzle money from the city, and working for the Sandoval cartel along with her husband Nicholas.

"There's something I never asked you," she said.

"Fire away."

"Why did you move into this, our house, after I left?"

"Two reasons. One, it was penitence. To be reminded every day, every second I was here of what I did wrong. Two, I was waiting for you."

She smiled. "Did you ever bring anyone here? A woman? You can tell me. I won't be mad."

"Bring another woman to our house? No, sweetheart, I never did that." Monty slipped the boxers on up to his trim waist.

Nibbling her lower lip, she couldn't tear her gaze from his marvelous body, strong legs, sculpted arms, washboard abs, a dusting of hair on his muscular chest. A spectacular specimen of a man. With his tawny hair a beautiful mess from their lovemaking and the evening stubble on his jaw, he looked rugged. Sexy. Perfect.

Squeezing her thighs together, she ached deep in her core to have him again. She glanced down at the diamond wedding band on her finger. Every time she looked at it her heart danced in her chest. *I'm Mrs. Montgomery Powell.*

An uncontrollable rush of pure joy suffused every cell in her body.

"What are you thinking right this second?" he asked, the expression in his eyes dark and alluring.

She loved the way he looked at her. Like she was the most beautiful, precious creature that he'd ever seen.

"About you. How happy I am to be your wife and that we got married on New Year's Eve."

It had been a gorgeous, candlelit evening ceremony at the ranch with the entire family and a few old friends from town. Some new ones too, such as Waylon. It had been small and intimate. She wore an empire-waist dress, her hair full of curls pinned high. He wore a tailored navy suit. They dined on filet mignon and sea bass and had three different flavors of wedding cake. Vanilla with passionfruit curd, a layer of purple huckleberry, and lemon with raspberry filling. Everyone danced until the stroke of midnight when fireworks burst into the sky, ringing in the New Year and celebrating their nuptials.

The only thing missing was her mother helping her get ready and her father walking her down the aisle, but Holly and Chance were pleased to fill in.

She missed her parents and her dad's meddling, but she'd worked through the stages of grief and was finally at the stage of acceptance.

Her life was full and rich and overflowing. She was grateful to be surrounded by so much love and support. To have such a large family where she got to see her nieces and nephews grow up. To be close to them. To have huge dinners where they all gathered, their lives inextricably intertwined. To call this ranch her home as her father always knew she would. Where their son would be raised.

Monty came back to the bed, leaned in, cupped her breast and gave her a deep, hot kiss. She pulled back and looked at him. Heat flickered in his eyes.

Laughing, she tapped his nose. "Don't even think about it,

mister. Holden will be dropping the kids off for us to baby-sit any minute."

Grace had given birth to the most beautiful little girl, Nova. Six pounds, seven ounces. The baby came two weeks early and she was only in labor for three hours. Another easy baby with a sweet temperament.

"You know, we could always get Mom and Dad to watch them." His timber-rough voice sent a shiver along her spine. He cupped her breast again and ran his thumb over her pert nipple.

Hot waves of awareness coursed between them.

"Don't you want to practice being parents, Monty? We're going to have our own soon."

"Oh, I want to practice all right. Practice making babies. This one might be a fluke."

Her smile fell as she realized they still hadn't discussed something.

"What's wrong, sweetheart?" He rubbed her arm. "Was it something I said? I don't want you to feel like I'm always all over you and you can't get a break. It's just you're so sexy." He beamed at her, sending a flutter through her chest.

"No, it's not that." Looking at the bed, she took his hand. "How would you feel if this baby was a fluke?"

"What do you mean?"

"The doctors told me it would be difficult for me to get pregnant. Next to impossible. Because I have a blocked fallopian tube as a result of surgery I had for endometriosis. What I'm saying is that this little guy is our miracle baby." She lifted her eyes to his. "He might be our only baby. I don't know if I'll be able to give you more children. I'm sorry. You wanted a big family. We should've talked about it before we got married instead of rushing."

He crushed his mouth to hers in a toe-curling, stomach-dropping kiss. "We already have a big family. Proof will be knocking at our door dropping off two babies in a minute. If our son is an only child, I guarantee he'll never be lonely. Not with his cousins living on the ranch." He smiled at her. "No imagining the worst. No regrets. It's you and me and this little one." He rubbed her belly. "No matter what. Right?"

A burst of all-consuming happiness rushed over her.

Monty stroked her cheek so tenderly that tears sprang to her eyes. "Don't be sad, sweetheart. This house is going to be full of kids we love. Trust me."

"I'm not sad. These are happy tears. I promise." She sat up and leaned against his chest.

Wrapping his arms around her, he hugged her tight, and she sank into the embrace, certain he would never let her go.

"Come on," he said. "We've got a reputation to earn. The best uncle and aunt ever. I want that top-dog status of *favorite*. Let's get dressed. We've got to entertain two kids under two until they run us ragged to the bone."

She laughed. "I can't think of anything else I'd rather do."

"Well, I've got a couple of ideas." He winked at her.

* * * * *

INTRIGUE

Seek thrills. Solve crimes. Justice served.

Available Next Month

Child In Jeopardy Delores Fossen
Mountain Captive Cindi Myers

....

Cold Case Discovery Nicole Helm
Shadowing Her Stalker Maggie Wells

....

Special Forces K-9 Julie Miller
Fugitive Harbour Cassie Miles

Keep reading for an excerpt of a new title
from the Romantic Suspense series,
FIND HER by Katherine Garbera

Chapter One

Lee Oscar didn't do regrets. She might have had a different life if her best friend, Hannah Johnson, hadn't gone missing two weeks before they graduated from high school. If she spent too much time dwelling on those mistakes, then she went down a rabbit hole that led to pain and destructive tendencies.

However, Boyd Chiseck was one of those people who *did* regrets. Hannah's disappearance when they'd all been seventeen had forged that in both of them. After living through that, Lee had learned there was no one who could keep her safe except herself. And had decided from that point on to arm herself with skills, both lethal and technical, to fight evil in this modern age.

She spotted him right away. He was just under six foot and had broad shoulders, but the years had softened his shape, giving him a bit of a dad bod even though he'd never had children. Boyd kept his brown locks trimmed short, but he still had a full head of hair even though he was in his forties. Her attention shifting to his face, she took in his neatly trimmed beard and preppy clothing. Today he was adorned in neat dark jeans that he'd probably pressed and a Ralph Lauren polo shirt.

His eyes were brown, not really remarkable except that he always had an intensity and sadness about him. The two were inexplicably twined, and whenever Lee sat across from him, she almost felt the weight of those emotions.

For Boyd, he'd gone into protection mode. Trained as a teacher while Lee had been going through training for an elite intelligence agency based in the US. Both of them determined to help people when they hadn't been able to save their good friend Hannah.

So when he called out of the blue asking her to meet him for coffee… Well, her first emotion wasn't excitement or nostalgia for catching up with an old acquaintance. Because Boyd would forever be tied to that one moment that had shaped her into the woman she was today.

At forty-two, she might have fooled herself into believing that what had transpired twenty-five years earlier would always stay firmly in her rearview, but as she walked into Zara's Brew, she knew that wasn't the case. There was never going to be a time when she and Boyd met up that Lee didn't remember Hannah Johnson and wish she'd done things differently.

But a seventeen-year-old's worldview was a lot different than a grown woman's.

He waved when he saw her and she moved through the café to take a seat at the booth that he'd selected. He had no way of knowing that she'd watched a shoot-out take place in that very booth six months earlier when her coworker and friend Kenji Wada and his fiancée, Daphne Amana, had been ambushed while the international rights lawyer had been trying to get evidence in a case she'd been working on.

No regrets, the voice in her head said dryly.

But, in reality, there always were. She'd been monitoring all the cameras and wasn't sure how she'd missed the sniper that had set up on the far side of the parking lot.

"Hiya. I ordered you an Americano with three sugars," Boyd said after he'd stood to give her a hug. "Told them to bring it when you got here."

"Thanks. Been here awhile?"

"Not really. You know me…thirty minutes early always feels late," he replied.

That hadn't always been the case, but she understood why it had become his habit. "I do. So you mentioned you needed some help."

"No small talk?" he murmured dryly. His dark brown hair had grayed over the years, and he was still in shape but not as muscled as he'd been when he played on their high school football team.

"How's the family?" she asked, a tinge of heat rising to her cheeks. "Sorry. I pretty much spend all of my time at my desk with monitors around me and only talk to the team when giving recon info or issuing a warning or order."

"Fair enough," Boyd said. "Parents are good. Dad finally retired and Mom is trying to push for that move to Arizona. We'll see what happens."

"And Daniella?"

"Good... I hear she's good," he muttered.

Lee lifted both eyebrows.

"She left about six months ago. I see her at work but we're separated," he told her with a shrug. "Mom suggested maybe marriage isn't for me."

"Wow. Sorry about that," Lee said. Daniella had been his third wife.

"Me too. She said I can't let go of the past."

Lee nodded. This wasn't news. She and Boyd both knew that he couldn't. That he would always blame himself for staying late at the gym to hang with the guys instead of going to meet Hannah. He'd always wonder if had he been there for his girlfriend she might not have been taken and would still be alive today. Lee wondered the same thing but about herself. If she'd left the computer lab with Hannah and gone to wait for Boyd with her instead of trying to get the program language for the algorithm she'd been working on to track grades and prove that her English teacher graded down on girls...

She reached over and squeezed his hand. There wasn't really anything she could say that would make him feel better. Or herself, for that matter. "So..."

The barista dropped off Lee's drink and then Boyd leaned closer. "One of my students hasn't shown up to class for the last three days. She has a rough home life and I'm not sure what happened. She might have run away. I called the number on file for her mom but haven't received an answer."

Lee wasn't exactly surprised by this. Boyd had come to her before when he thought things were odd with a student. "Name."

"Isabell Montez, but she goes by Izzie."

She pulled out her smartphone and started making notes on the notepad. Boyd gave her a physical description and Air-Dropped Izzie's yearbook photo to her. "I went to the cops and they said they'd do a wellness visit to her home," he added. "But I haven't heard back from them."

"Did you go by the house?"

He nodded. "I did. There's no sign of anyone there. I think the cops will probably just write it off, but my gut says there's more here."

Because of what they'd both been through, his gut was always going to say that, Lee realized. "Okay. I'll check into it. Does she have socials?"

He shrugged. "No clue. That's not really my thing."

Why did that not surprise her? Boyd wasn't exactly the Facebook type. "Fair enough. I'll check into this and get back to you when I hear something," Lee said.

He flashed a quick grin. "Which *is* your thing."

"What do you mean?"

"Just that you only come out from behind your computer when there's a crime to solve and then you go back."

She shrugged, not really able to argue with that.

They'd already exhausted the small talk, so she took a quick sip of her sweet, dark brew and then nodded at her old friend and got up, ready to start digging into Izzie Montez to find out where she'd gone.

A new puzzle to solve and hopefully a girl that could be saved. Van would say she'd joined Price Security to rescue people. Hell, everyone on the team had done that. But this time because Boyd was involved, the need to get this right and find that girl was stronger than it had been in a while.

Aaron Quentin liked life undercover. He didn't need a therapist to tell him that he used his work to hide from life. He knew that. However, over the last year, he'd started to get closer to his youngest brother, Xander, which was making him reevaluate some things.

He was British but worked for the DEA on their large criminal-gangs task force. Aaron had originally come to work for the DEA when he'd been on holiday in Miami. He'd been at loose ends, making money fighting in some underground clubs, when a fellow fighter had introduced him to his backers who were part of an East Coast drug syndicate.

Aaron had realized he was at another crossroad, and for the first time in his twenty-eight years, he'd decided to do the smart thing and not screw up again. He'd used a contact he had from his time in the SAS to get a meeting with a local DEA agent, and that had been it. Now ten years later, he was almost feeling like the work he'd done taking down two large criminal networks almost made up for the angry, tough youth he'd once been.

The accident was something he'd never be able to forgive himself for, and his family would never fully be healed. But looking at forty gave him a different perspective. Seeing Xander settled with his fiancée, Obie Keller, and working in private security was also helping. Also, having his brother back in his life... Well, it was making Aaron see his life through a different lens.

There was always that question of how long he could be effective undercover. He'd come out to the West Coast because after a high-profile bust in Miami, he felt he was getting too well-known.

Or at least that's what he *told* himself. The other reason, which he wasn't ready to delve into, was to be closer to Xander. The two of them, along with his future sister-in-law, had all gone home for Christmas. It had been...eye-opening to realize how much he'd missed the family, and after a long chat with Tony, he was starting to see himself in a different light.

Of course, it wasn't as easy as it always seemed on TV shows or in movies. The truth was, violence was where he was most comfortable—or had been. That's why undercover work suited him. He had no issues being a tough guy, or fitting in with the criminal element.

They were his people. He understood what it was like to

grow up in a crowd of testosterone and always fight to be the alpha. He was the third of four brothers who'd grown up wild.

He and Xander were the youngest and their older brothers never pulled punches. He'd learned to be resilient and to survive by example. Fighting to be the top dog was all he'd known until a rugby game where his second-oldest brother was left paralyzed after a tackle by Aaron.

He'd blamed himself. Hell, they all had in different ways. Could Tony and Abe, the older two, have stopped antagonizing him and Xander? Couldn't he and Xander have just walked away? Sure, but that wasn't the Quentin MO.

Aaron blew out a breath. All this wading through the past was making his skin feel too tight and itchy, had him wishing he could just down a bottle of whiskey to forget. But he hated being drunk and how that thin veneer that he called control would often slip away and he'd wind up in a fight—because he *always* did—and then would most likely add to his list of regrets.

As much as he'd told himself he was in LA because of Xander, he knew there was another reason. Lee Oscar.

She was the tech genius at Price Security. Hot as hell…as much as he didn't do romance because of his job and basic lack of good relationship skills. Still, he couldn't shake her from his thoughts.

She wasn't his usual type of woman, which didn't mean crap to his libido. Apparently faded tight jeans and T-shirts that skimmed her curves were what he was attracted to.

"Mate, what are you doing here?"

Aaron glanced over his left shoulder to see Xander striding toward him. His brother was just coming off a job—Price had let Aaron know and also let him into the building. He'd been waiting in what served as a guest lobby on the fourth floor.

"Hoping for some hang time. Obie called."

Xander rubbed the back of his neck as he dropped his duffel on the floor at his feet. Aaron walked over and hugged his brother. Not for a moment embarrassed by the emotion that swamped him. He'd been alone for too long.

"Yeah? I can hang. Gotta shower though, and Kenji and I have a *Halo* match."

Price Security was so much more than a workplace. Giovanni "Van" Price had created a family out of the loners he'd hired as first-rate bodyguards and security consultants, something that Aaron had seen firsthand in Miami.

For a moment, he was jealous of the found family that Xander had here. But then shoved that down. He was slowly trying to rebuild the brotherly bond that he'd ripped the hell out of when they'd been in their early twenties. "Cool."

"Great. Let's go up to my place. You in town for work?"

"Yeah. I start on Monday. Trying to lie low. Was going to hole up in a hotel but then… Obie."

"You didn't have to wait for her to call. You can always crash at my place," Xander said.

Aaron shrugged. He still wasn't used to this either. He'd made himself into a lone wolf after his pack had disintegrated. Convinced himself that he liked it better that way. But recently he was beginning to rethink it.

Starting to want to see Xander and his family more often. And wondering if maybe there was a different life out there for him.

When they got on the elevator, Lee Oscar was on there. Their eyes met and she lifted one eyebrow when his gaze lingered too long. Lee was about five-five and fit. She had long brown hair that she habitually wore pulled back in a ponytail and was whip-smart.

He'd talked to her in Miami after she and the rest of the Price Security team had helped him wrap a delicate case he'd been working. He'd noticed her as a woman the very first moment he met her. He leaned against the wall of the elevator, crossing his legs at the ankle as he watched her, trying to figure out what was different about her.

"Hey, babe, how's life treating you?" he asked. Noticing his brother shaking his head. But Xander hadn't been there in Miami when they'd done shots of tequila, and for a moment in the hot moonlight, something had passed between the two of them.

"Fine. You, babe?" she asked.

He noted Xander trying to hide a smile but ignored his brother.

"Same. Just starting a new gig."

"Are you staying here?" she asked him, not Xander.

"Do you want me to?" he asked. If she ever gave him the hint of an opening, he'd jump at it. But with Lee, it was like he had no game. None. Other women usually took one look at him and it was game on. But not Lee.

"Not really," she said.

"Ouch."

"Sorry. It's just your job is high-risk and it would mean extra security measures in place and that's more work for me."

"I don't want to cause that," he said. "Plus I'm undercover, and this building is a bit too high vis for my MO."

"Another case like Miami?" she asked.

"Something," he said. He couldn't divulge the details and didn't want to. His life worked because of the compartments he kept.

"Be safe," she said as she exited on her floor.

"You too, babe."

She paused, glancing back over her shoulder. "It's Lee, not babe."

He gave her a slow smile and arched one eyebrow at her. "Noted, Lee."

"Mate, seriously?"

"Seriously."

"She's not a casual-type woman," Xander said. "She's like a sister to me, so watch yourself."

"She's got her own back," Aaron said. He wondered if he should apologize to his brother but wouldn't have an idea where to begin. It was probably better he wasn't staying here.

Lee had his attention and it was clear that Xander wasn't down with that. But still he couldn't stop thinking about her... Something seemed different.

She looked worried. He hadn't seen her that way before.

Isabell Montez wasn't that hard to find. She had the regular socials and had been pretty active until about ten days ago. Thanks to Isabell's feed, Lee was able to pull together different photos and start running them through a facial recognition program that she had helped develop back when she'd been working for the government. She attended San Pedro High School, which of course Lee had been aware of since that was where Boyd worked. The program had been improved in the last fifteen years, and Lee had kept up with updates for herself and the government.

She thought about Boyd as she ran the search. That boy had never been the same after high school. She got it—she hadn't either—but it seemed to Lee that Boyd had been trapped in those four years. The good *and* the bad.

She couldn't get far enough away from her past. It was ironic that when she retired and started working with Van that she'd ended up only an hour away on the 5 from where she'd started her journey. Her grandpa had died a few years ago and Lee never went back to Ojai. She didn't want to. The past for her tended to stay there.

She was too busy doing her job and keeping her clients and the staff at Price Security safe. In a way, she was the opposite of Boyd. Having had that one lapse in judgment, she'd focused on never letting it happen again. Her old classmate, on the other hand, felt as if he were trying to fix what happened to Hannah. That if by being vigilant he could bring her back. But that wasn't ever going to happen.

Even though they'd never found her body, which of course made things more complicated. Like, maybe she was still alive. Though the years Lee had spent working in human trafficking made her doubt that. She'd looked for Hannah over the years. Had even used some software to age her old pictures and run them through every facial recognition program and came up with a few likenesses.

But they'd never panned out.

She stood and stretched as the program kept running, when the door behind her opened. Her office was a bank of computer screens and then, behind her, a big conference table that the team used when it was time to have a confab or for Van to hand out assignments.

She glanced over her shoulder to see her boss walking toward her. Van Price was a big-muscled bald man with intense green eyes that warmed when he laughed. He wasn't tall, just presented himself in a way that made everyone take a step back. When Lee had first met the security guru almost twenty years ago, she'd been intimidated until they'd been paired on an undercover assignment and she realized that the tough exterior hid a softy with a heart of gold.

She was one of a handful of people who knew that fact, which she also knew was intentional. Van was lethal, never hesitating to do what was necessary to keep his clients and his staff—or *family* as he called them—safe.

"How was old home week?"

She shook her head. "Painful. Boyd has another missing kid."

"*Another* one?"

"Yeah, every five years or so, he calls me about a kid he thinks has been taken," Lee said. Her mind naturally identified patterns, and even if they might be coincidences, she hadn't been able to ignore the fact that it was every five years since Hannah's disappearance that Boyd reached out.

"Was the kid taken?" Van asked.

"Not sure yet. I mean, the police definitely checked out her house after he called, and found nothing. The family was gone, so it could be they are just in the wind. But her socials went quiet too, which isn't normal for that age," Lee admitted. "So... what brings you by?"

"Just checking on one of my favorite girls," Van said, with that slow smile of his.

"Just checking in, huh?" She narrowed her eyes at him. "What do you need?" she asked, knowing Van never did anything without a reason.

"Kaitlyn Leo from the CIA reached out again asking for Kenji and Daphne's help. I thought we had an agreement. Can you look around and make sure they aren't active again?"

By "look around," he meant hack into the CIA's servers and check on the agent status. "Kenji would tell you."

"I know he would, but there is always a chance that Leo would go behind his back," Van grumbled. "We've both known that to happen."

They had. After they'd retired from the government, Kenji

and Daphne had been asked to do favors, which both of them had agreed to, but then their status had been changed to active until they notified their bosses that they were definitely inactive.

"I'll let you know what I find. Aaron's here, by the way. I bumped into him in the elevator." She was still buzzing slightly from the interaction with him. He got her that way. That insolent way he leaned casually against the wall of the elevator and then checked her out in a manner that was anything but casual. Mixed Signals should have been his name.

There was a quiet intelligence to him that drew her, but then he opened his mouth and came on like someone who spent too much time in a bar. Which should have made it easier for her to ignore him completely.

But it didn't.

"Yeah, I gave him access. He's working in LA and needs a safe place for his downtime."

"Cool. A heads-up would have been nice," Lee said. Since she kept the building secure, she liked to know when they had someone new on the premises. Especially someone like Aaron Quentin who was usually deep undercover with drug cartels.

"He just arrived a little while ago," Van pointed out. "You sure you're okay?"

She knew she was touchy. It was Boyd and of course Hannah and this young girl, who'd looked funny and happy in her social media photos, who was now missing. Her mind could easily supply all the scenarios where she might be and how they could find her. It made her edgy.

She just shrugged.

Van put his hand on her shoulder and squeezed.

They both knew that there was nothing to be said. That world—the murky crime-filled one—continued to thrive no matter what they did and nothing would change that.

Lee's best hope was to find Izzie before too much more time passed.

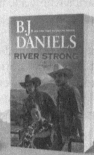
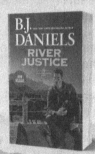